I've got the per

"Ah, hell," he muttered. It was ludicrous. Trish? A plant? A willing player in his mother's scheme to marry him off?

Or was she just a pawn?

Adam pushed away from his desk and began to pace. He stopped. Shook his head. Paced some more. Stopped again.

He was driving himself crazy.

Maybe it was just a happy coincidence that his previous secretary had left the company, replaced by a certain attractive woman who just might be capable of seducing him into love and marriage.

His eyes narrowed as he conjured up a picture of his mother meeting, scheming, conniving to pull it off.

Suddenly, it didn't seem at all far-fetched.

He had to hand it to them, he admitted with a short laugh. It was a nice try. Trish was definitely attractive. But while he might enjoy the seduction part, there was no way in hell he'd fall for the whole marriage package.

THE MILLIONAIRE MEETS HIS MATCH

BY
KATE CARLISLE

All the characters in this book have no existence outside the imagination of
the author, and have no relation whatsoever to anyone bearing the same name
or names. They are not even distantly inspired by any individual known or
unknown to the author, and all the incidents are pure invention.

Published in Great Britain 2011
by Mills & Boon, an imprint of Harlequin (UK) Limited,
Eton House, 18-24 Paradise Road, Richmond, Surrey TW9 1SR

© Kathleen Beaver 2010

ISBN: 978 0 263 88236 0

51-0711

Harlequin (UK) policy is to use papers that are natural, renewable and
recyclable products and made from wood grown in sustainable forests. The
logging and manufacturing processes conform to the legal environmental
regulations of the country of origin.

Printed and bound in Spain
by Blackprint CPI, Barcelona

To my fellow Desire™ author Maureen Child,
a marvelously talented writer and a truly wonderful
friend. I couldn't have done it without you…
and the lattes…and the doughnuts…the laughs…
and the trips to Vegas…and so much more. Love you!

New York Times bestselling author **Kate Carlisle** was born and raised by the beach in Southern California. After more than twenty years in television production, Kate turned to writing the types of mysteries and romance novels she always loved to read. She still lives by the beach in Southern California with her husband, and when they're not taking long walks in the sand or cooking or reading or painting or taking bookbinding classes or trying to learn a new language, they're travelling the world, visiting family and friends in the strangest places. Kate loves to hear from readers. Visit her website at www.katecarlisle.com.

Dear Reader,

I'm thrilled to welcome you to my first Desire™! I've been a Desire™ reader for years, so it's a dream come true for me to be writing for them.

The saying goes "man plans and God laughs." Well, this is a story of the best laid plans going awry. Trish James devises a simple plan of revenge when she goes to work for Adam Duke. She holds Adam responsible for destroying her home and family, and she'll stop at nothing to ruin him. Or so she thinks.

Adam has big plans, too, none of which includes marriage. But seduction? Absolutely. But as his desire for Trish grows, so does his suspicion that his mother might've had something to do with Trish getting the job. This mom is not above scheming and matchmaking if it means her three handsome sons will fall in love, marry and give her lots of grandbabies to love. So what happens when the plans of a vengeful secretary, a seductive millionaire and a matchmaking mama collide? Sparks fly, to say the least!

I hope you love reading Adam and Trish's story as much as I loved writing it. Let me know! You can reach me through my website, www.katecarlisle.com.

Happy reading!

Kate

One

"Consider this fair warning. Watch your back or I guarantee they'll take you down."

"You're making too much of this," Adam Duke said as he eased his black Ferrari into his parking space near the executive entrance of Duke Development International.

"You think so?" His brother Brandon's voice came through loud and clear over the car's state-of-the-art sound system. "I'll be sure to remind you of that after you've said your wedding vows and promised to live happily ever after with the girl of *Mom's* dreams."

"You need to chill out," Adam said. He shifted into Park and grabbed his briefcase before stepping out of his car.

"Hey, it's your funeral," Brandon groused. "Or wedding. Whatever. Just don't be surprised when you find yourself on a honeymoon with some woman who was planted right under your nose by our diabolically clever mother."

Adam laughed as he took a moment to straighten his tie before strolling inside. The ultramodern office building he owned with his brothers, Cameron and Brandon, was the headquarters of Duke Development International. "I think I'm safe," Adam said. "The chances of Mom sneaking anything past me while I'm working twenty-two hours a day on this closing are pretty slim."

His brother, Cameron, also in on the three-way conference call, spoke for the first time. "Despite Brandon's typical overkill, you know Mom. She's relentless. She thinks we should all be married and now she's playing hardball. That means she'll try every devious trick in the book to make it happen."

"Right, that's all I'm saying," Brandon said, apparently relieved that at least one of his brothers was getting the message.

"Okay," Cameron said. "Might be a good idea to stay alert for the time being."

"Yeah, be alert for the skirt," Brandon said, then added with a snicker, "or you could get hurt."

The brothers shared a laugh at Brandon's pitiful attempt at poetry.

"Look, I'll see you guys later," Adam said. "We can finish this conversation then."

Still chuckling, Adam disconnected the call and waved to the DDI security guard who stood at attention next to the wide, polished marble registration desk in the lavishly appointed lobby. He stepped inside an empty elevator car and ascended alone to the penthouse floor.

The fact that his mother was trying to set up Adam and his brothers was no surprise. She'd made it eminently clear on any number of occasions that she wanted grandchildren. But now Brandon was making it sound as if she were suddenly on a crusade and willing to use underhanded means to introduce new women into their lives.

"Take your best shot, Mom," Adam murmured as he made his way down the broad, open corridor toward the executive offices. He loved Sally Duke, the woman who'd adopted him when he was eight years old, but Adam Duke was the last person on earth who would succumb to her machinations when it came to marriage.

Whistling softly, he walked past his assistant's empty chair, noticed that her computer wasn't turned on yet, and marveled that he'd actually made it into work before her this morning. That was rare. Cheryl Hardy was a workaholic who loved her job. A good thing, because they'd be working night and day for the rest of the month, right up to the evening of the gala grand opening of the new Duke resort at Fantasy Mountain.

"What do you mean, she *quit*?" Adam demanded an hour later. "My people don't quit."

"This one did," Marjorie Wallace, his long-time Human Resources manager said.

"Impossible. We're about to close on a billion-dollar deal." Adam pushed back from the massive mahogany desk and rose to pace along the wall of windows that overlooked the craggy coastline of Dunsmuir Bay and the clear blue ocean beyond. It was a breathtaking view of the central California coast, one he saw every day and never grew tired of, but it mattered little now as he whipped around to confront Marjorie. "She's not allowed to leave."

"Actually, she is. It's not like she was an indentured servant," the older woman said drily. "She's gone, Adam. Let's move on."

"Did she say why?" Adam raked one hand through his hair. "Never mind. I'll double her salary. We can work this out."

He didn't appreciate Marjorie's dry chuckle. "Oh, really?" the HR manager asked. "How many times did Cheryl remind you that she needed a vacation and you convinced her she didn't? She told you she was getting married. You brushed her off."

"She never said a word. I would've listened."

"She told you every day."

"She didn't," Adam insisted, although he had a vague memory of Cheryl mentioning…something…about a wedding. Had she been talking about her own wedding? He couldn't remember. It hadn't seemed important at the time.

"She did," Marjorie maintained defiantly.

Adam rounded the desk and faced the insolent woman up close. "You're not supposed to argue with the boss."

Marjorie's laugh rang out. "Oh, Adam."

Adam scowled. "Remind me again why I haven't fired you for insubordination."

"Let's see." Marjorie's grin remained as she folded her arms across her chest. "Maybe because I'm so darn good at my job? Or maybe because I'm your mother's best friend and I've known you since you were eight years old? Or could it be because I've never told your mother who really hit the baseball that broke her office window when you were nine or who trampled her prize tulips that same summer? Oh, and what about the time you were grounded and I caught you sneaking out to—"

"All right, all right," Adam said irately, holding up his hand for her to stop. "There should be a statute of limitations on that kind of stuff."

"Sorry," Marjorie said with a grin. "Honorary aunties never forget."

"Tell me about it," Adam muttered. "Look, this is ridiculous. Get Cheryl on the phone."

"She quit," Marjorie said, enunciating the words so he couldn't ignore them. "She won't be back. She was three months' pregnant and working around the clock. Something had to give."

He stopped in midpace and turned. "Pregnant?"
Marjorie nodded.

Appalled, he threw his hands up. "She always insisted she was a shark. She loved the kill. Sharks don't get pregnant and run off in the middle of a deal."

Marjorie shrugged. "I guess she was a dolphin in shark's clothing."

"Very funny," he said coldly. "You can't trust anyone these days."

"So true."

"I don't have time for this," Adam said abruptly. "I need a replacement, now."

Marjorie smiled. "I've got the perfect person for you."

Adam stopped her with a look. "I'm warning you, Marjorie. Don't bring me someone who's going to get pregnant and leave without notice."

"Of course not," she said with a huff.

"And I don't want some bubble-gum-chewing bobblehead doll." He stalked back and forth in front of the desk, warming to his rant. "I want someone with maturity, someone who knows the damn alphabet well enough to file something in the right drawer. And I definitely don't want—"

"I know what you want, boss," Marjorie said quickly. "And I've got just the person for you. Trish has gotten rave reviews as one of our best special assignment assistants. Her credentials are—"

"A floater?" Adam said, shaking his head in disbelief. "Are you kidding me?"

"Special assignment assistant," Marjorie said through clenched teeth.

He waved her off. "I won't work with a floater. This job's too important to trust—"

"We don't have a choice," Marjorie said with a hiss, then added in a normal tone, "Trish's credentials are excellent. She graduated from a very good college, then went on to get her MBA. She's smart as a whip. I think you'll be pleasantly surprised."

"How smart can she be if she's in the floater pool?" he said stubbornly.

Marjorie straightened her spine and pierced him with a look. "Our floaters—I mean, special assignment assistants—are top notch and you know it."

"Of course they are," he said. It was true. Duke's floaters were an enthusiastic and skilled group. But that wouldn't be enough for this job.

"Now, you behave," Marjorie added in a hushed voice, making Adam feel like a ten-year-old who'd been caught stealing apples from old man Petrie's orchard. "Trish is very smart and pretty."

"Yeah, but can she type?" Adam muttered acerbically.

* * *

Trish James had heard more than enough from Adam Duke, who obviously hadn't noticed that she'd been standing in the doorway to his office for the last five minutes.

It's showtime, she thought, steeling her nerves as she pushed away from the door and crossed the wide, elegantly furnished office to introduce herself.

"I type 120 words per minute, Mr. Duke," Trish said brightly as she held out her hand to shake Adam Duke's. "It's nice to meet you. I'm Trish James, your special assignment assistant."

As their hands touched, Trish felt a jolt of heat and stared up at the man, hoping her apprehension didn't show on her face. She'd known from the start that the CEO of Duke Development would be a formidable opponent. She just hadn't realized that he'd be so tall and intimidating. Or so attractive—if you cared for the sort of potent, masculine toughness that must've appealed to every last woman in the known universe. Looking into his dark blue eyes, she felt her stomach take an unwelcome dip. Even seething with anger, Adam oozed sex appeal from every inch of his broad, muscular frame. Minutes ago, as she'd watched him from the office doorway, Trish had had to stifle an almost overwhelming urge to sneak away.

But Grandma Anna hadn't raised a coward, so she'd pushed ahead and here she was, ready to beard the lion in his own den.

"Trish dear," Marjorie said with a wink, clearly aware that Trish had overheard everything the HR manager and Adam had just said. "This is Adam Duke, of course. You'll be working together for the next few weeks. I know you'll do a wonderful job. Call me if you have any questions."

Marjorie gave Adam a final warning glance, then smiled again. "Have a good day, both of you." Then she turned and raced toward the door.

Trish almost laughed. Sure, have a good day. It was really starting out well. She tracked Marjorie's escape out the door, leaving Trish on her own to face the man who had haunted her dreams for the last year. A man who'd turned those dreams to nightmares.

A man who didn't even know who she was.

"Welcome," Adam said gruffly.

"Thank you," Trish said graciously, ignoring the insincerity in both their voices. They'd just started off on the wrong foot. Determined to right the situation and conduct herself professionally, she cleared her throat and said, "I appreciate that you'd rather not depend on a floater, Mr. Duke, but let me assure you that I know my way around an office."

His eyes narrowed. "We refer to them as special assignment assistants, Ms. James."

It took her a moment to realize he was joking. "Of course we do. My mistake."

He smiled reluctantly. "That's better."

Her entire system zoomed up to red alert. It was that devastating smile that did it. *Warning!* her nerve endings screamed. In that moment, she could see how his former assistant might've been seduced into working for him until she snapped in two.

Determined to follow through with her plan, she squared her shoulders. Despite his gorgeous face, Adam Duke was a shark. He personified the killer species, and Trish ought to know, since he'd cold-bloodedly destroyed everything she'd ever loved. Now it was payback time. That's why she was here.

Looking at him now, she had to admit he was the best-looking shark she'd ever seen. His eyes sparkled with both awareness and cynicism, but Trish could imagine them turning to blue ice if he ever discovered her true reason for being here.

"Ms. James?"

"What? Yes?" Trish blinked. The last thing she needed was to be caught staring soulfully at her unforgiving boss. "I'm sorry, I was taking mental notes. Could you repeat that?"

With a thoughtful nod, he glanced at his watch. "I've got to leave for a meeting shortly, but I'll show you around first."

As they crossed the luxurious space, Adam pointed out the locked cabinet where he kept some personal files, next to a sideboard with coffee and sodas to which she could help herself.

"Thank you," she said. "I appreciate that."

"I'm not sure you will when you have no time to go to lunch and this is all you're stuck with."

"At least we won't die of thirst," she said lightheartedly, but her grin faded as she met his gaze and was struck again by his sheer strength and masculinity. She had to force herself to get a grip.

Despite his good looks, she knew he was inflexible and demanding, knew he would be a formidable task-master. Frankly, she wished she could tell him to take this job and…well, she couldn't say it. She needed the job too much. She was on a mission and she would accomplish what she'd set out to do. Let Adam Duke look down on her, if it made him feel bigger and better. She didn't care. The worse he treated her, the more justification she would have for doing what she'd come here to do.

But why did he have to be even more gorgeous in person than in the newspaper photographs she'd studied? Honestly, didn't she have enough to handle without being bombarded by feelings of attraction for a man who had single-handedly brought so much pain and destruction to her life?

No, it didn't matter how handsome he was. All that mattered was, if not for Adam Duke, Trish would still have her home and her grandmother would still be alive.

Adam checked his wristwatch again and Trish snapped back to attention. "I'm sorry, Mr. Duke, but I don't know your schedule yet. Do you need to leave for your meeting?"

"I'll be cutting it close," Adam said distractedly. "Let me get you settled before I go."

He led the way out to the large alcove where she would work. He pointed out the wall of file drawers behind her desk that held most of his clients' personal information and all the deals he was currently working on.

"Arranged in alphabetical order," he added.

Remembering his comment to the HR manager, Trish smiled. "I assure you I'm familiar with the alphabet."

He managed a rueful chuckle. "Let's hope so, Ms. James."

Trish grabbed a pad and took fast notes as he gave her a list of names of people whose calls he would always take, along with his cell phone number.

"While I'm gone, you can get your desk arranged, then I've left a cost analysis to be typed up, as well as some other letters and documents that need revisions.

If you have time, you can start studying what's inside those file drawers. I'll need the Mansfield papers when I get back."

Trish wrote everything down, then smiled. "I'll take care of everything, Mr. Duke. You won't be sorry."

With a look that said he was already sorry, he said, "Call me Adam."

"And please call me Trish," she said.

"Right." He looked at her for a moment, his mouth set in a skeptical scowl.

She smiled expectantly.

"Don't forget the Mansfield papers," he said finally, then strolled out of the executive suite, leaving Trish more shaken than she wanted to admit.

"That went well," Adam muttered in disgust as he pounded the elevator call button. "Knucklehead."

As he contemplated the attractive brunette who was now assigned to be his interim assistant, three things bothered him. First, the woman had been able to sneak up on him without him even noticing, and that never happened. He attributed his lack of awareness to his angry reaction to the news that his formerly invaluable assistant had run off and left him in a bind.

It had been obvious by her sardonic smile as they shook hands that Trish James had heard every word of his tirade over Cheryl's untimely departure—and that was the second thing that bothered him. No one ever saw Adam Duke lose his cool. His control was legendary. Marjorie didn't count. He'd known the woman for almost as long as he'd known his adoptive mother.

But now Trish James had seen him ranting like an idiot and that was never a good way to begin a working relationship—not that they would have that lengthy a working relationship, he hastened to add. He would need someone much more highly qualified to take over the position of executive assistant, not some refugee from the floater pool.

He immediately backed away from that thought. Marjorie was right, the floaters in his company were all good workers with great attitudes, willing to pitch in wherever they were needed. But Adam would need someone with top skills and experience, a self-starter and a go-getter with enthusiasm for the long work hours and a deft hand at dealing with his very demanding clients.

The third thing that bothered him was that she didn't look like the usual matronly floater his company employed. Notwithstanding that mocking little grin, her mouth was a bit too wide and her lips too lush. Her almond-shaped, dark green eyes seemed to focus a little too knowingly on him. He'd noticed the confidence in her posture and the way she held her chin high, and found himself grudgingly admiring her. She seemed determined to make this work.

She wore her shiny, chestnut-brown hair pulled back from her face in a classic style, and her black, pin-striped pantsuit fit her tall, poised figure like a glove. He generally hated pantsuits on women, but hers wasn't so bad. If his instincts were right, and they usually were, Trish James's suit covered one fantastic set of legs.

His groin tightened uncomfortably at the thought and he smacked the elevator button again. Her touch had sent something hot and wicked blasting through him and Adam wasn't about to encourage it.

But hell, every time she'd smiled up at him, Adam had felt his pulse spike. Her eyes had glittered with natural humor and her smiling lips were moist and full.

"And you hightailed it out of there like you were being chased by the town bully," he muttered in annoyance as the elevator doors finally opened. Two tech guys exiting gave him a puzzled look, but he ignored them both as he stepped inside.

It was just as well that he'd rushed out of the office, he thought as the elevator descended to the lobby. It would've been a lot worse if he'd stuck around and she'd happened to notice the bulging evidence of his desire for her.

Adam rubbed his hand along his jaw in frustration. What the hell was wrong with him? He wasn't some hormone-driven kid out on a date with the prom queen. This was just lust, pure and simple, and easily conquered. He wouldn't be led around by his libido. Ever.

Shoving open the private entry door leading out to the parking lot, Adam realized what this sudden attack of lust was all about. He'd been working day and night for months in anticipation of closing the Fantasy Mountain resort deal. He just needed to get the job done, then he needed to get laid. And not by one of his own employees, he added silently. There were any number of willing women he could call for a night of casual sex. And he would. As soon as he closed the deal.

As he jumped into the driver's seat of the Ferrari, he remembered his earlier conversation with Brandon and Cameron. Something about Mom trying every trick in the book to set him up with a marriage-minded woman.

An image of Trish James flashed through his mind and Adam frowned. Okay, that was ridiculous. There was no way his mother had anything to do with Trish being hired. Yes, the timing was a bit coincidental, and

Adam didn't believe in coincidences. But the idea was ludicrous.

He turned the key and listened to the finely tuned, high-performance engine roar to life. It was beyond ridiculous to imagine his mother going to that much trouble. He realized that he was buying into Brandon's paranoia and he shook it off.

But, meanwhile, he would do everything he could to avoid spending too much time with the gorgeous brunette who seemed destined, through no fault of her own, to make his calm and ordered life a living hell.

After a quick glass of water and a few cleansing breaths, Trish was ready to get to work. After all, she was being paid well and her work ethic was strong, so just because she was out to ruin the man didn't mean she wouldn't do a good job for him while she was here.

She started by exploring her new workspace. It was bright and spacious, just outside the doors to Adam Duke's palatial office. Everything was big and impressive, befitting the executive assistant to the president and CEO of Duke Development International.

The cherrywood desk was almost as big as her apartment's actual living room. And while it wasn't quite as dramatic as the floor-to-ceiling view of the coast from Adam's office, Trish actually had a view of the ocean from the window directly across from her desk. If she wasn't careful, she could get used to all this extravagance.

"But you *will* be careful," she admonished herself. She wasn't here to get comfortable, to enjoy any perks of the job. Just as she wasn't here to sigh over Adam Duke like some starstruck teenager.

But really, why couldn't the guy look like a troll?

"Let it go, Trish," she said, rolling her eyes. "Just get to work."

Forty minutes later, after she'd finished revising Adam's letters and documents and completed the cost analysis he'd left, Trish faced the file drawers. She wasn't even sure what she was looking for, but the faster she found something incriminating inside these drawers, the faster she'd be able to give up this sham job and be on her way. Maybe she would find what she needed today. That would certainly save her from weeks of turmoil, working side by side with the most delectable man on the planet.

"He even smells good," she groused, recalling his subtle scent that reminded her of green forests and autumn rain. "You weren't going to dwell on that, remember?"

Resolutely she opened the first drawer and began to sort through the files. An hour later, after memorizing every client name from A to M, Trish came to the Mansfield file, the one Adam had requested. He still wasn't back from his meeting so she looked through the file, studied the issues involved in the deal, then laid the thick folder on Adam's desk.

Finished with the tasks he'd assigned her, Trish checked her e-mail, printed her list of job priorities. She vowed to be on time every day and to do her job to the best of her ability while creating a pleasant work environment for everyone around her. She would make herself an invaluable member of Adam's team.

And then she would destroy him.

TWO

"I'm telling you, the woman's gone off the deep end with this marriage thing." Brandon Duke paced in front of the Dunsmuir Bay Yacht Club's wide bay window, ignoring the picture-perfect view of sailboats and blue skies lying beyond the glass. "She's obsessed."

"Why is that a surprise?" Adam grinned, then took a quick sip of strong coffee. "And why are you so freaked out? It's not like this is the first time Mom's tried to talk us into getting married. She wants grandkids and we're not cooperating."

"That's right," his brother, Cameron, said, sitting back in the comfortable captain's chair. Despite the thousand-dollar business suit and silk designer necktie, Cameron looked completely relaxed. But Adam knew he never relaxed. A former Marine, Cameron was more driven, possibly more ruthless, than anyone Adam had ever known. Except himself.

"Remember when she forced us all to watch videos of her wedding day?" Cameron asked, shaking his head. "She thought it would soften us up or something."

"That was gruesome," Brandon agreed. "But the wedding cake looked good." He stretched his wide shoulders, glanced around the busy dining room, then sat down at the table and studied the yacht club breakfast menu. "Are we eating or what?"

"Are we breathing?" Adam said with a laugh.

"You're always eating," Cameron said to Brandon as he picked up the menu.

Brandon ignored his older brothers and signaled the waitress over. "I'll have pancakes, eggs and bacon. And toast. Better make it a double order of toast."

"I'll have the Denver omelet," Cameron said, and set the menu down. "And throw in a short stack, will you, Janie?"

"You bet, Mr. Duke," Janie, the waitress, said. She turned to Adam. "How about you, Mr. Duke?"

"I'll stick with coffee," Adam said. He needed the jolt to snap him out of the knee-jerk reaction he'd had to his new temporary assistant earlier. If he'd been more awake, she never would've caught him so off guard.

Janie poured more coffee, then scurried off.

Brandon said solemnly, "Look, guys, about Mom. This time it's different. She's serious. You should've heard her on the phone with her pal, Beatrice. She's lined up a whole squadron of friends to work on this thing. They've already got women lined up for each of us."

"Oh, yeah?" Cameron said with a leer. "I'm always on the lookout for new women. Remind me to thank her when I see her this weekend."

Adam raised an eyebrow. "If you really want to

date someone Mom picked out, there's always Susie Walton."

Cameron shivered visibly at the high school memory. "Why'd you have to go and spoil my appetite like that?"

"That's my job." Adam turned to Brandon. "Did you tell her you're on to her?"

"Hell, no," Brandon said. "The woman's a runaway train and I don't feel like getting flattened."

"Smart." Adam stared out at a sailboat passing by under motor power until it made its way into the marina channel. He shook his head. "What makes her think I'd marry any woman she threw at me?"

"Good question," Brandon said, stymied.

"What makes her think we'd marry *anyone,* ever?" Cameron said.

"She's Mom," Brandon said with a shrug.

"Yeah." Cameron sighed. "She's like a heat-seeking missile when she gets a bug up her butt."

"Interesting mixed metaphor," Adam said as he lifted his coffee cup. "But apropos nonetheless."

Cameron shot Adam a look of derision. "Dude, apropos? Nonetheless?"

Brandon slugged Cameron's arm. "Leave him alone. He's using his words."

Cameron snorted. "Right. Sorry."

Adam disregarded them. "The bottom line is, she's not setting me up," Adam said easily.

"That's my point," Brandon persisted. "She's not setting anyone up. It's going to be a surprise attack this time. She told Beatrice, and I quote, 'They won't know what hit them.'"

His two brothers shared a look of amusement, but

Brandon wasn't cowed. He shook his finger at Adam. "Ignore me at your peril, dude."

Adam glanced at Cameron, who raised his eyebrows at his brother's adamant tone but said nothing.

Brandon saw the exchange and held up his hands. "I'm just saying, watch out. You're first on her list, Adam. And if you fall…"

"I won't," Adam said.

"Good luck," Brandon grumbled. "The woman's diabolical."

Cameron took a sip of coffee, then wiped an imaginary tear from his eye. "It'll be so poignant watching Adam tie the knot."

Brandon grinned and joined in with a few fake sniffles. "Our little guy's all grown up."

"Very funny," Adam said tightly. "I'm not tying anything." He looked from Cameron to Brandon. "And neither are you two. We made a pact."

The men grew silent as Adam's words took them back to the day when three eight-year-old boys were forced to make peace with each other. They'd been fighting all morning until their foster mother, Sally Duke, had had enough. She put sandwiches, chips and boxes of juice up in the custom tree house she'd had built for them and warned them not to come down until they could learn to live as brothers.

They were up in that tree house for hours before the dark and dirty secrets began to spill out. Cameron confessed about life on the edge with his junkie mom. Brandon talked without emotion about his father, who beat him regularly until the man was killed in a bar fight. His mother had disappeared long before that, so Brandon was put into the foster care system.

Adam had never known his parents. He'd been

abandoned outside a hospital at age two, then raised in an orphanage and a series of foster homes, one worse than the next. He'd been thrown out of four homes and was on a collision course with juvenile hall when Sally Duke found him and took him home.

All three boys were considered bad risks, but that hadn't deterred Sally, a young, wealthy woman who had recently lost her husband and had plenty of love to share. Sally's beloved husband had been a foster kid, too, and she wanted to give back to the system that had produced such a fine, self-made man as her husband, William.

Up in that tree house, having divulged their secrets, the three boys swore allegiance to each other. From that moment, they were blood brothers and nothing would split them apart. As part of their pact, they swore they would never get married or have kids because, based on their experience, married people hurt each other and parents hurt their kids. Even if Sally kicked them all out of her big house on the bluff overlooking Dunsmuir Bay, they swore they'd remain brothers forever.

But Sally was determined to make sure the boys knew that her home was their home, that they were a real family now. She was strict when she needed to be, but always warm and loving, and all three boys had thrived in her care. Eventually, she was able to adopt them and give them her last name. The Duke brothers grew up as a force to be reckoned with.

"Here you go," Janie announced. She placed their breakfast plates down and Adam watched his brothers begin to eat with gusto.

Adam got a coffee refill and sat back in his chair to reflect on Sally Duke, his mother, the woman who'd given three boys a chance at a good life instead of them being dragged down by a system too overburdened to care. Sally had changed the direction of their lives and made it possible for them to grow up strong and self-assured.

Adam owed her his life. But that didn't mean he would roll over and play dead just because Sally wanted to hear the pitter-patter of little rug rats around the house.

"You want some of this bacon?" Brandon asked.

"No, thanks," Adam said. He checked his watch. "I'd better run. I've got a meeting with Jerry Mansfield in half an hour."

"Wait, what are we going to do about Mom?" Brandon said.

"You worry too much," Cameron said between bites. "Nothing's going to happen."

Brandon shook his head. "We are so screwed."

"Deb, I have to go," Trish whispered. Her best friend had called to find out how the job was going but Trish couldn't concentrate, knowing Adam would be back from his meeting any minute now.

"Just one more thing," Deb said. "Ronnie's taking me out for my birthday tomorrow night."

"Do you need me to babysit?"

"No, but thanks. My mom's coming over."

"Oh, my God," Trish said as realization dawned. "Is this the first time you've been out since the baby was born?"

"Yes, and I don't know what to wear," Deb whined. "My world is elastic waistbands and maternity bras. I want to look sexy again. Help!"

Trish mentally pictured Deb's closet. She knew it as well as she knew her own. "Haven't you lost enough weight to wear your red dress?"

"Probably, except my breasts are slightly too big."

"Gee, Ronnie will hate that," Trish said drily. "Wear it."

"I really want to knock his socks off."

"Trust me," Trish said, chuckling. "He'll never know what hit him."

The floor creaked.

Trish jolted and whipped around. "Mr. Duke."

He stood several feet away by his office door. "I need the Mansfield file."

She hung up the phone. Deb would understand. Then she stood, wishing the floor could swallow her up. She couldn't believe he'd caught her on the phone. "It's on your desk, Mr. Duke."

He looked as if he were about to say something, but then he just nodded. "Good. Thanks."

"You're welcome." Trish stood rigidly, hating that she was ready to jump at his smallest command.

But he said nothing. Instead, he stared at her, then strode slowly around her area, glancing with suspicion at her desk, the files, the window. His presence was intimidating and chilling, so why did she feel as if she were burning up?

Finally, he met her gaze again. "What have you done?"

Taken aback, she said, "I—I didn't do anything."

He shook his head. "No, it looks different. You moved stuff around."

Trish relaxed her shoulders slightly and exhaled. "I didn't think you'd mind. I rearranged a few things on the desk and I moved that plant. It was blocking the view."

He raised an imperious eyebrow. "Cheryl never had time to notice the view."

"That's a shame," she said, glancing at the window. "It's gorgeous."

He stared at her intently. "Yes, it is."

Trish felt her cheeks heat up. "You don't have to worry that I'll spend all my time staring out at the ocean, Mr. Duke. I'm here to work."

"Good to know." He seemed reluctant to leave. Did he not trust her to do her work despite the tempting view of the world outside her window?

He cleared his throat, then walked toward his office. At the double doors, he turned. "Buzz me when Jerry Mansfield arrives, will you?"

"Of course, Mr. Duke," she murmured.

"And call me Adam."

"Of course."

She almost collapsed as Adam closed the door to his office. What was wrong with her? It wasn't as if she'd never seen a good-looking man before. But for some reason, this one seemed capable of mesmerizing her. As he'd stared at her, she'd felt the electric attraction. She'd been unable to breathe, aware of his every movement. She could almost feel his touch.

How was that fair? In case she'd forgotten, Adam Duke equaled the Enemy.

She rose from her desk and stood at the window where she gazed out at the wide blue expanse of ocean. What she should do is go and dunk herself in the cold water. These feelings were utterly unacceptable and she would not give in to them.

"It's just chemistry," she mumbled. She refused to feel anything but contempt for the man. After all the pain and loss she'd suffered because of him, she couldn't afford to lose her nerve now that she was so close to achieving her goal.

"So snap out of it, right now," Trish lectured herself. "What would Grandma Anna say if she could see you now?"

Trish conceded that Grandma Anna would've taken one look at Adam Duke and said, "What a hunk." Her grandmother had always had an eye for a handsome devil and her favorite line had always been, "I may be old, but I'm not dead."

But then Grandma had suffered the heart attack that led to her death. And Trish laid the blame for her grandmother's death directly at the feet of Adam Duke and his company.

If not for his cutthroat business tactics, her grandmother would still be alive and she and Trish would still live in the spacious apartment above their lovely Victorian antiques and gift shop known as Anna's Attic.

Victorian Village, the charming row of connected three-story Victorians on Sea Cove Lane, had provided homes and livelihoods for six families over several generations. Trish had grown up there, and eight months ago, right after she obtained her MBA, she'd banded together with her neighbors to look into buying the building from the long-time landlord and applying for historic landmark designation. Then everything changed. The landlord died, and before the historic landmark paperwork could go through, a development company swept in with a better bid. The landlord's children had no sentimental attachment to Victorian Village so they sold it to the highest bidder. The development company bought the block-long building, threw out the occupants and demolished their homes and livelihoods in order to build a concrete parking structure.

That company was Duke Development International.

It seemed that Adam Duke needed more parking for his expanding company, so with one sweep of his powerful hand, he had single-handedly destroyed six families' dreams. Grandma Anna's heart had literally broken after she was forced to move from the only home and business she'd known and loved since she first married her husband all those years ago.

Trish shook away the unhappy memories and hurried back to her desk. It wouldn't do to be caught staring out the window, the very thing she'd sworn not to do.

The memories helped strengthen her resolve and she went to work. On her short breaks, she pored through more files, looking for something, anything, that would connect Adam Duke to the unsavory business dealings she knew he was involved in. So far, all she'd found were neatly organized files with legitimate documentation and clearly itemized fees and costs. No double billing, no questionable investments, no shady transactions. But she knew it was only a matter of time until she found something. The destruction of her home and livelihood couldn't have been the only underhanded deal he'd negotiated in all his years in business. She knew what Adam had done probably wasn't illegal per se, but it was sneaky and unfair and mean-spirited. And she would find something eventually, some kind of evidence that would expose him as the sleazy businessman she knew he was. Only then would she fulfill the promise she'd made at her grandmother's deathbed, finally put her memories to rest and go on with her life.

By the end of the day, Trish was no closer to finding anything she might use against Adam Duke than she had been that morning. She turned off her computer and grabbed her purse, then knocked on Adam's office door. When he called out, she poked her head inside. "If there's nothing else you need, I'll be leaving for the day."

"Dammit," he muttered.

With some alarm, she checked her watch. It was almost six o'clock. "My usual hours are nine to five-thirty but I'll be glad to stay later if you need me."

"What?" Adam looked up and frowned as if just noticing her. "Oh. Sorry. You're leaving? That's fine. Have a good evening."

"What's wrong?"

He paged through the file, his mouth set in a grim line. "Something's missing from this file."

Trish's eyes widened. "I—I put everything on your desk."

"I'm sure you did." He thumbed through both stacks of papers clipped into the file. "But there's a lease amendment missing. It's got to be somewhere in the files, or maybe it's around Cheryl's—er—your desk."

"I'll check." In a panic, she rushed back to her area and rifled through the desk drawers. Had she subconsciously sabotaged a file? Of course she hadn't. She stopped and took a deep breath. Tried to relax. Then she carefully checked the file drawer, nearest to the place she'd first found the Mansfield documents.

"I think I found it," she said, walking back into Adam's office.

He jumped up from his desk and met her halfway. "Where was it?" he demanded.

"It was tucked inside the Manning file."

He rolled his eyes. "Manning. Great. I suppose that's close to Mansfield."

"Next file over."

"Good to know." He walked back to his desk where papers were scattered everywhere. "Thanks for finding this. It would've been disastrous if the client found out we'd lost it."

"I'm glad I could help."

"I just wonder how many more mistakes like this one are waiting to be found."

"I can start checking through the files tomorrow if you'd like."

"Good idea." He rubbed his knuckles across his jaw. "I guess Cheryl was under more pressure than she let on. This never would've happened if she was on top of her game."

"Three months' pregnant and trying to plan a wedding?" Trish said. "I'd call that pressure."

Adam chuckled ruefully. "Yeah, yeah. I guess I didn't help much. Still, this could've been a costly mistake. I'd appreciate it if you'd start going through the files more closely tomorrow."

"Of course." Trish almost laughed out loud at the request. She now had a legitimate reason to pore through the files and he'd handed it to her on a silver platter. She almost felt guilty, but refused to let herself go there. "Do you need anything else tonight?"

"No, thanks," Adam said as he sat back down at his desk. "You go and enjoy your evening."

She watched as he rolled his sleeves up his muscular arms. He'd long ago removed his jacket and his tie was off now. His usually well-groomed thick, dark hair was unruly and looked as if he'd combed it with his fingers more than once that afternoon.

A shiver ran up her back that had nothing to do with any temperature shift and everything to do with the ruggedly handsome man sitting before her.

She realized that she was staring. Flustered, she said, "You're working late tonight?"

"It's not that late."

She checked her watch. "It's after six."

He shrugged. "That's not late. I'll be here another few hours getting these documents finished for another meeting tomorrow."

"I can stay if you need help."

He glanced at the work spread out on his desk, then looked at her. "You don't have to."

"At least let me order you dinner before I leave."

"Not necessary."

But it was necessary. She would feel guilty all night long if she left him working alone without food. "It's not a problem."

"Well, if you're sure," he said, then pulled his wallet out and handed her a $50 bill. "That would be great. Thanks. I think Cheryl's got Angelo's Pizza on speed dial."

"Pizza? Are you sure?"

"I always order pizza when I work late."

Trish's eyes narrowed. "How often do you work late?"

"Almost every night."

"You eat pizza every night?"

He calculated, then shrugged. "Just about."

"That's not very healthy."

He grinned. "It's got all the food groups."

She simply shook her head and walked out to her desk where she found the file folder of local restaurant menus she'd seen earlier. She placed an order with a nearby restaurant for grilled chicken and rice with green beans and a salad.

She busied herself by starting on the filing project,

going through each of the folders more closely, as he'd requested. It also gave her the chance to continue her search for something incriminating, but so far, there was nothing.

After forty minutes, the food delivery arrived. She found a tray in the kitchen down the hall, laid the food out and took it into his office.

He did a double-take when she placed the tray on his desk. "What's this?"

"It's real food," she said.

He grinned. "You're pretty bossy, aren't you?"

"I just believe in good nutrition," she said defensively, and waited while he tasted everything.

He watched her with amusement as he took the first bite of chicken. "It's good."

She nodded. "And good for you."

He took another bite. "No, it's really good."

"I'm glad." She sat on the edge of the chair in front of his desk. "It'll keep you going better than pizza will."

"You may be right." After a few more bites, he said, "Marjorie mentioned you have an MBA."

"You were listening?"

His lips twisted in a self-deprecating grin. "Okay, fine, I deserved that."

Her eyes widened. "Oh, I didn't mean—"

"It's okay," he said with a laugh. "But in my own defense, I've had to deal with some of our floaters before. You haven't."

"Did you mean special assignment assistants?" Trish said, biting back a smile.

He laughed again. "Okay, I was an ass."

She couldn't help but laugh. "I wouldn't say that."

"You didn't have to say it," he said wryly.

"But you had a right to be angry," Trish allowed. "I

can't imagine someone leaving you high and dry in the middle of such an important deal."

He bit into a green bean. "I'm still angry. But I suppose I'm somewhat to blame. Cheryl did mention getting married a few times, but I've been so wrapped up in the Fantasy Mountain deal, I guess I let it go in one ear and out the other."

"This is the ski resort I've heard so much about?" She'd seen the photographs of the resort lining the walls of the lobby downstairs.

"Yeah," Adam said, taking another bite of chicken. "We're closing the deal at the end of the month and we've planned a major celebration. The investors and their families will be staying there for a long weekend. There'll be a big formal party and lots of hoopla. If we can get our act together."

"I'm sure it'll come together nicely," Trish said. "The photos of the resort look beautiful."

He sat forward in his chair. "It's a great place, Trish. Top-of-the-line luxury, with a spa and a world-class restaurant, great trails and ski runs. It's fabulous. The rooms are rustic, but warm and beautiful and elegant at the same time. I can't wait to show it off."

Trish couldn't help but get caught up in his enthusiasm. "It sounds wonderful."

Adam looked thoughtful. "Cheryl was in charge of the big opening-night gala we're throwing for the investors."

"A gala?"

"Red carpet, formal ball, the whole bit."

"Sounds exciting."

He stabbed at a small piece of chicken. "It will be if we can still pull it off. That's something else I'll need to bring you up to speed on tomorrow."

"Oh, I'd love to work on something like that. I've always dreamed—" She stopped. Whoa. No dreaming, please. What was she thinking? She'd been drawn in by his charm again. She carefully checked her watch, then stood. "Naturally, I'll be glad to do whatever you need me to do. I'd better be going now. I'll see you in the morning."

Adam seemed surprised by her abrupt change in attitude, but said smoothly, "Of course, it's late. Thanks again for everything. See you tomorrow."

"Yes, good night." She hurried out of his office, grabbed her purse off her desktop and raced to the elevator. As she waited, she berated herself. What was wrong with her, sitting around chatting with him as though they were the best of friends? Lest she forget, Adam Duke was not her friend and never would be.

And furthermore, as far as the opening-night gala was concerned, if she managed to complete the *real* job she'd come here to do, she'd be long gone before the Fantasy Mountain formal ball ever took place.

Three

She should've quit yesterday.

It was now Trish's fourth day on the job. She'd been through every file drawer along one long wall of her workspace but had found absolutely nothing incriminating about Adam Duke. Nothing that could be used to create even the tiniest public outcry against him and his company. On the contrary, yesterday she'd stumbled upon a full drawer of files containing the many charitable foundations he served on, along with pages and pages of donations he'd given over the years. The man seemed to be a veritable paragon.

"He even wants to save the whales," she muttered.

But that's not why she should've quit. She wanted whales to have a good life, too. And it was great that he supported all those charities. But did Adam have to come across as such a Boy Scout? She knew he wasn't, knew all those good deeds were just a façade to cover up the slimier projects his company carried out. There were plenty more files to search and she knew she'd find something eventually. She had to. She'd been here almost a week and so far he'd treated her so nicely, she was racked with guilt.

But that wasn't the reason why she should've quit, either. No, the reason was that she was starting to *like* Adam Duke. And not just because he was beyond handsome, not just because her heart stammered whenever he got close to her and not just because she was starting to dream of him at night. God help her.

No. The problem was, she was starting to like *him*. The man himself. His sense of humor, his sense of right and wrong, his work ethic, the way he treated his subordinates. Everyone in the company seemed to adore him and as much as she'd fought it, she found herself teetering dangerously close to that slippery slope. And adoration was not, repeat, *not* listed on her business plan.

And even if she did adore him—which she *didn't*—Adam Duke was the last person on earth she would ever get involved with. Not that he'd asked her out or anything. He never would. She was his employee and he was probably too damn conscientious to ever cross that line. And that was fine, too. She'd heard enough office gossip to know that she wasn't his type at all. Meaning, she wasn't a supermodel, tall and thin and beautiful—if vapid. Nor was she the type to fall into bed with a man just because he took her out to dinner.

She fumed as she slammed shut another file drawer. Even if he did ask her out to that fancy dinner, she would say no. Because Adam Duke was the enemy.

"Remember, Trish?" she muttered fiercely under her

breath. "That's why you're here. The man is the *enemy*. Try to stay on track, would you?"

"Good morning, Trish," Adam said.

Okay, she might've let out the eensiest little squeal, but she applauded herself for not jumping more than six inches at the sound of his voice. Why did he continue to sneak up on her?

"Good morning," she whispered hoarsely, trying to catch her breath.

"You're trying to make me look bad, aren't you?" he said, gazing at her through narrowed eyes.

"What? Me? No." She glanced around quickly. The file drawers were closed. There were no incriminating notes on her desk. How had he grasped the true reason why she was here?

He laughed and every last synapse in her nervous system stood up and did the cha-cha-cha. Who needed coffee when Adam Duke was in the room?

She cleared her throat and moved to her desk. "I'm not sure what you mean."

"I thought I'd be the first one in the office," he explained. "But you've beat me to it every day this week and here you are again, already settled in and hard at work."

"Oh." She was such a moron. "Right." She tried to breathe evenly as she fiddled with the staple remover and almost gouged her thumb. "Um, well, I do like to get an early start on things."

"Great," he said with a wink and a crooked smile. "I like that, too."

She resisted the urge to check her pulse. She looked away, tried to swallow, but her throat was dry as dust.

"Everything okay this morning?" Adam asked.

"Uh, yes."

"Any calls?"

"No, sir."

"Sir?" He grinned. "I like the sound of that."

She shook her head. There was that teasing sense of humor again. And that, combined with a winning smile, was surely the most attractive quality in any man. Well, a perfectly shaped rear end helped, and Adam Duke had that going for him, too.

"Are you ready to go over the opening-night arrangements?" she asked as Adam turned toward his office.

"Absolutely," he said. "Grab your notes and come in."

Trish squelched the thought that her notepad wasn't the only thing she wanted to grab. As she followed him into his office, she took it all in: the perfect butt, the wide shoulders, his masculine scent, his powerful stride. The man exuded strength, charisma and incredible sex appeal, and his ethics had the appearance of being honorable. So what was she doing here? Besides tormenting herself, of course? Lust, forbidden and sweet, roiled inside her and she almost groaned. How could she be so stupid as to be falling for him?

She really should've quit yesterday.

Adam ignored the now-familiar tightness pulling at his groin and sat down behind the heavy mahogany desk. By now, he should've been used to this ridiculous lust and the physical manifestation it produced in him every time he walked into the office and feasted his eyes on the deliciously curvaceous Trish James.

Physical manifestation? He rolled his eyes in disgust. Why not call it a hard-on and be done with it? But hey, wouldn't his brothers be proud that he was using his words?

Despite the physical…whatever, Adam had to admit he got a kick out of seeing Trish every morning. She was adorable without even trying to be, and it was easy and fun to spook her. You'd think she was up to no good, the way she startled so easily.

His chuckle got lost somewhere in his chest as he watched her plant herself in the chair opposite him and cross her legs. She was wearing a dress today and it was just as he'd suspected: her legs were world class. Smooth, shapely and lightly tanned, they were accentuated by three-inch heels that made Adam wish they were all she was wearing. He would start at her ankles, kissing and licking his way up to—

"Before we go over my notes," Trish began, "there's a letter you should probably read." She pulled a piece of correspondence from his inbox and handed it to him. "It looks important."

Adam raised his eyebrows when he saw the law firm letterhead and was scowling by the time he finished reading the contents.

He grabbed the phone and hit the speed-dial number of the contractor on-site at Fantasy Mountain. Holding up one finger to let Trish know this wouldn't take long, he waited for his call to be put through. He and his brothers hired Bob Paxton Construction for all their projects because Bob was simply the best in the business. And the Duke brothers only worked with the best.

Ten minutes later, Adam hung up the phone.

"I take it the news is bad?" Trish asked.

He glanced over, noticed her look of concern and realized that he was grateful she was so in tune with him and his business. It felt good to have someone on his side. Almost instantly, he brushed that odd feeling away and stood to pace.

"Yeah, it's bad news," he said, walking across the room to the coffeepot. He poured himself a cup and held the pot out to Trish.

"No, thanks," she said, still wearing that look of consternation. "Did someone get hurt at Fantasy Mountain?"

"No," Adam said immediately. "You read the letter, right?"

"Yes," she said, making a face. "But the legalese made my eyes cross."

"I know what you mean." Adam chuckled and sat back down at his desk. "But I assure you, nobody was hurt."

"Then what happened? Can you discuss it?"

"Yeah. The ADA guidelines weren't followed for the parking structures." He set the coffee mug on the corner of his desk.

"ADA is the Americans with Disabilities Act?"

"Right," Adam said, impressed that Trish had heard of the federal act. He'd had to explain it more than once to Cheryl when she'd first started working for him. "We make every effort to comply with the ADA, not only because we don't want to get sued, but also, more importantly, because we want everyone to be able to enjoy the experience our resorts have to offer. It's a no-brainer. But somehow, the subcontractor who built the parking structure didn't comply with the guidelines."

"The guidelines tell you how many spaces you need for handicapped parking and that sort of thing?"

"Right," Adam said, pleased once again that she was aware of the issues involved. "It's a lot more complicated than that, though, right down to the angles of curbs and degrees of slope, the width of sidewalks, the height of sinks in the bathrooms. I could bore you to tears with all the details. But the bottom line is, the crew building the parking lot screwed up."

"How did this lawyer find out about it?" she asked, pointing to the letter.

"Good question," Adam said, taking another sip of coffee. "There are organizations that make it their business to check out new facilities like hotels, shopping centers, public spaces, to make sure that the ADA guidelines are followed to the letter. That way, they can assure their members that they'll have access to all areas."

"That's probably a good idea."

"Yes, it is," he said, and ordinarily he had no trouble with the inspections. Because the Dukes had never had a problem. Until now. "So now we've got to get it fixed before the resort opens."

"Can it be done that fast?"

"That's what the phone call was for. Bob's already on it. In fact, he's more furious than I am. He'll get the subcontractor back there to clean up their mess. I want them to start as soon as possible, but before anything can happen, this lawyer wants to survey the site with us and point out everything that's wrong."

She gave him an understanding smile. "You don't like lawyers."

"They're a necessary evil," Adam said, shrugging. Then he grinned. "Besides, my lawyers can beat up anyone else's lawyers any day."

Trish laughed. "I'm sure they can."

As pleased as he was to have made Trish laugh, he quickly sobered. "I don't want to make light of this situation. I grew up with plenty of handicapped kids in the orphanage, so I know the problems they face."

Whoa, where had that come from?

He rushed to change the subject even as Trish's eyes

widened in sympathy. "So while this problem is stupid and annoying, it's not irreparable."

She nodded slowly, but didn't say anything, and Adam knew that if he could've kicked himself, he would have. He'd never made a slip like that before. What was he doing, talking about the orphanage to someone outside of his own family? It was none of the world's business what his life had been like before Sally Duke had intervened. Sure, reporters had dug out the truth in the past, but he preferred never to discuss it at all.

"We'll need the jet," he said abruptly.

She blinked. "We have a jet?"

He simply nodded, then punched up his calendar on the computer. "Yeah, we've got a jet. I'll need you to call and book it for Wednesday morning."

She snapped back into business mode and began writing in her notepad. "Wednesday morning. Where and when?"

"Let's make it eight o'clock. Leaving Dunsmuir Airport and traveling to the Fantasy Mountain airstrip. They've made the flight before. Let them know what you want for breakfast, and tell them I'll have the usual."

She looked up, mystified. "The usual? Wait. Breakfast? Me? Why?"

He grinned as she tripped over her words. "Breakfast is the most important meal of the day."

She shook her head in exasperation. "You don't need me to go with you."

"Of course I do," he said, breezing over her protest. He strolled to the wet bar, placed the coffee mug in the little sink, then casually added, "And pack an overnight bag."

"What?" She jumped up from the chair and blocked his way back to his desk. "Why?"

He gazed into her beautiful, leaf-green eyes and almost forgot what they were talking about. Almost. "It might be a long day. We could get stuck on the mountain. You never know about the weather in November." He could hear the tension in his own voice and wondered why a discussion of travel arrangements made him feel as horny as a high school kid.

"I suppose," she said slowly, but she didn't look at all convinced. She obviously didn't want to go to Fantasy Mountain, but the more she protested, the more he wanted her with him. She was so close, he itched to take her in his arms and fuse her body to his. But that probably wouldn't help his cause just now.

"Besides bringing you up to speed on the ADA issues," he explained, "this'll be a good time for you to take a look at the space for the opening-night festivities."

"Really, Adam, I don't see why…" Her shoulders slumped and she blew out a breath.

Adam stared at her for a moment. "Trish, are you afraid of flying?"

"Of course not," she said indignantly, her chin held high.

"Good. Be ready to leave at eight o'clock Wednesday morning."

"Fine."

He sat down at his desk again and said, "We'll go over your notes for the opening-night festivities while we're in the air next week. I won't have time to do it until then. And right now, I need you to pull some files."

Once Trish left the office, Adam could breathe again.

Pensively, he stood up, strolled to the wide bank of windows and stared out at the coast. He'd been walking an increasingly narrow tightrope over the last few days, trying to keep his mind on business despite being barraged by sexual fantasies that featured his attractive new assistant.

"Dammit." He couldn't blame Trish. She was efficient, discreet and intelligent. She seemed to have a good sense of humor. Adam noticed he'd been laughing a lot more lately and wondered if too much laughter was rotting his brain.

The woman was not only good at her job, but actually seemed to care about him. Hell, she even made sure he ordered something healthy for dinner every night he worked late. She'd stood her ground on the health food issue again last night and he'd admired her style while at the same time he'd debated whether he could rip off her clothes, throw her onto his couch and satisfy his true hunger.

Adam had already identified the problem. Lust. Pure and simple. He knew it. He just didn't know what to do about it. Well, no, actually, he knew exactly what to do about it, he thought ruefully. He just couldn't figure out when he would have a free minute to find a willing woman and satisfy that particular itch until the Fantasy Mountain resort was a done deal.

He wasn't going to give in to what he felt for Trish. Not while she was working for him.

So it promised to be one hell of a frustrating month.

An hour later, the intercom rang and Adam grabbed the phone. "What?" he asked a little too curtly.

"It's your brother Brandon on line 2," Trish announced.

"Thanks."

Adam pushed the speakerphone button. "What's up?"

"Who was that?" Brandon asked immediately.

"My new assistant."

"Is she hot?"

"I'm hanging up now."

"She must be hot."

"Goodbye, Brandon."

"Wait," Brandon said quickly. "Just wanted to alert you to the fact that Mom had dinner with Marjorie last night."

"So what?"

"Don't you get it?" Brandon demanded. "Marjorie's one of Mom's oldest friends. She's got to be in on the scheme. Think about it. Mom's got our own Human Resources manager working to sabotage us from within the company. They're perfectly positioned to bring you down."

"You're nuts."

"Fine. But don't say I didn't warn you. Mom's turned desperate and ruthless. I actually heard her say that you're going down first, so you'd better be on your guard. Don't be surprised if they pull an inside job."

Adam shook his head as his brother's ranting came to an end. "When did you become so paranoid?"

"Call me names but heed my words," Brandon said in a serious tone, then added, "Mom wants grandkids and to get what she wants, she has to sacrifice us. You're her first target, so I'm just saying you might want to beware of strange and beautiful women running amok in your office."

Adam laughed. "Were you hit in the head with one too many footballs?"

"This is the thanks I get for watching your back?"

"Talk to you later, bro," Adam said, shaking his head.

"I can only hope so," Brandon said mournfully, then quickly reminded him about the weekend barbecue at their mother's house.

Adam was still chuckling when he hung up. He buzzed Trish and asked her to bring him the North Vineyard file. She entered his office and his gaze was immediately drawn to her legs. Again. The dress she wore was office appropriate. Almost too conservative, in fact. It shouldn't have been sexy, so why were his nerves humming as he watched how well the silky material clung to her curves and skimmed her knees as she made her way across the room?

Small silver buttons ran up the front of Trish's dress and Adam wondered how long it would take to unbutton them enough to allow the soft fabric to slide off her shoulders and reveal her enticing breasts. In no time, he would have her naked, under him, on his desk.

"Do you want it on your desk?" she asked.

Adam flinched. Could she read his mind? He looked up to see her smiling as she held the thick client folder out for him to take. He exhaled heavily. Chances were, she wouldn't be smiling if she knew which direction his mind drifted off to whenever she walked into the office.

"Adam?"

"Yeah." What the hell was wrong with him? He felt a headache brewing and pinched the bridge of his nose. "On the desk. Thanks, Trish."

"I didn't know your company owned vineyards."

"What?"

She pointed to the file. "North Vineyard is part of Duke Cellars. I never made the connection until now."

"Oh." He rubbed his forehead and tried to concentrate on the mundane topic. "Yes. We own a number of vineyards and we've just had our fourth press. It promises to be a good one. We'll be opening a resort in the wine country next year."

"Oh, that sounds exciting."

"Yeah, it should be a fantastic opening."

Her eyes glittered with interest and all he could think about was making them shine with passion.

"Are you all right?" she asked, concern in her voice.

"Oh, yeah, great," he said, clamping down on his urge to pull her onto his lap.

"Are you sure I can't do anything for you?"

Not unless she was willing to give him a full body massage. "Thanks, no. I'll be fine."

She didn't look convinced. "Okay, but I'm right outside and I have aspirin if you need it."

A cold shower would be more of a help, but Adam nodded. "I appreciate it."

She turned to leave and he caught the lightest scent of oranges and vanilla. Against his better judgment, he savored the sweetness as he watched her long-legged gait carry her across the thickly carpeted office toward the door. The sway of her curvaceous bottom hypnotized him completely.

Dammit, would he ever be able to relax in his own office again?

Beware of strange and beautiful women running amok in your office.

"What the—?" He looked around, then made a face as Brandon's words managed to filter through his distracted mind.

Trish turned. "Did you say something?"

"No," he said in a strangled tone he barely recognized as his own.

"Okay." She smiled, then slipped out and quietly shut the door behind her.

An inside job.

"Stop it," he said aloud, shaking his head in protest. Brandon was seriously deranged and Adam was buying into his obsession, that was all.

You're her first target.

"No, I'm not."

She's ruthless and desperate.

"There's no way." He shook his head again and cursed under his breath, then brusquely opened the North Vineyard file and started to study the lease terms. After reading the same convoluted sentence three times, he stopped, looked up and stared at the closed doors leading to Trish's work area.

They're perfectly positioned to bring you down.

He raked his fingers through his hair as he recalled Marjorie's words four days ago, the morning she brought Trish in to take Cheryl's place as his assistant.

I've got the perfect person for you, Marjorie had said. And she'd been damn cheery about it, too.

"Ah, hell," he muttered. There was no way his brother Brandon was right. It was ludicrous. Trish? A plant? A willing player in his mother's scheme to marry him off?

Or was she just a pawn?

Adam pushed away from his desk and began to pace. He stopped. Shook his head. Paced some more. Stopped again.

He was driving himself crazy.

How could his mother and Marjorie pull off something like this? First of all, they would've had to have orchestrated Cheryl's departure. Or would they? Maybe it was just a happy coincidence that Cheryl had left the company, and Marjorie, coerced by his mother, had jumped at the opportunity to bring in a certain attractive woman who just might be capable of seducing him into love and marriage.

His eyes narrowed as he conjured up a picture of Mom and Marjorie meeting, scheming, conniving to pull it off.

Suddenly, it didn't seem at all far-fetched.

Abruptly, he remembered Trish's own words, the ones he'd overheard her say to someone on the phone the other day.

Trust me, he won't know what hit him.

Had Trish been talking to his mother? Or Marjorie, perhaps? It was obvious from her words that something shady was going on.

Did he really need more proof than that?

No. He had all the ammunition he needed.

He had to hand it to them, he admitted with a short laugh. Nice try. Trish was definitely attractive, and while he might enjoy the seduction part, there was no way in hell he'd fall for the whole love-and-marriage package.

He stared out the window at the waves crashing against the cliffs south of Dunsmuir Bay. He and his brothers had bought this land and built their company in this spot specifically to take advantage of the view. Despite the advantages Sally Duke had given them, they'd worked their asses off to get their company to the place it was today. He wouldn't allow some gold digger to get her greedy paws on half of all that.

Raking a frustrated hand through his hair, he turned from the window and grabbed a bottle of water from the sideboard. It just figured that Mom would pick out someone smart and nurturing like Trish to be his mate. Yes, she was beautiful, too, but her beauty was fresh and healthy, nothing like the calculated, sophisticated, worldly women he'd always dated in the past. He knew his mother disapproved of those types of women, but they filled the bill as far as Adam was concerned. Women who wanted no strings, no obligations, just healthy, raucous sex when the spirit moved them. Nothing wrong with that.

He suddenly recalled his mother's face as he'd introduced her to one of those women at a charity ball they'd both attended a few weeks earlier. At the time, he thought he'd read disappointment in the way Mom stared at him, the way her lips were pursed and her jaw was set. But it wasn't disappointment at all, Adam realized now. It was determination. He'd seen a new sense of purpose in his mother's eyes that night.

Determination to marry him off at the earliest possible date.

Adam rubbed his jaw, unsure of his next move. It was beginning to sink in, what Brandon had been dealing with since he'd temporarily moved back in with their mother. Sally Duke was a force of nature and it would be dangerous to underestimate her.

The more Adam pondered the odds that Trish had been planted here by his mother and Marjorie, the more plausible the whole thing seemed. The only question that remained was whether Trish was aware of their scheme. If she was in on the plan, and landing a rich husband like Adam was the only reason she was working here, then that made her a gold digger—plain and simple. An attractive gold digger, to be sure. But that meant she was fair game and ripe for outmaneuvering.

Pacing the length of his office and back, Adam mused over the possibilities. Trish James was perfect, absolutely perfect. Not for him, certainly, but for Mom's imaginary view of what a prospective wife for her son should be like.

And the more he thought about it, the more he had to admit how impressed he was. His mother had almost pulled one over on him.

"Well played, Mom," Adam murmured with a calculated grin. "And don't worry, there'll be a seduction, all right."

He'd seduce the lovely gold digger, enjoy a few nights of hot, delicious sex, then send her on her way.

"But not right away," he murmured as the plan took shape in his mind. After all, he had Fantasy Mountain to consider, and Trish was doing a great job organizing everything that would make the opening gala an event that would be talked about for years to come. Once it was over, though, he would kiss Trish James goodbye. Literally. He'd send the gold digger packing while also sending a clear message to his meddling mother that he would not tolerate her interfering in his life again.

With any luck, that would put an end to this ridiculous matchmaking scheme once and for all.

Four

"So it's as horrible as you thought it would be?"

"No, no," Trish said, keeping her voice perky. "It's going great."

It was Friday night, the end of an exhausting week. Trish tried to relax with a glass of chilled chardonnay while her best friend Deb Perris coaxed her three-month-old baby to drink milk from a bottle. They sat in Deb's comfortable family room directly across the breakfast bar from the kitchen.

"You never were a very good liar," Deb remarked.

"Why would I lie?" Trish asked.

"Gosh, I don't know." Deb brushed a few soft strands of Gavin's hair off his forehead. "Maybe you're trying to hide something. But here's a little hint. If you think raising your voice two octaves higher than normal makes you sound happy, you're wrong."

Trish leaned forward to tug at little Gavin's tiny

foot. "Poor baby, you'll never be able to get away with anything."

"That's right," Deb said proudly. "So you might as well spill the beans. Is the man as bad as you thought he would be?"

"Worse," Trish muttered before taking another hearty sip of wine to dull the misery.

"Really? Worse? How thrilling." Deb pulled the bottle out of Gavin's mouth to check how much milk was left. The baby began to fuss.

"Don't worry, sweetie," she crooned. "There's plenty more." She popped the bottle back into his mouth, then looked at Trish, unable to hide her excitement. "You know, I'm not surprised. Everyone at DDI seems to love him, but it's always a different story when you get them behind closed doors. Figures the richest ones are always the biggest jerks."

"But that's the problem," Trish grumbled. "The big jerk isn't turning out to be quite the jerk we thought he'd be. Just the opposite, in fact. He's thoughtful and funny and a true Good Samaritan—if all those charity files are to be believed. You should've seen how angry he got when he found out the contractors messed things up for handicapped guests at the resort."

"You're kidding," Deb said. "He sounds like some kind of white knight."

"I know." Trish took another healthy gulp of wine. She wasn't about to mention the orphanage Adam had spent time in. Not that she cared about his sensibilities. But good grief, how was she supposed to deal with the man she'd declared her sworn enemy when, despite what he'd done to her home and her family, she was actually starting to like him?

"Huh," Deb said. "There's got to be *something* wrong with him."

"Not so far," Trish griped.

"Oh, come on," Deb persisted. "I can tell you're holding out on me and that's not fair. I'm stuck here blathering baby talk all day, every day. So throw me a bone, would you? A little gossip? Something? Anything?"

Trish laughed. "I've got nothing."

"I'm not above begging," Deb said as she fiddled with the baby's blanket. "I don't get out much. And not that it's an issue or anything, but let's face it, you owe me."

"Hey, I steered you toward wearing the red dress, didn't I?"

"Not good enough," Deb said, laughing. "Although Ronnie was a happy man. Come on, spill."

Trish sighed. It's true that if it weren't for Deb, she might never have been hired by Duke Development International in the first place. When Deb left her administrative job at DDI to stay home with the baby, she'd recommended Trish to Marjorie Wallace, the HR manager, who'd immediately hired Trish for the special assignment department. Trish never would've been able to infiltrate the company so quickly if not for Deb. So, yes, she owed her friend the truth—if only she could figure out exactly what the truth was.

"You could've warned me how dangerous this job could be to my health," she groused, getting up to pour herself another half glass of the delicious crisp, dry wine. As she pushed the cork back into the bottle and returned it to the refrigerator shelf, she noticed the label. *Duke Cellars*. Oh, great. She couldn't escape the man for one minute.

Deb gave her a quizzical look. "What do you mean, dangerous?"

Trish waved a hand to negate her words. "It's nothing."

Deb persisted. "Hey, if there's a problem, you don't have to handle it alone. You could—"

"It's just—" Trish exhaled heavily. "It's hard to breathe when he's standing by my desk."

Her friend's smile was smug. "He really is cute, isn't he?"

"Cute?" Trish repeated, stunned by the word. When had Deb become such a master of understatement? *Cute* was for puppy dogs and two-year-olds. *Devastating* would more accurately describe Adam Duke.

"But as I recall," Deb continued, "I *did* warn you. You just weren't ready to listen. You were on a mission, remember?"

Trish sipped her wine. "I still am."

"You still intend to go through with it?"

"I have to."

Deb shrugged, put the now-empty baby bottle on the side table, then lifted the baby to her shoulder. After a few pats, Gavin let out a healthy burp and they both laughed.

"What a good boy," Deb whispered, bouncing the baby lightly in her arms.

Trish couldn't prevent the pang of envy that tripped up her heart as she watched. Deb and she had been best friends since fourth grade when Deb's parents moved their family to Dunsmuir Bay. Two years ago, Trish had been maid of honor when Deb married her high school sweetheart, Ronnie, in a beautiful ceremony on the cliff overlooking the bay. Then little Gavin was born three months ago and Deb quit her job to stay home.

Trish smiled wistfully. She didn't really envy her friend's happiness, but sometimes she wished things had turned out differently in her own life. If Grandma were still alive, if Anna's Attic and the Victorian Village were still standing, her life might've taken another road, might've turned out more like Deb's. She might have a husband or even a baby of her own by now.

Resolve trickled through her as she reminded herself that whatever else he appeared to be, Adam Duke was the reason her world had fallen to pieces. And Trish wasn't the only one who'd been affected. There were others depending on her to keep her word to bring Adam down. If she ever wanted to face her old friends and neighbors again, she needed to be strong and follow through on her plan.

Maybe someday, when Adam Duke and his machinations had been dealt with and were a thing of the past, she might think about settling down. But not yet. Not until she could look herself in the mirror and feel some amount of pride at having fulfilled the promise she'd made to Grandma Anna on her deathbed.

Content that little Gavin was settled and happy in his infant seat, Deb sat back down. "I know this plan of yours is something you've thought about for a long time, but if you've had a change of heart, it's okay. You're free to change your mind anytime you want."

"I won't change my mind," Trish said.

"There's no shame in it," Deb insisted. "You've got an accounting degree and an MBA. You could get a job anywhere."

"I know, and I will," she said, gazing at her friend with renewed resolve. "But first things first. My personal feelings about Adam Duke don't matter. He deserves to be taken down and I won't give up until I've done just that."

* * *

Trish spent most of Saturday morning running errands. She stopped at the dry cleaners, the grocery store, the bank and finally the library where she returned two books, then strolled over to browse the new arrivals shelf.

"My goodness, is that you, Trish?"

She turned, then smiled and gave the chic, older woman a hug. "Mrs. Collins, how are you?"

"I'm as well as can be expected for an old gal." Selma Collins was a neighbor from Victorian Village. She'd owned the stylish clothing shop that had provided Trish with dresses for all the significant events of her life, from her first communion to her senior prom.

Today Mrs. Collins wore one of her vintage Chanel suits. It was almost as old as she was, but it was elegant and timeless, just as she was. Her subtle scent of Chanel No. 5 filled Trish's sense memory and, just for a moment, transported her back to a happier time.

"Oh, Mrs. Collins," Trish said with a grin, "you look as fresh and young as the day I met you."

The woman slapped Trish's arm. "My dear, you were a toddler when I first met you, so stop pulling this old gal's leg."

They both chuckled, then Trish wasn't sure what to say. Most of the neighbors knew her plan to infiltrate Duke Development and they'd applauded her for taking action. But if she came up with nothing, she didn't know how she would face them. And that outcome was looking more and more inevitable with every day she spent with Adam Duke.

"You probably heard that Claude and Madeleine had to declare bankruptcy," Mrs. Collins whispered.

The news hit Trish like a physical blow to the chest.

Claude and Madeleine Maubert had operated the Village Patisserie for over twenty years. Their chocolate croissants were the stuff of dreams. Trish had loved hearing Mrs. Maubert's stories of her life in Paris before she met her husband and they ventured "across the pond," as she always said. "Oh, no. Are they going to be all right?"

Mrs. Collins shook her head. "They went through most of their savings trying to set up another patisserie like the one they'd had at the Village, but they just couldn't make it work. I don't think their hearts were in it."

"I wish there was something I could do to help."

"Oh, dear girl, you're doing everything you can." Mrs. Collins squeezed her arm. "We have such great hopes for you."

Trish smiled thinly but said nothing. She wished now that she hadn't raised the expectations of her neighbors by telling them of her plan to find some dirt on Adam Duke. Even if she did discover something they could use against their nemesis, it wouldn't bring back their shops or their homes.

But eight months ago, after Grandma Anna died, Trish had been so angry and hurt that she'd stormed into City Hall and demanded to know why the city hadn't approved the historical designation for Victorian Village. They'd told her that renters couldn't apply for the designation; it had to come from the owners.

She remembered the overwhelming desire to throw something at the clerk. It shouldn't have mattered who applied for the designation. It was an objective fact that the block-long building was a town landmark, well over one hundred years old and lovingly preserved in the classic Queen Anne Victorian style. How dare the city allow it to be bulldozed into oblivion and replaced by a concrete slab?

After receiving no satisfaction at City Hall, she'd marched into the large Duke Development construction trailer that was camped on the site of her razed home and made silly threats. The head guy, a wormy little man who made her skin crawl, had warned her to get out or he would call security, so she left of her own accord, but not before foolishly ranting her intention to "take down Duke Development" if it was the last thing she did.

Now, she could only laugh ruefully at the memory but back then, she'd been carrying around a grudge that weighed her down like a stone. Soon after the embarrassing scene at the Duke construction trailer, Trish had attended a barbecue with her old neighbors. She'd shared her plan with them, boldly promising that she would find something—anything—that could be used to hurt the Dukes in some way. It had been rash of her, but her friends had hailed her as their heroine and bolstered her confidence, so she knew she had to give it her best shot.

And so she had. But so far, she'd found nothing remotely damaging to the corporation or to Adam Duke himself. On the contrary, the man appeared to be a saint.

Mrs. Collins hugged her again and told her to "keep the fight alive." Trish promised to arrange a get-together soon, then watched the older woman walk away. Trish knew she had no choice but to renew her pledge to continue her search. She just prayed that Adam never found out her true intentions because, if he did, she had no doubt that he would make it impossible for her to ever find work in this town again.

* * *

"Who wants hot dogs?" Sally Duke cried as she slid the patio door open while balancing two full platters of hot dogs and buns.

"Let me help you with that, Mom," Adam said, jogging over to grab something from her capable hands. He set the trays on the patio table.

"Thanks, sweetie," Sally said. "Could you make the hamburger patties? You're so good at that."

"I'll take care of them. You relax."

"Oh, and I think we'll need more sangria."

"You got it." Adam signaled to Brandon, who stood behind the tiki bar on the other side of the wide terrace, beyond the pool. "Mom needs more sangria."

"Coming right up," Brandon called.

Adam entered the big, sunny kitchen where Cameron stood at the stove, putting the finishing touches on the latest batch of his world-famous chili.

Adam snatched a pickle from the relish tray in the refrigerator and chomped it down before heading over to taste-test the chili.

"Needs salt," he said after the first spoonful.

"I know," Cameron said.

Adam pulled the hamburger meat from the refrigerator, grabbed a large glass bowl from the cupboard and cleared a spot on the kitchen island to work.

"I need to talk to you and Brandon some time today," Cameron said as he stirred the pot. "The environmental report came in on the Monarch Beach property and I want to take action on Monday."

"Sounds good," Adam said. "I've got an ADA issue going on at Fantasy Mountain, too."

"Speaking of fantasies," Brandon said as he walked

into the room carrying the empty sangria pitcher. "How's that sweet new assistant of yours doing?"

Cameron turned. "You've got a new assistant?"

"Mind your own damn business," Adam said gruffly to Brandon.

"Ouch," Brandon said, grinning as he ladled more sangria from the punch bowl into the pitcher. "I seem to have touched a nerve."

He left the kitchen to deliver the sangria but was back in less than a minute. "What did I miss?"

"I believe we were about to discuss Adam's new assistant," Cameron said drily.

Dammit, this subject wasn't going to go away. Might as well discuss it with people he trusted. Adam walked to the sink and pulled the kitchen curtain back in order to scan the patio. "Where's Mom?"

"Marjorie and Bea just arrived," Brandon said. "They're all out at the bar, drinking sangria and wolfing down chips and salsa."

"Good," Adam said, suddenly feeling almost as paranoid as Brandon had earlier in the week. "Let's make sure they stay out there."

"What's going on?" Cameron asked. "You don't want Mom to know about this ADA issue?"

Brandon snickered as he grabbed a beer from the refrigerator. "I'm betting he's not really worried about the ADA issue right now."

"Shut up," Adam grumbled as he kneaded garlic powder into the meat.

"He hates when I'm right," Brandon said, smirking.

"Luckily, that rarely happens," Adam said drily.

"Good one," Brandon said, too amused to counter the jibe. "So go ahead, just spill it."

It wasn't that easy, Adam thought, staring at his

brothers. They'd always shared their problems with each other. Despite Brandon's easygoing nature, he had instincts as sharply drawn as Adam's and Cameron's. Besides being his brothers, these two men were his business partners and the two people he most trusted with his life. So he took a breath and spilled his guts.

"It's this thing Brandon's been harping on," he said, glancing from Cameron to Brandon. "You know, about Mom's latest campaign."

Cameron looked puzzled for a second, then said, "The matchmaking thing?"

"Yeah."

"What about it?"

Adam hesitated, then said, "I've got this new assistant."

Brandon nodded. "She's very hot."

"You've seen her?" Cameron turned to Adam. "When did he get to see her?"

Adam rolled his eyes. "He hasn't seen her."

"No," Brandon said, "but I've talked to her on the phone. Her voice is very hot."

"So?" Cameron turned to Adam. "Is she hot or what?"

Adam shook his head as he added more seasonings to the meat. His brothers were nothing if not predictable when it came to women. "Yeah, she's hot. That's the problem."

"I don't really see that as a problem," Cameron said, grinning. "But that's just me."

Brandon chuckled, then took a sip of beer.

"Okay, I'll bite." Cameron shrugged. "So what does your hot assistant have to do with Mom and…" He stopped, stared at Adam, then Brandon, then back to Adam. "No way," he whispered in amazement.

"Way, bro," Brandon said, nodding sagely.

"She wouldn't," Cameron said. "Would she?"

"Wouldn't she?" Adam asked. "We are talking about Sally Duke, right? The woman known far and wide as the Steel Camellia?"

"Right," Brandon said, then added, "the woman everyone in town calls when they need to accomplish the impossible."

"But…how?" Cameron thought for another few seconds, then asked, "Wait a minute. You already have an assistant. Where's Cheryl?"

"She quit," Adam said flatly.

"Cheryl quit?" Cameron frowned at the chili, then glanced at Adam. "What's happening with the Fantasy Mountain opening?"

"Trish hit the ground running with that project," he said, realizing again that no matter what her reason was for being in his office, she was damn good at her job. "She's got it covered."

"Trish. Your new assistant."

"Yeah."

"So she's good."

"She's excellent."

"Where'd you find her?"

Adam paused, then admitted, "The floater pool."

Cameron whipped around. "What?"

"You didn't tell me that," Brandon said.

"I know what you're thinking."

Cameron's eyes narrowed. "I'm not sure you do."

"Does she know what she's doing?" Brandon asked.

"Completely," Adam said as he pulled a cookie sheet from one drawer and wax paper from another. "Possibly better than Cheryl."

"Wow," Brandon said. "Cheryl was great."

"I know."

Again Cameron stared at the chili, deep in thought, as though chili beans might hold the secrets of the universe. You just never knew, Adam thought.

Finally, Cameron looked up and said, "So let me get this straight. You think Mom got Trish a job as a floater, then arranged for Cheryl to quit, then made sure Marjorie put Trish in her place in hopes that you might fall…?"

"When you say it out loud, it sounds pretty far-fetched," Brandon admitted as he took a seat at the kitchen table.

Adam bit back an expletive as he formed the first hamburger patty. He watched Cameron stir the chili some more as his brother tried to work out this conundrum.

Cameron added a bit more salt while he muttered, "It doesn't make sense."

"Well, it's Mom," Brandon said, slouching in his chair as he took a long sip of beer.

"I know," Cameron said. "I'm trying to work out all the angles, but I'm coming up with nothing. There's no way she could've pulled this off. It's impossible."

"You sure?" Adam said, his eyes narrowing. Cameron always weighed the odds, studied all the angles. If he said it was impossible…

"I'm absolutely sure." Cameron nodded with conviction. "I mean, Mom's good, but that's really out there."

"Yeah, I know, but…" Adam pounded another lump of hamburger meat into submission and put it on the cookie sheet. "I can't help feeling it's all a little too coincidental."

"You're right," Cameron said as he added more salt and chili powder to the pot. "But how could she have arranged everything? The scenario borders on labyrinthine."

Brandon's eyebrows shot up. "Labyrinthine. Nice."

"Thanks," Cameron said with a nod. "Bottom line, it's impossible."

When the kitchen door opened and Sally popped inside, Adam couldn't help but grin. With her platinum-blond hair pulled back in a ponytail, their mother looked like a teenager in pink shorts, a white tank top and purple flip-flops. "I'm going to set the table, and the girls need more sangria."

"I'll bring another pitcher out in a minute, Mom," Brandon said.

"Thanks, sweetie." Sally began pulling knives and forks out of the drawer, then glanced around at each of the men. "What are you boys cooking up in here?"

Brandon gave her a look of complete innocence. "Chili, Mom."

Sally eyed him suspiciously, then looked at Adam. "Is that all?"

"I was just bringing them up to speed on Fantasy Mountain," Adam said. "We'll be out in a minute."

"I hope so." She grabbed napkins from another drawer and crossed to the backdoor. "It's a beautiful day outside and I don't want you spending it inside talking shop."

"Yes, Mom," all three men said in unison.

As soon as the door shut, Cameron said, "Where were we?"

"Mom's diabolical plot to take over the world as we know it," Brandon said, and pointed his beer bottle at Cameron. "You were saying it's impossible, but Adam still thinks it's a little too coincidental."

"Maybe I'm just being paranoid," Adam said.

"You can blame that on Brandon," Cameron said, grinning.

"Hey," Brandon said, straightening up. "I'm not paranoid, I'm just vigilant."

Cameron's smile faded as he leaned against the stove and crossed his arms. "I want to be clear. When I said it was impossible, I meant that there's no way Mom or Marjorie could've convinced Cheryl to quit. But we all know how determined Mom can be, so it's entirely possible that she had Marjorie scoping out the scene at DDI for possible replacements that might come up at any time, in any of our offices. They could've planted Trish in the floater pool with the intention of using her on any of us."

"And they got lucky with Cheryl," Adam finished.

"Exactly," Cameron said.

"I told you Mom was recruiting her friends to help her," Brandon reminded them. "This is sounding more and more plausible by the minute."

"Dammit." Adam looked at his brothers, each in turn, then said, "Somehow, some way, Mom's behind this. And if she is, then Trish is a willing participant. Which means, my brothers, she's fair game."

Brandon laughed. "You're gonna turn the tables on her."

"That's my plan," Adam said. "I figure if she's looking to seduce me, I'm going to head her off at the pass. I'll seduce *her*. Then, I'll let her know I'm in on her scheme with Mom just before I cut her loose."

"It's good," Cameron said with an approving nod. "I like it."

"It'll work," Brandon agreed with a look at Adam. "As long as you don't slip up."

Adam pierced him with a look. "Please."

"Hey, it's not just you on the chopping block here, bro. If Mom succeeds with you, the two of us are next. You're fighting this battle not just for the Dukes, but for all mankind."

"Amen," Cameron told him.

Brandon stared out the window at their mother and her friends laughing and talking. "They're probably toasting their victory as we speak."

Cameron snorted. "A bit premature to be celebrating, don't you think?"

"Trust me," Adam said through gritted teeth. "They're doomed for disappointment."

Five

"We're cleared for takeoff, Mr. Duke."

"Thanks, Pamela."

As the older flight attendant disappeared behind the partition that separated the passenger compartment from the galley, Adam glanced at Trish sitting next to him. Her face was pale but still lovely. She wore a severe navy business suit with a plain white blouse, yet still managed to appear feminine and sexy. His fingers itched to peel that suit off her as soon as humanly possible. "All buckled up, Trish?"

"Um…" She rechecked the buckle she'd checked six or eight times already. "Yes."

"Good." He glanced at his watch. "We should be there in an hour or so. We can use the time now to discuss the opening-night situation. Did you bring your notes?"

"Yes." She licked her lips as the jet engines began

to roar and the powerful Gulfstream G650 moved into position on the runway. "But if you don't mind, I need a minute or two."

"Why? What's wrong?"

"Nothing," she said, closing her eyes. "I just need a minute."

She gripped the armrests tightly as the jet picked up speed.

"I thought you weren't afraid of flying," he said.

Her jaw clenched. "Not afraid, just alert."

"If you were any more alert, you'd be spinning."

"My seat belt's on," she pointed out. "I won't spin very far."

He leaned in and whispered. "I hope not. I need you right here next to me."

Her eyes sprang open and she glared at him. "Are you trying to distract me?"

"Maybe. Is it working?"

She closed her eyes and settled back. "No."

"I could try harder," he said softly.

"Please don't," she murmured, biting her lower lip. "I'm trying to concentrate."

"On what? Keeping the plane up?"

"Yes," she admitted. "Do you mind?"

"Not at all," he said as he leaned his head back against the headrest. "In fact, I appreciate it."

"You're welcome," Trish said. Her eyes remained closed but a ghost of a smile formed on her lips.

Without thinking, Adam touched her hand to gauge how tense she really was. She immediately grabbed hold of his hand and held on for dear life.

He watched her face as the luxurious private jet soared to cruising altitude. Her demeanor remained serene but her grip on his hand grew more taut until he thought she might cut off the circulation to his fingers.

Then she licked her lips again and he felt his throat grow dry as his stomach tightened in a knot of arousal. He wondered if she would bring this same level of focus to their lovemaking. When he slipped inside her, would she grip him so tightly, he wouldn't know where he left off and she began? Would she call out his name as she reached her peak? Would her eyes flutter closed or would she watch him watching her as they both flew over the edge? He would have his answer soon, of that he had no doubt.

A few minutes later, Adam saw Pamela, the flight attendant, leave her seat. He took it as an indication that the plane had leveled off enough that they were free to move around.

"You can open your eyes now," he said. "Mission accomplished."

She blinked her eyes open and glanced around, then abruptly released his hand. When she realized he was staring at her, she sighed. "I suppose you think I'm nuts."

He smiled indulgently as he unlatched his seat belt. "Not at all."

"Right," she said acerbically, then muttered, "I'm not sure why you needed me to come along anyway."

She might not have seen the point of her presence here today, but Adam did. The point was seduction. He intended to keep her very close to him from now on. He was on a mission of his own and there was no doubt whether he would accomplish it or not. She would be his. His for as long as he desired her. Eventually he would let her know he'd guessed her true intentions and he'd send his sexy gold digger packing.

For now, he sat back in the streamlined chair and assumed a relaxed pose.

"I'll need you to take notes as we survey the problem areas of the parking structure. We'll have to turn those notes into a joint agreement with the lawyers. But I also want your point of view on things in general. You haven't been to the resort so I'd like to hear your first impressions of everything you see."

She thought about that for a moment, then nodded. "I'll do my best."

"I expect nothing less."

She smiled hesitantly. "Thank you."

Pamela arrived with a basket of muffins and croissants with butter and jam, then poured coffee and juice.

He watched Trish choose a flaky croissant, then slather it in butter and jam.

"I told you to order whatever you wanted," he said. "They must have some low-fat frittata thing with gloppy yogurt, or maybe some flavor-free granola? We could ask."

She had the good grace to laugh. "No, I told them I'd have whatever you were having."

"I'm in shock," he admitted, then stared at the rich chocolate croissant on his plate. "This stuff probably isn't the healthiest choice, but it's the easiest, and they taste great."

"We all have to indulge once in a while," she said, then took a bite of the croissant and almost moaned in delight. "Oh, it's so good."

He couldn't look away. She happily ate the entire pastry, savoring each little morsel on her plate. When he caught her licking a drop of jam off her finger, it took every last ounce of willpower he had to maintain self-control and not start licking her fingers himself.

Trish, meanwhile, seemed completely unaware of his precarious state. How was that possible? How could someone who'd agreed to play a part in his mother's matchmaking game be so oblivious to the effect she was having on him?

The only explanation was that she knew exactly what she was doing. It was all an act. Licking jam off her fingers, gripping his hand earlier—it was all part of the game. And if she wanted to play games, he was all for it. But he was the one who would decide precisely what game they'd play.

And the name of this game was hardball.

After twenty minutes of breakfast and business talk, the dishes were cleared and Trish excused herself. She made her way to the airplane's compact bathroom, where she washed her hands, then stared at herself in the mirror.

"What is wrong with you?" she whispered viciously. "Have you gone insane?" She splashed some water in her face to clear her brain before freshening her lipstick. She still couldn't believe she'd grabbed hold of Adam's hand earlier. Yes, she was a nervous flyer, but that was no excuse. He was her boss, for goodness' sake, as well as her sworn enemy.

But it had felt so comfortable and seemed so right to hold on to him. And he didn't appear to have minded at all. In fact, he'd been the one to touch her first, hadn't he? So it wasn't really her fault, was it?

"I don't care who started it," she berated herself, "There will be no more holding hands with the boss."

She needed to maintain some sense of dignity, after all. She still had to get through the day with him, not to mention the trip back home. What would she do for an encore on that flight? Kiss him?

"Oh, don't even go there."

But it was too late. She'd been thinking about it for days, wondering what it would be like to kiss him. How it would feel to be held and touched and made love to by him. Her thighs tingled at the image she'd conjured up and the desire threatened to overwhelm her.

She was in big trouble.

She exhaled heavily, knowing she had to shake those thoughts away. If she fell for Adam Duke, she wouldn't be able to live with the consequences. She wouldn't be able to face Mrs. Collins or Sam Sutter, the bike store owner, or the Mauberts or any of the others, having broken her vow to avenge their pain. She needed to remember their faces, remember her goal, her mission.

Shoring up her nerves, she fluffed her hair and straightened her suit jacket, then made her way back to her seat.

Adam had opened his briefcase while she was gone and was looking over some sort of legal document.

As she sat down, he looked up and shook his head. "I'm reading the specs and they're all correct. The ADA parameters are all spelled out. So why didn't the construction company get it right?"

"Will you consider a lawsuit?" she asked.

He laughed without humor. "We can't exactly sue a company that we own."

She blinked. "You own Parameter Construction?"

"Yeah." He didn't look happy. "Bought 'em last year, along with a few other small companies. We're still working out the kinks."

"Oh. Well, that's a problem, but maybe it won't be as bad as you think."

He shrugged. "We'll know soon enough. No matter what needs to be done, I refuse to delay the opening. The resort is booked to capacity for the entire season. I won't put that in jeopardy."

"Absolutely not," she said indignantly. "They'll just have to make it happen."

"Exactly," he said, then leaned a little closer to add, "I admire your passion."

It was a simple compliment, so why was she suddenly tongue-tied? Did he mean it as a double entendre or was it just her wild imagination again? When he said *passion,* did he mean *passion?* Or did he simply appreciate her enthusiasm for the work? Did it matter? And could she be a bigger dolt? She realized that he was staring again and scrambled desperately to collect her wits back from wherever they'd scattered off to.

"Anyone can see it's the right thing to do," she said weakly.

"Not necessarily," he said, tapping the document. "Some people don't have a problem cutting corners."

"Please fasten your seat belts, Mr. Duke, Ms. James," Pamela said. "We're beginning our descent and should be landing shortly."

Trish's nerves began to race in a whole new direction as she fumbled for the seat belt.

"All buckled up?" he asked, shoving the document back into his briefcase.

"I'm getting there," she said, annoyed to hear the tension in her own voice. Finally, she managed to connect the belt securely around her waist.

Without another word, Adam took her hand in his. The movement pulled her up close to his warm, solid shoulder and her fears gave way to heated cravings. She tried to concentrate on breathing, deeply, evenly, but his strong, masculine scent got in the way. It clouded her mind and turned her thoughts to mush. When he began to stroke her hand softly with his thumb in an apparent effort to calm her, Trish almost melted into a puddle right then and there.

The plane cleared the mountain, then leveled off as it descended toward the Fantasy Mountain airstrip. It could hardly be called an airport, although that was the Dukes' eventual plan for it.

Adam glanced over at Trish and noticed that she'd turned a delicate shade of green. It must've been that sharp bank over the last mountain range that did her in. Was she going to be ill? She had a death grip on his hand and was rubbing her stomach with her free hand. She seemed to be trying to swallow over and over, probably to keep her ears from popping.

A moment ago, a strange protective instinct had made him take hold of her hand in an attempt to reassure her that everything would be okay. Watching her now, he had an irresistible urge to pull her onto his lap, cradle her in his arms and soothe away her fears. But he resisted and the moment passed.

It wasn't his job to comfort her. Yes, it bothered him that she seemed to be suffering, but he had to keep in mind just why she was there in the first place.

Damn, she was the most unlikely gold digger he'd ever met. She should've been more sophisticated, more of a game player. She should've been the sort of woman who was used to flying off to exotic places and carrying on casual, flirtatious conversations with men. But she hardly seemed the type.

He wondered what Sally and Marjorie had promised her in exchange for her part in this charade. Besides Adam Duke, that is. Had they offered her money? A new car? A permanent job with the company?

But Adam knew his mother and the more he thought about it, the more certain he was that his mother would never try to buy off a woman with material goods. No, Mom would figure that marriage to her son would be a good enough lure for any woman.

And Trish had agreed. He supposed he should be flattered, but he wasn't.

Whatever devil's bargain she'd agreed to, she would ultimately fail. In the meantime, though, Adam was more than willing to play along. He would be lying if he said he only wanted to seduce her because of her part in Sally's matchmaking game. No, Adam just plain wanted her. Wanted his hands on her lush curves. Wanted his mouth on her lips, her skin. He wanted to feel her all over, inside and out. It had been this way ever since the first day she walked into his office. And he would have her, all of her. Soon.

And that's where the game would end.

Norman Thompson, the ADA lawyer, had a tendency to drone on and on.

"I've already told you that we'll make the changes, Norm," Bob Paxton said calmly. "Just give us your notes and cut the editorials."

"Did you get that last measurement, Trish?" Adam said, crossing the narrow walkway to stand beside her.

"Yes, I've got it," she murmured, grateful she'd brought a new legal pad with her on the trip. She'd filled almost every page. She was also grateful she'd borrowed

Deb's warm down jacket and thin, thermal gloves or she would've turned into a block of ice by now. Despite the sunny day, it was cold up here in the mountains and they'd been outside for almost five hours.

"Do you have anything more for us?" Adam asked the lawyer.

Thompson snorted in disgust. "Isn't that enough?"

"Yes, it is," Adam said easily. "Thank you for your input. We'll send you a complete list of the changes we make, along with photographs of the completed work. I assume you'll want to conduct a final survey of the grounds after the work is completed."

"Absolutely," he said.

"Good." He glanced from Bob to Trish to the lawyer. "We're finished here."

"I suppose," Thompson said, dropping his own notepad into his thin briefcase. "I'll expect your report within the month."

"You'll get it next week," Adam said briskly, holding out his hand. "Have a good day."

"Well." He shook Adam's hand. "You do the same."

They watched Thompson walk back to his car, then Bob turned to Adam. "Next week might be cutting it close, but we'll aim for it."

"I want it done," Adam said. "If you have any problems with the crew, I want to hear about it immediately."

"There won't be any problems," Bob said determinedly as he put his small, digital camera back in his pocket. "I'll e-mail you the photos as soon as I'm back in my office. And I'll find out exactly who was responsible for all the mistakes."

"I know you will," Adam said, shaking hands with the contractor. "Thanks, Bob."

"It was great to meet you, Bob," Trish said.

"Nice meeting you, too, Trish," Bob said, shaking her hand. Then she and Adam watched him head back to the construction trailer parked on the periphery of the resort property.

"Let's get up to the lodge," Adam said, placing his hand on the small of her back and leading her away from the parking structure. "It's freezing out here."

"I'm glad I'm not the only one who noticed," Trish said, but now she wasn't sure if her shivers were from the weather or from his touch.

As he guided her along the bark-covered shortcut to the lodge, Adam pointed out the beginnings of several trails to be used for cross-country skiing and snowshoeing once the snow began to fall. The downhill skiing trail was just a short hike away.

"It's so beautiful," Trish said, stopping to look in every direction.

"I think so," Adam said gruffly, looking right at her.

Trish felt herself blushing and would've looked away, but how could she? It was as if he were a magnet and she were metal. His eyes were so blue and knowing, so aware of everything. Did he know what she was thinking? What she wanted?

Trish blinked. What was wrong with her? She still couldn't believe she was here in this place with him. When she'd first seen that letter from the ADA lawyer, she wished she'd been the one to alert the man about the problems at the resort. It would've been sweet revenge indeed against Adam Duke. But after hearing Adam talk about the handicapped kids he'd known at the orphanage, she was glad she'd had nothing to do with it. It almost broke her heart to know Adam had spent part of his childhood so lonely and alone.

She was still determined to seek justice and closure. She owed that much to Grandma Anna and the others. But she wouldn't do it on the painful memories of a lonely child living in an orphanage.

There was no sign of that childhood pain now as she stared at Adam and saw the stark hunger in his eyes. Then the starkness disappeared as Adam glanced around the trail.

"Serenity Lake is just beyond the main building," he said, casually pointing over her shoulder as if they hadn't just shared a special, lust-filled moment. "We'll be able to see it from the lodge. In summer and fall, there's boating, kayaking, canoeing, fishing, hiking, bird watching, mountain biking. We also offer yoga, croquet, tennis, golf and horseback riding."

"Wow."

He grimaced. "I sound like a travel agent, don't I?"

She laughed. "Yes, you do. But I'm sold. This place is fantastic."

Trish stared up at the magnificent Arts and Crafts-style resort that rose six stories up the side of the mountain. Fantasy was a perfect name for it. The stone and timber façade, dark wood gables and carved willow balconies offset the forest-green pitched roof, covered walkways and tall stone chimneys. The overall effect was stunning, rustic yet aristocratic.

"It's amazing," she said.

"Wait'll you see the inside," Adam said, grabbing her hand to take her up the wide plank stairs and through the impressive double-door entrance.

"It's…" Trish slowly spun around to take in the massive main lodge. The huge fireplace at one end of the room was tall enough that Trish could walk inside it. She wouldn't, of course, since there was a roaring fire warming the space. But it was certainly big.

Throughout the room, golden brown leather chairs and sofas were grouped around hand-built twig tables. Thick carpets covered the hardwood floors and wide wood beams stretched across the immense cathedral ceiling. The walls were exposed timbers, bleached, then varnished to a rich, warm hue.

"It's dazzling," she said finally.

He chuckled. "Why don't you have a seat by the fire? I'll check where they put our bags and get the keys to our rooms for the night, then we'll take a tour, meet the chef and have dinner."

She stopped in her tracks. "Our rooms? Dinner? Aren't we flying back?"

"It's after four o'clock and we still have work to do here," he explained. "We'll spend the night and go back tomorrow morning. That way you can meet with the chef and we can talk about the opening."

"But that's crazy," Trish said before she could stop herself. "I can't spend the night here with you."

He studied her for a moment. "Is it spending the night away from home that worries you or the fact that you're here with me?"

"Neither," she said hastily. "I'm not worried. I'm just…hmm."

He moved closer and seemed to grow taller, stronger, before her eyes. "We're here to work, not play."

"I know," she whispered.

He was close enough that she could smell his scent, a heady combination of forest, citrus and Oh, dear lord, leather. If she moved another inch, their mouths would meet. It was tempting.

"Are you afraid of me?" he asked quietly.

She tried to laugh, but her throat was too dry. "Don't be silly."

"Because I assure you, Trish. You're in no danger from me."

"Of course not." She smiled weakly.

He stared at her face for another moment, looking for signs of what? Fear? She gave him her best blank look. He nodded once and went off to get the keys. Sinking into a plush leather chair near the warm fire, Trish swallowed uneasily. In no danger from him? Was he serious? Or simply blind? Oh, if he only knew how much danger she was in. She just hoped he would never find out.

Six

After a tour of the lodge and the behind-the-scenes facilities, Adam introduced Trish to Jean Pierre, the head chef. Together with the hotel and restaurant managers, they all sat down to discuss opening-night strategies. After an hour, Adam ended the meeting and took Trish off to enjoy dinner in the resort's most elegant restaurant.

Adam had already explained to Trish that although the resort wasn't yet open to the public, the entire staff was up and running at full power these last few weeks until the official opening. The kitchen prepared meals throughout the day and the waitstaff served them to other employees with the same professionalism they would show to a paying guest. The same procedure was followed by the other departments throughout the hotel, and everything was observed and graded by the management team.

When it came to running their resorts, the Dukes preferred to leave nothing to chance.

And when it came to seducing beautiful women, Adam Duke left nothing to chance, either.

It had occurred to him as he was picking up their room keys, that his strategy with Trish could use some fine-tuning. So far, she was playing the model employee, pretending confusion and uncertainty when he'd informed her they'd be spending the night in this remote, beautiful place. He'd ostensibly played right into her hands, practically delivering himself on a silver platter for her enjoyment. So why hadn't she taken the bait?

Why was she continuing to act so coy?

You'd never know she had her sights set on him, he thought with some disgust. She was obviously playing hard to get, but the goody-goody act was no longer working for him. He would have to find a way to break through her charade. He wanted to look into her eyes and see her hunger, her craving, her need for him.

That's when he would make his move.

Adam had been in the corporate world a long time and his business instincts were well-honed. He knew how to stoke the fires of desire—in both business and pleasure. He was aware that the surest way to drive up both price and demand was to make it clear that the item was unavailable.

It worked in property development, in sales and acquisitions—and it would work with Trish. With that in mind, Adam decided that he would be the one to play hard to get. He would wine and dine and flatter and cajole and work her into such a state of frenzied need that she would be the one to proposition him. And then he would decide whether to say yes or no.

And because he was such a nice guy, he would probably say yes. Make that *hell,* yes.

Accompanying Trish into the dining room, Adam stood close enough to hear her breath catch as he touched her shoulder. He felt her heartbeat flutter as his fingers glided over the pulse point of her wrist. He wondered what she was thinking. Was she as attracted to him as he was to her? Oh sure, she wanted him as a husband, but did she want him as a lover? If so, she was playing it awfully damn cool.

He looked forward to turning up the heat.

They were led to a beautifully set table in front of the wide, plate-glass window overlooking the shimmering lake. As Adam pulled out her chair, he deliberately touched the small of her back, then let his hand glide up to her neck as she sat down. He was pleased to feel her back arch in response, as though she wanted more.

He would not disappoint her.

As Trish gazed at the view, dusk turned to dark and the world outside the window turned magical. She gasped as strategically designed outdoor lighting twinkled to life, accenting the beauty of the nearby forest and surrounding mountains. All of it was reflected in the serene surface of the lake.

"It's so perfect," she said, gazing across the table at him.

"I'm glad you like it," he said, admiring the way her brown hair tumbled loosely around her shoulders and her green eyes sparkled in the candlelight.

"How could anyone not love it?" She smiled dreamily as she placed her napkin in her lap. "If I were you, I'd never want to leave."

Adam was glad he'd arranged in advance to have the stylish restaurant all to themselves. It should've felt odd or eerie to be the only diners, but it didn't. The room was beautiful and well-lit. Willow screens and feathery trees in large pots were used to create intimate dining spaces. The staff was attentive, yet discreet.

Again leaving nothing to chance, Adam had contacted Jean Pierre over the weekend and requested that the chef prepare an extensive tasting menu consisting of those items he was considering serving at the opening-night gala.

For the next two hours, Adam and Trish tasted tiny skewers of tender grilled baby vegetables and savory meats along with a wonderful assortment of delicate canapés. Tiny pancake pillows topped with smoked salmon, crème fraiche and dill, bite-sized pieces of rare roast beef in a pastry crust accompanied by dipping sauces of creamy, homemade horseradish and a savory chutney. There were decadent sauces, fluffy patés and fragile mini-soufflés.

To accompany the hors d'oeuvres, there were six different champagnes to choose from and a number of vintages of cabernet sauvignon to sip and enjoy.

The conversation was enjoyable, as well. Adam found Trish's opinions stimulating and thoughtful, so they had a spirited discussion on a number of issues. They discovered a mutual appreciation of both vintage jazz and the Sunday comics. She had a sense of humor and she was smart and most important, loyal.

When the conversation finally wound around to the issues plaguing the resort, Trish wondered aloud just how the construction snafu might have occurred. She offered to assist Bob with his investigation of the subsidiary that had cut corners.

"When the truth emerges," she said, shaking her finger at him, "heads will roll."

"I'm glad you're on my side," he said, chuckling.

"Oops," she murmured, realizing what she'd said. "I think I've had too much champagne."

"But you're having fun, aren't you?"

"Yes." She smiled. "Everything is just beautiful. Thank you for including me in your evening."

"I had no intention of dining without you." He sipped his wine. "But now I have to ask, why were you so concerned about staying overnight up here? Do you have a boyfriend waiting at home?"

"Good heavens, no."

He was relieved to hear her say so. "A hot date maybe?"

She frowned. "No, of course not."

"Why 'of course not'? Don't you date? You're a beautiful woman."

Despite the soft candlelight, Adam could see Trish's cheeks turn pink.

"You shouldn't say things like that," she said.

"Even if it's true?" Adam teased. His grin faded as he sipped his wine. "Were you nervous about being alone with me?"

She glanced around the room as if she might be looking for the waitstaff. "We're not alone."

He leaned in. "Yes, we are."

Biting her lower lip, she looked around again, then straightened up and gazed directly at him. "No, of course I'm not nervous about being alone with you. You're my boss. I know I'm perfectly safe with you."

He studied her. "I wish I could say the same."

"What do you mean?"

"I'm not sure how safe I am around you."

She swallowed. "Don't be silly."

"You're dangerous to my peace of mind."

Her brow furrowed. "But I'm...I'm harmless."

"Hardly," he said with a grin, then let her off the hook by changing the subject. "Did you grow up around Dunsmuir Bay?"

She hesitated, then said, "Yes."

He chuckled. "You don't sound sure about it."

She raised her chin. "I grew up down by the pier, with my grandmother."

"Oh, yeah?" Adam said, relaxing back in his chair. "I like that area."

"Yes, I loved living there."

"You moved?"

"Yes." She looked away, unwilling to say more.

It sounded to Adam as if there might be more to the story but he didn't push. Instead, he held his glass up, determined to lighten the mood. "Let's have a toast. To Fantasy."

Trish managed a smile as she tapped her glass to his. "To Fantasy." She took a sip, then put the glass down and groaned. "Everything has been delicious, but I can't put one more thing in my mouth."

A vivid image of what else she might do with her mouth almost brought Adam out of his seat. It was absurd. What was it about this woman that made his libido behave as if he hadn't gotten laid in five years? Perhaps it was because he knew they'd come together soon. Very soon, he'd be able to bury himself in her warm depths. It wouldn't be soon enough to suit him or his raging erection, however.

Had he honestly thought he could wait for her to make the first move? Impossible.

He was about to suggest that it was time to go, when Jean Pierre emerged from the kitchen with several small platters and began to explain all the desserts he'd chosen for them. Adam's ardor was effectively extinguished, probably a good thing.

Trish's eyes grew wider with each little morsel the chef pointed to. After he left them alone, she stared at Adam in dismay.

"This is crazy," she whispered. "Seriously, I can't eat another bite."

"I'm not sure I can, either, but we don't want to hurt Jean Pierre's feelings." Adam speared a succulent miniature fruit tart with his dessert fork and held it out for her to taste. "Just one more bite?"

She moaned and rubbed her stomach. "I can't do it."

"But how will we know if it's suitable for the gala?"

"Why don't you taste it?" she asked.

"Because I'm the boss and I say it's your job to taste the desserts."

Trish laughed. "I'm not sure I've ever seen that rule in the employee handbook."

Adam chuckled. "Okay, then do it for Jean Pierre."

"Oh, all right." She took a deep breath. "This is for Jean Pierre."

"Good girl," Adam said, moving the fork closer. "One little taste."

She took the bite and licked her lips. "Mmm, it's really delicious."

Beguiled, Adam scooped a small spoonful of creamy chocolate mousse and held it out for her to sample. "One more bite, babe. Open wide."

"Okay," she said, smiling. "but only because it's chocolate."

"That's my girl," he murmured.

Time stood still as he watched her close her eyes, open her mouth and take the bite. Then she sighed.

"Oh." She licked her lips and moaned. "Oh, my God. Oh, it's fabulous." She swallowed, then licked her lips again.

In an instant, Adam's body was tight and aching. So much for playing hard to get. He wanted her with a need that burned right through him. In his current condition, he'd never make it out of the restaurant alive. Fine with him. He'd send the staff home, then make love to Trish right here.

So much for his grand scheme of withholding sex until she begged for it. He was the one who would beg her if he had to. Without even trying, she was the sexiest woman he'd ever met.

She was saying something, but he couldn't hear her. All the blood that might've helped his brain function had recognized a more urgent need and rushed to his body's lower half.

Adam tossed his napkin on the table and stood. "Let's go," he said, almost growling the command.

"Don't we have to pay the bill first?"

"I own the place, sweetheart." He came around to pull her chair out. "There is no bill."

"I guess I really am tired if I forgot that." She smiled up at him.

But on the way out, she insisted on stopping to thank everyone who'd waited on them, then poked her head into the kitchen and called out her gratitude to Jean Pierre, who came running over to kiss her on both cheeks and thank her profusely.

She had a way of making everyone feel special, including Adam, he thought as he led her out of the restaurant. He was beginning to wonder just exactly who was seducing whom.

Riding up in the elevator, Trish could barely breathe. Her heart raced and she shivered with pleasure, he was standing so close. She should've backed away and cut herself off from his touch, but she couldn't bear to. Not yet. Once they were back in Dunsmuir Bay and reality set in, she would deal with these forbidden emotions. But right now she simply wanted to concentrate on his masculine scent, feel the soft pressure of his arm against hers, appreciate his tall, confident stance and wonder how it would feel to be wrapped up in his arms.

She shivered again.

"You're cold," he said, shrugging off his jacket and slinging it over her shoulders. Then he put his arm around her and pulled her closer. "The mountain air can sneak up on you."

"Thank you," she murmured, wondering if he'd read her mind. If so, couldn't he see that it wasn't the cold making her shiver? Good grief, she was burning up—couldn't he feel it? But it felt so good to be pressed against his hard body, she never wanted him to stop holding her.

Even though she knew it didn't mean anything. Could *never* mean anything. He was just being polite, after all.

Trish made an effort to keep her thoughts casual as she glanced around the elevator. Even in this small space, the hotel's rustic style prevailed, with a charming bench to sit on and kitschy antler sconces on the walls.

There had been a few times during dinner when she thought Adam might be attracted to her, thought he might even be tempted to kiss her good-night. But he was all business now, holding himself rigid even though he had his arm around her. It was just as well. She had no business thinking they could ever be more to each other than boss and assistant. And, lest she forget, she still had her mission to accomplish, even though at the moment, she could barely remember what that mission was.

It must've been the champagne, or maybe the chocolate mousse. She wasn't thinking clearly at all.

They left the elevator at the top floor and Adam stopped at a door halfway down the hall. Using a card key, he opened the door and held it for her to walk inside.

"Oh," she said on a quick intake of breath as she looked around the large king-size hotel room, then walked directly to the stone fireplace. A fire had been set recently and was going strong, radiating warmth throughout the room.

There were throw pillows piled on the wide stone hearth for cozying up close by the fire, and the mantel held a sweet display of old-fashioned portraits in small Victorian frames. Hanging on the walls on either side of the mantel were vintage tinted photographs of mountain and lake scenes.

"So pretty," she murmured, then turned away from the fireplace and noticed the carved wood king-size bed for the first time.

"Wow." It was a masterpiece, covered in richly brocaded silk with a colorful cluster of pillows. Whole logs made up the frame and headboard, and tall, braided willow branches acted as bedposts. The willows were adorned by gauzy drapes that looped from one branch to the next, giving the room a light, ethereal feel.

The room smelled of pinecones and forest rain. She breathed it all in.

"I'm in awe," she said, spinning around to see more. "I love it."

"I'm glad." He leaned against the sliding-glass door leading to the balcony. His arms were folded across his chest and he looked relaxed and confident and too sexy for her own good, Trish thought.

He unlocked the glass door and stepped outside. "I know it's cold, but you should come out and see the view."

She joined him, grateful for the chilly air. Maybe it would cool off the heat washing through her. Adam stood at the rail, staring out at the lake and the mountain rising on the opposite side—dark, vast and mysterious. The moon had risen and was reflected in the water's surface.

"It takes my breath away," she said. "I wish we could stay for a week."

"Do you?"

"Who wouldn't?" she demurred. "It's lovely."

"So are you."

She looked away. "No, I'm not."

"You take my breath away," he said slowly, his dark eyes shining with intent.

She looked up at him, in time to see him lower his head to hers. In time to tell herself to stop this.

"Adam, I'm not sure…" Trish's thoughts scattered as he covered her mouth with his. His lips were soft yet demanding and the thrill was instant, the warmth so all-consuming, she wondered if she might go up in flames.

"You're not sure what?" Adam murmured against her skin as his mouth traveled along her jawline.

Trish barely heard him through the cloud of sensation fogging her mind. "What?"

His deep chuckle reverberated as his hand cupped the nape of her neck. "I'm going to kiss you again."

She was aware of her heart pounding rhythmically in her chest as she pressed her hand against him. "You shouldn't."

He met her gaze. "You don't want me to kiss you?"

"Whether I want you to or not isn't the point," she whispered.

"Then it's settled," he said, and returned to ravage her mouth.

The vague thought that nothing was settled flitted away. A soft moan escaped her and her knees nearly crumpled as his tongue urged her to open for him. She obliged him, wanting to taste him, wanting to feel his touch everywhere on her body. He was all heat and hardness as he pressed against her. The world around her dissolved and all that mattered was his mouth on hers, his hands gripping her backside as he aroused and devoured her.

"Oh, Adam, I…"

"I want to make love with you, Trish," he said, his dark blue eyes gleaming.

She gulped and felt the last of her resolve drain away. "I—I want that, too, Adam."

"I'm glad," he said. "It's cold. Let's go inside."

He took her hand and led her back inside and slid the door closed. Still holding her hand, he walked to the bed, where he stopped, kissed her again with slow deliberation, then released her only to pick up his jacket and tuck it under his arm.

"What are you doing?" she asked.

"I'm saying good night."

She couldn't have heard him right. "You're what?"

"Saying good night," he said, cupping her cheek in the palm of his hand and stroking her skin with his thumb. "And thanking you for a fantastic evening."

He kissed her again and she met him with fervor and a need she'd never experienced before.

"But...but you can't go," she said, still not believing him. How could he get them both so wound up only to walk away? How could he kiss her, tell her he wanted to make love with her and then leave?

"Believe me, I don't want to," he said, resting his forehead on hers and staring into her eyes. "But I also don't want to rush you into something you might regret later."

She almost groaned, knowing she should be grateful for his thoughtfulness. Knowing she should appreciate that he was willing to take it slow. Knowing that she didn't want him to leave.

"But I warn you that the next time we kiss," Adam said, skimming his lips against hers, "it won't stop there."

He pulled back to meet her gaze. "And there *will* be a next time."

She blinked, stunned into silence by his words.

"Sweet dreams, sweetheart," he said, drawing her close. His hands skimmed down her back to her hips as his mouth hovered an inch from hers. She parted her lips in invitation but instead of kissing her, he whispered, "Until next time."

Then he opened the door and walked out, leaving her dazed and aching with need.

Seven

I must be out of my mind, Adam thought as the plane soared above the mountains and headed for home. He'd had her just where he wanted her and hadn't made a move. And though he could stand back and marvel at his own inner strength, he had to question whether he'd made a mistake or not. His body was still clamoring for her despite knowing that she was trying to play him.

Now, as he watched Trish squeeze her eyes shut and clutch his hand, Adam wondered if it was indeed inner strength or just plain *stupidity* that had caused him to walk away from her. Last night's kiss had proven that Trish wanted him as much as he wanted her. Sure, maybe she was a gold digger, but he didn't think she'd been faking the need he'd seen in her eyes. And if the look in her eyes hadn't been enough, she'd actually said so. *Out loud,* he reminded himself, replaying the moment over and over in his head. His memory was perfect, dammit. He could recall with absolute clarity the scent of her. The feel of her. The shine in her eyes as she looked up at him. And he could hear her whispered voice echoing in his mind.

I want that, too, she'd said, when he told her he wanted to make love with her.

I want that, too.

So, was he deaf, as well as stupid? She'd *wanted* him. And what had he done? He'd walked away. As a show of strength. To prove that he was his own man and to show the world that no one but Adam Duke would determine his own future. Certainly not some cute-as-hell gold digger. And definitely not his mother.

But what had he gotten for his troubles? A sleepless night, an aching body and a temper on the edge of snapping. Why the hell did it have to be Trish James who appealed to him on every level?

He'd walked away to prove that he wasn't the kind of man who would roll over and play dead just because Trish James said she *wanted* him.

"So how's that whole 'determine your own future' thing working for you?" Adam muttered under his breath. Then he shook his head, thoroughly disgusted. "It's not working well at all."

Because he hadn't determined anything, he told himself. In making his choice to thwart his mother's matchmaking attempts, he'd been *reacting,* not acting. He hadn't made the choice he'd wanted to make. He'd made the only one he *could* make. So, really, his interfering mother and the gold digger she'd set on his scent were still in charge. And the knowledge of that was enough to kick his determination into high gear. There was no way they would win this game. No way at all.

"Did you say something?" Trish asked, her eyes fluttering open.

"No," he said, irritated that she'd caught his muttering. "Just thinking out loud."

She nodded, then looked down at their hands and carefully pulled hers away. "Sorry. But thanks for the hand-holding. Again."

He refused to acknowledge that he missed the feel of her hand in his. Clearly, he was still wound too tightly.

"Whatever gets us off the ground," he said, smiling though his jaw was tense enough to crack walnuts.

"It seems to work." She smiled shyly, then didn't seem to know what to do next, so she pulled out her notes from yesterday, opened her laptop and began typing.

He watched her slim, graceful hands strike the keys, then glanced up to see her squint as she studied her notes. Absorbed in her work, she began to nibble at her bottom lip in concentration, and Adam had the most maddening urge to pull her into his arms and nibble that lip for her. Dragging her off to join the Mile-High Club probably wouldn't be the most professional way to start the business day, but at this point he really didn't care.

The jet leveled off and Adam forced himself to open his briefcase and get some work done. If he could focus on upcoming concerns, maybe his mind would stop wandering to Trish. He pulled out the documents he needed to study for a meeting later this afternoon and tried to concentrate on them. But it was impossible with Trish sitting so close to him. He glanced over and saw her staring at her computer screen, now filled with her notes from yesterday's survey with the ADA lawyer. She looked fresh and businesslike this morning in a blue-gray suit and a simple white shirt. She hadn't pulled her hair back so it hung loose and thick and wavy around her shoulders and she wore some sultry perfume that wafted into his brain and turned his thoughts to soggy oatmeal.

Who was he trying to fool? There's no way he was going to get any work done. He wanted her more now than he had the night before, which he wouldn't have thought possible. Now that he'd tasted her, he knew it was only a matter of time before he would have all of her.

A matter of time? No. He wanted her now. Wanted his hands on her curvaceous breasts, wanted his mouth on every single inch of her skin. He was rampant at the image of those long, shapely legs wrapped around him. Muttering a harsh expletive under his breath, he subtly adjusted himself in his chair.

He would have her tonight, of that he was certain. There would be no walking away from her this time.

With that settled, Adam ruthlessly squelched his desire for Trish and forced himself to get down to the business of running his company.

"This has got to be the longest day in history," Trish muttered as she sat at her desk later that afternoon. She'd been trying all day to forget about the night before, forget about that stunning kiss and focus on her job.

Earlier, she'd actually considered claiming she was ill and going home. But if she'd gone home, she'd just be staring at her four walls and slowly driving herself insane. But being here at the office, so close to Adam and not being able to do anything about it, was driving her batty.

"And just what would you do about it if you could?"

she asked herself bitterly. "He doesn't want you, re-member? You were practically begging him to make love with you and he walked out."

Granted, she didn't have much experience in making love, or with men in general, for that matter. But she was fairly certain that having the man walk out after the woman said she was all fired up and ready to go was not a good sign.

She cringed at the memory of her puckering up and practically begging him to kiss her before he left her room last night. But no. Instead of kissing her, he'd whispered, "Next time," then walked out.

What had he meant? Next time? Next time when? Tonight? Tomorrow? Next *year?* And why did she care? She wasn't here to be romanced. But in spite of her best-laid plans and against her better judgment, she wanted to be.

Needless to say, she hadn't slept well at all last night, despite the beautiful room and that plush bed.

Now she wondered, not for the first time, whether she should just quit her job with Adam Duke and deal with the pain of losing her home and her grandmother in some other way. She had to face the fact that the man she'd been seeking revenge from, the man who had ruined her life and destroyed her grandmother's dream, no longer stirred up the same anger and resentment inside her.

No, that man stirred up something very different inside her now.

"Oh, my goodness," Trish said, as tendrils of lust radiated through the pit of her stomach. She was in very deep trouble if simply thinking about the man could turn her insides to jelly.

Trish forced herself to remember that she was being

paid to work here and that's just what she needed to do. If nothing else, it would keep her from feeling sorry for herself. There was nothing worse than a pity party for one.

Bouncing up from her chair, she gathered a stack of documents that needed to be copied and carried them to the copier. For the next three hours, she buried herself in work, typing documents and letters, making copies, running to the mailroom. Thankfully, the work kept all her troubling thoughts from circling over and over in her mind.

The next time she looked up from her computer, Adam was staring at her from his doorway. "Do you mind staying late tonight? We've got some extra work to take care of."

"No, I don't mind," she said. "I'd planned on it. Shall I order dinner?"

"In a minute," he said. "Can you come into my office first?"

"Of course." It would give her a chance to tell him what she'd been thinking about all day.

He sat on the edge of his desk as she approached.

"I want to thank you for everything," she said tentatively. "Dinner last night was wonderful, the resort is magnificent and, um, I hope you'll accept my apology for what happened, you know, after."

Adam studied her for several long seconds, his face an expressionless mask. "No."

Okay, she hadn't expected that. Couldn't he see how hard it was for her to humiliate herself in front of him? *Again?* As confused as she was by his reaction, she was also a little steamed. For heaven's sake, she was apologizing to him, the least the man could do was be gracious about it.

"No?" Her eyes narrowed in puzzlement. "You won't accept my apology? But…you can't just say no."

"Yes, I can." He pushed away from the desk and approached her. He was so close and his look was so focused on her that for a moment, she thought he might kiss her again, right there in his office. And however crazy it was to think it, it was even crazier to hope he would do it. Which made her wonder just how unhinged she'd become.

But instead of kissing her, he took hold of her hand and led her to the sitting area at the far end of his office.

When they were both seated on the soft burgundy leather couch, Adam squeezed her hand. "Are you apologizing for our kiss last night?"

She couldn't meet his gaze but instead concentrated on an intriguing spot on the wall beyond his left shoulder. "I behaved completely unprofessionally. I can't even believe I did that. You should probably fire me, but maybe we could just move on and forget it ever happened."

"If anyone should apologize, it's me," he told her, dropping her hand and standing up. "I'm your boss. You don't owe me anything."

He pulled her to her feet, took her hands in his and held them tightly. "I should apologize, but I'm not going to."

"You're not?" She blinked at him. This wasn't going the way she'd expected it to.

"No. Because I'm not sorry at all. I really liked kissing you and I'd love to do it again, but I'll understand if you don't want to."

"Oh, but I do," she said in a rush, then felt her cheeks

burn. Very smooth, Trish, she told herself. Burble over him like a high school girl talking to the football star.

"I'll understand," he repeated quickly as his mouth spread into a grin. "I'll be extremely irritable and I'll have to take a cold shower or two, but I'll understand."

She breathed in, then out, slowly. "You'll understand."

"That's right. I won't like it, but you say no and this is done. Here. Now."

She pulled her hands away and tried to gather her thoughts. All she had to do was say no. It was up to her. He wanted her, just as she'd hoped. And she wanted him desperately, despite knowing what kind of man he was. Despite knowing it was a huge mistake. But, first, she had to say something.

"Adam, it's important that you know that I've never done that before. That is, I mean, I hope you don't think I'm…" She exhaled heavily and waved her hand in exasperation. "Oh, you know what I mean."

He laughed softly. "Are you trying to say you don't usually kiss the boss?"

She raised her chin and met his gaze. "Of course I don't."

He gazed at her with that crooked, boyish grin of his and she felt another unwelcome spark burst into flame in her belly. She reminded herself that she was flirting with the enemy, but it didn't help douse the flames. She wanted him. She knew better, knew she should stand up and walk out right then, but she couldn't. She wasn't going anywhere.

"Say no and we're done. But if you don't say it, Trish," he whispered, lifting one hand to skim her hair back from her face, "then there's no stopping once we start."

"I don't want to stop," she confessed, and closed her eyes as his fingertips trailed across her cheek.

He pulled her tight against him and covered her mouth completely in a hot, open-mouthed kiss that overwhelmed and inflamed her.

He held the nape of her neck firmly, keeping her close as their tongues tangled and parried in a wildly sensual paso doble. Trish met his passion with her own ardent desire, ignoring the voice in her head that warned her that if she wanted to survive, *she should walk away from Adam Duke, now.*

But how could she walk away when she was already lost in this sweeping rush of sensation and wanting? Already lost in the softness of his lips that belied the strength and confidence of his lean, hard body. He pressed her against his solid chest, causing her nipples to quiver and harden.

Oh, God, no, she wouldn't walk away.

"Adam, I…" She couldn't complete the thought but it didn't matter as he seemed to anticipate her every want.

"I know," he whispered, and laid her down on the wide couch. He covered her body with his and his mouth claimed hers with renewed urgency. His taste filled her senses, his taut body tempted hers. She could feel him lengthen and harden against her thigh and she wanted all of it, all of him.

She reached up to wrap her arms around his neck at the same time as his hand moved to cup her breast, drawing a soft moan from deep in her throat. He began to unbutton her blouse while his lips nipped and kissed their way along her jaw to her ear, then down her neck.

He pushed himself up and straddled her, staring at

her with a heated intensity that somehow gave her the courage to act more boldly than she felt. He watched intently as she eased her blouse off, then began to unhook her bra.

"I'll do it," he said huskily, and peeled back the white lace cups. His nostrils flared as he stared at her exposed breasts.

"Beautiful," he said, then took both breasts in his hands and used his thumbs to gently flick her nipples to a hard peak.

She caught her breath when he bent down and took her into his mouth, teasing one ultrasensitive nipple first with his teeth, then with his tongue, rolling and licking her firm tip until she groaned aloud.

He continued his tender assault on her other breast as he reached to unzip her pants and ease them down her legs. She took over, shimmying and finally kicking her pants to the floor to allow him full access to every part of her.

His eyes met her gaze and Trish saw a flicker of heat and pure masculine satisfaction in his dark eyes. He slipped his fingers beneath the elastic band of her thong and touched her most intimate spot. When he slid one finger inside her, she gasped.

"So hot and tight," he murmured, then eased out and back in again. He repeated the action over and over, creating friction against her sensitive flesh that aroused and devastated her.

"Adam," she whispered. "Please."

Instead of answering, he stood and made fast work of taking his shirt off, tearing off his shoes and socks before unzipping and removing his trousers.

Trish watched, mesmerized as she savored the sight of his long, powerful legs and well-toned body. She shivered with anticipation and her breath hitched as he pulled off his boxers and revealed his large, stiff erection.

She ached to touch him.

He was watching her now as he reached for his pants and pulled a foil packet from the pocket. He tore it open and slipped on protection, then stretched out on the couch and took her in his arms. He kissed her fiercely, carnally, at the same time as he found her moist core and entered her with one, strong thrust.

Trish's eyes opened wide and she cried out, but almost as quickly as the pain came, it was gone, replaced by a feeling of fullness, an intimate connection she'd never experienced before.

Adam stopped, held perfectly still, locked inside her and stared down into her eyes. "A *virgin?*" His words were strangled as if there were a fist clamped around his throat. "Why didn't you tell me?"

"Can we talk about this later?" she demanded, lifting her hips, drawing him deeper.

He hissed in a breath through gritted teeth.

"Don't stop," she commanded, and latched her ankles over his legs.

He gave her a tight grin. "I have no intention of stopping, but we'll talk about this."

"Later," she moaned. Her hands glided over his shoulders in an attempt to calm him down, urge him on, reassure him it was okay to keep going. *Please* keep going.

His lips found hers again and he kissed her tenderly as he began to move again. Pleasure grew and spread through her and she relaxed beneath him.

"Wrap your legs around me, sweetheart," he murmured. "Move with me."

She did so, matching his rhythm. She could feel his heart pounding against hers and it made her feel alive. She watched his face—beautiful, strong, straining as he gave her pleasure. She tightened her legs around him, then lost sight of everything but the lush heat that was threatening to consume her.

"Open your eyes," he said. "I want to see them turn dark when you come with me."

She was helpless to do otherwise as he plunged and filled her. Heat built within her and need ignited every nerve ending as she climbed higher and higher. She cried out his name as color exploded behind her eyelids and electric pulsations coursed wildly through her body.

Adam stiffened above her and shouted her name. He drove into her one last time, so deeply that she could've sworn she felt him touch her heart. Then he collapsed against her and his full weight pressed her into the couch. He murmured words she couldn't hear, but his warm breath against her skin soothed her.

For the next few minutes, all she could feel were the tremors moving in waves throughout her body and all she could hear was their ragged breathing. She was completely drained and satiated. She felt free, joyfully free and more alive than she'd ever been before.

Eight

Adam carefully shifted and stretched out alongside Trish. He tucked her closer to him and then, leaning on one elbow, stared down at her.

"Why didn't you tell me?"

Despite the fact that they were inches away from each other, she wouldn't meet his gaze. A virgin? Was she really that hungry to get her hands on his bank account that she'd given up something so precious?

Adam wondered what she was thinking. Was she getting ready to bolt? He wouldn't put it past her, but he wasn't about to let her walk out right then. Not until he knew what was going on. He wanted—no, he *needed*—to know what was going through her mind. If she'd felt so compelled to apologize for one measly kiss the night before, she must be drowning in guilt and regret now, after just having had wild, incredible sex on his office couch.

But that didn't mean she was going anywhere. No way. Not yet. His own guilt had ratcheted up a notch or two besides. Would he have taken her if he'd known she was a virgin? No. But that ship had sailed. Besides, he couldn't say why, but he wasn't ready to let her go. Not until he could taste her again. He thought of the private bathroom connected to his office, with a shower big enough for two. He could offer her the use of the shower, then join her there.

The soft curve of her thigh was nestled against his shaft, causing it to stir to attention. He almost groaned aloud. It wasn't bad enough that he'd taken her here, in his office, on the couch. Now he wanted her again.

"I'd better be going," she whispered.

"No," he said immediately, telling himself she was too vulnerable right now for him to allow her to leave—and he refused to dwell on why he cared one way or another. He'd never wanted a woman to stay with him any longer than absolutely necessary. But Trish was different. He wasn't prepared to say how or why she was different. She just was. Gold digger or not, he felt something for her. And besides, he wanted answers to some questions.

"You're not going anywhere until I find out why you didn't tell me you were a virgin."

"Why does it matter?" she asked, still averting her gaze.

"Because I wouldn't have taken you on a damn couch, that's why."

She glared at him. "Well, then, that's why I didn't tell you."

He frowned as he brushed a strand of hair back from her face. "But I could've gone slowly and not hurt you so much."

"You didn't hurt me," she insisted softly, shaking her head as she said it. Her eyelids fluttered and she finally smiled at him. "Well, not too much anyway. And after a few seconds, it was perfect."

"Not yet," he said with determination. "But it will be."

Trish sat at her desk early the next morning, torn between preening like a satisfied cat and crawling under her desk to hide in shame.

She'd had sex with the enemy.

If it had only happened once, she might've chalked it up to temporary insanity. But it hadn't happened just once. Not even twice. *Three times!* In three different ways. She shivered at the memory of everything he'd done to her. One thing was certain: she'd never look at his conference table the same way again. And she was considering erecting a small shrine in front of that awe-inspiring couch of his.

She knew it was wrong, knew what a mistake she'd made, but it had been amazing, wonderful, thrilling. She'd reveled in Adam's kisses, each caress and every whispered word. He'd made her feel like she'd never felt before.

Well, of course she'd never felt those things before. Up until last night, she'd been a virgin.

She couldn't have told Adam why she was still a virgin at the ripe old age of almost twenty-six, so it was a good thing he never asked. She'd grown up sheltered, surrounded and protected by her grandmother and her neighbors at the Victorian Village. Once she went off to college, she was working too hard to mix in much with the party crowd.

She graduated a year early, then came home and

enrolled in the MBA program at the local university. Grandma Anna was starting to slow down, so Trish tried to help out in the store every day. She took over the purchasing and handled all the shipments. She rotated the displays and dealt with advertising and promotions.

Grandma was always teasing her, telling her to go out and meet people, have fun, fall in love. And Trish always figured there would be plenty time to do just that.

But that was around the same time her grandmother and their neighbors applied for historic landmark designation for the Victorian building. And that's when their world came crashing down, thanks to Adam Duke's company.

That's why she was here. Because Adam Duke had destroyed their lives and now she was out to ruin him. If only she could remember that.

Trish sighed heavily and powered up her computer. It was still early enough that she could do some personal work without feeling too guilty.

"This is for you, Grandma," she murmured, then logged onto the company's Web site and did a search of their mergers and acquisitions over the past two years. She made a list of the companies Duke had acquired, and planned to search the Internet to see if any unsavory dealings had gone on during the transactions. She might even try to set up some interviews of the former employees of those companies to see how badly they were treated by the Dukes.

She sat back in her chair, feeling better now that she'd taken some small action toward avenging her grandmother. After the way she'd spent the previous evening, she wasn't sure she'd ever lose these feelings of guilt, but at least she could tell herself that her mission was still on track. She owed that much to her Village friends.

So why did her thoughts keep drifting back to Adam?

This morning it seemed that all she could remember was Adam's skillful moves, his talented mouth and the scent of his skin. Suddenly her loins tightened and fresh waves of excitement surged through her. She could barely suppress a moan.

"Oh, good grief," she muttered as she stood up. She had to get busy. What if someone caught her day-dreaming at her desk? What if *Adam* caught her? It was still early and he wasn't in yet, but he'd be walking down the hall any minute. She swept up a handful of correspondence and rushed off to the copy room to work.

Standing in front of the copy machine, Trish realized she had some serious decisions to make. Where would she go from here? What would she do? She leaned against the machine, closed her eyes and exhaled wearily. It was time to admit that she was in deep trouble.

After all, it wasn't bad enough that she'd slept with the man she'd once considered her worst enemy, the man she'd held responsible for destroying her happiness and the life of her beloved grandmother. And it wasn't bad enough that the man she'd slept with was her *boss,* the person whose company she'd infiltrated in order to destroy him. And it wasn't even bad enough that she'd made a promise to her grandmother on her deathbed that she would avenge the wrongs done to Grandma Anna and her neighbors, that she would find a way to make Adam Duke experience the same level of pain that she and Grandma Anna had known.

No, what was really, really bad was that she couldn't wait to be in his arms all over again.

But it couldn't happen again.

The copy machine stopped and Trish jolted at the abrupt silence. In that moment it became crystal clear exactly what she would have to do. A switch had been thrown inside her conscience. Even though she hadn't gotten a lot of sleep last night and now felt as though she were walking through a heavy fog, she knew at last the direction she must take. Deathbed promises were not to be treated lightly. She'd betrayed not only her grandmother but all her old neighbors by becoming involved with Adam Duke.

How could she ever face her old friends again?

There was only one thing to do.

She had to tell him she could never have sex with him again. If she didn't put a stop to it now, her goal of righting the wrong she'd set out to do would have to be written off as a total failure. Which meant that it wouldn't be Adam who was destroyed. It would be Trish.

As she walked back to her desk with the stack of copies, she concluded that she would talk to Adam as soon as possible. It shouldn't be difficult. After all, why would he care that she was refusing to sleep with him again? He had a million women waiting in line for the same opportunity.

She wrinkled her nose at the thought. Even if that was true, she didn't like to think about all the women in the world who were chomping at the bit for a chance to have wild jungle sex with Adam Duke. It was downright depressing.

As she sat down at her desk and began to check her e-mails, she shook her head in dismay. All those women.

Just waiting in line. Why in the world would he even give a hoot that plain old Trish James would never make love with him again?

"No, absolutely not." Adam had heard enough. He stormed across the office and halted within a foot of her. "I refuse to accept your resignation. You're still my assistant, Trish. There's work to do. So, go back to your desk and do…something."

"Do something?" she repeated, then had the nerve to smile at him.

"You heard me," he grumbled. "Go." He waved his hands as if to shoo her away. Dammit, he couldn't be this close to her without inhaling her luscious scent. He wanted to strip her naked and nail her against the wall. Probably not a good idea to bring that up, given her present mood.

"Adam, please," she said patiently, as if she were a wise parent and he a recalcitrant child. "I didn't say I was resigning. I said I'd been rethinking my job here at DDI."

"Yeah, I heard you," Adam said, crossing his arms tightly across his chest. "I just don't know what the hell you're talking about. Rethinking. I'll probably be sorry I asked, but what the hell's that supposed to mean?"

"It means that things have become complicated," she said carefully. "It means I don't think we should…" she huffed out a breath and fisted her hands against her thighs in frustration. "Do I really have to spell it out for you?"

He took another small step toward her. "Yeah, Trish. Spell it out for me."

"We can't have sex again," she shouted, then

slapped her hand over her mouth and stared at him in astonishment.

"Okay." He grimaced and rubbed his ear. "I don't think they heard you down on the third floor."

"See what you made me do? I didn't mean to yell." The apology was a bit muffled as she still had her mouth covered.

"That's okay," he said, and reached for the hand covering her mouth to coax it away. "I don't agree with your 'rethinking' plan but I appreciate your honesty."

"You do?"

"Of course I do," he said, keeping a strong grip on her hand. "And I've got to say, I also appreciate your feelings."

"Really?" She gave him a suspicious sideways glance. "Well, thank you."

He nodded. "You're welcome. And I'm really glad you're not quitting."

"I would never leave you in the lurch."

"I'm glad." He stroked her shoulder paternally. "I need you, Trish."

She nodded earnestly. "I know. And I won't let you down."

He continued the stroking, gradually moving his hand up to cradle the back of her neck. "You never have."

"Um." She craned her neck ever so slightly to allow him more access. "Thank you, Adam."

"No problem."

"Okay." She bit her bottom lip, then said, "Well then, I guess I'll just go…do…something."

"Yeah, one thing before you go," he said, then bridged the short distance between them by tugging her close to him.

"Um, what are you doing?" she asked warily as they stared at each other.

"Just testing a theory," he said, and nipped gently at her ear. It was gratifying to hear her moan.

"But—"

"You see," he murmured as he ran slow, nibbling kisses along her jaw. "In the interests of full disclosure, I should tell you that I absolutely do intend to have sex with you again."

"Oh," she said, breathing out a sigh as he licked the pulse point at the base of her neck. "But really, that's not a good idea. And I—I should get back to…um, work."

"Yeah, me, too," he said, eliciting a strangled sob from her as he cupped her breast through her silk blouse. "I won't keep you too long."

She arched her back, then groaned, "How can this be happening again?"

"I'll show you," he said, and covered her mouth with his in a devastating kiss that left no doubt about his intentions. Dammit, he'd missed the taste of her. Now he wanted to savor every inch of her skin, inside and out. In seconds, he was reaching to unzip her pants while she fumbled for his belt.

He'd thought after one night that he would've had his fill of her. He'd figured he'd be calling her bluff this morning, revealing her to be the gold digger that she was. But as soon as Trish had tried to call it quits, he'd known he wasn't ready to end it with her. The fact that she'd tried to end it first was something he'd have to think about.

Was she playing him? Was she deliberately being coy in hopes that he'd be the one to push for a relationship? A relationship that would lead to him standing at the altar watching her walk down the aisle?

While that vision should've been enough to send him running for cover, it didn't matter right now. He still wanted her, still needed her with a bone-deep passion that was relentless. And until the need faded, he wasn't about to let her go.

"Adam, touch me," she whispered.

"Glad to," he said. Picking her up, he walked her backwards, then pressed her against the wall and urged her to wrap her legs around his waist. "On second thought, I'm keeping you here all morning."

Her office telephone rang at five o'clock. Trish ran back to her desk, recognized Adam's cell phone number and grabbed the phone.

"Hey, Trish," he said, his deep voice sending waves of desire through her entire body. How could the sound of his voice make her so weak? Oh, she was such a goner.

"Listen," he continued, "I'd like you to stop by my house and drop off the Spirit file on your way home from work tonight. Will that be a problem?"

"No problem at all." Trish slid back into her chair and mentally smacked herself. Work. He was calling about work. What had she expected? He was her employer, remember? She worked for him. For goodness' sake, she really needed to get a life.

"If you don't have plans," he continued, "I can pay you back by cooking dinner."

Dinner? He wanted to cook her dinner? She knew she should say no. It was inviting trouble to continue seeing him. And dinner at his house? Oh, please, she would never make it home. *Come on, Trish. You can do it. Open your mouth and say, no. Say thanks, but no thanks.*

"I really shouldn't," she hedged, and wanted to kick herself for not being firmer in her refusal.

"Do you have plans already?"

Tell him yes!

"Uh, no," she said, then rolled her eyes. What was wrong with her? Why didn't she just lie? Because he would've seen right through it. She was a really bad liar, just as Deb always told her.

"Then stay for dinner."

"I just don't think it's a good idea."

"I thought you were into health and nutrition."

"I am," she said, frowning. What did that have to do with anything?

"You need to eat dinner," he cajoled. "It's not good to skip meals."

She shook her head. "I'm not skipping—"

"Look, Trish, you're bringing me work files. It's just business. I'd like you to stay for dinner so we can discuss the opening-night festivities."

She sighed. "Yes, okay, fine." *You wimp!*

"Great," he said jovially. "I'll grill some steaks. See you in a while."

She placed the phone down, then her head hit her desk with an audible thunk. What was wrong with her? What part of *we can't have sex again!* did she not understand? Of course, as soon as she'd thrown those words at him this morning, he'd taken up the challenge. And she'd bent to his will like a floppy licorice stick. But oh, God, that frenzied round of wild sex against his office wall? Sweet Georgia Brown, for as long as she worked for DDI, she would always look fondly on that particular wall.

"Excuse me," a soft, female voice said. "Is Adam Duke here?"

With a start, Trish lifted her head. She hadn't realized anyone was here, hadn't heard that woman's footsteps because of the thick carpet that covered the wide hallway.

"Hello." Trish stood, straightened her jacket and brushed her hair back as she surreptitiously studied the woman who was several inches shorter than Trish and definitely more voluptuous. She didn't recognize her and wondered who she might be. A client, maybe? The woman wore a lovely coral halter dress that accentuated her remarkable cleavage, and her perfectly highlighted blond hair was pulled up in a sexy updo. She was beautiful and from the looks of her diamond-encrusted watch, buttery soft taupe purse and matching open-toe high heels, she was wealthy, as well.

"I'm sorry," Trish said. "Mr. Duke is not available."

"Oh, dear," the woman said. "Are you sure?"

"Yes."

She sighed. "I was told he worked late most evenings, so I took a chance, hoping he might be available for cocktails tonight." She opened her purse and handed Trish a business card. "I guess we'll do it another night."

"Are you a friend of Adam's?" Trish asked warily as she gripped the business card. Even the woman's stationary was expensive.

"I'm Brenda," she said smoothly. "He'll know who I am. Are you sure he won't be back tonight?"

"I'm afraid not," Trish said. "He's gone for the day."

Brenda sighed again and glanced at her elegant watch. "Tonight really would've been ideal."

"I'll be glad to give him your card."

"Please do," she said, then flashed a knowing smile. "He'll want to know I came by."

"Of course, he will."

"Okay, then." She turned to leave, then stopped and looked back at Trish. She hesitated, then said, "Please let him know that I'm really looking forward to getting to know him better."

Trish smiled tightly. "I'll be sure to tell him."

"Thank you," Brenda said, then walked away.

"No, no, thank you," Trish murmured as she watched the woman stroll down the hall.

The potatoes were baking in the oven, the wine was opened and breathing, the steaks were marinating. As the doorbell rang, Adam put the salad he'd just made into the refrigerator to chill.

"Perfect timing," he murmured, then jogged to the front door, opened it and smiled. "Come on in."

"Sorry I can't stay," Trish said breezily as she shoved the thick Spirit file into his chest. He struggled to catch it.

"What's this?" Adam said, taken aback. "Why can't you stay?"

"I just remembered a previous engagement," she said through clenched teeth. "Oh, and by the way, Brenda said to say hi."

"What?" Adam shook his head. "Who's Brenda?"

"Oh, that's nice," she said tightly. "You date so many women, you can't even remember their names."

"No, I—"

"And she was so disappointed you weren't there. Here's her card. You be sure to call her for a good time. Oh, hey, maybe she'd like to come over for dinner."

"Trish, this is ridiculous. What's going on?"

"I've had my eyes opened." She seemed to deflate before his eyes. "Never mind. It's not your fault. It's mine. I never should've gotten involved. It was wrong. You're my boss."

"That doesn't matter," he insisted. "Please, Trish, don't—"

"Good night, Adam."

"Wait. Will I at least see you Monday?"

She sniffed. "I told you I wasn't going to leave you in the lurch. I don't go back on my word."

Adam couldn't be sure but he thought she looked close to tears. He grabbed her hand. "Trish, I don't know what happened but we can—"

"No. I'm sorry." She pulled her hand free and backed away from him. "I can't. I just can't do it."

"Move it a little more to the left, boys," Sally said, and Adam and Brandon groaned in unison. "I think it'll look beautiful centered on the window, don't you?"

"Yeah," Adam said, straining as he moved the heavy love seat one more inch. Then he dropped his end of the couch and swiped his damp forehead with the sleeve of his denim work shirt. "See, Mom? It's perfect. It's staying right here."

It was Saturday afternoon and his mother needed to rearrange her furniture. It did no good to ask why. Sally often got a wild hair up her butt to move stuff around for no rhyme or reason. But, hey, it meant free beer and pizza for lunch.

"Hey, Cam," Adam called, "bring me a beer, will you?"

From the kitchen, Cameron yelled back. "No problem."

Sally bent her head to the left, then the right, closing

first one eye, then the other, trying to make sure the love seat was exactly where she wanted it to be.

Ignoring her, Brandon plopped down on the couch and yelled, "Bring me a beer, too, will you?"

"Already on it," Cameron said, as he walked back into the den, holding three icy bottles. He handed one to each of his brothers, then took a long, satisfying swig from his own.

"I think it's perfect, right where it is," Sally said finally.

Adam chuckled. "Glad you think so, Mom, because it's not going anywhere else today."

"That stupid little thing weighs a ton," Brandon groused as he sat back and perched his bare feet on the ancient wide oak coffee table.

Sally sat down next to him and patted his biceps. "That's why I keep you around, sweetie. Now, take your feet off the table."

He did, but rolled his eyes. "Can you feel the love?" Brandon said, and his brothers laughed.

Cameron took a seat in one of the leather Buster chairs that faced the small couch. Glancing up at Adam, who slouched against the wall, he said, "Everything go smoothly with the Fantasy ADA survey?"

"Yeah," Adam said, taking a long sip of beer. "Trish had everything written up the next day and we sent the settlement letter off to the other side. Bob Paxton should have the renovations done within two weeks."

"That's fast."

"Yeah," Adam agreed. "He was motivated."

"By anger, I'll bet."

"Exactly." Adam grabbed a chair from the game table and sat. Just mentioning Trish's name made him worry and wonder for the hundredth time today, what in the world had happened to her last evening. She'd gone running off and before he could even think to go after her, she was gone. Now he would have to wait until Monday to find out how everything in his world had gone south between the time he called her at five o'clock and the time she showed up at his place less than an hour later. And who was Brenda?

He missed Trish, dammit. Not that it meant anything. It couldn't mean anything. He would never allow a woman to become so important that she had the power to disrupt his peace of mind. But Trish was his assistant. They worked well together. And yeah, okay, he wanted to be wrapped up in her naked, hot body more than he wanted to breathe again. But never mind all that. She was a valued employee. Of course he was worried about her. And that's the story he was sticking to.

"So, how is Trish?" Brandon asked casually. "How're things going?"

Adam flashed him a look of warning but said nothing.

Sally perked up. "Who's Trish?"

"She's my assistant, Mom," Adam said tightly. As if she didn't know.

"Oh, I've spoken to her on the phone. She sounds so sweet."

Cameron snorted as Adam slumped over in the chair, rolling his eyes.

"Who's Trish?" Brandon repeated with a chuckle. "That's real funny coming from you, Mom."

"It is?" Sally said. She glanced from one son to the other, then shook her head in confusion. "I guess I don't understand your male sense of humor."

"Brandon's humor is a world apart," Cameron said.

"True enough," she said. Again she stared at each

of the men, no doubt in search of the real story, then homed in on Brandon, clearly the weak link in this scenario. "So why don't you explain to me just how funny I am?"

Brandon exchanged glances with his brothers, then shrugged. "Guess it had to come out sometime."

"Ball's in your corner, dude," Cameron said, then stood. "I think this calls for more beers. Mom, you want something?"

"Chicken," Adam muttered under his breath.

"Got that right," Cameron said with a grin. "I can't watch."

"I'd better have a glass of white wine," Sally said, but didn't take her eyes off Brandon, who was starting to squirm.

"Coming right up," Cameron said, whistling as he left the room.

"Now, what in the world are you talking about?" Sally said. "What's going on?"

Brandon squeezed her hand patiently. "Mom, we know you arranged the whole thing."

"What whole thing?"

"With Trish." He shrugged again. "And Adam. We know Marjorie helped. We know the whole story."

She cocked her head and stared at him in complete befuddlement. Adam's stomach was beginning to sink. His mother wasn't that good an actress.

Cameron walked back in and handed her a glass of pale, straw-colored wine.

"Thanks, sweetie," she said, smiling up at him. "I think I'm going to need it."

"No problemo," he said, and quickly moved out of his mother's line of sight.

She took a sip of wine, placed the glass on the side

table, then cast a meaningful glance at Adam. "Can you explain what Brandon's talking about?"

Adam frowned as whispers of worry fluttered inside him and couldn't be stopped. Had he been wrong? Was his mother really not playing games? Impossible. He blew out a tired breath and said, "Trish is the woman Marjorie hired to be my assistant."

"What happened to Cheryl?"

Brandon chuckled. "Oh, you're good, Mom."

"Cheryl got pregnant and quit," Adam explained.

"Oh!" Sally said, clapping her hands. "Well, that's wonderful. I should send her a gift."

"Mom, focus," Brandon said, sitting forward. "We know you arranged for Trish to work for Adam."

She blinked. "I did what?"

"We know you're trying to set him up with women. You know, so he'll get married and have children and you'll have grandchildren and—" Brandon waved his arms around. "You know, blah, blah, blah."

"Ah." Sally's eyes narrowed. "Blah, blah, blah. Yes. Well, it's true I want grandchildren, but I'm not sure… well, tell me again how I arranged for—what was her name?"

"Trish," Brandon said. His patience was wearing thin.

"Right, Trish." Sally looked contemplative. "Tell me again how I arranged to get her into Adam's office."

Brandon cast an anxious glance at his brothers, not saying aloud what he was so obviously thinking. *Could their mother's memory be slipping?* Adam almost laughed out loud. He had no such doubts. Sally Duke was smart as a whip. She was pulling Brandon's chain. He shouldn't be enjoying the show, considering it was his ass on the line, but he just couldn't help himself.

"Remember, Mom?" Cameron spoke slowly. "Marjorie arranged it for you. She got Trish in there."

"Of course." Sally nodded. "Marjorie's a good friend."

"Exactly," Brandon said. "So you're not denying you set the whole thing up?"

"Why would I?" Sally asked. "It sounds like a very clever plan."

"We wouldn't expect anything less, Mom," Cameron said.

"Thank you, sweetie," Sally said, then glanced over at Adam with a sparkle in her eye. "All this talk of women and plans and setups reminds me, Adam. Have you gone out with Brenda yet?"

Alarmed now, Adam stood. "Who's Brenda?"

"Yeah, who's Brenda?" Brandon asked.

Sally sat back on the couch, seemingly enjoying herself. "Brenda is Geraldine Sharkey's doctor's daughter."

"Geraldine?" Cameron said, as he leaned against the back of the leather chair. "Your friend from the hospital guild?"

"Yes," she said, beaming at Cameron, pleased that he'd remembered. "We play canasta together now. She wanted to introduce Dr. Brisbane's daughter to some nice men, so I gave her Adam's office phone number."

"Oh, crap." Adam glowered. The mysterious Brenda. *She* was the one his mom had set him up with? But that would mean… "She didn't call. She just showed up."

"But, Mom," Brandon asked cautiously, "why would you send Brenda when you've already got Trish working for Adam?"

Sally started to answer him, then stopped. "What does Brenda have to do with Adam's assistant?"

"Very funny," Adam said, and started to pace the floor of the den. "Look, Trish is working for me and I'm happy with her. I don't want any more setups, so you can call off your dogs. Send Brenda somewhere else."

"Is she hot?" Brandon asked hopefully.

Cameron burst into laughter and Adam just shook his head.

Sally pushed herself off the couch and met Adam halfway across the room. She wound her arm through his and said softly, "Adam, you must know I had nothing to do with getting this woman a job in your office."

"I know that now, Mom," Adam said, leading her on a slow walk across the room.

He believed her. Which meant Trish was innocent. She hadn't been stalking him or playing him or lying to him. And Adam had treated her badly. Dammit, she'd been a virgin. He didn't like the guilt that had reared up inside him. He didn't like knowing he'd been wrong. And he didn't like admitting that he wanted Trish anyway. Wanted her now even more than he had before.

"It sounds as if you like her," Sally said cautiously.

"Don't get your hopes up," he warned.

She smiled up at him. "Honey, I always have my hopes up as far as you're concerned. And you've never let me down."

He let out a sigh. How could a man argue with the woman who'd given him everything? Even her meddling was a gift, he thought, because without Sally Duke in his life, he'd never have known what love was. "Thanks, Mom. You've never let me down, either."

"Oh, sweetie, you're going to make me cry." She wrapped her arms around him in a big hug and Adam felt like a complete ass. He wasn't about to tell her how badly he'd treated Trish. How he'd seduced a completely innocent woman. Innocent in every way.

Later, as he drove home from his mother's house on the cliff, he thought about how he'd sweet-talked Trish, flown her off to Fantasy Mountain and plied her with champagne. The following day, she'd given herself to him. In his office. On the couch. And various other places.

He should've been disgusted with himself, but the memory of taking her on his conference room table caused him to harden instantly and he wanted her all over again.

He had thought Trish was a gold digger, a willing accomplice in his mother's half-baked plan, anxious to get a piece of his hefty bank account. But she wasn't who he thought she was. She was the real deal. To complicate his predicament, he liked her. A lot.

"Dammit," he said, pounding his fist on the steering wheel. He would find a way to make it up to her. He would take her out, treat her like a princess. He would explain his mother's mistake in sending Brenda to the office. Then he would make love with Trish all night long. All week long. Hell, all month long.

He knew it wouldn't last between them. It couldn't. Adam didn't do forever. He would eventually let her go, but until that moment came, they could enjoy each other to the max.

Nine

Trish was losing ground.

It had been almost two weeks since that fateful evening when the elegant Brenda had shown up with her perfect hair and perfect shoes and ruined Trish's weekend.

But by Monday, Trish knew she had to thank the woman for opening her eyes to reality. She had no business dreaming of Adam Duke when he was the one responsible for all the unhappy turns her life had taken. From that day on, Trish had been on a campaign to find something, anything the least bit incriminating that she could use against Adam. So far there was nothing, but she'd vowed not to give up.

Meanwhile Adam had sworn that it was his mother who had tried to set him up with the voluptuous Brenda. And Trish believed him. Adam had explained that his mother wanted him and his brothers to settle down, so she had resorted to sending every woman she came across their way in hopes that one of them might lure the men into marriage. And that was never going to happen, Adam assured Trish.

Trish had laughed along with him when he described his mother's tenaciousness, and she accepted his apology, not that he needed to apologize. But since he was offering, she was willing to forgive him.

But she refused to forget.

Trish opened a file drawer and returned two folders to their rightful place, then pulled the file cart over to the next drawer. Adam was out of the office and Trish was all caught up with her work, so she was using this time to re-examine the client files in the hope that she'd missed something important the first time.

But her mind kept going back to Adam's apology about his mother's matchmaking efforts and his cold insistence that he would never marry. It's not as if Trish were looking for someone to tie the knot with, least of all Adam Duke, but it made her sad that he'd grown up to be so contemptuous of marriage.

And yet, despite his cynicism, he had been nothing but thoughtful and attentive to Trish in the two weeks since that fateful night. She'd tried but couldn't dismiss the memory of his arms wrapped around her. Every time she thought of his heated gaze, her insides twisted into curlicues.

For two weeks Adam had been relentless in his campaign to soften her up, weaken her resolve and change her mind. He'd been inventive and sexy and sweet, and Trish's resolve was slipping fast. He was fighting dirty, captivating her with his charm and consideration. Just when she thought she had a handle on her emotions and could withstand his latest salvo, he would slip through her defenses.

On Tuesday, he'd placed a single white rose on her desk and said it reminded him of her own unique style and beauty. Then he'd kissed her gently and she'd practically dissolved in his arms.

Trish buried her head in her hands. She had to be strong. She had to fight, not just for herself but for her grandmother and all the people who really mattered to her. And she *was* fighting, she thought, as she flipped open another client file and studied the lease agreement.

But every time Adam came near her, she was betrayed by her own body. Closing the client file, she sighed. Perhaps it was time to accept defeat. She just plain wanted him.

Oh, she knew it couldn't last. He was clearly not the type of man to settle down, get married and raise a family. Not with her, anyway. Not with the shopkeeper's granddaughter. Even with her MBA, she knew she wasn't the type of woman Adam Duke would ultimately marry—if he ever married at all. He would marry someone sophisticated and worldly, someone with whom he could travel the world. Trish's feet were firmly planted on solid ground. She wanted to live here forever. Sure, she'd love to travel someday, but it wasn't as important to her as home and family were.

And someday, she vowed, she would have a home and a family, but for now, none of that mattered.

For now, for today, Adam wanted *her*. And she wanted him. So for as long as it lasted, Trish would savor his desire to be with her. She wouldn't dwell on the future. She would live in the present, enjoy the moment and hope that her time with Adam Duke would provide enough lovely, exciting memories to keep her warm for a lifetime.

It had been one hellish day. Trish felt like a limp string of spaghetti, beaten and boiled and flung against the wall. She'd done nothing all day but put out fires and quell skirmishes that had been threatening to become full-scale wars. She'd definitely earned her paycheck and that was always a good feeling. It was just too bad she was way too tired to enjoy herself.

Once Adam had left the office for a dinner meeting with a visiting developer, Trish had dragged herself over to the file cabinets where she'd taken the time to go through a few more file drawers. Despite her overwhelming attraction to Adam, she was absolutely duty-bound to do something for Grandma Anna and her Village neighbors. So she continued her search for a scrap of something, anything she might be able to give to the local press, some story they could dig into in hopes of embarrassing Adam. It didn't have to bring down his entire company anymore. She just wanted to find something that would bring closure to the pain her family and friends had gone through. She owed it to them.

But tonight she simply didn't have the energy to scour the files. Her heart wasn't in it, even if her conscience nagged at her. She compromised between heart and conscience and worked diligently for almost an hour, going through and checking each file, before getting discouraged and calling it a day.

Knowing she had nothing at home in the way of dinner, Trish pulled into the local grocery store on her way home and parked. Before getting out of her car, she buttoned her coat because the nights were getting colder now. As she locked her car, she could see her breath in the air, and it reminded her of that cold night out on the balcony at Fantasy Mountain.

She shivered, remembering that it was out there on that balcony that Adam had first kissed her.

They would be going back to Fantasy Mountain in two weeks for the grand opening. Adam had promised that the two of them would go up two days early and take advantage of the spa and any activities they wanted to enjoy. There was only one activity she could think of, and that was making love for hours with Adam in that beautiful room with the luxurious, fantasy bed.

With that image in her head, she almost floated across the parking lot. As she reached the door, an older man bumped into her and she grabbed him before he could fall.

"I'm so sorry," she said. "Are you hurt?"

"Nah, I'm okay," the man said.

Trish did a double take. "Sam? Sam Sutter?"

"Trish?" Sam said, then laughed as she wrapped him in a bear hug. "Aren't you a sight for sore eyes."

"Oh, Sam, I've missed you so much."

His laugh turned to a cough that grew stronger and more deep-throated until he was doubled over.

"My goodness, Sam, are you all right?" Trish thumped his back, not sure what else to do. "Let's get inside."

Sam Sutter was an old friend of Grandma Anna's. He'd owned the bike shop in the Victorian Village, two doors down from Anna's Attic. His shop used to rent bikes and paddleboards and roller skates to the tourists who walked to the beach along Sea Cove Lane. Sam had given Trish her first bicycle and taught her how to ride it. Every bike she'd ever owned had come from Sam's shop.

Her old neighbor looked as though he'd aged ten years in the last few months since she'd seen him. She hoped it was just the cold that had him looking so worn down.

Sam stood up straight, the coughing jag over, but Trish could still hear him wheezing.

"Sam, you don't sound good at all," she said as she grabbed a cart and led him down the dairy aisle.

"No kidding," he said, blowing his nose with a linen handkerchief he'd pulled from his coat pocket. "I caught one of those winter colds and I think it's turning into bronchitis."

She placed a carton of milk in the cart, then threaded her arm through his as they walked down the next aisle. "You need to get to the doctor."

"I know, honey, but I just can't afford a doctor these days. I'll buy some cough syrup and aspirin. That'll have to do me for now."

"Did you get a flu shot this year?"

"Not yet, but I'll try to work it into my busy schedule." He grinned at her. "You're a sweetheart, Trish."

"Oh, Sam, I miss you," Trish said, and squeezed his arm.

"I miss you, too, honey," Sam said with a chuckle. "We had some good times back in the day. That reminds me, I ran into Bert Lindsay the other day."

Bert and his wife, Tommie had operated an upscale hair salon and beauty supply store in the Village.

"How are they doing?" she asked, as she maneuvered the cart around the corner and down the next aisle.

"Tommie's arthritis has been bugging her, but she's got a good attitude."

"I'll try to stop by and see them next week."

"You know they'd love to see you," he said.

"I would love that, too."

Sam waited while Trish picked out the best-looking zucchini she could find, then he said, "Bert tells me you're working for Duke."

Trish sucked in a breath, then exhaled carefully. "Yes, I am."

"I knew you'd find a way to get to him. You were always a smart girl." Then his eyes narrowed. "It's probably not very generous of me to say this, but I hope you come across something we can use to get his nose in a twist."

Guilt pooled inside her and sent hundreds of tiny ripples of shame out to every cell in her body. Here was one of her dearest friends, beaten down and destroyed by Adam Duke and all Trish could say was, "Oh, Sam, I'm not sure I can do that."

He touched her shoulder in understanding. "That's okay, honey. We all just appreciate that you'd care enough to try."

"I—I promise I'll do what I can."

They wandered over to the cold remedies aisle and Sam found aspirin and a box of extra-strength cough syrup. "Whatever you do, honey, I know it won't bring the Village back. But it would be nice if Adam Duke just had an inkling that what he did to us was wrong."

"That would be nice," Trish said halfheartedly, then wanted to crawl into a box. She could barely look Sam in the eye, knowing she'd betrayed them all by becoming romantically involved with Adam. What would they do if they knew the truth? They were all such sweet people, they'd probably forgive her. She just wasn't sure if she could forgive herself.

At the checkout stand, Sam began to pull cash and coins from the pockets of his old coat.

"Hey, I'm buying this," Trish said, pulling out her credit card.

"Don't be silly, honey."

"But it's the company card," she said lightly, hoping he'd believe her little white lie. "We'll let Duke pay for it."

Sam let out a rusty laugh. "In that case, okay."

As they walked out to the parking lot together, Trish asked, "Do you need anything, Sam? Can I help you in any way?"

"Ah, honey, I don't need a thing. It's just been great to see you."

"Are you limping?"

"It's nothing." He waved it off as he grumbled, "Doctor says I need a hip replacement. Can you imagine them cutting me open to stick a hunk of metal into my hip socket? That's not going to happen."

"Oh, Sam." She shook her head. "It might make a big difference and get rid of the pain."

"Maybe," he muttered, then he jabbed his finger in the air. "Let me tell you something: getting old ain't for sissies."

She chuckled. "That's what Grandma Anna always said."

"Yeah, I know." He laughed. "I miss your grandma a lot. She was a pip, that one."

"I miss her, too."

"Here's my truck." He gave her another big bear hug, then she helped him open the door. "You take care of yourself, honey, and don't let that Duke fellow get you down."

"I won't." She held his arm steady as he climbed into

the driver's seat. "You take care of yourself, too. Get rid of that cough."

"I promise." He grinned. "We're all so proud of you, Trish."

"Thanks, Sam."

She waited until he was tucked inside his truck and had started the engine. Then he waved. She smiled and waved back, watching until his truck disappeared out of the parking lot. As she walked to her car, she thought about Sam and how much she'd missed him. How much she'd missed her Village family. She was so glad she'd run into him. So why did it feel like her heart was breaking?

Adam shoved another thick lease document into his briefcase. "Are we all set with the orchestra? I know the union guy was giving you problems."

"It wasn't a real problem," she said, brushing off his concern. "The union rep just wanted to make sure we'd be giving the band two full breaks during the evening and I told him we would. So, no problem."

Trish had taken charge of hiring a big band orchestra for the gala. She'd never negotiated a deal like that before, never dealt with union issues or artistic temperaments. It had been exhilarating and scary and she'd pulled it off without a hitch.

Adam tapped his fingers on the edge of his case, thinking. "What do we do for music during the breaks?"

She smiled. "I've got a fantastic DJ to fill in. He'll also do some introductions and announcements. I've given him a script."

"You're amazing."

"I know." Her smile grew as he laughed. "I mean, thank you."

"You're welcome," he said, and glanced at his copy of her checklist. "So the music is set. And the hotel's taking care of the red carpet stuff. We've got limousines lined up to take guests from the airstrip to the hotel entrance. Photographers are set. Lighting is good. All the entertainment channels will be there."

"We've even got an actual red carpet."

"Oh, yeah. Can't forget that," he said, chuckling. "I think that's everything. Are you finished packing?"

"Almost." She thumbed through the pages of her list. "Oh, I've got the company jet flying your mother and her three friends to the resort the morning of the gala, then they'll be back to take your brothers and their dates up in the afternoon."

"Thanks for taking care of that." He pulled her into his arms and planted a kiss on her forehead. "I'm glad we're going up two days early."

"It'll take two days to get everything ready."

"We won't be working the whole time," Adam said. He'd already told her he wanted this time to be a mini-vacation just for the two of them. They could do whatever they wanted. If they were in the mood for some energetic physical activity, they could go cross-country skiing or ice-skating. Or they could just settle into the spa, get a couples massage, or while away the hours in the sauna or hot tub. He'd already scheduled a manicure and pedicure for her. He'd insisted that her every wish was his command, as long as she was pampered and fluffed and ready for him every night.

Trish doubted she would spend much time being pampered, but she couldn't help the tingles she felt when he described what he wanted to do to her.

She only had one more thing to do before they left the next day. She'd been putting it off forever, but the fact was, she needed a fabulous dress for the gala. Knowing there would be snow, she'd borrowed Deb's down coat and gloves again. But she still had to buy a dress. She planned to go shopping tonight after work, unless she could sneak off before that.

"That's it," Adam said as he closed his briefcase. "I'm off to meet with the SyCom people."

She handed him a thin folder. "Here are your notes for the meeting."

"What would I do without you?" he asked, then pulled her into his arms and kissed her. "Mmm, is it too late to cancel the SyCom meeting?"

Trish smiled. *If only.* "You'd better go."

"Yes, ma'am." He grinned and gave her a snappy salute, then grabbed his briefcase and strolled out the office door.

Trish sighed as she stared at the mess on Adam's desk. She would deal with all that later. Right now, she would take advantage of Adam's absence and go find a dress.

Two hours later, Trish returned to the office, ready to get back to work. She'd bought the most beautiful dress she'd ever seen. Why that made her feel guilty, she wasn't willing to say out loud, but at least she'd found it on sale.

After taking care of all the work on her desk, she headed into Adam's office. Files were piled everywhere on his desk, papers were askew. There was spilled coffee and a half-eaten cinnamon scone still sitting there. How could he possibly work in all that mess and jumble?

She began straightening things, starting with piling

the many files onto the file cart. She tried to match the loose papers with the files they went with. Pens and paper clips went back in the drawer, the scone was tossed out and dirty coffee mugs were hustled down the hall to the kitchen dishwasher.

After his desk was cleaned to her satisfaction, she pulled the file cart out to the cabinets by her desk and began returning them to the drawers. It took her nearly an hour, but she had almost reached the bottom of the pile. She picked up the next file wallet and checked the name. It was one she hadn't heard of. Vista del Lago. Curious, she thumbed through the thin folders and pulled out a piece of correspondence to see what it was all about.

She got through the first short paragraph before she had to fumble for her desk chair to slide down and sit. She examined the attached notice addressed to residents of Vista del Lago, informing the tenants that they had thirty days to vacate before the building was to be demolished.

The internal company letter to Adam was marked "Personal and Confidential" and listed the reasons why the building should be torn down. It was close to the beach, so the property was worth millions. It was an eyesore with paint peeling and wood trim crumbling, so it would take too much work to restore it. The tenants were mostly senior citizens on fixed incomes, so raising the rent had proved problematic. Better to just evict the tenants and level the building.

Trish's hands shook as she read the details of the coldly impersonal Notice to Vacate, which gave the elderly tenants thirty days to pack up all their worldly belongings and find somewhere else to live.

The letter reported that the Vista del Lago site would

be the ideal place to build luxury condominiums that would garner an excellent return on the company's investment.

She didn't know how long she sat there staring into space. She was struck dumb, frozen, unsure what to do next. This was it, the perfect sordid information she'd been seeking ever since she first came to work for Adam.

Her mind bounced back and forth between pretending she'd never seen the letter and shouting its discovery to the rooftops.

Part of her insisted that the letter was none of her business. She should just shove the file back into the drawer and forget she ever saw it.

But how could she do that?

It was documentation, clear and stunning evidence that Adam's company was about to tear down yet another building—this one filled with defenseless, low-income senior citizens—in order to build something more pleasing to the corporate eye, something like high-priced luxury condominiums with a view of the ocean. Much better than the ugly low-rent senior housing that was currently occupying the space.

Trish's stomach was doing backflips and not in a happy way. The letter and accompanying notice weren't exactly a smoking gun, but they were just the sort of dirt the local newspapers would devour like hungry hounds. It might not destroy Adam Duke, but if the press framed the story correctly, it would definitely be a blow to his company's reputation and Adam's personal pride would probably take a serious hit. If the news coverage was good enough and the public outrage strong enough, it might even prevent the project from going through.

It was the perfect weapon. Trish knew it. But how in

the world could she use it against Adam when she was in love with him?

"No." The word shuddered from deep in her throat as that realization sank in.

Trish rose from the chair and paced around her alcove. Feeling trapped, she went into Adam's office and walked to the window overlooking the coastline.

"Oh, no. Absolutely not." She whipped around, stumbling blindly back and forth across Adam's office. She didn't know where to go, what to do, where to hide from the stunning realization that she was in love with Adam Duke.

Barely able to take another step, she collapsed onto the couch.

How could she be in love with him?

She let out a moan, then bent over and buried her head in her hands. It couldn't be. Please, not Adam. Despite his good qualities, despite the fact that he was her lover, he was still the man responsible for forcing her small family and her beloved neighbors out of their homes. He was the man who'd destroyed the beautiful historic building where she and her grandmother had lived and worked their entire lives. He was the man who'd replaced that lovely, venerable Victorian building with an ugly, soulless concrete block-long parking structure.

He was the same man who would do it all over again to the residents of Vista del Lago, if Trish didn't stop him.

She sat up, glanced around. Maybe there was a reasonable explanation for his actions. Maybe he didn't know the whole story. But that was ridiculous. The evidence was sitting on his desk. He had to be familiar with the file.

It was staring her in the face. Adam Duke was about

to destroy the lives of yet another group of innocent people.

Sadness crept into Trish's heart as the inevitability of her situation settled over her. She had to do something. She had to take a stand.

No longer sure of her motives or her feelings, Trish scanned the Vista del Lago paperwork, transferred it onto a CD and slipped the disk into her purse.

Ten

They descended the jet stairway onto the tarmac and Adam inhaled the cold, pine-scented mountain air. He could finally relax and spend these next two days with Trish, uninterrupted by the work that had consumed them over the last few weeks. He planned to keep her busy in bed when he wasn't otherwise pampering her.

She'd been quieter than usual during the plane ride but Adam chalked that up to her usual anxiety over flying.

"I'm so glad to be back," she said softly, staring out at the mountains they had just flown over. Then she rubbed her arms. "Oh, but it's so cold."

"It's going to snow." He took hold of her hand and led her to the waiting limousine. "The driver will take us to the hotel, then come back for the bags."

He bundled her into the limo and held her close. As the driver sped toward the resort, he considered the woman sitting next to him. He was proud of the work she'd done and didn't mind admitting that she made him look good. She'd been thrown into the role of his personal assistant and she'd exceeded his wildest expectations. She was a hard worker and a good sport.

But more than that, she was sexy as hell and he couldn't get enough of her. He was amazed to realize that he hadn't grown tired of her, amazed that he still wanted her every day and night. He knew it couldn't last, knew that he would send her away eventually. He couldn't say when it would happen, but he knew it would. For now, though, he refused to question the fact that he wanted to be with her all the time.

He hoped that when the breakup finally happened, Trish would understand and not take it personally. He would be careful to make sure she knew that it wasn't her, it was him. Adam had vowed, long ago, never to become too involved with anyone. He didn't believe in forever, certainly didn't believe in love. He didn't trust it. After all, people might say they love you and promise to take care of you, but then they'd dump you off at a hospital entryway and never return. He ought to know. People lied.

After all the pain he'd seen growing up, first in the orphanage, then in all those miserable foster homes, he knew it was unavoidable that people grew to hate and hurt one another. He'd seen plenty of damage done and figured that for most relationships, it was just a matter of time.

Sally Duke had been different, he told himself. The exception to the rule.

But romantic love was doomed from the start. He wouldn't let that happen to him. And he wouldn't let it happen to Trish, either. He didn't want to hurt her so he was determined to avoid anything that remotely resembled a serious relationship.

And Trish had "serious relationship" written all over her.

But for now, for the next two days, he was looking forward to spending time with her and making love with her. And what better place to do that than Fantasy Mountain?

After the elevator delivered them to the top floor, he followed her into the presidential suite and watched with amusement as she twirled around, trying to take in everything. The room was spectacular, if he did say so himself. And needless to say, much bigger than the one Trish had slept in last time.

The walls were constructed of blond wood logs polished to a high sheen, except for one entire wall that was covered in river rock and formed a wide fireplace and hearth. A forest-green suede couch and charming bentwood chairs and tables made up a cozy conversation area. The wide, rounded balcony stretched the length of the suite with doors leading out from both the living room and the bedroom. In the bathroom, a soaking tub was planted in front of windows that looked out at the snow-capped peak of Fantasy Mountain.

Trish walked into the master bedroom and saw another small fireplace facing the king-size bed, framed in willow branches. She turned and faced him. "I didn't think it was possible but this room is even more fantastic than the one from before."

"That's because it's bigger," Adam said with a grin.

"It's definitely bigger," she said with a smile as she wandered back into the living room. "It's also different because we're seeing it in the daylight."

Adam followed her, content to watch her enjoying

herself. She peeked through the gauze curtains, then pulled the cord to open them, filling the room with more light. "Oh, the view from here is beautiful."

She turned to face him just as a shaft of sunlight bounced off her back, creating an aura of shimmering gold and bronze around her. It made him realize that she was the most stunning woman he'd ever seen.

"You're beautiful," Adam said, unable to keep the thought to himself.

She beamed at him. "So are you."

"First time anyone's ever said that to me." He approached her slowly. "I hope you didn't make any plans for the morning."

"Plans?"

"Yeah. Come here." He yanked her against him and kissed her in a soul-searing meeting of mouths and tangling of tongues. Then, in one swift move he lifted her into his arms and carried her into the bedroom, where he laid her down on the bed, then stood and began to unbutton his shirt.

Trish sat up to pull off her sweater, but Adam reached over to stop her. "I'll do that."

"Hurry," she said in a breathless whisper.

"Oh, yeah." Her mouth was already swollen and wet from his kiss and so damn tempting that he had to taste her again. He knelt on the bed and swept down to devour her, his tongue plunging in and around hers. He felt himself grow even more rigid and had to force himself to control the need that was consuming him.

He reached for her sweater and pulled it up and over her head. The slinky black bra was a surprise and he grinned as he used his finger to trace the shape of her breast, then dipped beneath the lace to play with her firm nipple.

"Adam, now," she demanded, then closed her eyes and raised her arms over her head. The movement caused her back to arch and her breasts to rise up. Adam swore under his breath and quickly unclipped her bra to reveal her soft, round breasts and tight nipples.

"Perfect," he said, and bent to take first one, then the other into his mouth.

He moved quickly to whisk off her pants, then left a trail of wet kisses along her belly. He gazed down at the strip of black lace she wore and swore again.

"You're so damn hot," he muttered. With one hand, he tugged at those skimpy lace panties and caused a tiny bit of friction against her soft folds. Hearing her whimper ignited his blood. He reached beneath the lace and touched her center, then dipped one finger into her. "So wet."

Tearing the lacy material away, he replaced it with his mouth, first kissing, then licking and finally feasting on her.

Her incoherent gasps fueled his own internal fire. He ran his hands up and down her strong, sexy legs, then grabbed her shapely ankles and hitched them over his shoulders. And continued his relentless onslaught of her hot, moist center.

The sensation of bringing her to a shattering peak was almost too much for him to take. Desire, painful and urgent, ripped through him as he crawled his way back up to look at her.

"You are the sexiest, most perfect creation," he said, unable to stop touching her.

"And you're wearing way too many clothes," she whispered, and grabbed his belt buckle.

He laughed, stood and stripped, pulling a condom out of his back pocket and donning it.

He had a moment to register her rich, brown hair tumbled around her delicate features, and her long, lush naked body stretched out on the luxurious bedspread, before kneeling back on the bed between her legs.

Holding her gaze, he positioned himself, then entered her slowly and had to grit his teeth to keep from exploding from her heated tightness.

It was all he could do to keep the rhythm slow, to feel each stroke move deep inside her, so deep that he began to lose himself in her, lose all sense of everything but her beautiful eyes and her lush heat. As his movements gathered speed, he felt a bone-deep need resound within himself, but refused to question it.

Her legs gripped him high on his waist, opening her up and allowing him to thrust even deeper. Her breath grew short, her breasts flushed dark rose and Adam knew she was ready to climax.

"Come for me, sweetheart," he said, his concentration focused, his thrusts slowing, teasing, until he withdrew almost completely. She opened her eyes in alarm just as he plunged back into her so deeply he thought he might lose himself in her. He rushed to kiss her, to swallow her screams, to savor her mouth as he thrust again, then withdrew. Then again, and again. Her eyes flashed hot and dark and he turned relentless, driving into her, plunging, stroking, their bodies damp with sweat and heat, his need savage and unremitting.

He saw her eyes cloud over seconds before she shattered gloriously. He crushed her lips again, tasted her passion, her pleasure, her sweetness, and lost control. His body tightened almost beyond endurance as he emptied himself into her.

Two days later, the night of the gala was picture-perfect in every way. It had snowed that afternoon, turning Fantasy Mountain into a glittering white winter wonderland.

Adam and Trish had reluctantly slipped back into work mode several hours earlier. Now Adam stood at the top of the wide main stairway leading into the hotel and greeted each guest personally. Wealthy investors and their families, old friends, a number of celebrities, even a few of his competitors, were all arriving to enjoy the opening weekend festivities. Adam's brothers and their top executives were already inside working the crowd.

The paparazzi swarmed outside, their flashbulbs and strobe lights turning the evening sky to daylight. Television interviewers were lined up along the red carpet that swept the entire length of the long carriage drive entrance. Heat lamps were posted at intervals to keep the arriving guests from feeling too much of the chilly night air.

From where he was standing, Adam could observe Trish with her walkie-talkie and her clipboard, co-ordinating limousine arrivals and valet service. She wore her jeans and boots and a down jacket as she worked the lines, running from one end to the other. She would stop to give an encouraging word to one of his staff, then laugh at a photographer's joke. She had a knack for making them all feel as though she were one of them while still giving orders and keeping everything on a tight schedule. She radiated confidence and warmth and it was obvious that everyone working the event had fallen in love with her.

Everyone.

Hell. Scowling, he ran a finger in between his collar and his neck. Why was it suddenly so damn hot?

Sally strolled up to him and put her arm around his

waist. "Darling, everything is simply fabulous. The hotel is magnificent."

"Thanks," he said, giving her shoulders a quick squeeze. "You look beautiful."

His mother wore a high-collared white satin tuxedo shirt with a black taffeta skirt and cummerbund—not that Adam would know taffeta if it walked up and bit him, but she'd described the dress in excruciating detail on the phone earlier in the week. Her hair was all scooped up in some kind of fancy French braided style, no doubt to show off her shiny, dangly earrings.

Sally beamed. "Thank you. Isn't it about time you got things started?"

"Twenty more minutes," Adam murmured, checking his wristwatch to be sure. He waved to catch the valet captain's eye, then tapped his watch and pointed to Trish. They'd worked out the signal ahead of time. Sure enough, within seconds, Trish came running.

"I'll make it on time," she said, bounding up the stairway and heading straight for the hotel door. On impulse, Adam stepped into her path and grabbed her in his arms. He swung her around, then kissed her and set her back down, breathless.

"You've got fifteen minutes to dress and get back down here," he said.

"You're not helping," she said, smacking his arm. Then her eyes widened. "Is this your mother?"

"Yes," he said, turning. "Mom, this is Trish."

"We've spoken on the phone," Sally said, shaking Trish's hand. "It's so nice to meet you in person."

"It's nice to meet you, too, Mrs. Duke."

"Oh, call me Sally, dear. Everybody does."

"Thank you," Trish said, smiling. "You look so beautiful."

"Oh, you're a sweet girl," Sally said, patting her hair.

"Yes, she is," Adam said. "Now get going." He kissed Trish again and she laughed as he patted her behind to push her along.

"So, that's Trish," his mother said a moment later.

"Yeah," he said, baffled and annoyed over the sudden and very public display of affection he'd just shown the world.

"She's absolutely perfect," she murmured.

His mother's tone had him eyeing her suspiciously. "What's that supposed to mean?"

She held up both hands innocently. "I'm just saying she's a perfectly lovely girl. And Marjorie tells me she's a hard worker."

His eyes narrowed. "What else does Marjorie tell you?"

"Oh, Adam," she said, with a soft chuckle. "If you only knew."

"Mother."

"Don't frown dear, you'll scare the guests."

He shook his head, then he held out his arm for her to hold. "How about if I escort you inside?"

"I'd be delighted."

With his mother by his side playing hostess, Adam worked the grand ballroom for the next twenty minutes. His guests raved about the rustically elegant resort and its beautifully designed ballroom and conference space. They gushed over the guest baskets placed in every room. Trish and the guest-services coordinator had selected the items to be included in the baskets and Adam had approved. Champagne, fresh fruit, cheeses and snacks, free spa treatments along with items from the hotel's exclusive line of hair and skin-care products, and a plush Fantasy Mountain bathrobe and towel.

Adam thought about his mother's earlier reaction to Trish. His suspicions were raised anew and he realized he would have to put an end to his affair with Trish as soon as he and Trish got back to town. The gala would be over and his life could get back to normal. He supposed he would miss her once in a while, especially around the office, but that's the way it had to be.

Having made his decision, he studiously ignored the tightening he felt in his chest.

As he greeted the mayor of a small town north of Dunsmuir Bay, he noticed the crowd begin to murmur.

"Oh," his mother whispered. "She's stunning."

He turned but couldn't say a word as he stared across the room. Trish wore a strapless black gown that molded to her breasts and fell in a graceful column to the floor, yet managed to show off every curve of her body. It was classic and elegant. And outrageously sexy. Her hair tumbled loosely around her shoulders and a thin row of diamonds draped her neck, bringing Adam's gaze right back to her stunning breasts. She looked like a goddess emerging from the sea.

She'd never looked more beautiful, if that was possible. It was Brandon who greeted her at the door, introducing himself to her and escorting her into the room. He snagged her a glass of champagne from a passing waiter and stayed by her side and talked.

Watching her sip champagne, Adam's insides tightened at the memory of their two days of pleasurable solitude ensconced in the hotel suite. They'd explored each other's bodies all day and throughout the night, finally falling into an exhausted sleep as dawn broke over the mountain.

Then waking up to start all over again.

The memory of her legs wrapped around him, her body arching into him, her sobs of need, caused a physical hunger in his gut and his jaw clenched as he forced himself to ignore it.

Adam checked his watch again. He had to determine exactly how long he'd have to stay at the party schmoozing with his guests before he could take Trish back to their suite. He could barely wait to strip that incredible dress off her.

"At the risk of repeating myself, she's very lovely," Sally said amiably, tucking her arm through his.

He looked at her squarely. "She's also a great assistant—smart, loyal, highly organized and very talented." And gorgeous in bed. Which is exactly where he wanted her. Now.

Sally touched his arm maternally. "I'm glad you have good people working for you, sweetie."

Adam exhaled slowly. "Me, too."

The orchestra began to play a big band favorite and Adam watched Brandon lead Trish out onto the dance floor.

"Crap," Adam said. Why was his brother holding her so close? He was going to cut off her breathing.

Sally chuckled. "Why don't you dance with me instead of standing here scowling? Your guests are going to think something's wrong with the plumbing."

"Good idea," he muttered, and led his mother onto the dance floor.

After a few minutes of gliding around, Sally smiled up at him. "You dance beautifully, Adam."

One of his eyebrows shot up. "I'd better. I risked my life to learn the damn fox trot."

Sally laughed. To this day, Adam couldn't believe she'd forced all three boys to attend cotillion when they were barely thirteen years old. Once word got out at school, the Duke brothers became targets and the fights began. The boys gave as good as they got, but often came home from school with black eyes and bloodied knuckles. Rather than cancel the dance lessons, Sally briskly enrolled them in marital arts and boxing classes, as well.

Chuckling, Adam recalled that she'd also forced them to learn how to cook and do their own laundry. She'd always said she was determined to raise well-rounded men who would make good husbands.

Adam was happy to be well-rounded, but that didn't mean he intended to be anyone's good husband.

"Every woman loves a man who can dance," Sally said suggestively, her eyes glittering with humor as she glanced across the ballroom.

Adam couldn't help but follow the direction of her gaze. His stomach tensed all over again as he spotted Trish, laughing and flirting and all wrapped up in the arms of his own brother.

The song ended. Trish and Brandon Duke applauded politely, then walked off the floor together.

"It was nice to meet you, Brandon," she said, and was surprised to realize she meant it. She'd been concerned when she found out that the outgoing man who'd met her at the door was Adam's brother. But as it turned out, he was a big friendly bear of a guy and a surprisingly good dancer. A former football player, he was several inches taller and a bit stockier than his brother. A very good-looking man, though not nearly as handsome as Adam.

"Great to meet you, too," Brandon said. "Especially after hearing so much about you."

"Really?" she said carefully. "Such as?"

"All good things," he assured her.

"Now I'm truly worried."

"Don't be," he said, laughing. "Listen, I'm going to try those Buffalo wings on the pier as soon as I can get there. Thanks for the recommendation."

"You're welcome," she said. "I've never been to Buffalo but I think they're pretty close to the real thing."

"That's what I've been looking for," he said. "Whenever my team played the Buffalo Bills, we'd always go to the Anchor Bar downtown to get our fix. I haven't been able to find the real thing since then."

"I hope you'll let me know what you think," she said.

As Brandon continued talking, Trish casually gazed around the crowded ballroom and ultimately homed in on Adam. A rush of warm longing rose from her toes all the way up to her ears as she realized he'd been watching her intently.

He stood with Sally, who stared up at Adam with a look of glowing pride and Trish couldn't blame her. Adam looked incredibly handsome in his custom-made tuxedo, and Trish shivered involuntarily as she remembered how the two of them had spent the early part of the day luxuriating in the soaking tub, washing each other's backs and making love. Then they'd dressed slowly. She helped him with his formal bowtie and cuff links. He zipped up her jeans, slowly, inch by inch, his fingers gliding along the zipper's path, touching her skin and sending ripples of heated desire throughout her body.

They almost didn't make it downstairs.

It was crazy. They'd spent the last forty-eight hours doing almost nothing but making love with each other. But now, gazing at him from across the ballroom floor, she realized she wanted him again. Would the wanting never cease?

It didn't matter. Once she returned home, she would turn the CD over to the local papers and quit her job at Duke Development. Grandma Anna would be avenged and Trish would move on with her life.

But for now she didn't want to think about that. For now, for this moment, there was only Adam.

She was about to make her excuses to Brandon and go to Adam, when a tall, dark and dangerously handsome man stepped in front of her.

"I'm Cameron Duke," he said in a deep, rich voice. "Obviously, my brother's too rude to introduce us."

"Not rude," Brandon insisted. "Just being considerate of Trish's tender feelings."

Trish grinned at Brandon, then shook Cameron's hand. "I'm Trish James, Adam's assistant."

"I know," he said, and his mouth twisted in a cynical grin. "I was wondering why we hadn't met you before, but now it's obvious."

"It is?"

"Yeah," he said. "You're beautiful."

Trish felt herself blush. The Duke brothers were formidable, to say the least, and each one was more good-looking than the next. The three of them must've fueled the dreams of every girl they went to high school with. Smiling up at Cameron, she said, "You're very kind."

"No, I'm not," he said bluntly.

"He's really not," Brandon said with an affable grin.

The band struck up the first notes of a sultry samba and Cameron held out his hand. "But I'm a good dancer. Shall we?"

"Oh." She cast a furtive glance across the room and saw Adam talking to someone else, so she smiled at Cameron and took his hand. "I'd love to."

"Mr. Duke. I must speak with you."

Adam turned, then had to look down at the short, thin man who'd addressed him. The middle-aged man wore a wrinkled black business suit with a worn purple tie and looked nervous and uncomfortable in the midst of all the festivities.

"Yes? What is it?"

"I'm Stan Strathbaum, former president of Strathbaum Construction, now a loyal employee of Duke Development."

"Yeah?" Was he supposed to know this guy? Adam couldn't say why, but he disliked him on sight.

"Yes." The man's lip curled up in a sneer as he pointed to the dance floor. "Mr. Duke, do you know that woman?"

Adam tried to follow the direction he was pointing and stared out at the dance floor.

"Which woman?" Adam said, his voice reflecting his annoyance.

"That one," Strathbaum said, his finger jabbing the air as he continued to point. "The one in the black dress."

What the hell? Was he pointing at Trish? Did

Strathbaum know how close he was to being tossed out
on his ass?

"What about her?" Adam asked.

"I don't know her name, Mr. Duke, but I'll never
forget her face. She stormed onto a Duke construction
site several months ago and threatened me with bodily
harm if I didn't halt the demolition of some old building
near the pier."

"Couldn't have been Trish," Adam said confidently.

"Oh, it certainly was, sir," Strathbaum said, and
pushed his glasses up his greasy nose. "It was her. She
was hostile and unstable and promised to take down
Duke Development if it was the last thing she ever did.
At the time I thought I'd have to call security, but I
managed to drag her out of my office myself."

He'd heard enough. How could this little creep stand
here, insulting Trish? Who the hell did he think he was?
"That's a ridiculous story."

"I'm warning you, sir, that woman is a security risk."
He folded his arms firmly across his chest. "The entire
resort and all the guests could be in serious danger."

"What are you talking about?" Adam said, a hint
of danger in his low, deep voice. "I'd like you to leave
before I call security to help you on your way."

The little guy swelled up like a self-important toad,
but still managed to look wary. "Sir, you may not like
what I say but I'm telling you the truth. I demand—I
mean—"

But Adam had stopped listening. Instead, he stared
at Trish, willing her gaze to meet his. He saw her eyes
turn warm, then cloud up in confusion, then widen in
horror as she seemed to recognize the obnoxious but
apparently *truthful* man who'd just revealed her deepest,
darkest secret to him.

* * *

From the dance floor, Trish noticed Adam talking to a slightly built man who looked alarmingly familiar. Her steps faltered.

"Is something wrong?" Cameron asked.

"I—I don't know." But suddenly she recalled where she'd last seen that man and his prune-faced sneer. It was at the construction site where she'd gone to beg someone—anyone—from Duke Development to put a stop to the imminent destruction of her home. At the site, she'd had the unfortunate luck to deal with Stan Strathbaum, the man who'd insulted her, threatened her and tossed her out of his office.

The same man who was talking to Adam. He was even sneering now as he pointed his accusing finger right at her.

Trish's blood turned to ice and her world flipped upside down.

Filled with dread, she pushed away from Cameron. "I have to go, I'm so sorry. Good night."

She quickly threaded her way off the packed dance floor and ran from the room.

By the time Adam made it up to the suite, she'd already called the concierge to arrange transportation back to Dunsmuir Bay. She'd packed away her beautiful dress and hurriedly changed into jeans, boots and a sweater.

He stormed into the bedroom. "Who are you?"

"You know who I am," she said wearily, tossing her underwear into her suitcase.

"No, I don't," he said. "Not anymore. Was that guy right? Did you threaten to destroy my company?"

"Don't be ridiculous."

"Trish, you went tearing off the dance floor the

minute you saw me talking to Strathbaum. What else am I supposed to think?"

"You're supposed to trust me," she said weakly, as she threw her toiletries into a small bag and stuffed them into her suitcase.

He grabbed her by the shoulders and forced her to stop. "Trish, answer me. Did you threaten to take down Duke Development? Not that you'd ever have a snowball's chance, but did you?"

She exhaled resignedly. "Yes, I suppose I did, but it's not what you think. I—"

"Not what I think?" he shouted. "Hell, you just admitted it to me. What else am I supposed to think? Somebody tells me you were threatening my company a few months ago, then lo and behold, you're on my payroll. What the hell? Were you honestly trying to destroy me?"

"No!" she cried, pulling away from him. "I just needed something to—"

"What did you need?" he demanded. "Money? Is that it? Are you actually the gold digger I thought you were all along?"

She stopped and stared at him. "You thought I was a gold digger?"

He shook his head. "That's not the point."

"You thought I was a gold digger?" Trish repeated more loudly, then came up close and jabbed him in the chest with her finger. "Let me tell you something, you arrogant jerk. I don't care anything about your money! Your company demolished my home. You destroyed my neighborhood, my grandmother's store, her livelihood and everything important in her life. You left us with nothing but rubble. My grandmother had a heart attack and died when you tore down the Victorian Village."

"Wait. Victorian Village?" he said, bemused. "I remember that place. It was like a landmark."

"Yeah," she said, squaring her shoulders. "It was. Until you showed up. I grew up in that landmark. That was my home. The home your company demolished eight months ago. And why did you do it? Because Duke Development needed a *parking lot*."

"What? That's not true."

"Oh, yes, it is," she said heatedly. "You bulldozed our beautiful homes and shops and replaced them all with an ugly block of concrete. You gave us thirty days' notice, then you evicted us. You threw my grandmother and all of our neighbors out into the street. They were good people, good friends I'd known my entire life. And for what? For a slab of concrete! My grandma died of a broken heart and I hated you for that."

"Wait a minute," he said.

"No." She gasped for air and realized that tears were streaming down her cheeks. She wiped them away angrily as she rounded the bed and pulled the rest of her clothes from the chest of drawers against the wall.

Adam followed her every step. "Wait a damn minute. I don't do business that way."

"Oh, really?" She looked up at him, saw confusion in his eyes and wished she could believe in it. Wished she could believe in him. But the facts were there. She'd *lived* the truth of how he did business. Maybe if she showed him that she had proof, he'd stop the ridiculous pretense of innocence.

She grabbed her purse, pulled out the Vista del Lago disk and thrust it at him. "You take a look at this, then talk to me again about how you do business."

"What is this?" he demanded, holding up the disk.

She stared at the disk. "It—it's something I was going to hand over to the newspapers."

"Then why are giving it to me?"

She laughed sadly and wiped away more tears. "Because even though you hurt me ten times over, it turns out I could never hurt you. I wanted to, Adam. I really did. But I just can't." She zipped her suitcase closed and stood it upright, pulled out the handle, threw her purse over her shoulder and started to leave the suite.

"You're not leaving," he said. "I want to talk about this."

"No more talk," she said, her world crumbling with each step she took. She stopped at the door and shook her head in misery. "You don't understand. I've betrayed my grandmother's memory by becoming involved with you. I've let down my friends and neighbors, the people you ruined." Her voice dropped another notch. "I can't believe I fell in love with a man who could do that to anyone."

His eyes were arctic blue as he stared at her in disbelief. "Do *what?*"

"That," she whispered, pointing to the disk, then she grabbed her suitcase and walked out.

Eleven

Adam had never considered himself a coward but he'd been avoiding doing something for more than a week and it was starting to eat him up inside.

He stared at the CD on his desk. The one Trish had given him. He'd put off viewing it for so long now, he was beginning to feel like a damn fool.

At first he hadn't wanted to look at it because he was just plain furious. At Trish, naturally. But also at himself for being sucked in by a woman who'd lied the entire time she'd been with him, then tried to blame him for her lies. He refused to accept that he'd been hurt by her betrayal. That was his mother's brilliant theory, once she realized Trish had left. Adam had less than politely cut her off, tersely explaining that no, he'd just been righteously pissed off.

The night Trish walked out on him, the night of the Fantasy Mountain gala opening, Adam had barely managed to return to the party where he maintained a semblance of civility—until he was ready to crack.

Once he was back home in Dunsmuir Bay, he'd buried himself in his office and worked day and night on other projects, other resorts, other deals. He had a business to run and didn't need some beautiful, treacherous woman running around distracting him. Even though every time he passed the desk where Trish usually sat, something inside him fisted in pain—that wasn't the point.

He knew his mother was concerned about him, but he couldn't deal with that right now. His brothers were another story. They'd made no bones about wanting to smack him out of this mood he was in, so they would occasionally show up at his house and drag him out for beers or otherwise try to cajole him into having some fun. One night, they showed up in his office with a twelve-pack and proceeded to berate him into easing up on the senior staff, some of whom had apparently been whining that Adam was taking out his problems on them.

Adam's solution had been succinct. They could suck it up. That's why they got paid the big bucks.

And besides, Adam wasn't the one with problems.

Meanwhile, Marjorie had quietly replaced Trish with Ella, a perfectly competent older woman who'd been with the company for ten years. She did her job, but didn't go out of her way to excel or make his life better. She didn't make him laugh. She never ordered him a healthy dinner on the nights he worked late.

"Like tonight," he grumbled, and reached for the phone to order a pizza. After three rings, he hung up the phone.

"Hell." Maybe he should order something more healthy from that upscale place Trish had found. He hadn't been sleeping well lately. Should he be eating more chicken? Or maybe a steak. He wasn't sure what he wanted, but it wasn't pizza.

The damnable woman had even managed to screw up his eating habits.

He shoved his chair back and stood by the window. Out on the bay, the full moon was reflected in the rippling water and the harbor lights twinkled in the distance. He swore under his breath.

It wasn't food that he wanted. It was her. He wanted Trish. Wanted her soft curves pressed up against him. Wanted her exquisite lips and tongue on his skin. And okay, he even wanted her clever mind solving his problems.

There, he'd admitted it. Satisfied? He slapped his hand against the wall of glass, then blew out a heavy breath. No, he wasn't satisfied.

Damn her for making him *want*.

He turned around and once again stared at the disk lying on the desk next to his laptop. He hadn't viewed it yet and he wasn't sure if he ever would. Why should he? She's the one who'd lied to him. So why should he believe anything he might see on that disk?

And speaking of lies, why should he believe she'd meant it when she told him she loved him?

Disgusted with his line of thought, Adam swept a piece of scrap paper off his desk and into the trash can. No, Trish didn't love him. No way. How could she love him and lie to him at the same time? Simple. She *didn't* love him, never had. Not that any of it mattered, he told himself. He didn't *do* love. Remember? Oh sure, he had cared for her. A lot. A small, pitiful part of him probably always would. But caring for someone wasn't the same as loving her.

And hell, it was a damn good thing he didn't love her because her betrayal would've hit him even harder than it already had. Not that he'd taken it that hard. It's just that, it could've been worse.

He eyed the disk again. Maybe he should throw the damn thing away. Or maybe he should return it to Trish. But he didn't know where she lived. Hell, he'd been sleeping with her and he didn't even have her address. He'd never picked her up for a date, never dropped her off, never kissed her good-night in front of her house. Didn't matter now.

He could probably get her address from Marjorie, although she'd been pretty annoyed with him lately. Still, he was the boss. He could get anything he wanted. Of course, even if he got Trish's address, it's not as if he'd go running after her.

"Oh, man," Adam muttered, spearing his fingers through his hair in exasperation. Knowing he wouldn't be getting any work done in his current state of aggravation, he shut down his laptop and left the office for the night.

That weekend, Sally Duke insisted that Adam come over for a special afternoon party she was throwing. He arrived an hour late to find the back patio deserted. When he walked into the kitchen, the only people he saw were his two brothers. Brandon stood at the stove, stirring and tasting Mom's homemade barbecue sauce.

Adam put the six-pack of beer and a bottle of white wine for his mother into the refrigerator. "Where's Mom?"

"She'll be out in a few," Cameron said.

Adam took a beer out and popped it open, then glanced around. "Anyone else show up yet?"

"Nope, this party's all about you, bro," Cameron said. Slouched against the kitchen counter, he took a pull of his longneck bottle of beer. "You've got Mom all freaked out. She can't stop worrying about you."

"Well, hell."

"Yeah. Which means we're going to have to kick your ass."

Adam rolled his eyes and drank his beer. "That's what this is all about?"

At the stove, Brandon shrugged. "Nothing personal you understand. It's our job."

"I do understand that," Adam said, picking up his car keys and slipping his sunglasses back on as he moved toward the kitchen door. "Enjoy the beer I brought. Say hi to Mom. I'll see you all around."

Brandon grinned. "And here I thought you'd be grateful for a chance to share your feelings."

"When pigs fly." Adam stepped outside and tried to close the door behind him, but Cameron caught it.

"You can run, but you can't hide," Cameron said calmly and stepped through the doorway.

"This should be fun," Brandon said, chuckling as he followed his brothers outside.

Adam stopped near the heated pool and turned to face his two closest friends in the world. "Guys, I love you, but if you come any closer, I'll have to kill you."

"Love you, too, bro," Cameron said, approaching him cautiously from the right. "But you're being an ass and we're tired of Mom bugging the hell out of us about it."

"See," Brandon said, taking a step toward him on the

left, "it's a matter of facing you down or dealing with Mom. You be the judge."

Adam had to admit they had a point. "Fine," he said, splaying his arms out. "Take your best shot. But I warn you, I'm taking you both down with me."

"As long as you go down first," Cameron said and rushed forward.

The explosion of water set off a mini-tsunami in the pool as all three brothers plunged into the deep end.

After some flailing and splashing and dunking of heads, Adam finally surfaced. He wiped his eyes of excess water and eventually focused on the pair of pink flip-flops standing at the edge of the pool. He looked up and saw his mother glaring down at him. She wore a goofy hat but her lips were set in a grim line and both hands were bunched up into fists perched on her pink shorts-clad hips.

"Hey, Mom, you're looking good," Adam said.

"Adam, I want to talk to you."

"Ouch," Brandon said. "She's mad."

"Yeah, that's going to leave a mark," Cameron agreed.

Adam sighed in resignation. He'd seen his mother's eyes before she walked away. She wasn't angry with him. She was worried. And that knowledge cut him in ways he couldn't begin to understand. He gripped the side of the pool and pushed himself up and out. Grabbing a towel, he followed him mother inside and found her in the kitchen, stirring the barbecue sauce on the stove.

"Everyone says you've turned into a bear at work," she said nonchalantly after a few moments.

"I've had a lot on my mind." He walked to the fridge and pulled out another beer, then sat down at the kitchen table, popped the top and took a long sip. "We're really swamped right now. Just opened Fantasy Mountain and now we've got Monarch Dunes opening in three months."

Sally sat down at the table next to him and Adam knew she was through beating around the bush. "Adam, what happened to Trish?"

He tried several ways of skirting the subject but eventually she wore him down, as she always did.

When he was finished telling his side of the story, she sighed. "Sweetie, even as a child, you didn't want to trust in love. But you're not a child any longer. Are you going to let Trish walk away, knowing you'll never be whole without her? Or will you find a way to convince her that you truly are the good man she once thought you were?"

"Let's get it straight, we're not talking about love." He realized his knuckles were turning white and loosened his grip on the beer bottle. "Besides, she lied."

"Maybe she had a good reason to lie. Did you ever ask?"

His jaw worked as he stared out at the wide expanse of grassy lawn that stretched all the way to the cliff. "No, I never asked. How could I trust her to tell me the truth?"

"Oh, Adam," Sally said. "Of the three of you, you were always the one who had the hardest time giving your trust."

"I trust you, Mom."

She sniffed a little and her eyes glistened. "Thank you, darling. I hope you always will. But more than anything else, I want you to trust yourself."

"I trust myself," he muttered. "It's the rest of humanity I have a problem with."

She laughed. "You're going to have to let that go." Sitting forward, she grabbed his hand. "Honey, if you want Trish, you have to dig deep, find out what happened there. Maybe it won't bring the two of you back together, but at least you'll be able to go on, having found out the whole truth. Until you do, I don't know if you can ever be happy. And if there's one thing I want in this world, it's for you to be happy. And you know I always get what I want."

Adam chuckled as he squeezed her hand with both of his. "You scare me to death, Mom."

"Oh, honey." She jumped out of her chair and gave him a tight hug. "That's the sweetest thing you've ever said to me."

He didn't go straight home but stopped at the office instead. It was a quiet Sunday so he knew he wouldn't be disturbed. Sitting down at his desk, he picked up Trish's disk and stared at it. "Vista del Lago" was written on it, probably by Trish, and he absently rubbed his finger over the script.

Swearing under his breath, he shoved the disk into his laptop and viewed the two pages of scanned documents.

When he was finished, Adam swiped his hand across his face. What the hell?

The letterhead was Duke Development's but he didn't recognize the name of the letter writer, Peter Abernathy. He logged in and used his special admin password to look up Abernathy's employment background and his record with DDI. The man had been president of Abernathy Construction up until a few months ago when Duke bought him out.

While Adam was logged on, he decided to look up

the same information on Stan Strathbaum. Turned out, Strathbaum had a background similar to Abernathy's. He'd been head of his own small company, Strathbaum Ltd., until Duke bought him out eight months ago.

After reading both men's employment histories, along with the DDI due diligence reports, Adam spent some quality Google time in order to get more information on both men and their business practices, as well as some details regarding certain historical landmarks in Dunsmuir Bay.

Finally, he sat back in his chair and thought about what he'd learned. For a long time, he stared out at the horizon where the pale blue sky met the cobalt blue of the ocean. He could now understand why Trish had been so upset by the thought that Adam would approve the plan to tear down Vista del Lago. She must've experienced a painful sense of déjà vu when she'd read that letter and notice, thinking Adam was out to destroy another small community of friends and neighbors, just like hers, all over again.

But what she didn't know was that Adam had never approved the Vista del Lago teardown. He never would. He didn't operate that way—not that she would ever believe him. And furthermore, he never would've approved the destruction of the Victorian Village if he'd known about it. That one had slipped through the cracks. Or rather, Strathbaum had shoved it through the cracks. The slimy little creep had rushed the demolition through before anyone at Duke could make a decision on the property one way or the other. And as furious as he was at the little toad, Adam had to admit that he was culpable, too. His company, his mistake. The mistake being that he hadn't been paying close enough attention. He'd taken his eye off the ball and people had been hurt.

With ruthless calm, he made a note to fire Strathbaum on Monday. Adam and his brothers didn't need someone like that working for Duke Development. But as satisfying as firing the man would be, it wouldn't bring back Trish's home or her grandmother. There was nothing he could do about the past. But there was plenty he could do about the future.

Trish drove to the hospital and handed the vase filled with two dozen perfect red roses to the clerk at the front desk. "Please give them to someone who needs them."

"They're so beautiful," the admissions clerk exclaimed. "But that's the third bouquet this week. Is it your birthday?"

"Not exactly," she hedged, then smiled. "Enjoy."

Actually, the bouquet of red roses was the fifth arrangement she'd received this week. Day one was daisies. They were so cheerful, she hadn't had the heart to give them away. Day two, pink roses. Day three, a beautiful spring bouquet. Trish had spent half the day mooning over that one before deciding it would be perfect for cheering up a sick hospital patient. Day four, shiny balloons and homemade chocolate-chip cookies. One balloon said, "I Miss You." She couldn't bear to give that one to the hospital so it was still bobbing around her tiny living room. How many more gifts and flowers would Adam send before he gave up and left her alone?

He'd called, too. Two, three times a day. She'd refused to answer or call him back. It was torturous enough just hearing his voice on her answering machine. If she actually spoke with him, how would she ever be able to block him from her mind and heart?

She should've been happy she'd proved him to be the bad guy she always knew he was. But she wasn't happy. She was miserable.

She pulled the car over and parked across the street from the pier. There weren't many tourists because it was winter, but the sun was still warm enough that she pulled a hat over her hair before walking across to the pier.

After buying a small box of caramel corn, she took the old wooden stairs down to the beach. The waves were forceful and the air was crisp and cold. She could smell the salt, feel the slight spray on her skin. She tried to think of happier times. Before Adam. She couldn't think about him because it hurt too much to wonder what might have been.

Was she being maudlin by coming down here? It was so close, only a block away from where the Victorian Village had stood. Now there was an ugly gray parking structure standing in its place, but Trish refused to look at it.

As she skipped through the waves that washed onto the shore, she thought of Grandma Anna, the only family she'd ever had. She barely remembered her father—killed in Operation Desert Storm when she was a little girl. Her mother died when Trish was nine and she and Grandma Anna mourned the loss together and grew to depend on each other.

Her grandmother had been her closest friend, her advisor, her teacher, her parent. Now she had no one, and it hurt so deeply to know that she was alone in the world. No family, no loved ones. Well, there was one man she loved, still. Even though he'd hurt her badly. She'd thought there was no greater pain than when Grandma Anna died, but she was wrong.

Losing Adam hurt even more.

She wasn't sure why it hurt so much. He'd never really been hers, after all. And she'd known his true nature all along. So why did it hurt so much now that she was alone again?

It had been three weeks since that fateful night at the Fantasy Mountain gala when that hideous man had spoken to Adam. If only she'd been able to stop him. If only Adam hadn't believed him. If only. Trish was sick and tired of moaning and groaning about things she couldn't change, things that could never be.

Such as the fact that she'd actually told Adam that she loved him. And he'd returned the favor by staring daggers at her as she walked out the door.

Oh, it was too humiliating to think about.

"So don't think about it," she grumbled, kicking up sand. "Do something. You need a job. You need to get on with your life. You need to do something about Grandma Anna's things."

She'd wondered what Grandma Anna would say about Trish falling in love with Adam, and now some words came to her mind. "Don't be ashamed for loving well."

Tears prickled her eyes. No, she wouldn't be ashamed. But it was definitely time to stop wallowing. She'd given love her best shot and she'd grieved over it. Now it was time to pick herself up, dust herself off and all that other stuff. What she needed was closure.

"That's a one-of-a-kind item," Trish said, wrestling the small treasure back from the woman who'd picked it up and shaken it. "An eighteenth-century pillbox. French, hand-painted with real pearls lining the edges. The cameo is carved ivory, inlaid on amber."

"Does it come in red?" the woman asked.

Trish wanted to smack her but resisted, much to her credit, she thought. Honestly, she'd wanted to smack so many of the people she'd dealt with today.

She didn't know what was wrong with her. She wasn't usually so short-tempered. She could understand people wanting a bargain, but didn't anyone in the world want something of quality that would last a lifetime or even longer?

Maybe it had been a mistake renting a booth at the local antique swap mart, but she'd decided she needed to sell Grandma Anna's antiques and collectibles, which had been in storage for the past seven months. She'd thought for a while that she would open another antiques store. After all, the reason she'd gone for her MBA, with a concentration in retail management, in the first place was to bring the Victorian Village shops into the twenty-first century. She'd had so many great marketing ideas for the whole neighborhood group, starting with obtaining the historical landmark designation.

So much for that pipe dream. It was time to move on with her life, time to clear away the clutter, but it still broke her heart to think of her grandmother's beautiful treasures going to somebody who didn't know a pillbox from a pop tart. She began to straighten the items on the back shelf.

"How much for everything you've got?" a man asked.

Adam.

Trish didn't have to turn around to know it was him. Every part of her knew it was him, including her stomach, which was performing somersaults at the sound of his voice.

It was vain, but her first thought was that she really

wished she'd worn something prettier instead of the T-shirt and jeans she'd decided to wear today. It was dirty business, setting up the booth every day, although visitors didn't seem to care much what anybody wore in the vast tented hall of the old fairgrounds.

She turned and took a moment to drink him in. Oh, God, would she always want to swoon whenever she saw him? Today he looked incredibly handsome in his high-powered suit and tie, even better than he looked in the dreams that continued to haunt her every night. Her throat was suddenly so dry that she grabbed her water bottle and gulped down the liquid. It barely quenched her thirst and didn't do a thing to calm her stuttering heart.

She forced herself to take even steps until she stood in front of him, separated only by the table filled with Grandma Anna's vast collection of antique pillboxes. With her chin rigid, she looked him in the eye and said, "I'm afraid you can't afford it."

His eyes narrowed as he stared back at her for what felt like minutes. Then he began to grin, slowly, calculatedly. Damn that cockeyed grin of his! It never failed to send her nerve endings spinning out of control.

"Hello, Trish," he said, his voice still as deep and sexy as she remembered. "You look good."

Well, she knew that was a lie, but it was a kind one. "What are you doing here, Adam?"

"Looking for a treasure," he said, gazing straight into her eyes.

She swallowed. Could he hear her heart breaking? Had he come to destroy her once again? It wouldn't take much.

"Look, Trish. I understand that I hurt you. I know

you don't trust me as far as you can throw me, but we need to talk and I need to show you something."

She sucked in a breath. "Adam, there's nothing you can show me or tell me that would change anything."

"I know you think so, but I want you—no, I need you—to give me a chance to change your mind."

She sighed. "Adam."

"You said you loved me."

She swallowed. So he was going to play dirty. "Oh, you heard that, did you?"

"Yeah, I heard you say it, so you can't take it back." Not breaking eye contact, Adam shoved the tables of knickknacks and collectibles aside and stepped inside her booth. In her space. Breathing her air. "I know you, Trish. You never would've said you loved me if you didn't mean it. Did you mean it, Trish?"

She tossed her hair back. "You thought I was lying about everything else. Why not that, too?"

"Let's just agree that I was an idiot."

"Okay, I can agree on that," she said, biting back a smile.

"I want you back, Trish."

Almost as quickly as it came, her smile was replaced by a frown. "Adam, it would never work between us. We're too different. You're wealthy and powerful and I'm just…me."

He took a step closer and said quietly, "I was dumped outside a hospital when I was two years old."

She hadn't known that and instantly, her heart wept for that tiny abandoned boy. "Oh, Adam."

"Believe me, Trish," he said. "My brothers and I have built a business and I'm proud of what I've done with my life. But I'm not all that wealthy and powerful on the inside. I'm just me. And all of me wants all of you with every last fiber of my being."

Tears threatened to erupt and Trish had to take some deep breaths before she could speak. "Adam, I don't know if I—"

He held up his hand. "I told you there was something I wanted to show you. Can you leave right now and come with me? I promise it won't take long."

Without another thought, she called out to her old neighbor, Sam, who was helping his friend Howie repair bikes in Howie's booth across the aisle. "Sam, can you watch my booth for a little while?"

Sam looked up and winked at them. "Sure, honey. You go on. I'll take care of things for you."

Adam said, "Thanks, Sam." Then he swooped Trish up in his arms.

She let out a little shriek. "Is this really necessary?"

"I don't want you to get away."

As he carried her down the aisle toward the door, people called out encouragement and a few ladies applauded.

"See?" he said, grinning. "It's a good thing."

She shook her head. "You're impossible."

"I just know what I want."

The drive to the beach in his Ferrari only took a few minutes. Adam turned onto a side street and drove another block, then pulled to the curb in front of a row of six lovingly refurbished Craftsman-style bungalows. They had all been converted into small retail businesses.

Each house was painted a slightly different muted shade of sage green or terra-cotta. Flowers bloomed along the walkways and charming signs were planted in the well-kept front lawns. Each house had a porch where goods were displayed, and each had a private owners' dwelling attached to the back.

"Oh, aren't they beautiful?" Trish whispered as she got out of the car. "I didn't know these were here."

"I didn't, either, until I started looking," he said, wrapping his arm around her shoulder and pulling her close. "But they were exactly what I wanted."

She gazed up at him. "You own one of them?"

"I own all of them."

"You—"

"Or rather, Sam Sutter owns that one." He pointed to the house on the end. "See the sign?"

Trish stared, then read, "Sam's Beachside Bikes."

"Oh, my gosh," she whispered, her voice shaking. "He never said anything."

Adam smiled. "The old guy's got the kind of poker face that could make him rich in Vegas. Mrs. Collins owns that one. Check out those mannequins on the porch. By the way, she's quite the diva."

Just then, Mrs. Collins walked out onto the porch and waved a huge scarf in their direction. "Yooohoo, Trish! Isn't this marvelous?"

Trish choked out a laugh but said nothing.

Adam pointed to the last house down the row. "Tommie and Bert Lindsay have already started moving their beauty supply inventory into the place on the far end. And Claude and Madeleine Maubert want the one next door for their patisserie. I think a French bakery and restaurant like theirs will do really well in this area. This is a well-traveled area, close to the beach, with a lot of small, upscale businesses and pedestrian traffic. I ran some demographics for all your friends' shops and—"

She launched herself at him and he managed to catch her. "Thank you," she said, as tears streamed down her cheeks. "I don't know how or why you did it and you're probably insane for doing it, but I can't thank you enough for this."

He stroked her hair, kissed her forehead, then turned with her in his arms and pointed again. "Did you notice this place here in the middle?"

Adam had thought it was the prettiest house in the row, painted three different shades of muted green with beveled glass windows in front. The door was old oak with wrought-iron fixtures and the porch was wide enough for a table and chairs and lots of potted plants.

"It's beautiful," she murmured.

"Read the sign, sweetheart."

Trish turned her gaze toward the white sign that swung from a post in the middle of the lawn. She gasped. The sign read "Trish's Treasures."

She stared dumbly at Adam.

"It's not Anna's Attic, but it's all yours," he said. "If you want it."

"Oh, Adam."

"There's one more vacancy," he explained quickly, hoping if he just kept talking she would change her mind and take a chance with him. "That's in case one of your other friends from the old building wants to move their business here. I tried to track them down, but I haven't heard back. Anyway, whoever claims the last place, I'll sign over the deed to them."

"But…why?"

He pulled her back into his arms. "Isn't it obvious? Because I love you, Trish." His gaze roamed over her face as he took in every inch of her. "I want to make you happy, sweetheart. I swear, I never would've torn down your beautiful home. It's my fault that I didn't keep better track of what my company was doing, but that will never happen again. I hope one day you'll believe me."

"I do believe you." She sniffled as she tried to blink away her tears. "The more I got to know you, the more I doubted you had anything to do with it. But that man, Strathbaum…"

"I fired him."

She bit her lip for a moment, clearly conflicted, then said, "Well, I hate to wish pain on anyone else, but I'm glad he's gone."

He stared into her eyes, so green and misty. "I hate that my name caused you so much pain. I wish more than anything that I could bring back your grandmother, but I can't. I just hope you'll be able to forgive me someday."

She reached up and stroked his cheek. "I've already forgiven you."

"Tell me I have a chance. Tell me you still love me."

Her bright smile lit up his heart. "Of course I still love you. I never stopped loving you."

"Marry me, Trish. Put me out of my misery and say yes."

"I thought you'd never marry anyone, ever."

He grimaced. "Did I mention earlier that I was an idiot?"

She laughed as one last tear rolled down her cheek. "You did."

He rubbed away the tear with his thumb. "You changed me, Trish. I want to be with you forever. Say you'll marry me."

"Of course I'll marry you." She reached up and

wrapped her arms around his neck. "I love you, Adam. I love you so much."

"Thank God." He kissed her, then grabbed her in a fierce hug and felt the formerly empty spot in his heart overflow with love.

* * * * *

Don't miss the next romance by New York Times
bestselling author Kate Carlisle
Featuring Cameron Duke
Coming September, 2011
from Mills & Boon® Desire™.

"That was your test?" she demanded. **"To see if we felt the inferno when we touched?"**

"No. Actually, I was going to kiss you."

She fell back another step, shocked as much by the statement as by the calm, businesslike way Rafe delivered it. "Why?"

"There's no point in becoming engaged if you aren't physically attracted to me," he explained. "My family would pick up on that in no time."

Larkin gazed down at her hand and scratched her thumbnail across the faint throb centered in the middle of her palm. "So whatever just happened when we touched is just an odd coincidence?"

"I sure as hell hope so."

DANTE'S
TEMPORARY
FIANCÉE

BY
DAY LECLAIRE

All the characters in this book have no existence outside the imagination of
the author, and have no relation whatsoever to anyone bearing the same name
or names. They are not even distantly inspired by any individual known or
unknown to the author, and all the incidents are pure invention.

Published in Great Britain 2011
by Mills & Boon, an imprint of Harlequin (UK) Limited,
Eton House, 18-24 Paradise Road, Richmond, Surrey TW9 1SR

© Day Totton Smith 2010

ISBN: 978 0 263 88236 0

51-0711

Harlequin (UK) policy is to use papers that are natural, renewable and
recyclable products and made from wood grown in sustainable forests. The
logging and manufacturing processes conform to the legal environmental
regulations of the country of origin.

Printed and bound in Spain
by Blackprint CPI, Barcelona

To Kathy Jorgensen, my sister in spirit.

USA Today bestselling author **Day Leclaire** is a three-time winner of both a Colorado Award of Excellence and a Golden Quill Award. She's won *RT Book Reviews* Career Achievement and Love and Laughter Awards, a Holt Medallion and a Booksellers' Best Award. She has also received an impressive ten nominations for the prestigious Romance Writers of America's RITA® Award.

Day's romances touch the heart and make you care about her characters as much as she does. In Day's own words, "I adore writing romances, and can't think of a better way to spend each day." For more information, visit Day on her website, www.dayleclaire.com.

Dear Reader,

At the heart of all romance novels is the issue of trust. No matter what form the conflict takes, the underlying problem is whether the hero and heroine can learn to trust one another with their deepest secrets, and ultimately, with their heart. Anyone who's been in love knows that giving those final pieces of yourself into the safekeeping of another person is the most difficult part of a relationship. *Dante's Temporary Fiancée* is no different.

Just as in real life, Larkin Thatcher and Rafaelo Dante must find a way to bare their secrets—as well as their hearts—to discover their soul mate. That can be a little tricky when each is keeping a secret from the other. Fortunately, Larkin and Rafe have a little help from an unlikely source—a "dog" named Kiko.

You might wonder why I used quotes when describing Kiko. That's because she isn't your average canine, but one who has reason to distrust humans as much as Larkin and Rafe distrust the feelings The Inferno has stirred between them. I hope you'll find yourself rooting for all three of them throughout this story—a tale that at its heart is about learning to trust in love.

All the best,

Day Leclaire

One

This time his family had gone too far.

Rafe Dante stared at the bevy of women being subtly—and not so subtly—paraded beneath his nose by various family members. He'd lost count of the number of women he'd been forced to shake hands with. He knew why they were doing it. They were all determined to find him a wife. He grimaced. No, more than just a wife.

They hoped to find his Inferno soul mate—a Dante legend that had gotten seriously out of hand. For some reason, his family had it firmly fixed in their heads that it took only one touch for some strange mythical connection to be forged between a Dante and his soul mate. Ridiculous, of course. Didn't they get it?

Not only didn't he believe in The Inferno, but he had no interest in ever experiencing matrimonial bliss-lessness again. His late wife, Leigh, had taught him that lesson in the short span of time from "I do" to "My lawyer will be in touch." Of course, that phone call had never come. Eighteen months ago his wife had chartered a private plane to Mexico to recover from the tragedy of her marriage to him and met a far worse fate when her plane crashed into a mountainside, leaving no survivors.

Rafe's younger brother, Draco, joined him and folded his arms across his chest. He stood silently for a moment, surveying the room and the glittering contents, both jeweled and female. "Ready to surrender and just pick one?"

"Get serious."

"I am. Dead serious."

Rafe turned on his brother, only too happy to vent some of his irritation. "Do you have any idea what the past three months have been like?"

"I do. I've been watching from the sidelines, in case you hadn't noticed. I'm also keenly aware that once you succumb to The Inferno, I'm next in line for the firing squad. As far as I'm concerned, feel free to hold out for as long as possible."

"I'm working on it."

Rafe returned his attention to the shimmer and sparkle and sighed. Dantes international jewelry reception possessed everything a man could ask for—wine, women and bling—and nothing he wanted.

The wine came from a Sonoma, California, vineyard just a few hours from the family's San Francisco home office. He knew the label on the bottles was as exclusive as the guest list. The women were beautiful, wealthy and shone as brilliantly as the wedding rings on display around the private showroom. As for the bling... Well, that often fell within his purview, at least it did when Dantes Courier Service transported the stunning array of gemstones and finished pieces.

And yet Rafe was nagged by a sense of utter boredom. How many times had he attended receptions similar to this one? Always observing. Always maintaining a vigilant eye from the shadows. Always the watchful lone wolf instinctively avoided by the guests, until one family member or another thrust a potential bride in his direction. It was a pattern that had repeated itself so many times he'd lost count.

This occasion celebrated the exclusive release of the latest Dantes collection, the Eternity line of one-of-a-kind wedding rings. Each was unique, combining the fire diamonds for which his family was renowned with the Platinum Ice gold from Billings, the company owned by Rafe's sister-in-law, Téa Dante, who'd married his older brother, Luc, three months earlier. Just seeing rings that symbolized love and commitment filled Rafe with bitterness.

Been there. Done that. Still had the scars to prove it.

And then he saw her.

The little blonde pixie working the reception as one of the caterers couldn't claim the title of most gorgeous woman in the room, but for some reason Rafe couldn't take his eyes off her.

He couldn't say why she attracted his attention or explain the vague sizzle she stirred. Granted, her features were quite lovely, delicate and fine boned with enough whimsy to make them interesting. Maybe it was her hair and eyes—hair the same shade as the ice-white sand of a Caribbean island and eyes the glorious turquoise of the rolling ocean waves that splashed and frolicked across those pristine beaches. Then there was that sizzle he couldn't explain, a vague compelling itch that urged him to get closer to her in every possible way.

She circulated through the display room of the Dantes corporate office building with a hip-swinging glide that made her appear as though she were dancing. In fact, she possessed a dancer's body, lean and graceful, if a bit pint-size, every delectable inch showcased by the fitted black slacks and tight red vest of her uniform.

She disappeared into the crowd, her tray of canapés held high, and he lost sight of her. For a split second he was tempted to give chase. A few minutes later, the pixie waitress reappeared with a fresh tray of champagne and circled through the guests in the exact opposite direction from where he stood.

For some reason it annoyed Rafe. Determined to force a meeting, he began to maneuver his way through the crowd on an intercept course, one circumvented by Draco's restraining hand.

"What?" Rafe asked, lifting an eyebrow. "I'm thirsty."

Draco shot him a knowing look. "Funny. I'd have said you look hungry. And with so many eyes on you, I recommend you avoid sating your appetite until a more appropriate time and place."

"Hell."

"Relax. Where there's a will…" Draco gestured toward one of the nearby display cases and deliberately changed the subject. "Looks like Francesca's latest line of Eternity wedding rings is going to be a huge success. Sev must be thrilled."

Caving to the inevitable, Rafe nodded. "I think he's

more thrilled about the birth of their son," he replied. "But this would probably rate as icing on the cake."

Draco inclined his head, then slanted Rafe a look of open amusement. "So tell me. How many of the lovelies fluttering around the room have our beloved grandparents introduced to you so far this evening?"

Rafe's expression settled into grim lines. "A full dozen. Made me touch every last one of them, like they expected to see me set off a shower of fireworks or light the place up in a blaze of electricity or something."

"It's your own fault. If you hadn't told Luc that you and Leigh never experienced The Inferno, the entire family wouldn't be intent on throwing women your way."

The fact that so many of his relatives had succumbed to the family legend only added to Rafe's bitterness toward his own brief foray into the turbulent matrimonial waters. Time would tell whether their romances lasted longer than his own. They might claim they'd found their soul mates, courtesy of the Dantes' Inferno. Rafe, the most logical and practical of all his kith and kin, adopted a far more simple and pragmatic—okay, cynical—viewpoint.

The Inferno didn't exist.

There was no eternal bond established when a Dante first touched his soul mate, no matter what anyone claimed, any more than Dantes Eternity wedding rings could promise that the marriages for which they were purchased would last for all eternity. Some hit it lucky, like his grandparents, Primo and Nonna. And some didn't, like his disastrous marriage to his late wife, Leigh.

Rafe stared broodingly at his older brother, Luc,

and his bride of three months, Téa. They were dancing together, swirling across the floor, gazing into each other's eyes as though no one else in the room existed. Every emotion blazed in their expressions, there for the world to witness. Hell, even when Rafe had been in the most passionate throes of lust, neither he nor Leigh had ever looked at each other like that.

In fact, he'd been accused by the various women in his life that his penchant for practicality and hard, cold logic—his lone wolf persona—bled over into his personal life with dismaying frequency. Possessing a fiery passion in the bedroom definitely compensated, as did his striking Dante looks, they conceded, but not when that passion went no farther than the bedroom door. Emotionally distant. Unavailable. *Intimidating.* For reasons that bewildered him, that word was always accompanied by a shudder.

What none of them understood was that he didn't do love. Not the brutal, I-married-you-because-you're-a-rich-and-powerful-Dante love his late wife, Leigh, had specialized in. Not the casual, melt-the-sheets-and-enjoy-it-while-the-bling-lasts type that characterized the women interested in an affair with him. And definitely not The Inferno brain-frying palm-burning happily-ever-after brand of bull spouted by his more emotional and passionate Dante relatives.

Rafe knew himself all too well. And he could state with absolute certainty that not only wasn't he hardwired that way, he never had and never would experience an Inferno love.

Which was just fine by him.

"It was annoying the first few times a potential bride was dangled in front of me," Rafe informed his brother.

"Since it was Nonna and Primo, I couldn't say much. But now everyone's gotten into the act. I can't move without having some gorgeous thing shoved under my nose."

Draco signaled to someone over Rafe's shoulder. "A fate worse than death," he said with a fake shudder.

"It would be if it were you under the gun."

"But I'm not." Draco leaned past Rafe and helped himself to a flute of champagne. "Want one?"

"Sure."

"Consider this your lucky day. The tray's right behind you." He offered a cocky grin. "And don't say I never did you a favor."

Confused by the comment, Rafe turned to take a glass and found his elusive pixie standing there, holding the tray of drinks. Close up she was even more appealing than from across the room.

He gestured to her with the flute. "Thanks."

Her smile grew, lighting up her face, the room and some cold, dark place in his heart. "You're welcome." Even her voice appealed, rich and husky with an almost musical lyricism.

Draco watched the byplay in amusement. "You know, if you want the relatives to leave you alone, there is one way."

That snagged Rafe's attention. "How?" he demanded.

Draco grinned. "Find your Inferno bride."

"Son of a—" Rafe bit off the curse. "I already told you. I'm never going to marry again. Not after Leigh."

He heard the pixie's sharp inhalation at the same time the flutes on her tray began to wobble unsteadily. The glasses knocked against each other, the crystal singing in distress. She fought to steady the tray, almost managed it, before the flutes tipped and cascaded to the floor. Glass shattered and champagne splattered in a wide arc.

Reacting instinctively, Rafe encircled the waitress's narrow waist and yanked her clear of the debris field. A tantalizing heat burned through the material of her uniform, rousing images of pale naked curves gilded in moonlight. Velvety-smooth arms and legs entwined around him. Soft moans like a musical symphony filling the air and driving their lovemaking.

Rafe shook his head, struggling for focus. "Are you all right?" he managed to ask.

She stared at the mess on the floor and nodded. "I think so."

She lifted her gaze to his, her eyes wide and impossibly blue, the only color in her sheet-white face. He didn't see any of the desire that had swept over him. Remorse and, oddly, a hint of panic, sure. But not so much as a flicker of passion. A shame.

"I'm so sorry," she said. "I started to step back so I could circulate some more and my foot slipped."

"You're not cut?"

"No." She blew out her breath in a sigh. "I really do apologize. I'll get this cleaned up right away."

Before she could follow through, another of the catering staff crossed the room to join them. He was clearly management, judging by the swift and discreet manner in which he took control of the situation and arranged to have the broken glass and champagne cleaned up. The waitress pitched in without a word, but when it was done, the manager guided her over to Rafe.

"Larkin, you have something to say to Mr. Dante?" he prompted.

"I want to apologize again for any inconvenience I may have caused," she said.

Rafe smiled at her, then at the manager. "Accidents happen. And in this case, it was entirely my fault. I'm afraid I bumped into Larkin, causing her to drop the tray."

The manager blinked at that and Rafe didn't have a doubt in the world that he'd have accepted the excuse if Larkin hadn't instantly protested, "Oh, no. The fault is entirely mine. Mr. Dante had nothing to do with it."

The manager sighed. "I see. Well, thank you, Mr. Dante, for your gallantry. Larkin, please return to the kitchen."

"Yes, sir, Mr. Barney."

Rafe watched her walk away. As far as he was concerned, she was still the most graceful woman in the room. "You're going to fire her, aren't you?"

"I wish I didn't have to. But my supervisor has a 'no excuses' policy for certain of his more exclusive clientele."

"I gather Dantes is on that list?"

Barney cleared his throat. "I believe you top the list, sir."

"Got it."

"It's a shame, really. She's the nicest of our waitresses. If it were up to me…"

Rafe lifted an eyebrow. "I don't suppose we can forget this incident took place?"

"I'd love to," Barney replied. "But there were too many witnesses and not all of our help is as kindhearted as Larkin. Word will get out if I do that and then both of us will be out of a job."

"Understood. I guess it would have helped if she'd allowed me to take the blame."

"You have no idea" came the heartfelt comment. "But Larkin's just not made that way."

"A rare quality."

"Yes, it is." Barney lifted an eyebrow. "If there's anything else you or anyone in your family needs…?"

"I'll let you know."

The two men shook hands and Barney disappeared in the direction of the kitchen, no doubt to fire Larkin. Rafe frowned. Maybe he should intercede. Or better yet, maybe he could arrange for a new job. Dantes was a big firm with plenty of branches. Surely he could find an opening for her somewhere. Hell, he was president of Dantes Courier Service. He could invent a job if one didn't already exist. The thought of Larkin's sunny smile welcoming him to work each day struck him as appealing in the extreme.

Draco approached. "So? Have you given my idea any thought?"

Rafe stared blankly. "What idea?"

"Weren't you listening to me?"

"It usually works best if I don't. Most of the time your suggestions only lead one place."

Draco grinned. "Trouble?"

"Oh, yeah."

"Well, this one won't. All you have to do is find your Inferno bride and everyone will leave you alone."

Rafe shook his head. "Apparently you're not great at listening, either. After that disaster of a marriage to Leigh, I'm never going to marry again."

"Who said anything about marriage?"

Rafe narrowed his eyes. "Explain."

"You know, for such a smart, analytical-type guy, there are times when you can be amazingly obtuse." Draco spoke slowly and distinctly. "Find a woman. Claim it's The Inferno. Maintain the illusion for a few months. Act the part of two people crazy in love."

Rafe's mouth twisted. "I don't do crazy in love."

"If you want everyone to leave you alone, you will. After a short engagement, have her dump you. Make it worth her while to go a long way away and stay there."

"You've come up with some boneheaded ideas in your time. But this one has to be the most ludicrous—" Rafe broke off and turned to stare in the direction of the kitchen. "Huh."

Draco chuckled. "You were saying?"

"I think I have an idea."

"You're welcome."

Rafe shot his brother a warning look. "If you say one word about this to anyone—"

"Are you kidding? Nonna and Primo would kill me, not to mention our parents."

"You?"

Draco stabbed his finger against Rafe's chest. "They wouldn't believe for one minute you were clever enough to come up with a plan like this."

"I'm not sure *clever* is the right word. Conniving, maybe?"

"Diabolically brilliant."

"Right. Keep telling yourself that. Maybe one of us will believe you. In the meantime, I have an Inferno bride to win."

Rafe headed for the kitchen. He arrived just in time to see Larkin refusing the wad of money Barney was attempting to press into her hand. "I'll be fine, Mr. Barney."

"You know you need it for rent." He stuffed the cash into the pocket of her vest and gave her a hug. "We're going to miss you, kiddo."

One by one the waitstaff followed suit. Then Larkin turned toward the exit and Rafe caught the glitter of tears swimming in her eyes. For some reason a fierce, protective wave swept through him.

"Larkin," he said. "If I could speak to you for a minute."

Her head jerked around, surprise registering in her gaze. "Certainly, Mr. Dante."

Instead of exiting into the reception area, he escorted her through the door leading to the hallway. "Is there a problem?" she asked. "I hope you don't blame Mr. Barney for my mistake. He did fire me, if that helps."

Ouch. "It's nothing like that," he reassured. "I wanted to speak to you in private."

Leading the way to the wing of private offices, he reached a set of double doors with a discreet gold plaque that read "Rafaelo Dante, President, Dantes Courier Service." He keyed the remote control fob in his pocket and the doors snicked open. Gesturing her into the darkened interior, he touched a button on a panel near the door. Soft lights brightened the sitting area section of his office, leaving the business side with its desk, credenza and chairs in darkness.

"Have a seat. Would you like anything to drink?"

She hesitated, then gave a soft laugh. "I know I'm supposed to say no, thank you. But I'd love some water."

"Coming right up."

He opened the cabinet door that concealed a small refrigerator and removed two bottles of water. After collecting a pair of glasses and dropping some ice cubes into each, he joined her on the couch. Sitting so close to her might have been a mistake. He could sense her in ways he'd rather not. The light, citrusy scent of her that somehow managed to curl around and through him. The warmth and energy of her body. The way the light caught in her hair and left her eyes in dusky blue shadow. He'd hoped the business setting would dampen his reaction to her. Instead, the solitude served only to increase his awareness.

He gathered his control around him like a cloak, forcing himself to deal with the business at hand. "I'm sorry about your job," he said, passing her the water. "Firing you seems a bit severe for a simple accident."

"I don't normally work the more exclusive accounts. This was my first time." She made a face. "And my last."

"The catering firm won't switch you over to work some of their smaller parties?"

She released a sigh. "To be honest, I doubt it. The woman in charge of those accounts isn't a fan of mine right now."

"Personality conflict?"

The question made her uncomfortable. "Not exactly."

If he was going to hire her, he needed to gather as much information about her as possible, especially if she didn't deal well with authority. "Then what, exactly?" he pressed.

"Her boyfriend was on the waitstaff, and…"

"And?"

"He hit on me," Larkin reluctantly confessed.

"Something you encouraged?"

To his surprise, she didn't take offense at the question. In fact, she laughed. "JD doesn't require encouragement. He hits on anyone remotely female. I hope Britt figures out what a sleaze he is sooner, rather than later. She could do a lot better."

Rafe sat there for a moment, nonplussed. "You're worried about your supervisor, not your job?"

"I can always get another job, even if it's washing dishes," Larkin explained matter-of-factly. "But Britt's nice…when she's not furious because JD's flirting with the help. I just got caught in the middle."

Huh. Interesting assessment. "And now?"

For the first time a hint of worry nibbled at the corners of her eyes and edged across her expression. "I'm sure it will all work out."

"I overheard Barney say something about rent."

She released a soft sigh, the sound filled with a wealth of weariness. "I'm a little behind. What he gave me for tonight's work should cover it."

"But you need another job."

She tilted her head to one side. "I don't suppose you're hiring?"

He liked her directness. No coyness. No wide-eyed, gushing pretense or any sort of sexual over- or undertones. Just a simple, frank question. "I may have a job for you," he admitted cautiously. "But I'd need to run a quick background check. Do you have any objections?"

And then he saw it. Just a flash of hesitation before she shook her head. "I don't have any objections."

"Fine." Only, it wasn't fine. Not if she were hiding

something. He couldn't handle another deceptive woman who faked innocence and then demonstrated avarice. *Refused* to deal with that sort of woman. "Full name?"

"Larkin Anne Thatcher."

She supplied her social security number and date of birth without being asked. He pulled out his cell and texted one of his brother's former security associates, Juice, with the request. He'd have gone through Luc, but there might be uncomfortable questions when he later presented Larkin as his Inferno bride. Better to keep it on the down low. In the meantime, he'd get some of the preliminary questions out of the way.

"Have you ever been arrested?" Rafe asked.

Larkin shook her head. "No, never."

"Drugs?"

A flash of indignation came and went in her open gaze before she answered in a calm, even voice. "Never. I've needed to take drug tests for various jobs in the past, including this latest one. I have no objection to taking one here and now if you want."

"Credit or bankruptcy issues?"

Indignation turned to humor. "Aside from living on a shoestring? No."

"Health issues?"

"Not a one."

"Military history?"

"I haven't served."

"Job history?"

Now she grinned. "How much time do you have?"

Rafe eyed her curiously. "That many?"

"Oh, yeah. The list is as long as it is diverse."

"Any special reason?"

She hesitated again, but he didn't pick up any hint of evasion, just thoughtfulness. "I've been searching."

"Right job, right place?"

She seemed pleased that he'd understood so quickly. "Exactly."

"I can't promise to offer that, but I might have something temporary."

For some reason she appeared relieved. "Temporary will work. In fact, I prefer it."

"Not planning on staying in San Francisco for long?" He tried to keep the question casual, but conceded that as attractive as he found her, he'd feel better about his proposition if she intended to move on a few months from now.

"I don't know. Actually, I'm looking for someone. I think he may be here."

"He." That didn't bode well for his little project. "Former lover?"

"No. Nothing like that."

He pressed. "Who are you trying to find?"

"That's not really any of your business, Mr. Dante," she said gently. "What I will tell you is that it won't have an impact on any job you might offer me."

He let it go. For now. "Fair enough."

His cell vibrated and he checked it, surprised to find that Juice had completed his preliminary check. Had to be a new record. Either that or Larkin Thatcher didn't have much history to find. The text simply said "Clean," but he'd attached an email that went into more specifics.

Rafe excused himself long enough to access his computer and scan it. Nothing unusual other than a long and varied work history. Considering she was only twenty-five, it was rather impressive.

"Still interested in offering me a job?" she asked.

It was the first time she'd betrayed any nerves, and it didn't take much thought to understand the cause. "How far behind are you on your rent?"

She tapped her pocket. "As I said, this will catch me up."

"But it won't leave you anything to spare for utilities or food, will it?"

She lifted a narrow shoulder in a wordless shrug that spoke volumes.

He took a moment to consider his options. Not that he had many. Either he made the offer and put Draco's plan into action, or he forgot the entire idea. He could still find a position for Larkin. In fact, there was no question that he'd do precisely that. The question was… Which job?

If it weren't for the Parade of Brides, it would have been an easy question to answer. But the unpleasant truth was, he just didn't know how much more of his family's interference he could handle. It had gotten to the point where it wasn't interfering just with his private life, but with his business life, as well. These days, he couldn't turn around without running into one of his many relatives. And for some reason, they were always accompanied by a young, single woman.

He needed it to stop…and soon.

Before he could decide, Larkin stood. "Mr. Dante, you seem hesitant." She offered an easy smile. "Why don't I make it easy for you? I really appreciate your concern, but this isn't the first time money's been tight.

I'm sort of like a cat. One way or another, I always land on my feet."

"Sit down, Larkin." He softened the demand with a smile. "My hesitation isn't whether or not I have a job available for you. It's which job to offer."

She blinked at that. "Oh. Well…I can handle most general office positions, if that helps. Receptionist. File clerk. Secretary or assistant."

"What about the position of my fiancée?" He folded his arms across his chest and lifted an eyebrow. "Do you think you could handle that?"

Two

For a split second Larkin couldn't breathe. It was as though every thought and emotion winked off.

"Excuse me?" she finally said.

"Yeah, I know." He thrust his hand through his hair, turning order into disorder. For some reason, it only added to his overall appeal. Before, he'd seemed a bit too perfect and remote. Now he looked wholly masculine, strong and authoritative with a disturbing edginess that most women found irresistible. "It sounds crazy. But actually it's fairly simple and straightforward."

Larkin didn't bother to argue. Nothing about this man was the least simple or straightforward. Not the fact that he was a rich and powerful man. Not his connection to one of San Francisco's leading families, the Dantes. Not his stunning good looks or the intense passion he kept so carefully hidden from those around her. How did the scandal sheets refer to him? Oh, right. The lone wolf who was also, ironically, the "prettiest" of the male Dantes.

True on both counts.

To her eternal regret, it was also true that he was still so madly in love with his late wife that he never wanted to marry again. Too bad he'd married a woman who, while as beautiful to look at as the man pacing in front of her, possessed a single imperative—to take and use whatever she wanted in life, regardless of the cost or harm it might do to others.

"I overheard you, you know," she warned. "I heard you tell your brother you never wanted to marry again. Not after Leigh."

"Leigh was my late wife," he explained. "And you're right. I don't ever want to marry again. But I do need a fiancée. A temporary fiancée."

She wasn't usually so slow on the uptake. Even so, none of this made the least bit of sense to her. "Temporary," she repeated.

He took the chair across from her and leaned forward, resting his forearms on his knees. Having him so close only made it more difficult to think straight. She didn't understand it. Of all the men in San Francisco, he should have been the very last she'd find attractive. And yet, every one of her senses had gone screaming onto high alert the instant he'd turned those brilliant jade-green eyes in her direction.

"You'd have to understand my family to fully appreciate my situation," he said.

Larkin fought to keep her mouth shut. How many times had she gotten herself into an awkward predicament because of her particular brand of frankness? More times than she could count. Despite her determination, a few stray words slipped out. "Your family does have a knack for hitting the gossip magazines."

To her surprise, he looked relieved. "Then you've read about The Inferno?"

"Yes." Excellent. That was short and sweet, and yet truthful. Added bonus…he seemed pleased with her answer.

"Then I don't have to explain what it is or that my family—most of them, anyway—believe implicitly in its existence."

Something in his manner and delivery clued her in to his opinion of the matter. "But you don't?"

A wickedly attractive smile touched his mouth. "Have I shocked you?"

"A little," Larkin admitted. She couldn't come up with a tactful way to ask her next question, so she tossed it out, not sure if it would land with all the explosive power of a grenade or turn out to be a dud. "What about your wife?"

"Never. We never experienced The Inferno. Nor would I have ever wanted to. Not with her."

Larkin's mouth dropped open. "Wait a minute—"

He cut in with cold deliberation. "Let me make this easy for you. My wife and I were about to divorce when she died. Any version of The Inferno we might have shared was the more literal, hellish kind, not this fairy tale my family's dreamed up."

"When you say you never want to marry again…" she probed delicately.

"It's because I have no intention of ever experiencing that particular level of hell again."

"Okay, I understand that." Considering how well she'd

known Leigh, she didn't blame the poor man. "But that doesn't explain your need for a temporary fiancée."

"My family recently discovered that Leigh and I never felt The Inferno toward each other."

Larkin was quick on the uptake. "And now they're trying to find the woman who will."

"Exactly. It's interfering with every aspect of my life. And since they won't stop until she's found, I've decided to take care of that for them."

His smile broadened. It would have turned his stunning good looks into something beyond spectacular if it hadn't been for the coldness in his green eyes. The smile stopped there, revealing a wintry barrenness that tugged at Larkin's heart. She'd always had a soft spot for strays and underdogs. In fact, some day she hoped to work full-time for an animal rescue organization. She suspected that for all his wealth and position, and despite the loving support of his large family, Rafe Dante qualified as both a stray and an underdog, which put her heart at serious risk.

"You want to pretend that you've experienced this Inferno with me?" she clarified.

"In a nutshell, yes. I want all of my relatives to believe it, too. We'll become engaged, and then a few months from now, you'll decide that you can't marry me. I'm sure I'll give you ample reasons for calling off our engagement. You dump me and disappear. I, of course, will be heartbroken to have found and lost my Inferno bride. Naturally, my family will be sympathetic and won't dare throw any more women my way." He smiled in satisfaction. "End of problem."

"And why won't your family throw any more women your way?"

"How can they, since you were my one true soul mate?" he pointed out with ruthless logic. "They can't have it both ways. Either you were my once-in-a-lifetime Inferno match or The Inferno isn't real. Somehow I suspect that rather than admit that the family legend doesn't exist, they'll decide that my one shot at Inferno happiness decided to dump me. I'll then have no other choice but to continue my poor, lonely, miserable existence never having found matrimonial bliss. A tragedy, to be sure, but I'll do my best to survive it."

Larkin shook her head in mock admiration. "A trouper to the end."

"I try."

She released her breath in a gusty sigh. "Mr. Dante—"

"Rafe."

"Rafe. There's something you should know about me. A couple of things, actually. First, I'm not a very good liar."

She opened her mouth to explain the second reason, one that would not just put a nail in the coffin of his job offer, but bury that coffin six feet down. He didn't give her the opportunity, cutting her off with calm determination.

"I noticed that about you earlier. I admire your honesty. In my opinion, it's the perfect way to convince my relatives that we're in the throes of The Inferno."

Her thoughts scattered like leaves before a brisk fall wind. "Excuse me?"

"We're going to try a little experiment. If it doesn't work, we'll forget my plan and I'll find someone else. I'll still offer you a job, just a more conventional one." He eyed her with predatory intent. "But if my experiment works, you agree to my plan."

"Experiment?" she asked uneasily. "What sort of experiment?"

"First, I want to set up a few parameters."

"Parameters."

How could Leigh ever have hoped to control a man like this? Through sex, of course. But somehow Larkin suspected that would work for only so long and solely within the confines of the bedroom. She didn't need more than five minutes in Rafe's company to figure out that much about him.

"I'm a businessman, first and foremost. Before we move forward, I want to make sure we have a clear meeting of the minds."

Larkin struggled not to smile. "Why don't you explain your parameters and then we'll see what sort of agreement we can come to."

"First, I need to make it clear that this is a temporary relationship. When either of us is ready to put an end to it, it ends."

She gave it a moment's consideration before shrugging. "I suppose that's no different than a real engagement."

"Which is my next point. You don't want to lie. I don't want you to lie. So if we become engaged, from that moment forward it *is* real. The only difference will be that at the end of the engagement—and our engagement will end—I'll see to it that you receive fair compensation for your time."

"The engagement will be real, but we preplan the ending." She lifted an eyebrow. "I swear I'm not being deliberately obtuse, but I don't see how those two are mutually compatible."

He hesitated, a painful emotion rippling behind his icy restraint. "I don't do relationships well," he confessed, "or so I've been told. I suspect you'll discover that for yourself soon enough and be only too happy to end our involvement. Until then, it will be the same as any other engagement, right down to a ring on your finger and making plans for an eventual wedding day." His mouth twisted. "I'd rather it be a far distant eventual wedding day that doesn't involve actual dates and deposits."

Her sense of humor bubbled to the surface. "We don't want to rush into anything. Not after your first experience. Better to have a long engagement and make sure."

"See? You already have your lines down pat."

A matching humor lit his face and even crept into his eyes. If she hadn't been sitting, she didn't doubt for a moment that her knees would have given out. He had to be one of the most stunning men she'd ever met. It didn't seem fair to have all of that rugged beauty given to one man. From high, arching cheekbones to squared chin to a mouth perfectly shaped for kissing, it didn't matter where she looked, it was all gorgeous. Even his hair was perfect, the deep brown offset by streaks of sunlit gold. But it was his eyes that fascinated her the most, the color a sharp jade-green that seemed to darken like a shadow-draped forest depending on his mood.

"So how do we handle this?" she finally managed to ask. "Assuming I agree to your plan."

He frowned, and even that was appealing. "It may not work," he admitted. "I think we can figure that out easily enough. But you'll have to trust me."

She took a deep breath and jumped in with both feet. "Okay. What do you have in mind?" she asked.

"A simple test. If we don't pass, we scrap the idea and I'll find you a job within the organization. If it does work, we take the next step forward."

"What sort of test?" she asked warily.

"Just this."

He stood and circled the coffee table between them. Reaching her side, he held out his hand. She stood as well and took the hand he offered. Her fingers slipped across his palm. Instantly, heat exploded between them, a stunning flash that seemed to burrow into flesh and bone with unbelievable swiftness. It didn't hurt. Not precisely. It…melded. With a gasp of disbelief, Larkin yanked free of his touch.

"What did you just do?" they asked in unison.

Rafe took a step back and eyed her with sharp suspicion. "You felt that, too?"

"Of course." She rubbed her palm against her slacks, trying to make the sensation go away. Not that it worked. "What was it?"

"I have no idea."

She lifted her hand and stared at the palm. There weren't any marks, though based on the explosion of heat she'd experienced, it should still be smoking. "That wasn't…" She cleared her throat. "That couldn't have been…"

She could see the emphatic denial building in his expression. At the last instant he hesitated, an almost calculating glitter dawning in his eyes. "The Inferno?" he murmured. "What the hell. Why not?"

She stared at him, stunned. "You're joking, right?" she asked.

"I don't personally believe in it, no. But I've heard

The Inferno described as something along the lines of what we just felt."

"That was your test?" she demanded. "To see if we felt The Inferno when we touched?"

"No. Actually, I was going to kiss you."

She fell back another step, shocked as much by the statement as by the calm businesslike way he delivered it. "Why?"

"There's no point in becoming engaged if you aren't physically attracted to me," he explained. "My family would pick up on that in no time."

Larkin gazed down at her hand and scratched her thumbnail across the faint throb centered in the middle of her palm. "So whatever just happened when we touched is just an odd coincidence?"

"I sure as hell hope so."

Huh. She lifted her head and looked at him. Their gazes clashed and the heat centered in her palm spread deeper. Hotter. Swept through her with each beat of her heart. A dangerous curiosity filled her and words tumbled from her mouth, words she'd never planned to speak. But somehow they popped out, hovering in the air between them.

"I believe you were going to kiss me," she prompted.

He approached in two swift strides. She knew what he planned, could see the intent in the hard lines of his body and determined planes of his face. He gave her ample opportunity to escape. But somehow she couldn't force herself to take the easy way out. Another personality quirk…or flaw, depending on the circumstances. Instead, she held perfectly still and allowed him to pull her into his arms.

This was wrong on so many levels. Wrong because

of Leigh. Wrong because it wasn't real. Wrong because even while she wanted to deny it, desire built within her like a tide building before a storm. Waves of it crashed over and through her until she couldn't think straight and common sense fled. He hadn't even kissed her yet, and already she could feel the helpless give of her surrender.

He leaned in and she waited breathlessly for his kiss, a kiss that didn't come. "It feels real, doesn't it?" The words washed over her like a balmy breeze, stirring the hair at her temples. "Maybe it is real. Maybe this engagement isn't such a bad idea. We can figure out what all this means."

"All what?" she managed to ask.

"All this…"

The kiss when it came hit with all the force of a hurricane. She didn't doubt he meant to keep it light and gentle. A tentative sampling. An initial probing. Instead, the instant he touched her, hunger slammed through her and she arched against him, winding her arms around his neck and hanging on for dear life.

It didn't surprise her in the least to discover he kissed even better than he looked. With a mouth like that, how could he not? His lips slanted across hers, hard enough to betray the edginess of his control, and yet with a passionate tenderness that had her parting for him and allowing him to sample her more fully.

All the while, he molded her against his body, the taut, masculine planes a delicious contrast to her slighter, more rounded curves. His hands swept down her spine to the base. There he hesitated before cupping her backside and fitting her more tightly between his legs. She gasped at the sheer physicality of the sensation.

The scent and taste of him filled her and she shuddered, overwhelmed by sensations she'd never fully realized or explored before.

How was it possible that a simple kiss—or even a not-so-simple kiss—could have such a profound effect on her? She'd kissed any number of men. Had contemplated sleeping with a few of them. Had allowed them to touch her and had satisfied her curiosity by touching them in return. But they'd never affected her the way Rafe Dante did with just a single kiss.

Is this how it had been for Leigh?

The stray thought brought Larkin to her senses with painful swiftness. With an inarticulate murmur, she yanked free of Rafe's arms and put half the distance of the room between them. Unable to help herself, she lifted trembling fingers to her lips. They were full and damp from his kisses and seemed to pulse in tempo with the odd beat centered in her palm. She stared at Rafe. If it hadn't been for the rapid give and take of his breath, she'd have believed him unaffected.

"I think we can safely say that we're attracted to one another," she informed him.

"Hell, yes."

His voice sounded rougher than normal, low and edged with an emotion that was reflected in his eyes like green fire. He crossed to the wet bar and removed the stopper on a cut-glass decanter. Splashing some of the amber liquid into a tumbler, he glanced over his shoulder and raised an eyebrow.

"Want some?"

She shook her head. She didn't dare. She'd always been a frank person. Alcohol tended to remove all caution and strip her of the ability to control her tongue.

There was no telling what she'd say if she had a drink right now.

He downed the liquor in a single swallow, then turned to face her. "That was…unexpected."

"Blame it on The Inferno," she attempted to joke.

"Oh, I intend to."

She stared at him, not quite certain of his mood. She couldn't tell if he was annoyed by what had happened, or relieved. Or maybe he just didn't give a damn. Perhaps a little of all three. Annoyed because their reaction to one another was a complication and he'd been as close to losing control of the situation as she had. Possibly even more so, since she'd been the one to finally end their embrace. Relieved because that same attraction would allow him to execute his plan. As for not giving a damn…

No. She was wrong about that. He might hide the fact he cared, bury it deep, but she was willing to bet the Dante passion ran hotter in him than all the others.

She had a decision to make. She could turn around and walk out of the room and never return. She could tell him who she was and what she wanted. Or she could go along with his plan and see how matters developed. Every instinct warned her to get out while the going was good, or at the very least explain why this insane idea of his would never work. Maybe she'd have made the smart choice, the far less dangerous choice…if only he hadn't kissed her.

"I gather we just became engaged?" she asked lightly.

He hesitated. "Something like that."

"And will your family believe that you've gone from

a total nonbeliever to an Inferno fanatic after one simple kiss?"

"Considering it happened just that way with each and every one of the Dante men in my family, yes."

"None of them believed?"

Rafe shrugged. "My cousin Marco did. He's probably the most romantic of all the Dantes."

"But not the rest of you."

"It isn't logical," he stated simply. "It's far-fetched at best and bordering on ludicrous when you look at it from a serious, rational point of view."

"I think it's sort of sweet."

His mouth curved upward. "Most women do."

A distinct awkwardness settled over her. "So, what now?"

"Now I take you home. First thing in the morning we'll get together and plan our strategy."

"Strategy." She couldn't help but laugh. "Let me guess. You're one of those organized, I-need-to-mold-the-world types, aren't you?"

"Somebody has to." He released a sigh and returned his glass to the wet bar. "Let me guess. You're one of those seat-of-the-pants, take-life-as-it-happens types, aren't you?"

She wrinkled her nose. "This might be a case of opposites attract."

"Don't worry. I'll organize everything and you just go with the flow."

Her amusement grew. "Control is an illusion, you know."

He appeared every bit as amused. "Whatever you say. How about if I control us out of here and you let it happen?"

"I think I can handle that."

Larkin gathered up her purse and circled the couch toward the door. Rafe joined her, his hand coming to rest on the base of her spine in a gesture that should have been casual. Instead, it was as though he'd given her another jolt of electricity. She stumbled and her purse dropped from her hand. Turning, she could only stare helplessly at him.

"Larkin." Her name escaped on a groan and then he pulled her into his arms again.

How could something so wrong feel so right? She had no business making love to Leigh's husband. None. But she couldn't seem to resist, any more than she'd resisted his bizarre proposal. When he touched her, it all made perfect sense. Probably because she couldn't think straight. All she could do was feel.

He pulled her close, so close she could hear the thunder of his heart and the rapid give and take of his breath. Or maybe she wasn't hearing his, but her own. He covered her face with kisses, swift and hungry, before finding her mouth and sinking inward. Oh, yes. *This*. This was what she craved. What she needed as desperately as sweet, life-sustaining air. Where before he'd controlled the kiss, now she took charge, giving him everything she possessed.

She heard his voice. Heard raw, guttural words. Words of want and need. And then her world tipped upside down as he swung her into his arms and carried her back to the couch. She hit the cushions with a soft bounce before he came down on top of her, his body pressing her deeper into the silken material.

"We just met," she managed to gasp.

He shifted against her, fitting them one to the other like two pieces of a puzzle. "Sometimes it's like that."

"When? With who?"

"Now. With us."

None of this made any sense. Rafe was supposed to be the rational one. The one in control. And yet, whatever had ignited between them had swept him away as completely as it had her. She wanted him with a bone-deep need that grew with each passing moment.

He made short work of the vest of her uniform, slipping buttons from their holes with a speed and efficiency that took her breath away. Parting the edges, he tackled her blouse next, button after button, before yanking the crisp black cotton from her slacks and shoving it half off her shoulders.

Rafe paused then, his hand hovering over the delicate bones of her shoulder, his dark skin tones at odds with her pale complexion. "My God," he whispered. "You're breathtaking."

No one had ever described her that way before. But seeing his stunned expression—seeing herself through his eyes—she felt beautiful. He traced the edges of her bra, a simple, durable black cotton, sculpting the curves of her breasts. She could feel her nipples peaking through the material. An intense heat shot through her, echoed in the throbbing of her palm and sinking deep into her feminine core.

"Rafe…"

It was her turn to touch. Her turn to explore. She cupped his face and gave in to the irresistible compulsion to trail her fingertips over those amazing planes and angles. To revel in the sheer masculine beauty of him. When she'd first seen him in the reception area, he'd appeared so self-contained, so remote. Never in a million years would she have imagined herself in this position. Who knew if the opportunity would ever present itself again? When they regained their sanity she wouldn't be the least surprised if he instituted a "no touching" rule, especially when touching was so incredibly, gloriously dangerous.

Unable to resist, she wove her fingers into his hair to anchor his head and then rose to seal his mouth with hers. He tasted beyond delicious and she couldn't get enough of him. Not his touch. Not his kisses. Not the press and drag of his body over hers.

Her hands darted to his shirt and she tugged at his tie, managing after a small struggle to rip it free from its anchor. Next she tackled the buttons that blocked her access to the rich expanse of flesh and muscle she yearned to caress. He groaned against her mouth, levering himself upward to give her better access. Her hands hovered over his belt buckle and the bulge that lay beneath.

And that's when they heard it.

"Rafaelo?" A deep, gruff voice came from the far side of the office door, accompanied by a brisk knock. "Where are you, boy?"

Rafe swore beneath his breath. Vaulting off Larkin, he helped her to her feet. "Just a minute," he called.

She stood, swaying in place, dizzy from the swift transition from passion to normalcy. Or the attempt at normalcy. "Who's there?" she whispered.

"My grandfather Primo."

Her eyes widened in alarm and her hands shot to the buttons of her blouse at the same time his did. Fingers clashed and fumbled. She could hear the murmur of voices coming from the far side of the door. Not just his grandfather, she realized. A woman's voice, too.

"Nonna," Rafe confirmed grimly. He let her finish working on straightening her clothing while he tackled the mess she'd made of his. "My grandmother."

"Do not be ridiculous" came Primo's rumbling bass. "This is an office. It is not as though he is in a meeting, not this late. Why should I stand on the doorstep like a beggar?"

"Because he has not invited you in."

"Then I will invite myself in" was the indignant retort.

With that, he turned the knob and stepped into the room. Rafe must have anticipated his grandfather's intent because he stepped in front of her, shielding her from his grandparents' eyes while she finished buttoning her blouse and vest. Not that it really helped, considering that his shirt was open and hanging out of his trousers.

"I have been looking for you, Rafaelo," Primo announced. "I have someone I wish you to meet."

Rafe sighed as he finished making repairs to his clothes. "I don't doubt it. But it's no longer necessary."

Primo planted his fists on his waist. "Of course it is necessary. You must meet as many women as possible. How else will you find your Inferno soul mate?"

Larkin peeked out from behind Rafe's broad shoulders and saw Nonna's eyes widen with a combination of surprise and dawning comprehension. "And who is this?" she asked.

Snatching a deep breath, Larkin skirted Rafe and stepped into the light, wincing at their stunned expressions. She didn't doubt for a single moment that she looked as if she'd been doing precisely what she *had* been doing. Guaranteed her mouth was bare of lipstick and swollen a telltale rosy-red from Rafe's impassioned kisses. And Rafe didn't look much better, not when she compared his businesslike appearance earlier to his current rough and rumpled manifestation. And guaranteed one or both of his grandparents had caught that…and more.

Primo's gaze swept to a point midway down the line of buttons holding her vest closed and his fierce golden eyes narrowed. Either she hadn't buttoned them correctly or she'd skipped one. Maybe more than one.

Nonna, on the other hand, hovered between shock and amusement at whatever hairstyle Rafe had left in his wake when he'd plowed his fingers through the tidy little knot Larkin had fashioned at the start of her evening. She could feel part of it dangling over her left ear, while stray wisps were plastered to the right side of her face and neck.

"Hello." She gave them a wide, brilliant smile. "I'm Larkin Thatcher."

"You are with the catering service?" Primo asked, giving her clothing another assessing look.

"Not any longer. They fired me."

Apparently they didn't know what to say to that, so she hurried to breach the silence. She couldn't help it. It was another minor personality flaw. Leigh had always called it babbling, which was a fair if somewhat blunt assessment.

"It was my own fault. I dropped a tray of drinks and that's a big no-no. The good news is that if I hadn't, I wouldn't have met Rafe and we wouldn't have gotten to know each other. I don't think we've finished discussing it yet. But we kind of got engaged."

Three

"Engaged," Primo and Nonna repeated in unison. Primo sounded outraged, Nonna shocked.

"Sort of." Larkin shot Rafe an apprehensive glance, as though aware that she'd jumped the gun a bit. "Or maybe not anymore. To be honest, I'm not quite sure what we are because we… Well, to be honest…" Her hands fluttered over her hair and the mismatched buttons of her vest. "That is to say, we got distracted."

Beside her, Rafe groaned. "Hell."

Her gaze darted from him back to his grandparents. They didn't seem pleased with his response. "Actually, it was rather heavenly," she hastened to reassure them.

Rafe took charge of the situation. "Let's just say that the minute we touched, things got out of hand. Or in hand, depending on your viewpoint."

"The Inferno?" Primo demanded. "It has finally happened?"

Rafe hesitated. He couldn't help the hint of resistance that undoubtedly shadowed his expression. He'd experienced something when he and Larkin had first touched. But The Inferno? A connection that would last a lifetime? Sorry. Still not buying it. "Time will tell," he limited himself to saying.

To his surprise, the reluctance implicit in his tone and attitude sold the idea with impressive ease, and he couldn't help but suspect that a more overt declaration would have had the opposite effect, giving his grandparents pause in the face of such a dramatic turnaround from his previous attitude.

He spared a swift glance in Larkin's direction and winced. Hell. Primo and Nonna weren't the only ones who'd picked up on his reluctance. So had Larkin. But wasn't that what they'd agreed to? Wasn't that why he'd hired her? To be his *temporary* fiancée? That's all it was for both of them. A transient relationship that would be nice while it lasted and, when it ended, give them both what they wanted. He'd be left the hell alone and she'd receive a nice bump to her bank account.

So why did she react as though she'd lost out on a special treat? Why that wistful look of longing, a deeply feminine look, one that spoke of childhood dreams and magical wishes? A look that caused him to respond on some visceral, wholly masculine level, that seemed to compel him to give her her heart's desire. Not that he could, even if he wanted to. He'd been up front with her from the start. He could never fulfill her deepest desires because he was incapable of fulfilling any woman's. The sooner Larkin accepted that, the better.

"I need to take Larkin home," he informed his grandparents. "We can discuss The Inferno once I've had time to explain it to my—" He broke off with a small smile. "My fiancée."

Primo instantly began to protest, but Nonna shushed him. "We will call tomorrow and arrange a proper meeting with Larkin," she said. "I am sure your parents would also like to meet her, yes?"

"I think we should take this slowly." Rafe stalled. "Now, if you'll excuse us?"

"First you will promise to drop her off and then leave. No more of what we interrupted here," Primo demanded. "Otherwise, you will find yourself with a wife instead of a fiancée, just like Luciano."

Rafe grimaced. Damn it. He knew that look, as well as the tone. And the reminder about his brother and Téa was a timely one. Hadn't the two of them been forced to the altar within twenty-four hours of being caught in the act? "Yes, Primo. I promise. I'll drop her off in the same condition in which I found her."

"*Era troppo poco e troppo tardi*. Too late for that, I suspect. But there will be no more…" He waved his hand to indicate Larkin's uniform. "No more button mishaps until there is a ring on her finger."

"I understand."

"And agree?" Primo shot back.

Rafe sighed. He was going to regret getting boxed in like this. "Yes. *Accosento*."

"Very well. Take her home. Your grandmother will call in the morning to arrange a convenient time for your Larkin to meet the family."

Larkin stepped forward and held out her hand to Primo. "It was a pleasure meeting you."

"I do not shake hands with beautiful women," Primo informed her. He enfolded her in a bear hug, swamping her diminutive form, and planted a smacking kiss on each of her cheeks.

Larkin then turned to Nonna and the two women embraced. To Rafe's concern, he caught the glint of tears in Larkin's eyes and realized that she'd reached her breaking point. The events of the day must have caught up with her. First the stress of working a high-profile client, then losing her job, his proposition, followed by what had almost happened on the couch. It all added up to…too much, too fast.

He didn't waste any time. Sweeping up her belongs in one hand and Larkin in the other, he ushered everyone out of the office. Not giving his grandparents time for any further questions, he wished them good-night and urged Larkin toward the elevators. They made the ride to the subterranean parking garage in silence. But as soon as they were enclosed in his car, she swiveled in her seat to face him.

"What did your grandparents mean about Luciano? About his ending up with a wife instead of a fiancée?"

He winced at the memory. "They were caught in the act, if you know what I mean."

Larkin's eyes widened in horror. "By Primo and Nonna?" she asked faintly.

"By Téa's grandmother and three sisters. Madam is Nonna's closest friend," he explained. "When Primo heard what had happened, he stepped in and insisted Luc do the right thing."

"Meaning…marriage?"

Her voice had risen ever so slightly, and Rafe flashed her a look of concern. "It all worked out. They were in love. They even claim to have experienced The Inferno the first time they touched." He hadn't succeeded in reassuring her and gave it another try. "My marriage may not have been a shining example of happily-ever-after, but Luc and Téa seem genuinely in love. Hell, for all I know, their marriage might last as long as my grandparents'."

She fell silent for a moment, which he took as a bad sign. If there was one thing he'd learned about Larkin, she didn't do silence. Sure enough, she leaped into speech. "I don't think I can do this," she announced in a rush. "I don't like deceiving people, especially people as kind as your grandparents. They take marriage and this Inferno stuff seriously."

He started the car and pulled out of his assigned parking space before replying. "That's what makes this so interesting. We're not deceiving anyone." He paused at the exit and waited for Larkin to relay her address before pulling onto the one-way street. "Admit it. We felt something when we touched."

The overhead streetlight filled the car with a flash of soft amber, giving him a glimpse of her unhappy profile. She stared down at her palm, rubbing at the center in a manner he'd seen countless times before by each and every one of his Inferno-bitten relatives.

The sight filled him with foreboding. As far as he knew, no one outside the family was aware of that intimate little gesture, one that his relatives claimed to be a side effect of that first, burning touch between Inferno soul mates. God forbid he ever felt that tantalizing itch. His palm might throb. It might prickle. That didn't mean it itched or that he'd find himself rubbing it.

"Okay, so I felt something," she murmured. "But that

doesn't mean it's this family Inferno thing you have going, does it?"

"Absolutely not," Rafe stated adamantly. Though who he was so determined to convince, himself or Larkin, he couldn't say. "The point is… We can't rule out the possibility that it's The Inferno. Not yet. Until we do, that's what we're going to assume it is and that's what we're going to tell my family."

"And they'll believe it?" He could hear the doubt in her voice.

"Yes. Implicitly."

"But *you* still don't."

"I have no idea," he lied without hesitation. "It could be The Inferno. Or it could have been static electricity. Or just a weird coincidence. But telling my family that we think it might be The Inferno won't be a lie. And until we discover otherwise, we go forward with our plan."

"Your plan."

He drew to a stop at a red light and looked at her. She sat buried in shadow, her pale hair and skin cutting through the darkness while her eyes gleamed with some secret emotion. He didn't know this woman, not really. Granted, he had a mound of facts and figures, courtesy of Juice. But he hadn't yet uncovered the depth and scope of the person those dry facts and figures described. Just in the short time he'd spent with her, he'd gained an unassailable certainty that he'd find those depths to be deep and layered, the scope long-ranging and intriguing.

And he couldn't wait to start the process.

The light changed and he pulled forward. "It started

out as my plan. But as soon as you told my grandparents that you were my fiancée, it became *our* plan."

"But it's a lie."

"First thing Monday I plan on putting a ring on your finger. Will it still feel like a lie when that happens?"

He heard her sharp inhalation. "A ring?"

"Of course. It's expected." He spared her a flashing grin. "In case you weren't aware, we Dantes specialize in rings, particularly engagement rings."

A hint of a smile overrode her apprehension. "I think I may have heard that about you."

"When our engagement ends, you can keep the ring as part of your compensation package."

"When," she repeated.

"It won't last, Larkin," he warned. "Whatever we felt tonight is simple desire. And simple desire disappears, given time."

"That's a rather cynical viewpoint." She made the comment in a neutral tone of voice, but he could hear the tart edge to it.

"I'm a cynical sort of guy. Blame it on the fact that I've been there, done that."

"Maybe you were doing it with the wrong woman."

"No question about that."

"Maybe with the right woman—"

"You, for instance?" He pulled to the curb in front of an aging apartment building and threw the car into Park. "Is that what you're hoping, Larkin?"

"No, of course not," she instantly denied. "I just thought…"

He wasn't paying her to think. He almost said the bitter words aloud, biting them back at the last instant. He wasn't normally an unkind person and she didn't deserve having him dump the remnants of his marital history on her, even if the subject of Leigh brought out the worst in him.

Nor would it pay to alienate her. Not now that he'd introduced her to his grandparents. If she chose to pack up and disappear into the night… He hesitated. Would it make any difference? Would his family believe he'd found his Inferno match and lost her, all in one night? Or would they think he'd concocted the story…or worse, that it hadn't been The Inferno that he'd experienced, but a nasty case of lust?

No, better to stick to the plan. Better to allow his family to come to the conclusion over the next few months that he'd experienced The Inferno. Then Larkin could dump him and his family would finally, *finally* leave him alone to get on with his life. Until then, he would do whatever it took so that his Inferno bride-to-be stuck to the game plan.

"What are you thinking?" Her soft voice broke the silence.

"Tomorrow is Saturday. Since you've been fired from your job, I assume you have the day off?"

She hesitated. "I really should be looking for a new job."

"You have a new job," he reminded her. "You're working for me now, remember?"

"A real job," she clarified.

Didn't she get it? "This is a real job and it's one that's going to take up every minute of your time, starting tomorrow."

A dingy glow from the windows of Larkin's apartment building illuminated her face, highlighting her apprehension. "What happens tomorrow?"

"I formally introduce you to some more of my family."

"Rafe…" She shook her head. "Seriously. I can't do this."

He reached out and took her hand in his. The tingling throb surged to life, intensifying the instant their palms came into contact. "This is real. All I'm asking you to do is help me figure out what it is. If my family is right and it's The Inferno, then we'll decide how to deal with it."

"And if it's not?"

He shrugged. "No harm done. Our mistake. We go our separate ways. You'll be compensated for the time I've taken away from your search for your mystery man. And I have the added benefit of being left the hell alone."

"Is that what you really want?" He could see her concern deepen. "Is that what she did to you? She turned you into the Lone Wolf the scandal sheets call you?"

"It's who I am. It's what I want." He refused to admit that Leigh had played any part in his current needs. She didn't have that sort of power over him. Not anymore. "And it's what I intend to get."

Larkin gave it another moment's thought and then nodded. "Okay, I'll do it, if only to see if I can mitigate some of the damage done by your late wife." He opened his mouth to argue, but she plowed onward. "But it's just until we know for certain whether or not it's The Inferno."

If the only way she'd agree to his plan was by turning it into some sort of "good deed," he supposed he could live with that. And who knew? Maybe it would work. Stranger things had happened. "Fair enough." He exited the car and circled around to the passenger side. "I'll see you in."

"That's not necessary."

He waited while she climbed the steps of the front stoop and unlocked the door to the apartment building. "I insist."

He held the door open and a wide, gamine smile flashed across her face. "You think I'm going to run, don't you?"

"The thought did occur to me," he admitted.

Her smile faded. "You don't know me well enough to believe this, but I always honor my promises. *Always.*"

"So you're finally here, Ms. Thatcher. I'd begun to think you'd skipped." The voice issued from the open doorway of the manager's apartment. A heavyset man in his sixties stood there, regarding Larkin with a stern expression, his arms folded across his chest. "Do you have your rent money?"

"Right here, Mr. Connell." Larkin dipped her hand into her pocket and pulled out the money, handing it over.

He counted it, nodded, then jerked his head toward the stairwell. "You have ten minutes to clear out."

Larkin stiffened. "Mr. Connell, I promise to pay on time from now on. I've always— "

For a split second his sternness faded. "It's not that and you know it." Then he seemed to catch himself, retreating behind a tough shell that years of management had hardened into rocklike obduracy. "You know the rules about pets. In ten minutes I'm calling animal control. And somehow I suspect they'll have questions about your…dog."

She paled. "No problem, Mr. Connell. We'll leave immediately."

Again Rafe gained the impression that the apartment manager would have bent the rules for Larkin if it were at all possible. "San Francisco is no place to keep her, Ms. Thatcher. She needs more room."

"I'm working on it."

Rafe cleared his throat. "Perhaps a little extra rent will help clear this up. Would you consider a generous pet deposit in case of damages?" he asked.

Connell caught the underlying meaning and shot him a man-to-man look of understanding. Then he shook his head. "It isn't about the money. And it isn't about the late rent. Ms. Thatcher is as honest as the day is long." He broke off with a grimace. "At least, she is when it comes to paying her debts. The animal, on the other hand—"

"I didn't have a choice," Larkin cut in. "It was the only way to save her."

The landlord wouldn't be budged. "You'll have to save her elsewhere."

"I don't suppose you could give me until the morning?"

She hadn't even finished the question before he was shaking his head again. "I'm sorry. If it were just me, sure. But others are aware of the situation, and I could lose my job if the owners found out I hadn't acted immediately once I knew about the animal."

"I understand." Rafe wasn't the least surprised at Larkin's instant capitulation. She had to possess one of the softest hearts he'd ever known. "I wouldn't want you to lose your job. It'll just take me a minute to pack."

Rafe blew out a sigh. He was going to regret this,

mainly because it would make keeping his promise to Primo almost impossible. "I know a place you can stay," he offered.

Hope turned her eyes to an incandescent shade of blue. "Kiko, too?"

"Is that your dog's name?"

"Tukiko, but I call her Kiko."

"Yes, you can bring Kiko. The landlord won't object. Plus, he has a huge backyard that's dogproof."

"Really?" She struggled to blink back tears. "Thank you so much."

She turned to Connell and surprised him with a swift hug, one he accepted with an awkward pat on her back. Then she led the way upstairs. Rafe glanced around. The complex appeared shabby at best, with an underlying hint of desperation and decay. He suspected that it wasn't so much that the manager was lazy or didn't care, but that he fought a losing battle with limited funds and expensive repairs.

They climbed to the third floor and down a warren of hallways to a door painted an indeterminate shade of mold-green. Larkin fished her key out of her purse and unlocked the door to a tiny single-room apartment.

"Hey, Kiko," she called softly. "I'm home. And I brought a friend, so don't be afraid."

Rafe peered into the gloomy interior. "I gather she doesn't like strangers?"

"She has reason not to."

"Abused?"

"That…and more."

Rafe didn't so much hear the dog's approach, as sense it. A prickle of awareness lifted the hairs on the back of his neck. And then he caught the glint of gold as the dog's eyes reflected the light filtering in from the hallway. A low growl rumbled from the shadows.

"Kiko, stand down," Larkin said in a calm, strong voice. Instantly the dog limped forward and crouched at her feet, resting her muzzle on her front paws.

Rafe groped for a light switch, found it and flicked it on. *Son of a—* This was not good. Not good at all. "What sort of dog is she?" he asked in as neutral a voice as he could manage.

"Siberian husky." Larkin made the statement in a firm, assured voice.

"And?"

"A touch of Alaskan malamute."

"And?" He eyed the animal, certain that at least one of its parents howled rather than barked, ran in a pack and mated for life.

Larkin wrapped her arms around her waist, her chin jutting out an inch. "That's it." Firm assurance had turned to fierce protectiveness overlaid with blatant lying.

"Damn it, Larkin, that's not all she is and you know it." He studied Kiko with as much wariness and she studied him. "Where the hell did you find her?"

"My grandmother rescued Kiko from a trap when she was a juvenile. But the trap had broken her leg. Gran even managed to save the leg, though it left Kiko with a permanent limp and, despite all the love and care lavished on her, it made her permanently wary of people. But she's old now. When Gran was dying, she asked me to take care of Kiko. Since Gran raised me, I wasn't about to refuse. End of discussion."

Compassion shifted across his expression. "How long ago did your grandmother die?"

"Nine months. And she was ill for about a year before that. It's been a bit of a struggle since then to keep a job while honoring my grandmother's dying wish," she found herself admitting. It had her stiffening her spine, pride riding heavy on her weary shoulders. "I've had to move around. A lot. And take on whatever jobs have come my way. But we're managing. That doesn't mean I don't have goals I hope to accomplish. I do. For instance, I'd love to work for a rescue organization that specializes in helping animals like Kiko. I just need to take care of something first."

"Finding your mystery man."

"Yes."

"Larkin—"

She cut him off. "We don't have time for this, Rafe. Mr. Connell gave me ten minutes and we've wasted at least half that already. I still need to pack."

He let it go. For now. "Where's your suitcase?"

"In the closet."

Instead of a suitcase, he found a large battered backpack and damn little else. It took all of two minutes to scoop her clothing out of the closet, as well as the warped drawers of an ancient dresser. Larkin emerged from the bathroom with her toiletries and dumped them into a small zipped section.

"What about the kitchen?" He used the term loosely, since it consisted of a minifridge, a single cupboard containing dishware for two and a hot plate.

"It came with the apartment. It'll just take me a minute to gather up Kiko's stuff and empty out the refrigerator."

She attempted to block his view of the contents, but it was difficult to conceal nearly empty shelves, especially when it took her only a single trip to the trash can to dispose of what little it contained. After she fed Kiko a combination of kibble and raw beef, she bagged up the trash and put a leash on the animal. Rafe picked up her bag. He felt a vague sense of shock that all her worldly possessions fit in a single backpack. Hell, half a backpack, since the other half contained supplies for her dog. He couldn't have fit even a tenth of what he owned in so small a space.

"You ready?" he asked.

Larkin snatched a deep breath and gave the apartment a final check before offering a resolute nod. After that it was a simple matter to lock up the apartment, turn in the keys to Mr. Connell, dispose of the trash and exit the building. Once there, Larkin gave Kiko a few minutes to stretch her legs. Then Rafe installed the dog in the back of his car, along with the bulging backpack, while Larkin returned to her seat in the front.

"So where are we going?" she asked as he pulled away from the curb.

"My place."

She took a second to digest that. "I thought you said you knew of a place Kiko and I could stay," she said in a tight voice.

"Right. My place."

"But…"

He shot her a quick, hard look. "If it were just you, I could make any number of arrangements, even with it pushing midnight. But your dog—and I use the term loosely—is a deal breaker. There isn't a hotel or motel in the city that would allow Kiko through their doors. And I suspect the first place you tried would have the police coming at a dead run. Is that what you want?"

She sagged. "No," she whispered.

"Then our options are somewhat limited. As in, I can think of one option."

"Your place."

"My place," he confirmed.

Traffic was light and he pulled into his driveway a short twenty minutes later. He parked the car in the detached garage and led the way along a covered walkway to the back entrance. He entered the kitchen through a small utility room.

Larkin hovered on the doorstep. "Is it all right if Kiko comes in?"

"Of course. I told you she was welcome."

"Thanks."

The two walked side by side into the room and Rafe got his first good look at Kiko beneath the merciless blaze of the overhead lights. The "dog" was a beautiful animal, long and leggy, with a heavy gray-and-white coat, pronounced snout and a thick tail that showed a hint of curl to it—no doubt from the husky or malamute side of her family. Her golden gaze seemed to take in everything around her with a weariness that crept under his skin and into his heart. He suspected that she'd have given up and surrendered to her fate, if not for her human companion.

Larkin stood at her side, dwarfed by the large animal, her fingers buried in the thick ruff at Kiko's neck. She fixed Rafe with a wary gaze identical to her dog's. "Now what?"

"What does Kiko need to be comfortable?"

"Peace and quiet and space. If she feels trapped, she'll chew through just about anything."

He winced, thinking about some of the original

molding and trim work in his century-old home. "I didn't notice any damage to your apartment. I wouldn't exactly call that spacious."

"She regarded that as her de—" Larkin broke off with a cough. "Her retreat."

"Right. Tell me something, Larkin. How the hell did you smuggle her into your apartment in the first place?"

"Carefully and in the wee hours of the morning."

"I'm sure. And no one noticed her when you took her out for a walk? They never complained about her barking or howling?"

"Again, we made as many trips as possible while it was still dark. But I guess she did make noise, since we've now been kicked out." She shrugged. "It doesn't matter. Kiko isn't crazy about the city, and I wasn't planning to stay long. Just until I finished my search. Then we were going to move someplace less crowded."

"Good plan. You do realize that if anyone catches you with her she'll most likely be put down."

"I have papers for her."

He lifted an eyebrow and waited. "You do remember that you're a lousy liar, don't you?"

For the first time a hint of amusement flickered in her gaze. "I'm working on that."

An image of his late wife flashed through his head. "Please don't. I like you much better the way you are." He gestured toward the refrigerator. "Are you hungry?"

"I'm fine."

"What about Kiko?"

"She's good until morning."

"Come on, then. There's a bedroom you can use on this level with doors that open to the backyard."

"It's fenced?"

"High and deep. My cousin Nicolò has a St. Bernard who's something of an escape artist. Brutus has personally certified my fence to be escapeproof."

A swift smile came and went. "We'll see if Kiko concurs."

He could see the exhaustion lining her face, her fine-boned features pale and taut. He didn't waste any further time in conversation. Turning, he led the way toward the back of the house, throwing open the door to a suite of rooms that was at least three times the size of her apartment. She seemed to stumble slightly as she entered the room, favoring her left leg.

"You okay?" he asked.

"Oh, this?" She rubbed her thigh. "I broke my leg when I was a kid. It only bothers me when I get too tired."

"My brother Draco has a similar problem."

"I feel for him," she said, then turned in a slow circle. "Wow," she murmured. "This place is amazing."

"Nothing too good for my fiancée."

She spared him a swift, searching glance, but didn't argue. "Thank you, Rafe," she said.

He couldn't resist. He approached and tipped her face to his. From the doorway he caught a soft, warning rumble, one silenced by a swift gesture from Larkin.

"It'll take Kiko a while to realize you're safe," she explained.

His thumbs swept across the pale hollow beneath her cheekbones to pause just shy of the edges of her mouth. "Somehow I think it'll take you a while, too."

"You could be right."

He leaned down and captured her lips in a gentle caress. She moaned, the sound a mere whisper. But it conveyed so much. Hunger. Passion. Pleasure. And maybe a hint of regret. More than anything he wanted to pull her into his embrace and lose himself in her softness. She swayed against him, and it took a split second to realize her surrender came from exhaustion rather than desire.

Reluctantly he pulled back. "Wrong time, wrong place," he murmured.

She sighed. "The story of my life."

He rested his forehead against the top of her head. "I also promised Primo that I wouldn't unbutton you any more tonight."

"I believe he meant from now on, not just tonight," she informed him gravely. "And I also believe you agreed to honor that promise."

He released her and took a step back, allowing them both some breathing space. "Actually, what I promised was that I wouldn't unbutton you again until I put a ring on your finger." He flashed her a suggestive grin. "Come Monday, I plan to have that ring right where I need it to be. Then prepare yourself to be thoroughly unbuttoned."

Four

Larkin awoke to someone knocking on her door. Kicking off her covers, she stumbled to her feet and blinked blearily around. What in the world? This wasn't her shabby little apartment, but something far more sumptuous and elegant. Something a world away from her realm of experience.

Memory crashed down around her. Getting fired. Rafe's proposal. Their shocking first touch. Their even more shocking kiss. His proposition. Her losing her apartment. And finally, her arrival here with Kiko. The knock came again and she jumped.

"Just a minute," she called.

She yanked open her bedroom door, only to discover that the knocking came from farther away. She stumbled in that direction, realizing there was someone at Rafe's front door. A very determined someone. She hovered in the foyer, debating whether or not to answer. Better not to, she decided, considering it wasn't her house. Unfortunately, the unexpected guest had a key and chose that moment to use it.

The door swung open and a woman poked her head inside. "Rafe?" She caught sight of Larkin and her eyes widened. "Oh. Oh, dear. I'm so sorry. Nonna said—"

"What is wrong, Elia?"

Larkin recognized Nonna's voice and shut her eyes. This could not be good.

"We've come at an inconvenient time," Elia turned to explain. "Rafe has a guest."

Nonna replied in Italian, the sound knife-edge sharp. Then the door banged open and Nonna marched into the house. "Larkin? I am surprised to find you here."

"I'm surprised to find me here, too," Larkin admitted. "In fact, I'm surprised to find us both here."

"What the *hell* is going on? Can't a man get a decent night's sleep?" Rafe's voice issued from on high and he appeared at the top of the staircase leading to the second story. "Mamma? Nonna? What are you doing here?"

He stood there, hands planted on his hips, his chest bare, a loose pair of sweats riding low on his hips. Larkin stared, dazzled. Despite his obvious annoyance, she'd never seen anything more gorgeous.

"Oh, my."

The comment escaped, along with her breath, her common sense and every last brain cell she possessed. To her utter humiliation, his mother took note, suppressing a smile of amusement at her reaction.

But really… His body was an absolute work of art, sculpted with hard muscle that filled out his lean frame. His shoulders were broad, with strong, ropey arms, though she'd suspected as much when he'd lifted her in them last night and carried her to the couch in his office. His abdomen was flat and sporting the type of six-pack that she would have been only too happy to spend an entire night sampling. His mane of hair fell in rumpled abandon, the colors a lush mixture of browns and golds.

"We came over to arrange a time to meet Larkin," Elia explained. Her smile wavered. "Surprise! We met."

Rafe thrust his hands through his hair and Larkin suspected by the way his lips moved that he was swearing beneath his breath. "Let me get dressed and I'll be down." His gaze sharpened, arrowing in on Larkin. "May I suggest you do likewise?"

"Oh, right." She glanced down at her own shorts and cropped T-shirt with something akin to horror before offering Rafe's mother and grandmother a weak, embarrassed smile. "Excuse me, please."

She dashed in the direction of her bedroom and closeted herself inside. Kiko stared at her alertly from where she lay in one corner, curled up on a thick, cozy rug. "What do you say we try out the backyard again and see what you think about it in the daylight," Larkin suggested.

She opened the French doors leading outside and watched while Kiko limped into the yard. She kept an eye on the dog for several minutes to assure herself that the fence would withstand all escape attempts before taking a swift shower and throwing on the first set of clean clothes to come to hand. The fact that a night spent in a backpack had pressed a thousand wrinkles into them couldn't be helped.

Calling to Kiko, Larkin headed in the direction of

the coffee scenting the air. She found Rafe and the women in a low, heated conversation. Since it was in Italian, she could only guess what they were saying. Nonna appeared to be offering the strongest opinion, and Larkin could make a fairly accurate guess what that opinion might be. They broke off at the sight of her and smiled in a friendly manner, though Larkin picked up on the tension that underscored their greeting.

She pretended not to notice, returning their smiles with a broad one of her own before zeroing in on Rafe. "I just want to thank you for giving me a place to stay when I lost my apartment. If you hadn't, I think Kiko and I would have been wandering the streets all night."

"What is this?" Nonna asked sharply.

"I've been trying to tell you—" Rafe began.

"No." He was cut off with an imperious wave. "I wish Larkin to tell me."

"I wasn't allowed to have a pet in my apartment building. The landlord found out about Kiko last night and kicked me out. Thank goodness Rafe insisted on walking me inside. If it hadn't been for him…" She shrugged. "Obviously we didn't have the time to find a place that would accept a dog, so Rafe thought the smartest option would be for Kiko and me to use his guest room for the night. I'm just relieved that he has a Brutus fence." She offered a quick grin. "Turns out it's also Kiko proof."

Rafe grimaced. "After last night, I don't know whether to be disappointed or relieved."

"Last night?" Elia asked sharply.

His eyes narrowed on Kiko in open displeasure. "Full moon," he said as though that were all the explanation necessary.

"Would it be okay if I fed her now?" Larkin hastened to interrupt. "I have some kibble for her, but she needs a little bit of raw beef mixed in."

"No problem." He crossed to the refrigerator and rummaged through the contents. "Before you joined us, we were talking and Nonna and my mother would like to take you out today so you three can get to know each other."

With his head buried in the refrigerator, Larkin couldn't get a good read on either his voice or expression. "I thought I might look for a job," she temporized.

"Time enough for that on Monday." He emerged with a small packet of steak and carried it to the cutting board. "In fact, I might have something for you at Dantes."

"Oh, I don't think—"

"Perfect," Elia declared with a friendly smile. "This engagement is all so sudden it's taken my breath away."

"That makes two of us," Larkin answered with utter sincerity.

Elia's smile wavered. "Then this should give us time to catch our breath, yes?"

Larkin's gaze swiveled in Rafe's direction where he stood at the counter slicing up the raw meat. "Not unless Mr. Organize and Conquer plans on changing his personality by the time we get back."

The two Dante women glanced at each other and then at Larkin before breaking into huge grins of amusement. "It would seem you know my Rafaelo surprisingly well, given the short amount of time you have known him," Nonna commented.

"Perhaps that's because he doesn't bother to hide that aspect of his personality," Larkin replied.

"In case you three haven't noticed, I'm standing right here," Rafe said.

He combined Kiko's kibble with the slices of meat. The dog sat at attention, watching his every move. When he placed the food on the floor, she approached it cautiously, sniffing at the floor and around the bowl before attacking the contents.

"That's a most unusual dog you have," Elia said with a slight frown. "If I didn't know better I'd swear she was part—"

"Definitely not," Larkin hastened to say. "She belonged to my grandmother, who raised her from the time she was a youngster."

Rafe broke in, rescuing her from any further questions. "I gather I'm Kiko's designated sitter?"

Larkin turned to him in relief. There were times his take-charge personality came in handy. This was one of them. "Do you mind?"

"Will she eat me?"

"I don't think so."

He lifted an eyebrow. "Color me reassured."

His dry tone brought a flush to her cheeks. "She's very sweet natured. Very beta."

"Well, if that's settled?" Elia asked.

Not giving Larkin a chance to come up with a reasonable excuse for avoiding their girl-bonding session, Elia urged Nonna to her feet and swept everyone toward the front door. Once there, she gave her son an affectionate kiss, one Larkin noted he returned with equal affection. Then they were out the door and tucked into Elia's car. The next instant they pulled out of Rafe's drive and headed toward the city. Larkin couldn't help tossing a swift glance over her shoulder.

Elia must have caught the look, because she chuckled. "Don't worry, Larkin. We'll return you safe and sound before you know it."

Right. It was that nerve-racking time between now and then that worried her. How in the world had she gotten herself into this mess? Yesterday she'd been free as the proverbial bird. No entanglements. No men. Just one simple goal. Find her father.

And now… Larkin shot one final desperate look over her shoulder before settling in her seat. Now she had a fiancé to deal with, his family, no job and was expected to spend the day bonding. Bonding! With Leigh's former mother-in-law, of all people. Not to mention this bizarre ache centered in her palm. She rubbed at it, which for some strange reason caused Nonna and Elia to exchange broad smiles.

Larkin sighed. What an odd family. Almost as odd as her own.

Rafe stared, thunderstruck. "What the *hell* have you done to my fiancée?"

"We've been doing what women have done for centuries in order to bond," Elia said. "Shopping."

"Makeover." Nonna enunciated the word carefully, then smiled broadly, though Rafe couldn't tell if it was due to the word—one he'd never heard his grandmother utter before—or the results of said makeover. "This is something girls do together," she added with an airy gesture. "You are a man. You would not understand."

Larkin's eyes narrowed. "Don't you like it?" she asked in a neutral voice. "Your mother and grandmother went to a lot of time and expense on my behalf."

He hesitated. Damn. Okay, this was familiar territory.

Dangerous, familiar territory. The sort of territory men discovered during their first romantic relationship. Most poor saps of his gender stumbled in unaware of the traps awaiting them until they'd fallen into the first one, impaling themselves on their own foolhardiness. Having several serious relationships plus one disastrous marriage beneath his belt, Rafe had figured he'd safely skirted or uncovered all the traps out there.

Until now.

"You look lovely." And she did. Just…different.

Larkin's mouth compressed. "But?"

Behind her, Nonna and his mother also regarded him through slitted eyes and tight lips. "But?" they echoed.

"But nothing," he lied. Time to regain control of the situation. First item on the agenda…get rid of Larkin's backup. He gathered up his mother and grandmother and ushered them toward the door. "It's late. Nearly dinnertime. You've spent the day bonding with Larkin and I appreciate all you've done. I know this has been very sudden, and yet you've made her feel like one of the family."

"Of course we made her feel like one of us," Nonna said. "Soon she will be."

"Not too soon," he soothed. "This Inferno business is new to both of us and a bit of a shock. We need time to get to know each other before jumping into marriage."

Nonna turned on him. "Where will she stay until then?"

"Right here in my guest room."

She shook her head. "That is not proper and you know it."

He gave her his most intimidating look. Considering

she was his grandmother, it met with little success. "You think I'd break my promise to Primo?"

She lifted a shoulder in a very Italian sort of shrug. "The Inferno is difficult to resist."

"If it becomes too difficult, I'll make other arrangements."

Nonna gave a dainty snort. "We will see what Primo has to say about that."

No doubt. Giving each woman a kiss, he sent them on their way before going in search of Larkin. He found her in the kitchen brewing a pot of coffee. Unable to help himself, he stood in the doorway and watched, vaguely blown away by her grace.

There was a gentle flow to her movements, as though each step was choreographed by some inner music. What would it be like to dance with her? At a guess, sheer perfection. She was made to dance, and the idea of holding her in his arms while they moved together in perfect symmetry filled him with a longing he'd never experienced with or toward any other woman.

Another image formed, a picture of another sort of dance, one that also involved the two of them, but this time in bed. She had such a natural sense of rhythm, combined with a lithe, taut shape. How would she move when they made love? Would she drift the way she did now, initiating a slow, sultry beat? Or would she be fast and ferocious, pounding out a song that would leave them sweaty and exhausted?

"Coffee?"

The mundane question caught him off guard and it took him a moment to switch gears. "Thanks."

"Cream? Sugar?"

"Black."

She poured two mugs. "Do you really hate it?"

Rafe hesitated, still off-kilter. It wasn't until she ruffled her hair in a self-conscious gesture that he realized what she meant. "No, I don't hate it at all. It suits you."

And it did. Before, her hair had been long and straight, and the two times he'd seen her, she'd worn it either pulled back from her face in a braid or piled on top of her head with a clip. The stylist had cut it all off and discovered soft curls beneath the heavy weight of her hair, curls that clung to her scalp and framed her elegant features. Few women had the bone structure to get away with the stark style. She was one of them. If anything, it made her look even more like a creature from fantasy and make-believe.

"And the clothes?" she pressed.

"I suspect I'd like you better without them."

Startled, she looked at him before grinning. "There speaks a man."

"Well, yeah."

He sipped his coffee and circled her. He had to admit that his mother had done a terrific job orchestrating the change. Between the haircut, the stylishly casual blouse, the three-quarter-length slacks and the scraps of heeled leather that passed for sandals, Larkin had settled on an eclectic style that was uniquely her own. No doubt some of that was due to his mother's influence. She had a knack for seeing the true nature of a person and giving them a gentle nudge in the appropriate direction, rather than simply layering on the current fashion, regardless of whether or not it suited. But the rest was all Larkin.

"How did she convince you to accept the clothes and salon treatment?"

A hint of color streaked across Larkin's cheekbones and she buried her nose in her coffee mug. "Your mother isn't an easy woman to refuse," she muttered.

"Engagement present?"

Larkin sighed. "It started out that way. Of course I said no. After all, we're not officially engaged." She set the mug on the counter with a sharp click and eyed him in open confusion. "I'm not quite sure what happened after that. All of a sudden it was a pre-engagement gift or welcome-to-the-family gift or—"

"Or a bulldozing gift."

Larkin's mouth quivered into a smile. "Exactly."

"And before you knew it you'd had a total makeover."

"Is she always like that?"

"Pretty much. She's sort of like a tidal wave. She sweeps in, snatches up everyone in her path and carries them off. There's no resisting her. You just sort of ride the wave and hope you can slip up and over the swell before you get caught in the curl."

Larkin groaned. "I got caught in the curl. A couple curls."

He ruffled her hair. "They look good on you."

"Thanks." She picked up her mug and studied him through the steam. "Now I know where you get certain aspects of your personality. You're just like her, you know."

"Don't be ridiculous—I'm far worse."

She grinned, the tension seeping from her body. "Thanks for the warning." Kiko slipped into the room just then and came to sit at Larkin's feet, leaning against her legs. "How was she?"

He regarded the dog with a hint of satisfaction. "Let's just say we came to terms."

Laughter brightened Larkin's eyes. "Let me guess. You gave her more steak."

He didn't bother to deny it. After all, it was the truth. "The Dantes are firm believers in bonding over food. You'll see for yourself tomorrow night."

He'd alarmed her. Not surprising, considering how much had happened in so short a time. "Tomorrow night?" she asked. "What's tomorrow night?"

"Every Sunday night the family has dinner at Primo's."

She swallowed. "The whole family?"

"Anyone who's available."

"And who's going to be available tomorrow night?"

"It varies week to week. We'll find out when we get there, but I'm guessing my parents, at least one of my brothers, my sister, Gianna, and a couple of my cousins." She turned away, busying herself at the sink rinsing her coffee mug. But he could tell he'd upset her. Where before she was poetry in motion, now she moved in jerks and stops. "What's wrong?" he asked.

She set her cup down and turned. Turbulence dimmed her gaze and shadowed her expression. "Look. You don't know me and I don't know you. We jumped into this crazy idea without thinking it through. Everything's been moving so fast since last night that we haven't even had time to discuss the details or come up with a solid game plan. I just don't think it's going to work."

"Nonna and my mother must have grilled you today."

Larkin lifted a shoulder. "Sort of."

"You must have told them something about your-self."

"Bits and pieces," she conceded.

Based on her expression, he figured she'd told them as little as she could get away with. "Clearly, nothing you said concerned or alarmed them. Stands to reason I won't be concerned or alarmed, either."

She caught her lower lip between her teeth in a gesture that was becoming familiar to him. "I didn't tell them a lot," she said, confirming his suspicion.

"Here's what I suggest. Why don't we spend tonight and tomorrow getting to know each other? If we decide it's not going to work, we'll call the entire thing off." Hell. If anything, his offer had somehow made it worse. "What now?"

"Your mother spent a fortune on my hair and clothes. I can't just leave. I owe her."

"I'll reimburse her."

Larkin's chin jerked upward. "Then I'll owe you."

"You can work it off at Dantes or we can just call it even for the time you've invested."

"I'm not a taker," she insisted fiercely.

He fought to keep his voice even. "I never said you were."

He could see the frustration eating at her. "There are things you don't know about me." She began to pace. Kiko paced with her. "I got so caught up in your job offer and then your kisses that I haven't been able to stop long enough to catch my breath. To...to explain things."

He zeroed in on the most interesting part of her

comments, unable to suppress his curiosity. "My kisses?"

She whirled to face him. "You know what I mean. I understand that it's simple sexual chemistry, but I'm not... That is, I've never..." She thrust her hands through her hair, ruffling the curls into attractive disarray. "I flunked chemistry, okay?"

"Okay."

"The whole Inferno thing made me lose my focus. I got off course."

Something was seriously upsetting her and his humor faded, edging toward concern. "It's not a problem, Larkin."

"It is a problem."

She practically yelled the words, pausing to control herself only when Kiko whimpered in distress. The dog paused between the two of them, at full alert, her ruff standing up, giving her a feral, dangerous appearance. Larkin made a quick hand gesture and the animal edged closer, rubbing up against her hip.

She forced herself to relax. "I'm sorry," she said, though Rafe couldn't tell if the apology was directed at him or the dog.

Okay, time to approach the situation the same way he did a business dilemma and apply some of his infamous Dante logic. "You told me you came to San Francisco to find someone. Is that what's upset you? You feel like this job is distracting you from finding this person?"

"Yes. No." She crouched beside Kiko and buried her face in the dog's thick coat. "My search is only one of the reasons I'm here."

"That's not a problem," he argued. "There's no reason why you can't continue with your search while working for me. In fact, I might be able to help. I know someone who is excellent at finding people. He's the one who ran the security check on you last night."

"It's…complicated."

Rafe hesitated. "And you don't trust me enough to explain how or why or who."

"No," she whispered.

"Fair enough."

He approached and crouched beside her. Kiko watched him but no longer appeared distressed, and he slipped his fingers through the dog's thick fur until he'd linked his hand with Larkin's. He could feel the leap and surge of their connection the instant they touched. Though he continued to reject the possibility that it was The Inferno, he couldn't deny that something bound them together, something deep and powerful and determined.

"Here's what I suggest," he said softly. "Let's do what we told my mother and Nonna we'd do. Let's take this one day at a time. We'll also give my suggestion a shot and get to know each other a little better. You tell me about yourself. Or at least, as much as you're comfortable telling me. And I'll reciprocate."

She peeked up at him. "An even swap? Story for story?"

"Sounds fair."

She considered for a minute before nodding. "Okay. Who goes first?"

"We'll flip for it. Winner's choice." He lifted an eyebrow. "Agreed?"

She considered for an instant, then nodded. "Agreed."

Satisfied to have them back on course, he released her

hand and stood. "It's getting late. Why don't we throw together a simple meal, open a bottle of wine and sit outside and enjoy the evening? I think we'll find it more comfortable to reveal personal details in the dark."

"Definitely."

They worked in concert after that. He grilled up most of the portion of the steak he hadn't fed Kiko while Larkin threw together a salad. Then he nabbed a bottle of wine, a pair of glasses and a corkscrew on the way out of the kitchen. He set everything on the glass-and-redwood table on his patio. "There's some crackers in the cupboard and cheese in the fridge," he called to Larkin. "Oh, and Kiko will want the last of the beef that's in there. Middle shelf."

"She will, will she?"

"Absolutely. I'm sure that's what I heard her just say."

Larkin appeared in the doorway. "Kiko talks now?"

He lifted an eyebrow. "What? She doesn't talk to you? Ever since you left this morning, I haven't been able to get her to shut up."

To his satisfaction, the final vestiges of distress leached from Larkin's body. While she carried the last of the food to the table, he opened the cabernet and set it aside to breathe. Then he fed Kiko, who gave a contented grunt and settled down closest to where Rafe stood, no doubt hoping for another treat in the near future.

"You've corrupted her," Larkin accused. "You're going to make her fat."

"I'm trying to keep from getting eaten. There's another full moon tonight."

"She's not a wolf," Larkin muttered.

"And you're a lousy liar."

"I'll have to work on that."

"Don't." A terseness drifted through the word. "I was married to an expert, so you have no idea how much I appreciate the fact that you don't lie."

For some reason his pronouncement had the opposite effect of what he'd intended. She shot to her feet and faced him with a desperate intensity. "You're wrong. I am a liar. My being here is a lie. Our relationship is a lie. And I've told you any number of lies of omission. If you knew the truth about me, you'd throw me out right now. This minute." She shut her eyes. "Maybe you should. Maybe Kiko and I should leave before this goes any further."

Five

Larkin waited anxiously for Rafe's response. To her surprise, he didn't say a word. Instead, she heard him pour a glass of wine. The instant she opened her eyes, he handed it to her.

"I believe lying by omission is called dating," he explained gently. "No one is completely honest when they date—otherwise no one would ever get married. All of that changes once you're foolish enough to say 'I do.'"

"Marriage equals truth time?" Is that what he'd discovered when he'd married Leigh?

"Let's just say that the mask comes off and you get to see the real person. Since we're not getting married, that shouldn't be a problem for us. Relax, Larkin. We're all entitled to our privacy and a few odd secrets."

His comments were like a soothing balm and she sank onto her seat at the patio table, allowing herself to relax and sip the wine he'd poured. The flavor exploded on her tongue, rich and sultry, with a tantalizing after bite to it. "This is delicious."

"It is, isn't it? Primo got a couple of cases in last week and spread them out among the family to sample. It's from a Dante family vineyard in Tuscany that belongs to Primo's brother and his family."

"Huh." She went along with the drift from turbulent waters into calmer seas, even though her intense awareness of him followed her there. "And does his brother's family have that whole Inferno thing going on, too?"

"I don't know. It's never come up in discussion. Though I suspect most of the Dantes are fairly delusional when it comes to The Inferno."

Rafe settled into the seat beside her and stretched out his long legs. He was close. So deliciously close. Her body seemed to hum in reaction, flooded with a disconcerting combination of pleasure and need.

"You still don't believe it exists, despite…" She held out her hand, palm upward.

He hesitated, shrugged, then cut into his steak. "That's what we're going to spend the next month or so figuring out."

Careful and evasive. It would appear she wasn't the only one being a bit cagey. "Are you just saying that so I'll stick with the job?" she asked, tackling her salad.

"Pretty much."

She couldn't help smiling. "Devious man."

A companionable silence fell while they ate their dinner, though she could also feel a distracting buzz of sexual awareness. It seemed to hum between them, flavoring the food and scenting the air. She forced herself to focus on the meal and the easy wash of conversation, which helped mitigate the tension to a certain extent. But there was no denying its existence or the gleam of awareness that darkened Rafe's eyes to an impenetrable forest-green. It added a unique dimension to every word and interaction, one that teetered on the edge of escalation…or it would have if they hadn't both tiptoed around the various land mines.

After they'd finished eating they cleared away the dishes and returned to the patio with their wine. Larkin released a sigh, half contentment, half apprehension. "Okay. Story time," she announced. "Explain to me again how this is supposed to work."

"Winner of the coin toss asks the first question. Loser answers first."

"Ouch. That could be dangerous."

"Interesting, at the very least." He tossed the coin. "Call it."

"Heads."

He showed her the coin, tails side up. He didn't hesitate. "First question. Tell me about Kiko—and I mean the truth about Kiko. Since she's going to be around my family for the next month or two, I think I deserve the truth."

It was a reasonable question, if one she'd rather have avoided. "Fair enough. To be honest, I don't know what she is. She's definitely not pure wolf, despite her appearance. I'd guess she's probably a hybrid wolf dog." Rafe's eyebrows shot upward and Larkin hastened to add, "But I don't think she's very high-content wolf. She has too many of the traits of a dog, as well as the personality."

"Explain."

Larkin winced at the gunshot sharpness of his response and chose her words with care. "Some people breed dogs with wolves, creating hybrids. It's highly controversial. Gran was violently opposed to the practice. She considered it 'an accident waiting to happen' and unfair to both wolves and dogs, since people expect the hybrids to act like dogs." At his nod of understanding, she continued. "But how can they? They're an animal trapped between two worlds, living in a genetic jumble between domestication and wild creature. So both wolf and dog get a bad rep based on the actions of these hybrids whenever they respond to the 'wild' in their makeup."

"Got it," he said, though she could tell he wasn't thrilled with her explanation. "What about in Kiko's case? How likely is she to respond to her inner wolf?"

"She's never harmed anyone. Ever." Larkin leaned on the word. "Can she? Potentially. So can a dog, for that matter. But she's more likely to run than confront, especially now that she's so old."

"How did you end up with her?"

Larkin switched her attention to the animal in question and smiled with genuine affection. Kiko lay on the patio, her aging muzzle resting on her forepaws, watching. Always watching. Alert even at this stage of her life. "We think Kiko must have been adopted by someone who either couldn't take care of her or were living someplace where they couldn't keep her because of her mixed blood. They dumped her in the woods when she was about a year old. Gran found Kiko caught in an illegal trap, half-starved."

He shot a pitying look in the dog's direction. "Poor

thing. I'm amazed she let your grandmother anywhere near her."

"Gran always had a way with animals." She spared him a flashing smile. "And Kiko didn't have much fight in her by the time Gran arrived on the scene. The trap had broken Kiko's leg. She was lucky not to lose it."

"Did your grandmother set the leg herself?"

Larkin shook her head. "That would have been well beyond her expertise. She took Kiko to a vet who happened to be a close personal friend. He set the leg and advised Gran on the best way to care for Kiko. It was either that or have her put down. Since neither Gran nor I could handle that particular alternative, we kept her."

"And my family? How safe will they be with her?"

Larkin leaned forward and spoke with urgent intensity. "I promise, she won't hurt you or your family. She's very old now. The longest I've heard of these animals living is sixteen years. Most live fewer than that. Kiko's twelve or thirteen and very gentle. Except for the occasional urge to howl, she's quiet. Just be careful not to corner her so she feels trapped. Then she might turn destructive, if only in an attempt to escape what she perceives as a trap." Pleased when he nodded his acceptance, she asked a question of her own. "What about you? No dogs or cats or exotic pets?"

He shook his head. "We had dogs growing up, but I'd rather not own a pet."

She couldn't even imagine her life without a four-legged companion. "Why not?"

"You're talking about taking responsibility for a life for the next fifteen to twenty years. I'd rather not tie myself down to that sort of commitment."

It didn't take much of a leap to go from pets to a wife. If he'd thought owning a pet was an onerous commitment, how must it have felt to be married to Leigh? Larkin suspected she could sum it up in one word.

"I guess Kiko isn't the only one who doesn't like feeling trapped," Larkin murmured. "Is that what marriage felt like?" *Or was it just marriage to Leigh?*

"It didn't just feel that way. That's what it was." He raised his glass in a mocking salute. "One good thing came out of it. I realized I wasn't meant for marriage. I'm too independent."

That struck her as odd, considering his tight-knit family bonds. In the short time she'd known the Dantes, one aspect had become crystal clear. They were all in each other's business. Not in a bad way. They just were deeply committed to the family as a whole. And that just might explain Rafe.

"What made you so independent?" she probed. "Is it an attempt to keep your family at a distance, or something more?"

He tilted his head to one side in open consideration. "I don't feel like I need to hold my family at a distance. At least, I didn't until this whole Inferno issue came up." He frowned into his glass of wine. "I'm forced to admit they do have a tendency to meddle."

"So if it's not your family that's made you so independent, where did it come from?"

He returned his glass to the table and shook his head. "That's more than the allotted number of questions. Four or five by my reckoning. If we're playing another round, you have to answer one for me first."

"Okay, fine." She slid down in her chair and sighed.

"Just make it an easy one. I'm too tired to keep all my omissions straight."

He chuckled. "Since we're not even engaged, I wouldn't want any deep, dark omissions to slip out by accident."

"You have no idea," she muttered. "Come on. Hit me. What's your question?"

"Okay, an easy one… Let's see. You said you broke your leg at one point. I guess that gives you something in common with Kiko."

"More than you can guess."

"So tell me. What happened?"

She tried not to flinch. She didn't like remembering that time, even though everything worked out in the long run. "I was eight. I was in a school play and I fell off the stage."

"I'm sorry." And he was. She could hear it in the jagged quality of his words. "Unless someone saw you when you were as tired as you were last night, no one would ever know. You're incredibly graceful."

"Years of dance lessons, which helped me recover faster than I would have otherwise. But I was never able to dance again." She couldn't help the wistful admission. "Not like I could before."

"Were you living with your grandmother at the time?"

"Yes." Before he could ask any more questions, express any more compassion, she set her glass on the table with unmistakable finality. "It's been a long night. I should turn in."

"Don't go."

His voice whispered into the darkness, sending a shiver through her. It was filled with a tantalizing danger—not a physical danger, but an emotional one that threatened to change her in ways she couldn't anticipate. Indelible ways from which she might never recover. She hesitated there, tempted beyond measure, despite the ghost of the woman who hovered between them. And then he took the decision from her, sweeping her out of her chair and into his arms.

"Rafe—"

"I won't break my promise to Primo. But I need to hold you. To kiss you."

A dozen short steps brought him to the French doors leading to her suite of rooms. Kiko followed them, settling down just outside, as though guarding this stolen time together. Even though an inky blackness enfolded the room, Rafe found the bed with unerring accuracy. He lowered her to the silken cover. A delicious weight followed, pressing her into the softness.

Despite Larkin's night blindness, her other senses came alive. She heard the give-and-take of their breath, growing in urgency. Felt her heart kicking up in tempo, knowing it beat in unison with Rafe's. Powerful hands swept over her and she caught the agitated rustle of clothing that punctuated the tide of desire rising within her. And all the while, the flare of energy centered in her palm spread heat deep into blood and bone, heart and soul.

"Are you sure this isn't breaking your promise to Primo?" she whispered.

His hand slipped around behind her and found the hooks to her bra. One quick twist and the scrap of lace loosened. He released a husky laugh. "I'd say we were teetering on a thin line."

She pulled her arms out of the sleeves of her blouse

and the straps of her bra and wrapped them around his neck. "A *very* thin line. Maybe a kiss tonight before you leave?"

Even as the words escaped, his mouth found the joining of her neck and shoulder. Her muscles locked and her spine bowed in reaction. She'd never realized that particular juncture of her body was so sensitive. She released a frantic gasp, a small cry that held the distinct sound of a plea. How was it possible that such a simple touch could have such an overpowering effect? She couldn't seem to wrap her mind around it.

He cupped her breasts and drew his thumbs across the sensitive tips. Tracing, then circling, over and over until she thought she'd go crazy. He hadn't even kissed her yet, and already she was insane with a need she couldn't seem to find the words to express.

"Rafe, please."

She couldn't admit what she wanted. It was all twisted into a confused, seething jumble of conflicting urges. The urge for more. Far more. The need to stop before she lost total control. Or was it already too late for that? The sheer, unadulterated want to wallow in the heat and desire of his touch. This was wrong—not that she dared admit as much to Rafe. But she knew. And the knowledge ate at her. She shifted restlessly beneath him and he stilled her with a soothing touch.

Cupping her face, he took her mouth, obliterating the wrong beneath a kiss of absolute rightness. It was sheer perfection. Where their earlier kisses were filled with heat and demand, this one was far different. It soothed. Gentled. Offered a balm to the senses. The desperation eased, grew more languid, and she found herself relaxing into the embrace.

"You know I want to take this further," he murmured against her lips.

"You also know we can't. I couldn't look your grandparents in the face if—" She broke off with a shiver.

"Then we won't." She could hear the smile in his voice and feel it in the kisses he feathered across her mouth. "But that doesn't mean we can't come close."

She squeezed her eyes closed. "That's torture. You realize that, don't you?"

"Oh, yeah. But I can take it if you can." A warm laugh teased the darkness. "I think."

"We're playing a dangerous game."

"Do you really want me to stop?"

She considered for an entire five seconds. What had happened to her willpower? She'd never found it difficult to hold a man at arm's length. Until now. But with Rafe… For some reason he affected her in ways she'd never expected or experienced before. Everything about him attracted her. His looks. His intelligence. His sense of humor. His strength. His compassion. Even his family ties—especially his family ties. They all appealed. And then there was her physical response to him. She'd come here wanting something specific from Rafe. What she'd gotten in its stead had been totally unexpected.

She slid her arms downward, surprised to discover that at some point his shirt had disappeared. "What if this isn't real? What if The Inferno is causing us to feel this way?"

She sensed his surprise at the question. "Is that what you think? That your response is caused by a myth?"

Larkin attempted to control her hands, but they had a mind of their own, sweeping over the sculpted muscles of his chest. They were so hard and distinctly masculine, so deliciously different from her own body. "I…I've never felt like this before. I'm just trying to understand—"

"You mean rationalize what's happening." His laugh contained a wry edge. "Trust me, I understand completely. I'm not interested in another emotional entanglement. Not after Leigh."

She stilled, the reminder an icy one. "Emotional?"

He leaned in until his forehead rested against hers. "Hell, Larkin. Do you think I want this to be anything more than physical? Pure chemistry?"

"I can pretty much guess the answer to that," she said drily.

He rolled off her and onto his back, scooping her against his side. She rested her head on his shoulder and allowed her hand to drift across the flat expanse of his abdomen. He sucked in his breath, lacing her fingers with his in order to stop their restless movement. "Since the minute I met you, I've been telling myself it's a simple physical reaction. That's all I want it to be. That's all I can handle at this point in my life."

"But?"

"But then you told me about your broken leg and how you'd never been able to dance again.…"

"I can dance. Just not the way I did before." She shrugged. "So?"

"It just about killed me to hear you say that," he confessed roughly. "To see how it affected you."

"Is that why we ended up here?"

"Pretty much." He tugged at her short crop of curls. He blew out his breath in a sigh. "Go to sleep, Larkin."

"What about…?"

"Not tonight. I'm not sure I could stop once we got started. Hell, who am I kidding? I *know* I won't be able to stop."

Nor would she. "Are you going to stay here with me?"

"For a while," he compromised.

She hesitated, not sure she should ask the next question. But it slipped out anyway. "What happens from this point forward?"

"I don't know," he answered honestly. "I guess we take it one day at a time."

"You think this feeling is going to dissipate over time, don't you?"

"Don't take this the wrong way, but I hope so."

"And if it doesn't?"

"We'll deal with it then."

She fell silent for a moment, then warned, "Whatever this is, Inferno or simple lust, it can't go anywhere. You aren't the only one who isn't interested in a permanent relationship."

"Then we don't have anything to worry about, do we?"

She wished that were true. But once he found out who she was, that would all change.

Rafe woke in the early hours of the morning to the haunting sound of a howl. He glanced down at the woman sprawled across him and smiled. It usually took several nights to get comfortable sleeping with a woman. But with Larkin, all the various arms and legs had sorted themselves out with surprising ease. He couldn't remember the last time he'd slept so soundly.

If it hadn't been for Kiko, he doubted he'd have woken until full daylight. Speaking of which…

Ever so gently, he eased Larkin to one side. She murmured in protest before settling into the warm hollow left by his body, her breath sighing in pleasure. Desire coursed through him at that tiny, ultrafeminine sound. Is that what she'd do when they made love? Would she use that irresistible siren's song on him? He couldn't wait to find out.

Deliberately he turned his back on the bed and crossed to the French doors. A full moon shone down on the fenced yard, frosting the landscape in silver and charcoal. Kiko sat in the middle of the lawn, her head tipped back in a classic pose, her muzzle raised toward the moon.

She exhibited an untamed beauty that drew him on some primitive level. Part of him wanted to run, free and natural, driven by instinct rather than the intellectual side of his nature, a side he clung to with unwavering ferocity. To be part of that other world, the world that called to the untamed part of the animal before him.

Knowing he couldn't, that *she* couldn't, filled him with sadness. She was wildness trapped in domestication…a trap he'd do whatever it took to avoid. Before she could voice her mournful song again, he gave a soft whistle. She hesitated another moment, gave a sorrowful whine, then padded in his direction.

"It makes me so sad." Behind him, Larkin echoed his thoughts.

He turned to glance at her and froze. The moonlight bathed her nudity in silver. She was a study in ivory and charcoal. Her hair, shoulders and breasts gleamed with a pearl-like luminescence, while shadows threw a modest veil across her abdomen and the fertile delta between her thighs. Rational thought deserted him.

She inclined her head toward Kiko. "She feels the pull of the wild, but can't respond the way she wants because she's been trapped in a nebulous existence between wolf and dog, unable to call either world her own." She fixed her pale eyes on him. "Is that how you feel? Trapped between two worlds?"

He still couldn't think straight. He understood the question, but his focus remained fixed on her. On the demands of the physical, rather than the intellect. "Larkin…"

She made the mistake of approaching, the moonlight merciless in stripping away even the subtle barrier of the shadows that had protected her. "Your family is such an emotional one, but you're not, are you?"

He couldn't take his eyes off her. "Don't be so sure."

A slow smile lit her face and she tilted her head to one side. With her cap of curls and delicate features, she looked like a creature of myth and magic. "So you *are* one of the emotional Dantes?"

It took him three tries before he could speak. "If I touch you again, you'll find out for yourself." The words escaped, raw and guttural. "And I'll have broken my promise to Primo."

For a long moment time froze. Then with a tiny sigh, she stepped back, allowing the shadows to swallow her and returning to whatever fantasy world she'd escaped from. Everything that made him male urged pursuit. He knew it was the moonlight and Kiko's howling that had ripped the mask of civilization from his more primitive instincts. He fought with every ounce of control he possessed.

As though sensing how close to the edge he hovered, the dog trotted past him to the open doorway. There she sat, an impressive bulwark to invasion.

"You win this time," he told her. "But don't count on it working in the future."

With that, he turned and walked away from a craving beyond reason. And all the while he rubbed at the relentless itch centered in the palm of his hand.

She'd lost her mind. Larkin swept the sheet off the bed and wrapped herself up in its concealing cocoon. There was no other explanation. Why else would she have stripped off her few remaining clothes and walked outside like that, as naked as the day she'd been born? Never in her life had she been so blatant, so aggressive. That had been Leigh's specialty, not hers.

Leigh.

Larkin sank onto the edge of the bed and covered her face with her hands. What a fool she was, believing for even a single second that she could embroil herself in the Dantes' affairs and escape unscathed. Maybe if she'd been up front with Rafe from the beginning it would have all worked out. That had been the intention when she'd asked to be assigned to the Dantes reception.

Her brow wrinkled. How had it all gone so hideously wrong? He'd touched her, that's how. He'd dropped that insane proposition on her and then before she could even draw breath or engage a single working brain cell, he'd kissed her. And she'd lost all connection with reason and common sense because of The Inferno.

The Inferno.

She stared at her palm in confusion. She wanted to believe that it was wishful thinking or the power of suggestion. But there was no denying the odd throb and itch of her palm. She couldn't have imagined that into existence, could she?

A soft knock sounded on her door. It could be only one person. She debated ignoring it, pretending she was asleep. But she couldn't. She crossed to the door and opened it, still wrapped in the sheet. He'd pulled on a pair of sweatpants and seemed relieved to see that she'd covered up, as well.

"It's late," she started, only to be cut off.

"I'm sorry, Larkin. Tonight was my fault." He leaned against the doorjamb and offered a wry smile. "I thought I could control what happened."

"Not so successful?"

His smile grew. "Not even a little. I can't allow it to happen again." He waited a beat. "At least, not until I have a ring on your finger."

Her eyes widened. "Excuse me?"

"Let's just say that once you're wearing my engagement ring, I'll consider my promise to Primo fulfilled."

The air escaped her lungs in a rush, and she fought to breathe. "And then?" she asked faintly.

"And then we'll finish what we started tonight." He reached out and wound a ringlet around his finger. "One way or another we'll work this out." His mouth twisted. "Of course, getting whatever this is out of our systems will take a lot of work."

"What if I don't want to make love to you?"

He chuckled. The rich, husky sound had her swaying

toward him. "Somehow I don't think that'll be a problem."

He leaned in and snatched a kiss, leaving her longing for more. And then he released her and left her standing there, clutching the sheet to her chest.

He was wrong. So wrong. Making love would be far more than a problem. It would be a disaster. Taking their relationship that next step would forge a deeper connection. No matter how much he wanted to deny it, it would create a bond between them that could offer nothing but pain.

Because the minute she told him that Leigh was her sister—*half* sister—and he discovered the real reason she'd approached him, he wouldn't want anything further to do with her.

Six

"Nervous?" Rafe asked as he downshifted the car.

They climbed farther into the hills overlooking Sausalito along a winding road that led to Primo and Nonna's. Each bend showcased breathtaking views one minute and then equally breathtaking villas the next. It was pointless to pretend she wasn't nervous, so Larkin nodded.

"A little. Your grandparents can be rather intimidating. And now there's the rest of the Dantes to contend with...."

She trailed off with a shrug that spoke volumes. A far greater concern was whether any of them would somehow make some sort of quantum leap and connect her to Leigh. With such a large contingent of Dantes present for Sunday dinner, she'd be lynched for sure.

Rafe spared her a flashing smile. "Try not to worry. The intimidation factor is aimed at me, not you. I've already received a half dozen lectures from various family members who are worried about my intentions toward you. Afraid I'll corrupt you or something." Pulling into a short drive, he crammed his car behind the ones already parked outside his grandparents' home. "Other than that, I have a terrific family."

"Big. You have a big family."

He glanced at her, curious. "Is it the size that worries you?"

"Everything about your family worries me," she announced ominously.

He chuckled at that. "Just do what I do and ignore all the drama. You don't have to answer any questions you don't want to."

"I'll tell them you said that, but somehow I doubt it'll work."

She opened the car door and climbed out, smoothing the skirt of her dress—something she rarely, if ever, wore. It was new, a purchase that both Nonna and Elia had insisted on making, despite her hesitation. In all reality, it was more of an oversize shirt than an actual dress, right down to the rolled-up sleeves and button-down collar. Unfortunately, she felt as if she'd forgotten half her outfit. Still, she couldn't deny it suited her.

A dainty gold belt cinched her waist, making it appear incredibly small, while the shirttail hem flirted in that coy no-man's-land between knee and thigh, drawing attention to her slender legs. She just hoped it didn't also draw attention to the thin network of silvery-white scars that remained a permanent reminder of her broken leg.

"Stop fussing. You look amazing." Rafe circled the

car and took her hand in his. "They're all going to love
you as much as Mamma and Nonna."

Despite her nervousness, she couldn't help finding
the Italian inflection that rippled through his voice
endearing, especially when he referred to his mother
or grandmother. It was as beautiful as it was lyrical.

"I'm being ridiculous, aren't I?" She blew out a
breath. "I mean, even if they don't like me it really
doesn't matter. It's not like this is re—"

He stopped the words with a kiss, the unexpected
power of it almost knocking her off her legs. Every last
thought misted over, vanishing beneath his amazing
lips. She shifted closer and wound her arms around his
neck, giving herself up to the delicious heat that seemed
to explode between them whenever they touched. She
couldn't say how long they remained wrapped around
each other, doing their level best to inhale one another.
Seconds. Minutes. Hours. Time held no meaning. When
he finally lifted his head, she could only stare at him,
dazed. He grinned at her reaction.

"Interesting," he said. "I'll have to remember to do
that anytime I want to change the subject."

"Who…? What…?" She took a tottering step backward. "Why…?"

His grin broadened at her helpless confusion. "You
were about to say something indiscreet," he explained
in a low voice. "I kissed you to shut you up. You never
know who might be listening."

Larkin's brain clicked back on, along with her
capacity for speech. "Got it."

It was so unfair. For her their embraces felt painfully
real. But for Rafe… Didn't the heat they generated melt
any of his icy composure? She could have sworn it did.

She sighed. Maybe that was just wishful thinking on her part, which meant she was putting herself in an increasingly vulnerable position if she didn't find a way to keep her emotions in check.

"I'll be more careful from now on," she added, as much for her own benefit as for his.

She drew in a shaky breath and aimed herself toward a large wooden gate leading to the back of the house. To her profound relief, she discovered she could walk in a more or less straight line without falling down. Rafe opened the gate, and they stepped into a beautifully tended garden area filled with a rainbow of colors and a dizzying bouquet of fragrances. An array of voices greeted them, coming from the people who spilled across the lawn or sat at a wrought iron patio set beneath a huge sprawling mush oak.

The next hour proved beyond confusing as Rafe introduced her to an endless number of Dantes. Some were involved in the retail end of the Dantes jewelry empire. Others, like Rafe and his brother Luc, ran the courier service. Still others handled the day-to-day business aspects. She met Rafe's father, Alessandro, who was as easygoing as his son was intense. And she met the various wives, their radiance and undisguised happiness filling her with a wistful yearning to enjoy the sort of marital bliss they'd discovered with their spouses. Not that it would happen. At least, not with Rafe.

"Have all of the married couples experienced The Inferno?" she couldn't help but ask at one point.

Rafe gave a short laugh. "Or so they claim." She considered that with a frown, one that he intercepted. "What?"

"Well, you're the logical one, right?"

"No question."

She indicated his relatives with a wave of her hand. "And every couple here, including your parents and grandparents, claim that they've experienced The Inferno."

He shrugged. "What can I say? I've come to the conclusion that the Dante family suffers from a genetic mutation that causes mass delusion. Thank God I was spared that particular anomaly." His gaze drifted toward his younger brother and sister. "Time will tell whether Draco and Gia escaped, as well."

That earned him a swift grin. "Mutations and anomalies aside, Primo mentioned that he and Nonna have been married for more than fifty years. And I gather your parents must have been married for thirtysomething years, right?"

"Your point?"

She suppressed a wince at the crispness of his question. "Despite your unfortunate genetic anomaly, doesn't logic suggest that, based on all the marriages you've seen to date, The Inferno is real? I'd also think that the fact that you *didn't* experience it with Leigh and your marriage failed only adds to the body of evidence."

He didn't have a chance to answer. Draco dropped into the conversation and into the vacant chair beside them. "You're not going to convince him. Rafaelo doesn't want to believe. Plus, he's a dyed-in-the-wool cynic who isn't about to allow something as messy and unmanageable as The Inferno steal away his precious self-control."

"If you mean I refuse to be trapped in another marriage, you're right," Rafe responded in a cool voice.

Draco leaned toward her. "Oh, and did I happen to mention that he doesn't want to believe?"

Despite the pain that Rafe's comments caused, Larkin's lips quivered in amusement. "You may have said something to that effect once or twice."

"Tell me you're any different," Rafe shot back at his brother. "Are you ready to surrender your current lifestyle to the whims of The Inferno?"

Something dark and powerful rippled across the even tenor of Draco's expression. Something that hinted at the depths he concealed beneath his easygoing facade. Larkin watched in fascination. *The dragon stirs* came the whimsical thought.

Draco took his time responding, taking the question seriously. "Answer me this…. If your Inferno bride dropped into your arms out of the blue, would you push her away?"

Rafe spared Larkin a brief glance. "Is that what you think happened to us?"

"To you?" Draco seemed startled by the question. His dark gaze flashed from his brother to Larkin. "Sure, okay. Let's say it happened to the two of you. Are you going to turn away from it?"

"It didn't happen to us," Rafe stated with quiet emphasis. "It didn't because there is no such thing as The Inferno, so there's nothing to turn away from."

Draco flipped a quick, sympathetic look in Larkin's direction before responding to his brother. "In that case, either you deserve an Academy Award for your performance tonight, or you're a lying SOB. I can't help but wonder which one it is."

Rafe regarded his brother through narrowed green

eyes. "You should know which one, since you're responsible for staging this little play."

"I may have orchestrated the opening scene," Draco shot right back, "but that's where my participation in this comedy of errors ended. Your role, on the other hand, appears to have taken on an unexpected twist."

Draco struck with the speed of a snake, snagging his brother's wrist. Larkin's gaze dropped to Rafe's hand and she inhaled sharply. He'd been caught red-handed—literally—rubbing the palm of his right hand with the thumb of his left, just as she'd been doing ever since they'd first touched.

"Part of the act," Rafe claimed.

But Larkin could see the lie in his eyes and hear it in his voice and feel it in the heat centered in her palm.

"Keep telling yourself that, bro, but in case you're wondering, I'm choosing Option B. That's lying SOB, in case you've forgotten." Draco deliberately changed the subject. "Hey, sister-to-be, I see I'm not the only one with an eventful childhood."

The change in subject knocked her off-kilter. "Sorry?"

He gestured to the nearly invisible network of scars along her leg. "We match. Mine was due to falling out of a tree. How about you?"

He asked the question so naturally that she didn't feel the least embarrassed or self-conscious. "Did a pirouette off a stage."

He winced. "Ouch." He nudged Rafe. "Of course, my ordeal wasn't anywhere near as bad as Rafe's."

"Rafe's?" She turned to him. "Did you break your leg, too? Why didn't you tell me?"

"I didn't break anything."

"Except a few hearts," Draco joked. "No, I meant what happened to him when I broke my leg. Didn't he tell you?"

Larkin shook her head. "No, he hasn't mentioned it."

"Oh, well, since we're all going to the lake next week, not only can he fill you in on every last gory detail, but he can show you the very spot where it went down. I'd point out the tree that started the trouble, but Rafe went crazy one year and chopped it down."

"It was infested," Rafe responded with a terrible calm. "It needed to come down before it infected other trees."

"You know, I've finally figured it out," Draco marveled. "If reality doesn't match the way you want your world to exist, you simply change your version of reality. Well, I've got news for you. That doesn't make it real. That just makes *you* delusional."

Larkin flinched at the word. She didn't know what had happened to Rafe all those years ago, but she could feel the waves of turbulence rolling off him, his impressive willpower all that held the emotions in check.

"I think we're being called to dinner," she said, hoping to defuse the situation. Standing, she offered her hand to Rafe. "I can't wait to sample Primo's cooking. Everyone I've spoken to has raved about it."

To her shock, he scooped her close. Lowering his head, he took her mouth in a slow, thorough kiss that caught her off guard and had her responding without thought or hesitation. "Thanks," he murmured against her lips.

"Anytime," she whispered back. Especially if it meant being rewarded with a kiss like that.

The kiss hadn't escaped the notice of Rafe's relatives, nor did she miss the gentle laughter and whispered comments that followed the two of them inside. She might have been embarrassed if not for the relieved delight on their faces. It didn't take much guesswork to understand why. Clearly, Leigh had done quite a number on Rafe and they were thankful that he'd finally put the trauma of his marriage behind him. She winced.

If they only knew.

"You didn't mention that we were expected to join your family at the lake next week," Larkin said.

"Sorry about that." He opened the door leading into the utility room off the kitchen and held it for her. "Is going to the lake with me a problem?"

With the exception of the few monosyllabic replies she'd offered in response to his various attempts at conversation, she hadn't spoken a word since they'd left Primo's. Rafe couldn't decide whether to be relieved or concerned that she'd finally started talking again. Clearly, something was eating at her. If their visit to the lake was her main concern, he could handle that and would chalk the evening up as a reasonable success. Otherwise…

"No. I just would have appreciated a warning."

Damn. She still wasn't looking at him, which meant her silence wasn't because of the trip to the lake. A lead-in, perhaps, or an oblique approach to the actual problem. But definitely not the problem itself. She crouched to greet Kiko, scanning the area as she did so.

"I don't see any damage in here. Maybe we should do a quick walk-through, just to be on the safe side."

"I'm sure she was fine." He stooped beside the pair and gave Kiko a thorough rub. The dog moaned in ecstasy. "Weren't you, girl?"

Sure enough, a quick inspection of the house revealed no damage. Once Larkin satisfied herself that Kiko had behaved while they were gone, he inclined his head toward the patio. "I'm not ready for the evening to end. Why don't we go outside before turning in for the night?"

She hesitated, another ominous sign. "Okay."

He removed a bottle from the refrigerator and nabbed a pair of crystal flutes, then followed her into the moonlit darkness. "Hmm. For some reason this has a familiar feel to it."

She tossed a smile over her shoulder, one filled with feminine enchantment. "Been there, done that?"

He set the bottle on the table. "Close, though a bit different from what I have planned for this evening."

She eyed the bottle and stilled. "Champagne?" A frown worried at the edges of her expression. "Are we celebrating something?"

"I guess that depends on how well this goes over." He removed a small jewelry box from his pocket and flipped it open, revealing the glittering ring within. "I couldn't wait until Monday," he explained in response to her look of shock. "Hell, I barely made it through last night."

She drew in a sharp breath. "Oh, Rafe. What have you done?"

His eyes narrowed. "You knew this was coming. I just moved up the timetable by a day or two. After last night…"

She actually blushed, which he found fascinating. At

a guess, she didn't often wander around naked in the moonlight. A shame. It suited her. It also suited him.

She took a quick step backward. Not a good sign. "It's just…" She trailed off with a shrug.

"Just what?"

He resisted the urge to follow her. Instead, he set the ring on the table beside the bottle of champagne, realizing that he'd been so focused on his own needs, he hadn't taken Larkin's into consideration. The ring and all that went with it could wait. He wanted her to enjoy their first time together, not be distracted by worries he could help ease.

"Honey, you barely spoke a word the entire way home. So either it's that, or it's the trip to the lake, or there's something else worrying you. Why don't you tell me which it is?"

He closed the distance between them and gathered her hands in his. It felt so right when he held her like this, felt the wash of warmth that flowed between them. Why did his family have to take something so basic, so natural, and wrap it up in myth and superstition? It was simple sexual attraction. Granted, the connection between them felt amazing. But couldn't they just call a spade a spade and let it go at that? Did they have to cloak a simple chemical reaction behind a ridiculous fairy tale?

"What's wrong, Larkin?"

Her gaze swept past him to fix on the table. "The only reason you bought me champagne and a ring is so you could make love to me."

He winced. Stripping it down to the bare-bones truth tarnished what he'd considered a romantic overture. "I thought—"

She cut him off without hesitation. "You thought that since you were buying my services, a bottle of champagne and a ring were sufficient. That you didn't have to turn it into some sort of big romantic gesture. I get that. It's not real, so why pretend it's anything more than sex, right?"

He released her hands. "Hell."

"I want to make love to you. But this…" She shivered. "An engagement ring is real, Rafe. It's a serious commitment, just like marriage. You're treating it like it's some sort of casual game or a fast, easy way to get me into bed."

Anger flashed and he struggled to contain it. "I'm well aware that marriage isn't a game. Cold, hard experience, remember?"

She stepped away from him, melting into the surrounding shadows, making it impossible to read her expression. "You hired me to do a job. You hired me to play the part of your fiancée for your friends and family and I've agreed to do that even though it goes against the grain to lie to them. You didn't hire me to sleep with you."

The comment had his anger ripping free of his control. "I'd never reduce it to something so sordid. One has nothing to do with the other. I wouldn't dream of putting a price tag on that aspect of our relationship. It would be an insult to both of us."

"And yet, you're only offering me that ring so you can get me in bed. Seems to me that's a hefty price tag."

He went after her and pulled her from the shadows and into his arms. "You know damn well why I offered you that ring. I made a promise to Primo, a promise I won't break. Do I want to make love to you? Hell, yes!

But I can't and won't do it unless you're officially my fiancée. It's going to happen eventually. Why not now? So I woke Sev this morning to open up Dante Exclusive and I picked out a ring for you. And not just any ring. A ring that reminded me of you. That seemed tailor-made for you."

He could tell his words had an impact. Her attention strayed to the table, her eyes full of curiosity and something else. A wistfulness that tore at his heart. "I won't be bought."

"And I'm not buying you. Not when it comes to this part of our relationship." His anger dampened, allowing him to rein it in. He didn't understand how she could rouse his emotions with such ease. He'd never had that problem with any other woman. "As far as I'm concerned, what happens in bed has nothing to do with your posing as my fiancée. If we'd met under different circumstances, we'd still have ended up there. You just wouldn't have had my ring on your finger."

She took a deep breath, conceding the point. "Show me the ring."

He took that as an encouraging sign. Crossing to the table, he collected the jewelry box. Removing the ring, he gathered her hand in his and slid it onto the appropriate finger. Even in the subdued lighting, the stones took on a life of their own.

The central diamond—one of the fire diamonds that made Dantes jewelry so exclusive and world renowned—sparkled with a hot blue flame. On either side of it were more fire diamonds, each subsequently smaller and bluer, the final one as pale and clear and brilliant a blue as Larkin's eyes. The stones were arranged in a delicate filigree Platinum Ice setting that seemed the perfect reflection of her appearance and personality.

"It's…" She broke off and cleared her throat. "It's the most beautiful ring I've ever seen."

"It's from the Dantes Eternity line."

Her gaze jerked upward. "The ones that were being showcased at the reception?"

"The very same. Every last one is unique and each has a name."

She hesitated before asking, "What's this one called?"

It was such an obvious question. He didn't understand her reluctance to ask it. But then, what he didn't understand about a woman's emotions could fill volumes. "It's called Once in a Lifetime."

"Oh. What a perfect name for it." To his concern, tears filled her eyes. "But you must see why I can't accept this."

Okay, it was confirmed. He did not—and never would—understand women. "No, I don't see. Explain it to me."

"It's Once in a Lifetime."

"I get that part." He fought for patience and tried again. "Just to clarify, you can't accept a ring from me? As in any ring? Or you can't accept this specific ring?"

A tear spilled out, just about sending him to his knees. "This one." It took her an instant to gather her self-control enough to continue. "I can't—won't—accept *this* ring."

He planted his fists on his hips. "Why the hell not?"

Now her lips and chin got into the act, quivering in

a way that left him utterly helpless. "Because of the name."

"You have got to be kidding me." He snatched a deep breath, throttled back on full-bore Dante bend-'em-till-they-break tone of voice and switched to something more conciliatory. "If you don't like the name, we'll just change it. No big deal."

She shook her head, loosening another couple of tears. They seemed to sparkle on her cheeks with as much brilliance as the diamonds in the ring she couldn't/wouldn't accept. "I'm sure you can see how wrong that would be."

"No, actually I can't." He tried to speak calmly. He really did. For some reason his voice escaped closer to a roar. So much for conciliatory. "It's a prop. Part of the job. And it's yours once the job ends."

She tugged frantically at the ring. "Absolutely not. I couldn't accept it."

His back teeth locked together. "It's compensation," he gritted out. "We agreed beforehand that it would be."

Her chin jerked upward an inch. "It's excessive and taints the meaning of such a gorgeous ring." She managed to tug it off her finger and held it out to him. "I'm sorry, Rafe. I can't accept this."

Damn it to hell! "You're required to wear it as part of your official duties. Once the job ends you can keep it or not. That's up to you."

"I won't be keeping it."

He shrugged. "Then I'll give you the cash equivalent."

She caught her lower lip between her teeth in obvious agitation. "I think it's time we amended our original agreement. In fact, I insist we amend it. When you initially mentioned my keeping the ring, I didn't realize we were talking about something of this caliber."

"If I offered you anything less, my family would know our engagement isn't real."

"Which is the only reason I'm willing to wear your ring." She drew back her hand and gazed down at her palm with a hint of longing. "Maybe a different one? Something smaller. Something that doesn't have a name."

"Sev knows which ring I chose. It'll cause comment if we exchange it." He didn't give her the opportunity to dream up any more excuses. Plucking the ring from her palm, he returned it to her finger. To his relief, she left it there, though his relief was short-lived.

"About that amendment…" she began.

He folded his arms across his chest. He should have seen it coming. Now that she had him between a rock and a hard place, she could name her terms and he'd be forced to agree. Or so she thought. He'd soon disabuse her of that fact. Just as he had Leigh when she'd pulled a similar stunt.

"Name your demands."

Larkin blinked in surprise. "Demands?"

"That's what they are, aren't they? I've introduced you to my entire family as my fiancée. We're committed to seeing this through. And now you want to change the terms of our agreement." He shrugged. "What else am I supposed to call it?"

Everything about her shut down. Her expression. The brilliance of her gaze. Her stance. Even the way she breathed. One minute she'd been a woman of vibrancy and the next she might as well have been a wax figurine.

"I don't want your money, Rafaelo Dante." Even her voice emerged without inflection. "You can keep your ring and your cash. I only want one thing. A favor."

"What favor?"

She shook her head, her features taking on a stubborn set. "When I've performed my duties to your satisfaction and the job has ended, then I'll ask you. But not before."

"I need some sort of idea what this favor is about," he argued.

"It's either something you can grant me, or not. You decide when the time comes."

He considered for a moment. "Does this have something to do with the person you're looking for?"

"Yes."

Her request didn't make the least sense. "Honey, I've already said I'd help you with that. I'm happy to help. But I hired you for a job and you deserve to be paid for that job."

She cut him off. "It's not just a matter of my giving you a name to pass on to Juice. There's more to it than that. For me, that something is of far greater value to me than your ring or cash or anything else you'd offer as compensation."

"I think I'll make that determination when the job is over. If your request doesn't strike me as a fair bargain — fair for you, I mean—then I'm going to pay you. If you don't want the ring, fine. If you don't want the money, fine. You can donate it all to charity or to the animal rescue group of your choice."

Even that offer had little impact. "Do you agree to my terms?" she pressed. "Yes or no?"

Depending on the favor, it struck him as a reasonable

enough request, though he suspected he'd discover the hidden catch at some point. There had to be one. He'd learned that painful fact during his marriage, as well as from a number of the women who'd preceded his late wife, and also those who'd followed her. When you were an eligible Dante, it was all about what you could give a woman. Once they'd tied the knot and Leigh had dropped her sweet-and-innocent guise, she'd made that fact abundantly clear. Well, he'd deal with Larkin's hidden catch when it happened, because there wasn't a doubt in his mind that it would be a "when" rather than an "if."

"Sure," he agreed, wondering if she could hear the cynicism ripping through that single terse word. "If it's within my power to give you what you ask, I'm happy to do it."

"Time will tell," she murmured in response. "I do have one other request."

"You're pushing it, Larkin." Not that his warning had any impact whatsoever.

"It's just that I was wondering about something." She continued blithely along her path of destruction. "And I was hoping we could discuss it."

He gestured for her to finish. "Don't keep me in suspense."

"What happened at the lake when Draco broke his leg?"

"Hell. Is *that* what's been bothering you all night?"

"What makes you think anything was bothering me?" she asked, stung.

"Gee, I don't know. Maybe it was that long stretch of silence on the trip back from Primo's. Or the fact that you've been on edge ever since our conversation with Draco."

He shouldn't have mentioned his brother. It brought her lasering back to her original question. "Seriously, Rafe. What happened to you that day at the lake? The day Draco broke his leg?"

When he remained silent, she added, "Consider it a condition of my leaving this ring on my finger."

Damn it to hell! "Now you're *really* pushing it."

"Tell me."

"There's not much to tell."

He crossed to the table and made short work of opening the bottle of Dom. Not that he was in the mood for a celebration. What he really wanted was to get rip-roaring drunk and consign his entire family, the bloody Inferno and even his brand-new, ring-wearing fiancée straight to the devil. Splashing the effervescent wine into each of the two flutes, he passed one to Larkin before fortifying himself with a swallow.

"Rafe?"

"You want to know what happened? Fine. I was forgotten."

Larkin frowned. "Forgotten? I don't understand. What do you mean?"

He forced himself to make the admission calmly. Precisely. Unemotionally. All the while ignoring the tide of hot pain that flowed through him like lava. "I mean, everyone went off and left me behind and didn't realize it until the next day."

Seven

"*What?*" Larkin stared at Rafe in disbelief. "They left you there at the lake? Alone? Are you serious?"

Rafe smiled, but she noticed it didn't quite reach his eyes. They'd darkened to a deep, impenetrable green. "Dead serious."

"I don't understand. What happened?" she asked urgently. "How old were you?"

She could tell he didn't want to talk about it. Maybe she should have let him off the hook. But she couldn't. Something warned her that whatever had happened was a vital element in forming his present-day persona.

"I was ten and our vacation time was up, so we were getting ready to leave. My cousins and brothers and I were all running around doing our level best to pack in a final few minutes of fun while my sister, Gia, chased after us doing *her* level best to round us up. Since she was the youngest and only five, you can imagine how well that worked."

"And then?" Larkin prompted.

He lifted a shoulder in a casual shrug, though she suspected his attitude toward that long-ago event was anything but casual. "Draco climbed a tree in order to tease Gia. I knew it would take a while for my parents to get him down, so I took off to check on this dam I'd built along the river that fed the lake. Apparently while I was gone Draco fell out of the tree and broke his leg."

She rubbed at her own leg and winced in sympathy. "Ouch. How bad a break was it?"

"Bad. All hell broke loose. Mamma and *Babbo*—my mother and father—took Draco to the hospital. Gia was hysterical, so Nonna and Primo took her with them. My aunt and uncle grabbed Luc and their four boys."

He was breaking her heart. "No one wondered where you were? They just…forgot about you?"

"There were a lot of kids running around." He spoke as though from a memorized script. "They each thought someone else had taken me. Draco was in pretty bad shape, so my parents stayed overnight with him at the hospital, which is why they didn't realize I'd been overlooked."

She could sympathize with his parents' decision, having gone through a similar ordeal. Only, in her case her mother hadn't stayed with her. Gran had been the one to stick by her side day and night. "When did they figure out you were missing?"

"Late the next day. They didn't get back to the city until then. When they went to round us all up, they discovered I was nowhere to be found."

"How hideous." Larkin gnawed at her lip. "Poor Elia. She must have been frantic."

Rafe glared in exasperation. "Poor Elia? What about poor Rafe?"

"You're right." So right. "Poor Rafe. I'm so sorry."

He reminded her of a snarling lion, pacing off his annoyance, and she couldn't resist the urge to soothe him. She approached as cautiously as she would a wild animal. At first she thought he'd back away. But he didn't. Nor did he encourage her, not that that stopped her.

Sliding her hands along the impressive breadth of his chest, Larkin gripped his shoulders and rose on tiptoe. His mouth hovered just within reach and she didn't hesitate. She gave him a slow, champagne-sweetened kiss. Their lips mated, fitting together as perfectly as their bodies. It had been this way from the start and she couldn't help but wonder—if circumstances had been different, would their relationship have developed into a real one?

It was a lovely dream. But that's all it was. The realization hurt more than she would have believed possible. He started to deepen the kiss, to take it to the next step. If the ring and champagne and engagement had been real, nothing would have stopped her from following him down such a tempting path. But it wasn't real and she forced herself to pull back.

She wasn't ready to go there. Not until she came to terms with the temporary nature of their relationship. Rafe might not realize it yet, but the "if" of their lovemaking would be her decision alone. The "when" on her terms.

He released a sigh. "Let me guess. More questions?"

She offered a sympathetic smile. "Afraid so."

"Get it over with."

"What in the world did you do when you returned and discovered everyone gone?" she asked, genuinely curious.

"I sat and waited for a couple of hours. After a while I got hungry, but the summerhouse was all locked up. So I decided maybe I was being punished for running off instead of staying where I'd been told and my punishment was to find my own way home."

Larkin's mouth dropped open. "Oh, my God. You didn't—"

"Hitchhike? Sure did."

"Do you have any idea how dangerous that was?" She broke off and shook her head. "Of course you do. Now."

"It all seemed very simple and logical to me. I just needed to get from the lake to San Francisco. The hardest part was walking to the freeway. And finding food."

Larkin couldn't seem to wrap her head around the story. "How? Where?"

"I came across a campsite. No one was there." He shrugged. "Probably out hiking, so I helped myself to some of their food and water."

She stared in disbelief. "You made it home, didn't you?"

"It took three days, but yes. I made it home on my own. Walked some. Snuck onto a bus at one point. The toughest part was coming up with acceptable excuses for why I was out on my own—excuses that wouldn't have the people who helped me calling the authorities."

"Your parents must have been frantic."

He crossed to the table and poured himself a second glass of champagne, topping hers off in the process. "To put it mildly."

"And ever since then?"

He studied her over the rim of the crystal flute. "Ever since then…what?"

She narrowed her eyes in contemplation. "Ever since then, you've been fiercely independent, determined not to depend on anyone other than yourself."

He shrugged. "It didn't change anything. I've always been the independent sort."

"Seriously, Rafe. You must have been terrified when you discovered you'd been left behind."

"Maybe a little."

"And hurt. Terribly hurt that the family you loved and trusted just up and deserted you."

"I got over it." Ice slipped into his voice. "Besides, they didn't desert me."

"But you thought they did," she persisted. "It explains a lot, you know."

"I don't like being psychoanalyzed."

"Neither do I. But at least now I understand why you hold people at an emotional distance and why you're so determined to control your world." It must have been sheer hell being married to someone like Leigh, who was a master at manipulating emotions and equally determined to be the one in control. "Did you ever tell your wife about the incident?"

"Leigh wasn't interested in the past. She pretty much lived in the now and planned for the future. Even if I had mentioned it to her, I doubt it would have made any difference."

True enough. "It makes a difference to me," Larkin murmured.

"Why?"

Because it clarified one simple fact. Their relationship would never work. His independent nature would rebel against any sort of long-term connection. Deepening that problem had been his experience at the lake all those years ago, when he'd learned to trust only himself during that three-day trek home. He wouldn't dare put his faith in someone he couldn't trust. And once he knew the truth about her, he'd never trust her. She strongly suspected that once that trust was lost, it could never be regained.

She also found it interesting that he was running away from what she'd spent her entire life wishing she could have. Family. An ingrained knowledge that she belonged. Hearth and home. Though her grandmother had been a loving, generous woman, she hadn't been the most sociable person in the world. She lived on a small farm, happy with a simple, natural existence far from the nearest town. While love and obligation had kept Larkin by her grandmother's side until her grandmother's death and news of Leigh's death had reached her, through the years she'd begun to long for more. The sort of "more" that Rafe had rejected. During the last year of Gran's life, Larkin had created a game plan for attaining that something more. First on her agenda was to track down her father. Then she intended to obtain a job at a rescue organization and pursue her real passion—saving animals like Kiko.

The only remaining question was… How did she get herself out of her current predicament? Of course, she knew how. All she had to do was tell him that she was Leigh's sister—*half* sister—and their temporary engagement would come to a permanent end. Then he'd either agree to what she required in lieu of payment, or he wouldn't. End of story.

What she really needed to know was how much longer he intended to drag out their engagement, and what sort of exit strategy he had planned. Knowing Rafe, there was definitely a plan.

"I have one last question," she began.

"Unfortunately for you, I'm done answering them. There's only one thing I want right now." He set the flute on the table with enough force to make the crystal sing. He turned and regarded her with a burning gaze. "And that's you."

How had she thought she could control this man? It would seem she was as foolish as Leigh. "I don't think—"

"I'm not asking you to think." Rafe approached, kicking a chair from his path. "I don't even care whether you choose to wear my ring or not. There's only one thing that matters. One thing that either of us wants. And it's what we've wanted from the moment we first met."

Without another word, he swept Larkin into his arms. The stars wheeled overhead as her world turned upside down. She clutched at his shoulders and held on for dear life. Her lion was loose and on a rampage and she doubted anything she said or did would change that fact.

"You're going to make love to me, aren't you?"

"Oh, yeah."

"Even though it breaks your promise to your grandfather?"

He shouldered his way into her bedroom. "I'm not breaking my promise to Primo. I put a ring on your finger. If you decide to take it off again, that's your choice. As far as I'm concerned, we're officially engaged."

"Rafe—"

He lowered her to the bed and followed her down. "Do you really want me to stop?"

The question whispered through the air, filled with temptation and allure. It was truth time. She didn't want him to stop. Just a few short days ago she'd never have believed herself capable of tumbling into bed with Leigh's husband. It was the last thing she wanted from him. But now…

Now she couldn't find the willpower to resist. It was wrong. So very wrong. And yet, she'd never felt anything so right. Every part of her vibrated with the sweetness of the connection that flowed between them. It danced from her body to his and back again, coiling around and through her, building with each passing second.

"I don't want you to stop," she admitted. "But I don't want you to regret this later on."

"Why would I regret it?" Despite the darkness, she could see the smile that flirted with his mouth and hear it penetrate his voice. "If anything, this should ease the tension between us."

"Or make it worse."

He leaned into her, sweeping the collar of her dress to one side and finding that sweet spot in the juncture between her neck and shoulder. "Does this feel worse?"

A soft moan escaped. "That's not what I meant."

"How about this?"

She shuddered at the caress. So soft. So teasing. Like the brush of a downy feather against her skin. "I mean when we go our separate ways. When the job ends. This will make it worse. Harder."

"It just gives us some interesting memories to take with us when we part."

"But it will end, right? You understand that?"

He traced a string of kisses down the length of her neck, pausing long enough to say, "I thought that was supposed to be my line."

"I just want to be clear about it. That's all."

"Fine. We're both clear about it."

"There's one other thing I should tell you before we go any further."

He sat up with a sigh, allowing a rush of cool air to pour over her, chilling her. A second later the nightstand lamp snapped on, flooding the room with brightness. "The timing's wrong, isn't it?"

Larkin jackknifed upright. "No, not at all." She twisted her hands together. "Do you think you could turn off the light?"

"Why?"

"I'd just find it easier to say this next part if the light were off."

"Okay." A simple click plunged the room back into the safety of darkness. "Talk."

"I think it's only fair to warn you. What we're about to do?"

"You mean, what we *were* doing but aren't?"

"Oh, no. It's definitely *are* doing. Or rather, about to do. Unless you change your mind."

"What the hell is going on, Larkin?"

"I've never done this before, okay?" she confessed in a rush.

Dead silence greeted her confession. "You mean you've never had an affair with someone after such a short acquaintance. You've never had a one-night stand. That's what you mean, right?"

"That, too."

He swore. "You're a virgin?"

"Pretty much."

"Last time I checked, that question required a yes or no answer. It's like pregnancy. Either you are or you're not. There's no 'pretty much' or 'sort of' involved."

She blew out a sigh. "Yes, I'm a virgin. Does it really matter that much?"

"I want to say no. But I'd be lying." He stood. "Looks like Primo didn't need to make that stipulation after all. All you had to do was say three simple words and you're officially hands-off."

She couldn't let it end like this. She didn't want it to end. She'd waited all this time for the right man and despite all that stood between them, she couldn't imagine making love with anyone else. If she didn't do something to stop him, he'd leave. Who knew if she'd be given another opportunity?

Larkin didn't hesitate. Grabbing the tails of her shirtdress, she tugged it up and over her head and tossed it to one side. She fumbled for the bedside lamp and switched it on, then froze, overwhelmed by her daring.

Her actions seemed to have a similar effect on Rafe. He froze as well, staring at her with an expression that should have had her diving under the covers. Instead, it heated her blood to a near boil.

She stood before him in a silvery-blue bra and thong that were made of gossamer strands of silk, clinging to her breasts and hips like a glittering cobweb. The set was the most revealing she'd ever owned. The bra was low cut, lovingly cupping her small breasts and practically serving them up for Rafe's inspection. Even more revealing was the thong. The minuscule triangle of semitransparent silk did nothing to protect her modesty. It just drew attention to her boyish hips and the feminine delta of her thighs. If she turned so much as a quarter of an inch, he'd also have a perfect view of the ripe curve of her backside.

It was as though he'd read her mind. "Turn around." The demand was low and guttural, filled with uncompromising masculine promise. Or was it more of a threat?

She rotated in place, feeling the heat of his gaze streak across her, burning with intent. When she faced him again, he hadn't moved from his position and her nervousness increased. Why wasn't he reacting? Why hadn't he taken her into his arms and carried her back to the bed?

"Rafe?" Anxiety rippled through the word.

"Take them off. No more barriers between us."

This was not what she'd planned. "I thought you—"

He cut her off with a shake of his head. "I want you to be very certain about this. I don't want there to be any lingering questions in your mind, now or later. If you want to make love with me, if you're absolutely certain this is right for you, then take off the rest of your clothes."

The light continued to blaze across her, ruthless

in slicing through the protective barrier of darkness. She understood his point. It wasn't that he didn't want to touch her. She could see the desire blazing in his expression, could feel the palpable waves of control stretched to the breaking point. Every instinct urged him to take her. To lay claim.

But he wouldn't. Not until she convinced him that she'd made this decision of her own free will, without his influencing her with one of his world-shattering kisses or beyond-delicious caresses.

She smiled.

There wasn't any hesitation this time. She reached behind her and unhooked the bra. The straps slid down her arms and clung for a brief instant, as did the cups. Then it drifted from her body to disappear into the pool of shadows at her feet.

A low moan escaped Rafe, and the tips of her breasts pebbled in response. "Finish it," he demanded.

She lifted an eyebrow, daring to tease. "Are you sure you wouldn't like to take care of this last part yourself?"

He took a swift step forward before catching himself. "Larkin—"

She put him out of his misery. Tiny bows held the thong in place and she tugged at them, allowing the scrap of silk to follow the same path as her bra.

"Is this enough to convince you?" She held out her hand, the one where The Inferno throbbed with such persuasive insistence. "Please, Rafe. Make love to me."

Rafe didn't need any further encouragement. In two rapid strides he reached her side and wrapped her in an unbreakable hold. Together they fell backward onto the bed. His mouth closed over Larkin's, hot with demand. She slid her fingers deep into his hair, anchoring him in place, as though afraid he'd leave her again if she didn't. Foolish of her. Now that he had her naked in his arms, he intended to keep her that way for as long as humanly possible, and hang the consequences. All that mattered right now was making it the best possible experience for her.

"I'm feeling a bit overdressed," he murmured against her mouth.

Her laugh was sweet and gentle and, for some reason, drove him utterly insane. "I think I can help you with that."

She made short work of the buttons of his shirt, yanking the edges open and sliding it from his shoulders. He shrugged it the rest of the way off and sucked in his breath when her hands collided with his chest. She had a way of touching him, of stroking her fingers across him. Just. So. This time the strokes took her farther afield, tracing the center line of his abdomen downward until she collided with his belt.

"I can take care of that," he offered. It might kill him to let go of her even for that brief a time. But considering the rewards of stripping off his trousers, he'd manage it.

"I'd like to do it." She laughed. "At the risk of totally freaking you, I've never stripped a man before."

It didn't freak him. In fact, it had the opposite effect. He wanted her to experience it all, anything and everything she wanted. Whatever would please her. He only hoped it didn't kill him in the process.

"Tell me if I do anything that makes you uncomfortable and I'll stop."

"I don't think that'll be an issue."

He captured her hands in his before she could finish removing his clothes. "I'm serious, Larkin. It could happen. I want this to be as perfect as possible for you."

She paused in her efforts long enough to cup his face. "See, here's how I figure it. It isn't the making-love part that needs to be perfect."

Rafe choked on a laugh. "No? In that case, I've been wasting my time all these years."

"Yes, you have," she retorted. "What needs to be perfect is who you're making love with."

He closed his eyes and swallowed. Hard. "Hell, sweetheart. Don't say that. I'm not perfect."

"No, you're not." He caught the tart edge underscoring her words and couldn't help chuckling. "But in this moment, you're perfect for me. Right man. Right place. Right time."

"But no pressure."

Her laughter bubbled up to join his. "None at all."

She made short work of his remaining clothing, removing the last of the barriers separating them. He gathered her up, spreading her across the bed. Moonlight picked a path into the room through the French doors leading into the yard. It was almost as though she drew the light to her. It seemed to rejoice in her presence, gilding her with its radiance and turning her skin and hair to silver. Only her eyes retained their vibrancy, glittering a glorious turquoise-blue that rivaled the most precious gem in his family's possession.

He studied her with undisguised curiosity. Had she always been this small? This delicate? How could something so ethereal contain such a huge personality?

Slowly he traced her features, finding a whimsical beauty in the arching curve of her cheekbones and straight, pert nose, her wide, sultry mouth and pointed chin. Then there was her body, superbly toned and supple.

"I don't think I've ever seen anyone more beautiful," he told her.

She shook her head. "Lots of women are more beautiful."

He stopped her denial with a slow, thorough kiss. "Not to me. Not tonight." He pulled back a few precious inches, reluctant to separate them by even that much. "Shall I prove it to you?"

Her eyes widened and she nodded, a delighted grin spreading across her mouth. "If you must."

"Oh, I must."

He cupped her breasts, their slight weight fitting comfortably in his hands. Then he bent and tasted them, one after the other, scraping his teeth across the rigid tips. Her breath escaped in a gasp and she arched beneath him, offering herself more fully. She shifted beneath him, fluid and flowing, parting her legs to accommodate him. And all the while her hands performed a tantalizing dance, tripping and teasing across him, one minute urging him onward, the next startling him with an unexpected caress.

It became a game, each trying to distract the other, their need and tension escalating with each passing moment. He discovered that her legs were incredibly sensitive, and that if he traced a line along the very top of her thigh and eased inward to the moist heart of her, she'd quiver like the wings of a newly hatched butterfly.

Their game came to an abrupt end when she darted

downward between their bodies and cupped him, delighted by his surging response. "Larkin," he warned. "I can't wait much longer."

She squirmed in anticipation. "I don't want you to wait."

He snagged the condom he'd had the foresight to stash in her nightstand table. An instant later, he settled between her thighs. He lifted her knees, opening her for his possession. But he didn't take her immediately. Instead, he slowed, making sure that the culmination of their lovemaking would be as pleasurable as the dance that had preceded it. Gently he parted her, found the secret heart hidden within and traced the sensitive nubbin.

She shuddered in reaction, lifting herself toward his touch. He slipped a finger inward, then two, and felt the velvety contraction of impending climax. "Rafe, please," she whispered. "Make love to me."

He carefully surged forward, claiming her as his own. She reached for him and he laced her hand in his. Their palms joined, melded, just as their bodies joined, melded. Heat flashed between them, sharp and penetrating, building with each thrust of his hips.

Larkin rose to meet him, singing her siren's song, calling to him in a voice that penetrated straight to his heart, straight to his soul. It lodged there. Her sweet voice. Her heartbreaking gaze. The tempered strength of her body as it surrounded him, held him. Refused to let him go.

Never before had he felt anything remotely similar to this. Not with any other woman. It was as though the mating of their bodies had mated every other part of them, forging a connection he'd never known existed.

Heat blazed within his palm, while an undeniable knowledge blossomed.

This night had changed him and he'd never be the same again.

Eight

Larkin stirred, moaning as tender muscles protested the movement.

"You okay?" Rafe asked.

She lifted her head and forced open a single bleary eye, blinking at him. "I think that depends on your definition of 'okay.' I'm alive. Does that count?"

"It counts."

"It's the strangest sensation."

"What is?"

"Most of my body is screaming, 'Don't move.' But there are a few regions that are saying, 'Again. Now.'" She decided to experiment and shift a fraction of an inch. "I'd be an absolute fool to listen to the 'Again. Now' crowd."

"'Kay."

He started to roll off the bed and she shot out her hand to stop him. "Call me a fool."

A sleepy grin spread across Rafe's face. "Call us both fools."

She went into his arms as though she belonged, which maybe she did, despite all that stood in their way. He'd been so careful with her, so attentive, determined to make certain she enjoyed her first sexual experience. No matter what happened from this point forward, she'd always have the memory of this night to cling to.

"Thank you," she told him.

He lifted an eyebrow. "For what?"

"For being perfect. Or at least, perfect for me."

It took him a moment to reply. "You're welcome."

She lifted her mouth for his kiss, shivering as it deepened and grew more intense. Kissing she knew about. She'd kissed a fair number of men. But those experiences paled in comparison to what she shared with Rafe. With the merest brush of his lips, Rafe seduced her. That's all it took for her to want him. To feel the rising tide of desire crash over and through her. One single kiss and she knew she was meant to be his. One single kiss and she knew...

She loved him.

The breath caught in her throat. No. That wasn't possible. She pushed against his shoulders and tumbled away from him, fighting to drag air into her lungs. Sex was one thing. But love? No, no, no! How could she have been so foolish?

"Larkin?" He reached for her. "Sweetheart, what's wrong?"

She evaded his hand. It was *that* hand. The hand that had started all their trouble. The one that had damned her with a single touch. The touch that had infected her with The Inferno.

She snagged the sheet and wound it tightly around herself, for the first time abruptly and painfully aware of her nudity. "How are we going to get out of this?" she demanded, her voice taking on a sharp edge.

He watched her, a wary glint in his eyes. "Get out of what?"

She shook her hand at him. Sparks from the diamond ring he'd placed there sent jagged shards of fire exploding in all directions. "Get out of this. Get out of our engagement. What's your exit strategy?"

He shrugged. "I don't know. Does it matter?" He patted the mattress. "Come on back to bed. It's not like there's any hurry."

She ignored the second part of his suggestion and focused on the first. For some reason, his admission filled her with panic. "What do you mean, you don't know? You must have a plan. You *always* have a plan."

He stilled, his eyes narrowing. "What's with the sudden urgency, Larkin?"

"I need to know how this is going to end. I need to know when."

He vaulted from the bed and padded across the room to where his trousers lay in a crumpled heap and snagged them off the floor. "You're having regrets."

She thrust her hand through her hair, tumbling the curls into even greater disarray. "I don't regret making love to you, if that's what you're getting at."

He grunted in disbelief. "Right."

Kicking the sheet out from beneath her feet, she came after him. "I'm serious. I don't have any regrets about that. None. Zero."

"Then what?" He tossed his trousers aside and cupped

her shoulders. Dragging her into his arms, he examined her upturned face, his expression hard and remote. "One minute we were kissing and the next you're freaking out about exit strategies. What the hell happened?"

She clamped her lips shut to hold back the words. That worked for an entire twenty seconds before the truth came spilling out. "I liked it."

He stared blankly. "Liked what?"

"Making love to you."

His lips twitched and then he grinned. "That's good. I liked making love to you, too."

"No, you don't understand." She attempted to tear free of his hold, but he wouldn't let her. Why in the world had she elected to have this conversation with his stark nakedness hanging out all over the place? It made rational thought beyond impossible. "I *liked* making love to you. A lot."

"I'm still right there with you."

She groaned in frustration. "Do I really have to spell it out for you?"

"Apparently you do."

"I *liked* making love with you. I *loved* making love with you. I want to do it again, as often as possible."

He reared back. "Well, hell, woman. No wonder you want to end our engagement. Who would want to make love as often as possible?"

"Stop it, Rafe." To her horror, she could feel the rush of tears. "You're supposed to be the logical one. You're supposed to have life all figured out. Hasn't it occurred to you that if we keep doing—" she shot a look of intense longing over her shoulder toward the bed "—what we've been doing, it might be sort of tough to stop?"

"Who said anything about stopping?"

Didn't he get it? "Don't you get it? That's generally what happens when engagements end. The two unengaged people stop making love." She pouted, something she hadn't done since she was all of three. "And I don't want to stop. So what happens when it's time to stop and we don't want to?"

"What usually happens is that those feelings ease up or wear off." He said it so gently that it made the pain all the worse. "It's just because you've never gotten to that stage of a relationship before. But trust me, I have it on good authority that excellent sex and mounds of bling aren't enough to make a woman want to stick around once she walks out the bedroom door."

That didn't make a bit of sense. "Now *I* don't understand." She waved her hand in a dismissive gesture when he started to explain again. "I get that you think the physical end of things will gradually grow ho-hum."

"I didn't say ho-hum," he retorted, stung.

"But what I don't get is what that has to do with the rest of it. What's bling got to do with sex, and what changes between us once we leave the bedroom? Is there a manual somewhere that explains these things? Because I have to tell you, I'm clueless."

He gave a short, hard laugh. "Are you serious? You don't know what bling has to do with sex?"

She shot him a knife-sharp look. "No. And if you do, then you've been hanging with the wrong sort of women."

He ran a hand along the nape of his neck. "I have to admit you've got me there."

"Look, I don't give a damn about bling. If the sex gets ho-hum, bling sure as hell isn't going to fix the problem, now, is it?" She planted her hands on her hips, only to make a frantic grab for the sheet when it started a southward migration. "What I need you to explain is what's going to happen after we leave the bedroom that will make our relationship turn sour?"

"I believe it has something to do with my being a loner," he explained a shade too calmly. "Too independent. Not domesticated. Emotionally distant. *Intimidating.*"

The rapid-fire litany worried her. It sounded as if he was quoting someone, and she could take a wild stab as to the identity of that someone. "Is that what Leigh told you?" Larkin asked, outraged.

"She wasn't the only one." He scrubbed at his face, the rasp of his beard as abrasive as the conversation. "How the hell did we get on this subject anyway?"

"Let me get this straight.… You think that once I've gotten bored with having sex with you, I'll actually want to leave you?"

"Yes." Humor turned his eyes a brilliant shade of jade. "Though I'll do my best not to bore you while we're in bed."

"And that's your exit strategy? One day I'll be here and the next day I'll be gone and you'll tell your relatives that I got bored and left."

His expression iced over. "I don't explain myself to my relatives."

She cocked an eyebrow in patent disbelief. "Something tells me that you'll need to do a lot more than explain the situation to them if—*when*—I leave." He didn't argue, which told her that he privately agreed with her assessment. Sorrow filled her when she realized that even if he didn't have a plan, she did. "I'll tell you what. I'll take care of it for you."

He frowned. "You'll take care of our breakup?"

"Yes."

"And how do you intend to accomplish that?"

Stupid. Very stupid of her. She should have anticipated the question. "It's better if you don't know."

He shook his head and folded his arms across his chest. Standing there, nude and intensely male, she could see how some women might find him intimidating. Not her. She swallowed. Probably not her.

"I happen to think it's better if I do know your plan," he insisted. "Now, spill."

"If I explain beforehand, you won't be in a position to react appropriately."

"I won't let you cheat on me." The fierceness behind his comment had her stumbling back a step. "Nor will they believe you, if that's what you're going to try to tell them."

"It isn't," she instantly denied. "That never even occurred to me."

Her bewildered sincerity must have convinced him, because he nodded. "Okay, then." He throttled back a notch or two. "Give me some sort of idea so I can decide whether or not it'll work."

She didn't dare tell him, or he'd find out how well it would work right here and now. "Trust me, it'll work. Not only will they believe it, but they'll rally around you. You won't have to worry about anyone trying to find another Inferno bride for you ever again."

She looked him straight in the eye as she said it. Could he see the bleakness she felt reflected in her gaze? He must have, because he took a swift step in her direction.

"Larkin? What is it?" Concern colored his voice. "Are you ill? Is something wrong with you?"

"It's nothing like that," she assured him. Time to move this in another direction before he broke her down and forced the truth from her. She planted her splayed hands on his chest and maneuvered him backward toward the bed. "Why don't we table this discussion for now and in the meantime, I suggest you get busy and bore me."

His legs hit the edge of the mattress and he reached out to snag her around the waist as he toppled backward. She tumbled on top of him, laughing as she fell. It still hurt whenever she thought about the future. Hurt unbearably to realize that this couldn't last. But she'd known it wouldn't when she'd agreed to an affair. And until the moment came when he found out who she was and what she wanted from him, she'd enjoy every single second of their time together.

Would he consider it a fair bargain? Somehow she doubted it and it distressed her to think that she'd make him any more of a loner than he was already. That he'd continue to turn from people because he no longer trusted them. She'd never forgive herself if that happened. But maybe he'd understand. Maybe he'd help her and they could part on good terms.

And maybe baby pigs around the world would sprout gossamer wings and use them to fly straight to the moon.

He tunneled his fingers through her hair and thrust the wayward curls away from her face. "What are you thinking about?"

She forced out a smile. "Nothing important."

"Whatever it was, it made you look so sad."

"Then why don't you give me something else to think about?"

He didn't need any further prompting. He took her mouth in a hot, urgent kiss, one that drove every thought from her head except one. Rafe. The way his lips drove her wild with desire. The hard, knowing sweep of his hands across her skin. Those magical fingers that left her weeping with pleasure. It was an enchantment from which she never wanted to escape.

She gave herself up to pleasure, exploring him with an open curiosity that he seemed to find intensely arousing. She'd never realized how hard and uncompromising a man's body could be in some areas and how flexible and sensitive in others. But she didn't allow a single inch of him to go uncharted.

One minute laughter reigned as she painted her way across his shape with her fingertips and the next minute it all changed. "I can't imagine ever becoming bored with you." She whispered the confession.

It took him a moment to reply. "I'm not sure it's possible for me to be bored, either. Not with you."

What should have been a light and carefree exchange took on a darker aspect, shades within shades of meaning, filled with a bittersweet yearning. She kissed him. Lingered. Then she began to paint him into her memory again. Only this time she did it with her mouth and lips and tongue, sculpting him with nibbling bites and soothing kisses. Arms. Chest. Belly. He called to her, the cry of the wolf for its mate. But all it did was drive her onward to the very source of his desire.

He didn't allow her to linger as long as she would

have liked. Instead, he became the sculptor, shaping and molding her until they became one. He linked his hands with hers, just as he had before. She knew why, could see it in his eyes and in the emotions he didn't dare express. Even though he would have rejected its existence with every ounce of his intellect, it throbbed between them, giving lie to his denial.

She opened herself to him, took him deep inside her until they flowed together in perfect harmony. She wrapped herself around him, surrendering to the explosion of passion, swept away like a leaf before a whirlwind. Tumbling endlessly into the most glorious sensation, a sensation made perfect because she wasn't alone. She was there with Rafe.

The people in his life called him a lone wolf and he'd more than lived up to his reputation, to the point where he believed it himself. But there was something he'd never considered. Something he either didn't know or had forgotten. But she knew. She understood. Because she was as much a lone wolf as he was.

Wolves mate for life.

The next week proved one of the most incredible of Larkin's life. Making love to Rafe shouldn't have made such a difference. But somehow it did. Whenever she bothered to analyze the situation—which wasn't often— she realized that it wasn't the sex itself that accounted for that difference, but the level of intimacy. It deepened, became richer, added a dimension to their relationship that hadn't existed before.

They spent hours in conversation, discussing every topic under the sun, except the few she avoided in order to keep him from connecting her to Leigh. Art. Science.

Literature. The jewelry business. It all became rich fodder for the hours they spent together.

How could anyone consider him emotionally distant? Or unavailable? Or even intimidating? It defied understanding. To her delight, he'd taken to Kiko, the two becoming firm friends. Even more amusing, she'd come across him a time or two conducting a lengthy one-way conversation with the animal.

"You will let me know if she answers, won't you?" Larkin teased when she discovered him discussing the merits of raw versus cooked beef with Kiko.

"I don't know what it is about that dog, but she insists on eating her food raw."

"She likes it the way nature intended. That might not be the healthiest for us, but it works for her."

He set Kiko's bowl on the ground. "Have you finished packing for the lake?"

"I have. Not that there's much to pack. Even with your mother supplementing my wardrobe, I can still fit everything into my backpack." She winced. "I think."

"Mamma does seem intent on filling up your closet."

Larkin smiled, though it felt a bit forced. "Every time I go in there I find another new outfit."

"Don't sweat it," he reassured her. "She's enjoying herself."

"I realize that." She shifted restlessly. "But it bothers me because she doesn't know our engagement is a sham. I don't want her to spend all this money on me when I'm never going to be her daughter-in-law. It's not right."

Rafe turned to face her, leaning his hip against the counter. "We've had this discussion before." He fixed her with his penetrating green gaze, his expression one that no doubt sent his employees scurrying in instant obedience. "I don't see any point in having it again."

It was the second time she'd caught a glimpse of the more intimidating aspect of his personality. Not that he hadn't warned her. She'd just been foolish enough not to believe him. She should have known better. Rafe didn't pull his punches.

"In that case, I'll wear a few of the outfits and leave the rest," she said lightly. "You can return them after I'm gone."

He shoved away from the kitchen counter and approached. "Why all this talk about leaving?"

"Well…" She forced herself to hold her ground even though a siren blared in her head, urging a full-scale retreat. "It occurred to me that since everyone's going to be at the lake, that might be a good time to stage our breakup."

"In front of all my relatives?"

"Bad idea?"

"Very bad idea, since I'm willing to bet that the majority of them would take your side in any fight you might care to initiate."

She cleared her throat. "I wasn't thinking of a fight, so much as an announcement."

"I don't do fights or announcements. Not in public. And I sure as hell don't do them in front of my entire family."

He closed to within inches of her. No matter how hard she tried, she couldn't keep herself from falling back a pace or two. Kiko looked on with intense curiosity and Larkin suspected that if it had been anyone other than Rafe proving his intimidation skills, the dog would have objected in no uncertain terms.

"Are you bored already, Larkin? Is that the problem?"

Her mouth parted in shock. "No! How could you even think such a thing?"

If shrugs could be sarcastic, Rafe had it nailed. "Oh, I don't know. Maybe it has something to do with your wanting to break off our engagement after one short week."

"In case I didn't make it clear enough last night, I'm not bored." Images of what they'd spent the time doing flashed through her head and brought a telltale blush to her cheeks. "Not even close."

"I'm relieved to hear it. But if it's not boredom…" He raised an eyebrow and waited.

Naturally, she broke first. Would she *ever* learn to control her tongue? "I'm afraid, okay?"

It was his turn to look shocked. "Afraid?" Shock became concern. "Of me?"

"No!" She flew into his arms, impacting with a delicious thud. "How could you even think such a thing?"

He wrapped her in a tight embrace. "Hell, sweetheart." He rested his chin on top of her head. "What else am I supposed to think?"

"Not that. Never that."

He pulled back a few inches and snagged her chin with his index finger, forcing her to look at him. "Then what are you afraid of?"

She didn't want to explain. Didn't want to tell him. But she didn't see what other choice she had. And maybe if he understood, he'd let her go before it was too late.

"It's what we were talking about before. I'm afraid to drag out our engagement," she admitted. "I'm afraid that it'll hurt too much when the time comes to walk away."

Something dark and powerful moved in his gaze. How could any woman have believed for one little minute that he was emotionally distant? It wasn't distance, but self-control. Larkin had never known a man whose emotions ran deeper or more passionately than Rafe's. And because they were so strong, he'd learned to exert an iron will over them to keep them in check. Intimidating? Okay, she'd give Leigh that one. But not distant. Never that.

"I won't let you go." The words came out whisper-soft and all the more potent because of it. "I can't."

He didn't give her the opportunity to reply. Instead, he swept her into his arms. Instead of carrying her in the direction of the guest suite, he climbed the stairs to his own bedroom. They'd never made love there before and she'd understood without it ever being said that his inner sanctum was off-limits.

He lowered her to her feet once they were inside and she looked around, curious. If anything, the room confirmed her opinion of him. The furnishings were distinctly masculine, powerful and well built, with strong sweeping lines. But there was also an elegance of form and a richness of color both in the decor and the warmth of the wood accents and trim. If she'd been shown a hundred different rooms and asked which belonged to Rafe, she'd have chosen this one in an instant.

The door swung shut behind her with a loud click and she turned to discover him watching her, the intensity of his gaze eerily similar to Kiko's. "Welcome to my den," Rafe said.

She attempted a smile, with only limited success. "Am I your Little Red Riding Hood?"

He approached, yanking his shirt over his head as he came. There was something raw and elemental in the way he moved and in the manner in which he regarded her. "Not even close."

Her smile faded. The wash of emotions thickening the air between them was far too potent for levity. She responded to the scent of desire, to the perfume of want, feeling it stir her blood and feed her hunger. Her body ripened in anticipation, flowering with the need to have him on her and in her. To be possessed and to be the possessor.

"Then what am I?" she whispered.

"Don't you know?" He backed her toward the bed. "Haven't you figured it out yet?"

In that instant she understood. Knew what he was to her and she to him.

She was his mate.

She could see it in his stance and in the possessiveness of his gaze, in the timbre of his voice and the strength of his desire. By bringing her here, he'd lowered his guard and allowed her into the most private part of his home… into the most private part of himself.

Even as she surrendered to his touch, a part of her wept. He'd finally opened himself to her, and in a few short weeks—possibly in just days—she was going to destroy not just his trust, but any hope of his ever loving her.

Nine

The closer they came to the lake house over the course of the three hour drive, the more Larkin's tension increased. Rafe could feel it pouring off her in waves. It didn't take a genius to guess the cause.

"No one's going to know," he told her.

She tilted her head to one side and peered at him over a spare set of his sunglasses, since she didn't own a pair of her own. "They're not going to know that we're sleeping together? Or they're not going to know that our engagement is a sham?"

His mouth twitched in amusement at the way the glasses swamped her delicate features. "Yes."

She considered that for a moment before releasing a low, husky laugh. "You're right. Blame it on an overly active sense of guilt."

"Guilt because you're sleeping with me, or guilt because our engagement's a sham?"

She shot him a swift grin. "Yes."

"Let's take care of your first concern." He spared her a heated look. "Sex."

"I believe you take care of that on a regular basis," she responded promptly.

"I do my best," he replied with impressive modesty. "Fortunately for you, you're about to discover that the engagement ring you're wearing is magical."

She held it out, admiring the way it caught and refracted the light. "It is?"

"Without question. The minute I put it on your finger, it created a net of blissful ignorance."

"Funny. I don't feel blissfully ignorant."

He snorted. "Not you. My family."

"Ah." To his relief, she began to relax. "And I assume this magical net keeps everyone from knowing we're sleeping together?"

"Without question. They may suspect, but the ring will cause them to turn a blind eye to it."

"Even Primo and Nonna?"

"Especially Primo and Nonna," he confirmed.

"And my other concern?"

That eventuality continued to hover between them like a malevolent cloud. "The reality—or lack thereof—of our engagement is also a nonissue."

"And why is that?" she asked.

He could hear the intense curiosity in her voice, along with a yearning that he found quite satisfying. "I have a plan."

"Which is?" she asked uneasily.

He debated for a moment. "I don't think I'm going to tell you. Not yet." At least not until he figured out how to convince her it would work. It would be a huge step for both of them. Only time could prove whether that step was the right one. "My plan needs a while to ripen."

She shifted in her seat, betraying her nervousness. "You do remember that I also have a plan, right?"

"We'll consider that plan B."

"I'm not sure that'll work," she murmured.

"Why not?"

She released a sigh filled with regret. "It's sort of on automatic. Eventually it's going to go off by itself."

"What the hell does that mean?"

But they arrived at the lake before she responded, which caused her as much relief as it caused him annoyance. He filed the information away for a more opportune time to drag out the details. One nice thing about his fiancée was that she found it impossible to keep secrets from him. A single, tiny nudge and it all spilled out.

They pulled up to the main residence, a huge sprawling building. When he'd been a kid, the place had looked far different, more rustic. But in recent years the family had rebuilt and expanded it, cantilevering the newer two end wings out over the lake. They'd also added private cabins, which dotted the shoreline and were better suited for the privacy issues of newly married couples.

Larkin leaned forward, her breath catching. "My God, it's magnificent."

He smiled in satisfaction. "Maybe you can understand why we all make the effort to come here each year."

"I'd never want to leave."

He parked in the gravel area adjacent to the storage

shed and workshop. "We'll be expected to stay at the main house."

"In separate rooms, I assume."

"Guaranteed. Don't let it worry you. I know plenty of places where we can find some privacy."

She appeared intrigued by the possibility. "I've never made love in the woods before."

"Only because there hasn't been the opportunity until now. I look forward to correcting that oversight."

She shot him a mischievous look. "So do I."

The next several days proved enlightening. After an initial shyness, both Larkin and Kiko took to his family with impressive enthusiasm. It made him realize that she never talked about her family, other than the occasional reference to her grandmother, and he couldn't help but wonder why.

Where he had always found his family somewhat intrusive, particularly when it came to certain personal issues such as women and romance, Larkin soaked in the love and attention as though it were a new and wondrous experience. Over the days they spent at the lake, he noted that she blossomed the most beneath the attention of his mother and father and he remembered her mentioning that she'd been brought up by her grandmother. She'd always taken pains to change the subject whenever the conversation turned to the topic of her parents, which raised an interesting question. What had happened to them?

Toward the end of their stay, he finally found a private moment to ask. He'd arranged for a picnic lunch that he'd set up on one of the rafts dotting the lake, this one offering the most privacy from curious eyes. She laughed in surprised delight when they swam out to the raft and discovered lunch waiting for them.

"What have you been up to, Rafaelo Dante?" She knelt on the raft and opened the lid of the basket, peering inside. Freezer packs kept the chicken and Primo's uniquely spiced potato salad icy cold, as well as the bottle of white wine Rafe had tossed in at the last minute. She rocked back on her heels. "This is… This is amazing."

Something in her voice alerted him and he took her chin in his hand and tilted her face toward him. Sure enough, he caught the telltale glint of tears. "What's wrong?"

"Nothing's wrong," she instantly denied. "It's…" She gazed out across the lake, emotions darting across her face, one after another. Longing. Sorrow. Regret. Then they vanished, replaced by a grateful smile. "Thank you for bringing me here. This week has been like some sort of beautiful dream. I've enjoyed every minute of my time here."

"I gather the ring is working? No one's given you any trouble?"

She stared down at it in open pleasure. "Your family hasn't given me a moment's trouble. And they were all so excited to see me wearing it." Then the sorrow and regret returned. "I hope they won't be too crushed when our engagement ends."

Time for the first step of his plan. "There's no rush to end it," he remarked in an offhand manner. "In fact, I think it may be necessary to continue the engagement for a while longer. Would that be a problem?"

"I—I'm not sure."

He didn't give her a chance to invent a list of excuses.

No doubt she'd come up with them, but he had a plan for that, too. Hoping to distract her, he filled their plates with food. Then he opened the wine and poured them each a glass.

They sat in companionable silence, soaking up the August sun while they ate and sipped their wine. It gave him plenty of opportunity to admire the sleek red one-piece she wore and the way it showcased her subtle curves. She was beautifully proportioned. Magnificent legs. A backside with just the perfect amount of curve to it. Narrow hips and an even narrower waist. And her breasts, outlined in the thin Lycra of her swimsuit, were the most delectable he'd ever seen. A dessert he planned to savor at the earliest possible opportunity.

"Tell me something, Larkin."

"Hmm?"

He gathered up their empty plates, slipped them into a plastic bag and returned them to the basket. "Why were you raised by your grandmother? What happened to your parents?"

The instant his question penetrated, she stilled. It was like watching a wild animal who'd caught the unexpected scent of a predator. She didn't say anything for a long time, which was so out of character for her that he knew he'd stumbled onto something important. She pulled her legs against her chest and wrapped her arms around them, her grip on the stem of her wineglass so tight it was a wonder it didn't shatter.

She remained silent for long minutes, staring toward shore where Kiko chased a flutter of butterflies. "Gran raised me because my mother didn't want me."

"*What?*" It was so contrary to his way of thinking,

he struggled to process it. "How could someone not want *you?*"

She buried her nose in her wineglass. "I don't like to discuss it."

She didn't actually use the words *with strangers,* but she might as well have. If anything, it made him all the more determined to pry it out of her. Hadn't she done the same for him when it came to his relationship with Leigh, as well as those long-ago events at the lake when Draco had broken his leg? He understood all too well what it felt like to have a poison eating away inside. Larkin had lanced his wound. It was only fair he do the same for her.

"What about your father?"

She shifted. "He wasn't in the picture."

"He left your mother?"

To his relief, Larkin allowed the question, even smiled at it. "My mother wasn't the sort of woman you leave. Not if you're a typical red-blooded male. No, she left my father to return to her husband."

He couldn't hide how appalled he was, couldn't even keep it from bleeding into his voice. "That's how you ended up living with your grandmother?"

Larkin nodded. "My mother discovered she was pregnant with me shortly after she returned home. She and her husband already had a daughter, a legitimate one. Naturally, he wasn't about to have proof of her infidelity hanging around the house, or have my presence contaminating his own daughter. So Mother kept my half sister and turned me over to Gran. She even gave me her maiden name, so her husband wouldn't have any connection to me. Considering some of the alternatives, it wasn't such a bad option."

In other words, her mother had abandoned her. He swore, a word that caused her to flinch in reaction. "And your father? What happened to him?"

She didn't reply. Instead she lifted a shoulder in an offhand shrug and held her glass out for a refill.

He topped it off. "You don't know who your father is, do you?"

"Nope," she confessed. "Barely a clue."

It killed him that she wouldn't look at him. He didn't know if it was embarrassment or shame or the simple fact that she was hanging on to her self-control by a thread. Maybe all of those reasons.

He took a stab in the dark. "I gather he's the one you're looking for."

She saluted him with her glass. "Right again."

"So what's his name? If you'd like, I'll pass it on to Juice and we'll have him tracked down in no time."

"Well, now, there's the hitch."

Rafe winced. "No name."

"No name," she confirmed.

"I can't think of a tactful way of asking my next question...."

"Let me ask it for you. Did my mother even know who he was? Yes, as a matter of fact, she did."

"And she won't give you his name?" Outrage rippled through Rafe's voice.

"She died before she got around to it, although she did let it slip one time that he lived in San Francisco. And Gran remembered her calling him Rory."

"Granted, that's not a lot to go on," Rafe conceded. "Even so, Juice may be able to help. Was there anything else? Letters, perhaps, or mementos?"

"You don't want to go there, Rafe," she whispered.

"Of course I want to go there. If it'll help—"

She set her glass on the raft with exquisite care. "Remember when I told you that my plan for an exit strategy from our engagement was on automatic? If you keep asking questions, the countdown begins."

"What the hell does finding your father have to do with ending our engagement?"

Darkness filled her eyes, turning them sooty with pain. "I can explain, if you insist. But don't forget I did try to warn you."

"Fine. You warned me. Now, what's going on?"

"My father gave my mother a bracelet shortly before she left him. I was going to use that to try to find him, assuming he wants to be found. It was unusual enough that it might help identify him."

"Go on."

"It was an antique bracelet."

"Great. So we'll give Juice the bracelet—"

She cut him off. "Small problem." He could see her struggle to maintain her composure. "I don't have it."

"Did you sell it?"

"No! Never."

"Then where is it?"

"My sister took it. My *half* sister."

Son of a bitch. Did he have to drag every last detail out of her? "Okay, I really don't understand. How did she end up with your father's bracelet if he wasn't her father and the two of you didn't grow up together?"

"Every once in a while, Mom would drop by for a visit with my sister in tow. On one of the visits, Mom gave me the bracelet. My sister—*half* sister—was *not* happy. She had everything money could buy, except that one thing. And she wanted it. It ate at her. I realize now that she couldn't stand the idea that I possessed something she didn't. She threw a temper tantrum to end all temper tantrums."

"And your mother gave in? She gave the bracelet to your sister?"

"Nope. She dragged my sister, kicking and screaming, out of my grandmother's house. The few times they visited after that everything seemed fine, though one time I caught her snooping around in my room. But years later, long after Mom died, she showed up out of the blue. I thought it was an attempt to mend fences and reconnect." Larkin's laugh held more pain than amusement. "After she left I discovered that the bracelet had left with her."

"Can you get it back?"

"I don't know yet. Maybe."

"Is there anything I can do to help? Perhaps if we were to approach her, offer to purchase it?"

For some reason the kindness in his voice provoked a flood of tears and it took her a minute to control them. "Thanks."

"Aw, hell."

He swept her into his arms and she buried her face against his shoulder, her body curving into his. He couldn't understand how a parent could abandon her child. But then, he couldn't imagine making any of the choices Larkin's mother had. No wonder Larkin took such delight in his family and the way they encouraged and supported and—yes—interfered in each other's lives.

Larkin had never had any of that. Worse, she'd been abandoned by her mother, never known the love of her father and been betrayed in the worst possible way by her half sister. Well, that ended. Right now.

"We'll take care of this, sweetheart. We'll get your bracelet back and use it to track down your father. If anyone can do it, it's Juice." He pulled back slightly. "Let's start with finding the bracelet. What's your sister's name? Where does she live?"

Larkin caught him by surprise, ripping free of his embrace. Without a word she dived from the raft and struck out toward shore, cutting through the water as though all the demons of hell were close on her heels. He didn't hesitate. He gave chase, reaching the shore only steps behind her. Catching her by the shoulder, he spun her around.

"What the hell is going on?" he demanded, the air heaving in and out of his lungs. "Why did you take off like that?"

She struggled to catch her breath. Water ran in thin rivulets down her face, making it impossible to tell whether it was from her swim or from tears. "I warned you. I warned you not to go there."

A hideous suspicion took hold. "Who is she, Larkin? Who has your bracelet? What's her name?"

"Her name is…*was*…Leigh."

"Leigh," he repeated. He shook his head. "Not my late wife. Not that Leigh."

She closed her eyes and all the fight drained from her. "Yes, your late wife, Leigh. She was also my half sister." She looked at him then, her eyes—those stunning aquamarine eyes—empty of all emotion. "And I wondered, assuming it's not too much trouble, if you could give me back the bracelet she took from me."

For a split second Rafe couldn't move, couldn't even

think. Then comprehension stormed through him. "All this time you've been with me, you've kept your relationship to Leigh a secret? All so you could find her bracelet?"

"*My* bracelet. And no! Well, yes." She thrust her hands into her wet hair in open frustration, standing the curls on end. "I didn't move in with you in order to search for it, if that's what you're suggesting. But yes. I asked to be assigned to the Dantes reception in order to get an initial impression of you. To decide the best way to approach you."

She'd been sizing him up. Right from the start she'd been figuring out the perfect bait for her trap. And he'd fallen for it. Fallen for almost the exact same routine Leigh had used on him. The poor innocent waif. In Larkin's case, abandoned by her mother, searching for her father. Raised by her grandmother. Was any of it true? None of Leigh's stories had been. Or was this Larkin's clever way to get her hands on whatever valuables his late wife had left behind?

"What a fool I've been."

"I'm sorry, Rafe. To be honest—"

"Oh, by all means," he cut in sarcastically. "Do be honest. It would make such a refreshing change."

"I was going to tell you the truth the night you offered me a job."

He paced in front of her, more angry than he could ever remember being. Somehow Larkin had gotten under his skin in a way that Leigh never had, making the betrayal that much worse. "If you had told me that night, I'd have thrown you out then and there."

"I know."

"So you didn't mention it."

Her mouth tilted to one side in a wry smile. "I think it had more to do with your asking me to be your fiancée and then kissing me. That pretty much blew every other thought out of my head."

The fact that his reaction had been identical to hers only served to increase his anger and frustration. "You still should have told me."

"Then your grandparents arrived on the scene and I got kicked out of my apartment." She continued the recital with relentless tenacity. "Maybe I should have confessed then, but to be hon—" She winced. "The reason I didn't was because I didn't feel like spending a night on the streets."

"I wouldn't have thrown you out in the middle of the night." He smiled grimly. "At least, I don't think so."

"Then in the morning I got swept off by Elia and Nonna. I really didn't want to make the announcement in front of them." She captured her lower lip between her teeth and a line of anxiety appeared between her brows. "But I shouldn't have let them spend any money on me. That was totally wrong, and if it's the last thing I do I'll repay every dime."

"Would you forget about the damn money?" Rafe broke off and scrubbed his hands across his face. What the hell was he saying? Money was the reason she was here. She just had a different routine than Leigh, a far more effective one, as it turned out. "You had ample opportunity to tell me in the time we've been together. Why didn't you?"

She squared her shoulders. In her halter-top bathing suit they looked breathtakingly delicate and feminine—a fact he couldn't help but notice despite all that stood between them. "You're right. I should have told you. My only excuse is that I knew it would change everything between us." Her chin quivered before she brought it under ruthless control. "And I didn't want our relationship to change."

He did his best to ignore the chin. She might look like a helpless stray, but he didn't doubt she was every bit as conniving as her sister. *Blood will tell,* as Primo always said. Of course, he'd been referring to The Inferno. But maybe greed and deceit and a lack of honor ran in some families the way The Inferno ran in his. Like mother, like daughter.

"You want Leigh's bracelet? Fine. You'll have it first thing tomorrow. After that, I expect you to clear out."

His final comment kept her from replying for a moment. Her distress shouldn't affect him. Not anymore. But for some reason it did. "Then you have it?" she asked in a low voice. "I wasn't sure whether it had been lost when Leigh's plane went down."

"It was at Dantes at the time, having the catch repaired. Right now it's in my office safe." He whistled for Kiko, then inclined his head toward the lake house. "Come on. We're leaving. I'll tell everyone there's been an unexpected emergency."

She didn't argue. "Of course." Her tone turned formal. "I'll find somewhere else to stay as soon as we get back to the city."

The comment only served to spin his anger to an all-time high. "As much as I'd love to have you gone, it'll be far too late to find a place for both you and Kiko tonight. Tomorrow I'll get your damn bracelet and find you a hotel or apartment willing to house you both." He cut her off before she could argue. "Enough, Larkin. This discussion is over. From now on, we do things my way. And my way means you're out of my life as soon as I can arrange it."

Rafe didn't waste any time putting his plan into action. Nor did he give his family the chance to do more than express confused concern before he had the two of them and Kiko packed and loaded and flying down the road toward San Francisco.

The instant they arrived home, Larkin made a beeline for her bedroom. Rafe followed. It wasn't the smartest move, but he had some final questions he wanted answered. He paused in the doorway, struggling to see through the pretense to the woman she'd revealed herself to be—a woman ruled by greed and avarice and dishonesty.

It was as though she read his mind. "I'm nothing like Leigh." She threw the comment over her shoulder.

"No? Time will tell." He stared at her, broodingly. "Once I slipped a ring on your sister's finger she went from sweet and innocent—like you—to cold and calculating. I have to hand it to her, she put on a great act leading up to our wedding. I guess I'm an easy mark when it comes to the helpless waif type of woman. Leigh was a more sophisticated version, granted, but that changed soon enough. It didn't take long to realize she wanted what every other woman wants from a Dante, the good life and everything my money could provide. I suppose I could have lived with that. For a while."

"Then what went wrong?"

"It was the adultery that I refused to tolerate."

The fluid lines of Larkin's body stiffened and she slowly turned to face him. "She cheated on you? *You?*"

He supposed he should be flattered by the way she said that. "Hard to imagine?"

"Yes, it is."

His eyes narrowed and he approached, swallowing up the narrow bones of her shoulders in his two hands. "How do you do it?"

She stared up at him, eyes huge and startling blue, her expression one of stark innocence. Bambi in human form. "Do what?"

"Look the way you do, so trustworthy and ingenuous, when everything you say is a total lie. How do you do that?"

"I'm not Leigh." She spoke calmly enough, but a hint of steel and temper washed across her face. "You're trying to tuck us into the same little box and I refuse to allow it. *I am not Leigh!*"

"And I might have believed you if you'd been candid about your connection to Leigh from the start. Just out of curiosity, was any of your story true? Were you really abandoned by your mother and raised by your grandmother?"

Exhaustion lined her face, along with a heart-wrenching despair. "I've never lied to you, Rafe. I simply didn't tell you about Leigh and the bracelet. I even told you I had secrets. Omissions. Remember?" She searched his face, probably looking for some weakness she could use to her advantage. "You said lying by omission was part of dating. Everything else I told you was the truth."

"And I'm supposed to just believe it."

"You know what, Rafe? I don't care what you believe. I know it's the truth and that's all that matters." She lifted her chin an inch. "You should be grateful to me, you know that? I've given you the perfect excuse for staying emotionally disconnected. I betrayed you. Now you can go back to being independent. The original lone wolf. You should be celebrating."

"Somehow I don't feel like celebrating." She attempted to pull back and he tightened his hold. "I can still feel it. Why is that?"

She didn't pretend to misunderstand. A hint of panic crept into her gaze, combining with a wealth of longing. "Maybe it really is The Inferno."

"You'd love that, wouldn't you?"

She hesitated. "I'd love it if it were real," she admitted with brutal frankness. "But I'm not that thrilled about it given the current circumstances."

He uttered a humorless laugh. "There's one good thing that's come from all this."

Her breath escaped her lungs in a soft rush. "I'm afraid to ask.…"

"Once I explain the facts to my family they'll finally leave me alone. No more Inferno possibilities paraded beneath my nose. Not only that, but they'll understand completely why I can't marry my Inferno soul mate. How could I, when she's Leigh's sister?"

Bone-deep temper ignited in Larkin's eyes, turning the color to an incandescent shade of cobalt-blue. "*Half* sister. And I'm getting really tired of being hanged for her crimes. You want something to be angry about? I'll give you something."

She swept her hands up across his chest and into his hair. Grabbing two thick handfuls, she yanked his face down to hers and took his mouth in a ruthless kiss. Desire roared through him at her aggressiveness. Her mouth slanted across his, hot and damp with passion.

Gently she parted his lips with hers. Teasing. Offering. Beckoning him inward. He didn't hesitate.

He tugged her closer, melding them together. Her thighs, strong and slender, slipped between his while her pelvis curved snugly against him. He could feel the shape and softness of her breasts against his chest, feel the pebbled tips that spoke of her need. And her mouth. Her mouth was as sweet and lush and tasty as a ripe peach.

He staggered forward a step, falling with her onto the bed. The instant they hit the mattress, he shoved his hands up under her shirt and cupped the pert apple roundness of her breasts. He traced his thumbs across her rigid nipples, catching her hungry moan in his mouth. The sound was the final straw.

He lost himself. Lost himself in the fire that erupted every time they touched. She wrapped her legs around him, pulling him tighter against her. Her breath came in frantic little gasps and she snatched quick bites of his mouth.

"Tell me this is a lie," she demanded. "Tell me I'm lying about what happens whenever you kiss me. Tell me this isn't real."

It took endless seconds for her words to penetrate. The instant they did, he swore viciously. "Not again."

"Yes, again." She wiggled out from underneath him and shot to her feet. "Do you think I want it to happen? You're Leigh's husband. I've never before wanted anything that belonged to her. But you—" Her voice broke and she turned away.

"I never belonged to her."

"You were married to her." She lifted a shoulder in

a disconsolate shrug. "There's not much difference as far as I can tell."

He stood, aware that nothing he could do or say would restore order to his world. He wanted a woman he didn't trust, probably would have made love to her again if she hadn't put a stop to it before it went any further. He'd already had his life turned upside down once, courtesy of his former wife. He wasn't about to let it happen again.

"I don't belong to any woman. And I never will."

"A lone wolf to the end?" she whispered.

"It's better than the alternative."

With that he turned and left. And all the while his palm burned in protest.

Ten

Larkin spent the night curled up in the middle of the bed counting the minutes until dawn.

Rafe was right about one thing. She should have told him she was Leigh's sister—*half* sister—right from the start. That had been the plan all along. If only she hadn't gotten distracted. No, time to face the truth. She hadn't been all that distracted. She hadn't wanted to reveal her identity to him because living the lie had filled her with more joy than she'd ever before experienced.

She swiped at her cheeks, despising the fact that they were damp with tears. She'd discovered at an early age that feeling sorry for herself didn't help. Nor did it change anything. Not that she had much to feel sorry about. She'd had Gran, who'd been a wonderful substitute parent.

Even so, she'd be kidding herself if she didn't acknowledge that some small part of her felt as though she were always on the outside looking in. That she'd never quite measured up. More than anything, she'd wanted to be loved by her mother. To belong. To have known the love of a father, as well. Instead, what had Leigh called her? A Mistake. Capital *A*. Capital *M*. Underlined and italicized. As a result, Larkin had held men at a distance, determined not to visit upon a new generation the same mistakes of her parents. If you didn't fall in love, you couldn't create A Mistake.

But her lack of a real family, a "normal" family, one that consisted of more than a loving grandmother, had filled her with an intense restlessness, a need to belong. Somewhere. To someone. To find the elusive dream of hearth and home and family. To finally fit in. But how did you find that when you were too wary to let people approach? Beside her, Kiko whimpered and bellied in closer.

"I know I wasn't a mistake, any more than you were," she told the dog. "We just don't quite fit in anywhere. We're unique. Special. Caught between two worlds, neither of our own making."

But no matter how hard her grandmother had tried to convince her of that fact and fill her life with love, there'd always been a part of her that had conceded there was a certain element of truth to Leigh's words. Bottom line… She wasn't good enough for her mother to keep. She'd been thrown away. Dispensable.

Until Rafe.

For a brief shining time she'd discovered what it meant to belong to a family, one who'd welcomed her with open arms. Until she'd ruined it. "I should have told him." Kiko whined in what Larkin took as agreement.

"But then he'd never have made love to me. And I'd never have fallen in love with him."

Tears escaped no matter how hard she tried to prevent them. It was worth it, she kept repeating to herself. No matter how badly it ended, the days she'd had with Rafe were worth the agony to come. If she had to do it all over again, she would.

Without a minute's hesitation.

Dawn finally arrived, giving Rafe the excuse he needed to give up on pretending to sleep and dress for work. He would have skipped breakfast, but Kiko padded out to join him, and well, damn it. He couldn't let the poor girl starve, could he?

He didn't see or hear any sign of Larkin, which was fine by him. The sooner he concluded their remaining business, the sooner he could get his life onto an even keel again. Go back to the way things had been before Larkin had stormed into his life and ripped it to shreds. Avoid further emotional entanglements and just be left the hell alone.

"It's what I've always wanted," he informed Kiko.

She gave his comment the attention it deserved, which was none at all. Aware he didn't have a hope in hell of gaining any support from that quarter, he downed the last of his coffee and rinsed the mug. Then, refusing to consider the whys and wherefores of his actions, he started up a fresh pot before heading out the door.

He wasn't expected at the office, since the entire Dante family was still officially on vacation. He'd also given his assistant the time off, which provided him complete privacy to closet himself in his office, undisturbed. He wasted a couple of hours taking care of business emails and paperwork, knowing full well they were his way of avoiding the inevitable. Finally he shoved back his chair and stared at the display rack that concealed his office safe.

He sighed. *Just get it over with!*

It took him only minutes to punch in the appropriate code and verify his thumbprint. The door swung open and he sorted through the various gemstones and jewelry samples stored there until he found the plain rectangular box he'd stashed in the farthest recesses.

Removing it, he relocked the safe and carried the box to his desk. Flipping open the lid, he stared down at the bracelet. It was a stunning piece. The setting gave the impression of spun gold, delicate filigree links that appeared to be straight out of a fairy tale. The original stones had been a lovely mixture of modest diamonds of a decent quality, and amethysts that weren't bad, if a shade on the pink side. Not good enough for Leigh, of course, but then few things were.

She'd insisted he replace the amethysts with emeralds because they were her birthstone, and the smaller diamonds with oversize fire diamonds because they were more impressive, not to mention expensive. He'd never felt either complemented the setting. But since he'd still been in the throes of lust, he'd agreed to her demands. She'd even wanted to have the setting altered, but there he'd drawn the line. It was perfect as is. Instead, she'd gone behind his back and made the adjustments without his knowledge. It wouldn't take much to return it to its original form, he decided, studying the bracelet. Sev's wife, Francesca, could do it in her sleep.

A knock sounded at the door and his sister, Gia, poked her head into his office. "Hey, you. Larkin said I could find you here."

He leaned back in his chair. "Did she, now."

"Yes, she did."

Gia entered the room and closed the door behind her. He and his sister had always been dubbed the "pretty" Dantes, identical in coloring, with matching jade-green eyes. While he'd despised the moniker, Gia had simply shrugged it off, neither impressed nor dismayed by the description. He, on the other hand, had been offended on her behalf, since his sister wasn't merely pretty. She was flat-out gorgeous.

"To be honest, I'm relieved Larkin's still at your place," she continued. "When the two of you left the lake I was a little worried you were on the verge of breaking up."

"So you followed us home?" Her shrug spoke volumes. "It's none of your business, Gianna."

"Then you *are* on the verge of breaking up. Oh, Rafe." She approached and slid a slim hip onto the edge of his desk. Leaning in, she examined the bracelet. A delaying tactic, no doubt. "Huh. Definitely not Francesca's work. Almost beautiful. Or it would be if it weren't so—" she made a fluttering gesture with her hands "—over the top. It also needs softer stones."

"Amethysts."

"Exactly." She nodded, impressed. "Good eye. Whose is it?"

"Leigh's." He corrected himself. "Larkin's, I guess." Confusion lined Gia's brow. "Come again?"

"Leigh and Larkin are sisters. *Half* sisters." Though why he bothered to make the distinction he couldn't say.

Gia's mouth dropped open. "Is this some sort of joke?"

"I wish." He gave her the short version. "Now she wants her bracelet. Once she has it, she'll be on her way. She can use it to try to find her father, or sell it, or do whatever the hell she wants with it." He flipped the case closed with a loud snap. "And that brings to an end my very brief Inferno engagement."

"I don't understand. Why does any of that put an end to your engagement?"

He glared at his sister. "What do you mean, why? Because she's Leigh's sister." He grimaced. "Half sister."

"So? It's not like she's Leigh. You only have to talk to her for five minutes to realize that much."

"She lied to me."

"Did she? She claimed she wasn't Leigh's sister?"

"Half sister," he muttered.

"I'll take that as a no." She waited for him to say more, blowing out her breath in exasperation when he remained stubbornly silent. "Fine. Be that way. But you can tell Larkin that if she needs somewhere to stay while she searches for her father—"

"Assuming there is a father and she's actually searching for him."

Gia inclined her head. "Assuming all that. She's welcome to crash at my place." She slipped off the desk. "Larkin loves you, you know."

He stilled. "She used me."

Gia shrugged. "It happens. But I'll tell you one

thing…" She paused on her way out the door. For some reason she wouldn't look at him. "I'd give anything to have what you're throwing away."

Rafe returned home to find Larkin perched on the edge of a chair in his living room, dressed in one of her old outfits. Kiko lay at her feet, the dog's graying muzzle resting on her paws. Her brilliant gold eyes shifted in Rafe's direction and she watched him with unnerving intensity. He caught a similar expression in Larkin's gaze. Beside the dog sat her backpack. It didn't take much thought to add two and two and come up with…Larkin was running. At least she'd done him the courtesy of waiting until he returned home. But then, it wasn't likely she'd leave without her bracelet.

She drew in a deep breath and blew it out. Rising, she gathered up her backpack, shifting it nervously from hand to hand. "Do you have it?"

He removed the box from his suit-jacket pocket and held it out to her. Without a word she accepted it and turned her back on him, her spine rigid and unrelenting.

"That's it?" he asked, though he didn't know what more he expected.

"Thanks." She threw the words over her shoulder. "But if it's all the same with you, Kiko and I will be on our way now."

He let her go. It was better this way. Easier. Cleaner. Safer.

An instant later she slammed her backpack to the ground. Whirling around, she came charging toward him. "Rafaelo Dante, what the *hell* have you done to my bracelet?" She shook the box he'd given her under his nose. "What are you trying to pull? You were supposed to give me *my* bracelet. Not this…this…*thing*."

"That is your bracelet."

Larkin popped open the top and held out the glittering spill of gold and gems. "Look at it, Rafe. What happened to it? It's ruined!"

How was it possible that she could put him on the defensive with such ease? "Leigh had me switch out the stones. Don't worry—it's even more valuable than it was before."

"Valuable? *Valuable!*" She stared at him as though he'd grown two heads. "What has that got to do with anything?"

"I just thought—"

Larkin's eyes hardened, filling with a cynicism he'd never seen there before. And something else. Something that twisted him into knots and filled him with shame. It was disillusionment he read in her gaze. It was as though he'd told her there was no Santa Claus. No Easter Bunny. No magic or fairies or wishing on stars. As though he'd taken every last hope and dream and crushed it beneath his heel.

"I know what you thought," she stated in a raw, husky voice. "You assumed I'm like Leigh. That it's the dollar-and-cent worth of an item that's important."

It hit him then. She wasn't Leigh. How could he ever have thought she was? It was like comparing an angel to a viper. Where Leigh had demanded and taken, Larkin had given him the most precious possession she owned—herself. And he'd thrown that gift back in her face. Accused her of the worst possible crime—being the same as her sister. *Half* sister. She'd given him her heart and he'd tossed it aside as though it were worthless, just as her mother had done.

"Don't you get it?" she whispered. Pain carved deep lines in her expression. "This bracelet is my only connection to my father. How am I supposed to use it to find him when it looks nothing like he remembers?"

Face it, Dante, you screwed up.

And now he had a choice, a choice that was vanishing with each passing moment. One path led back the way he'd come. Returned him to where he'd been just weeks ago. The other option... Well, if he chose that one, he'd have to risk everything he'd always considered most precious. His independence. His need to control his world and everything within it. The barriers he'd spent a lifetime erecting to protect himself.

But the potential reward...

He looked at Larkin. Truly looked at her. That's all it took. He burrowed the thumb of his left hand into the throbbing center of his right palm and surrendered to the inevitable. He'd risk it all. Risk anything to have her back in his life. And just like that, a plan fell into place. It would take days to accomplish, possibly weeks. It would take extreme delicacy and exquisite timing. But it just might work.

Now for step one. "I can put the bracelet back the way it was," he offered.

Tears welled up and she brushed at them with a short, angry motion. "Forget it. I don't want anything from you."

She turned to leave, whistling to Kiko. Instead of following her, the dog darted forward, snatched the backpack in her jaws and took off at a dead run up the steps to the second story.

"Kiko!" she and Rafe called in unison.

Together they raced after her, finding her crouched in the center of his bed, guarding the backpack. She barked at the pair of them.

"Looks like she doesn't want you to leave," Rafe said.

"She'll get over it." Larkin approached the bed and picked up the backpack. "Let's go, Kiko."

Though the dog allowed Larkin to take the backpack, she hunkered down on the bed in a position that clearly stated she wasn't planning to budge anytime soon. Okay, this could work to his advantage.

"Let her stay," Rafe suggested.

"What?" Larkin turned on him. "Why?"

"You both can stay here until we get the problem of your bracelet sorted out."

She instantly shook her head. "That's not going to happen."

Rafe wasn't surprised. That would have been too easy, and something told him that nothing about regaining her trust would prove easy. "In that case, Gia has offered you a room while you search for your father. The only problem is that her place isn't suitable for Kiko. Leave her here for the time being."

Tears filled Larkin's eyes. "It's not enough that you ruined my bracelet? Now you're taking my dog, too?"

Hell. "I'm not taking her," he explained patiently. "I'm letting her stay until our business is settled."

Her chin jutted out. "I thought our business was settled."

"Apparently not. I still owe you for your time and the damage to the bracelet."

"Forget it."

"Somehow I had a feeling you were going to say that," he muttered. "In that case, the least I can do is have your bracelet fixed so it's returned to its original condition. Will you consider that a fair exchange?"

She looked doubtful. "You can do that?"

"Francesca can handle anything."

"Francesca." Her eyes widened at the reminder, filling with horror. "I forgot about the engagement ring."

She yanked the ring off, holding it out to him. When he refused to take it, she crossed to his bedside table and placed it there with unmistakable finality. "If you'll have my bracelet repaired, I'll consider us even."

He wouldn't. Not by a long shot. She squared her shoulders and turned her back on Kiko. The expression on her face almost brought him to his knees. Despite the love and support she'd received from her grandmother, everyone else in her life had abandoned her. So many rejections in such a short life. And here it was happening to her again.

Well, not for long. No matter what it took, he intended to make things right.

The next couple of weeks were absolute agony for Larkin. Rafe made no attempt to get in touch. Nor did she go to the house, even though she missed Kiko fiercely. She made noises a couple of times about sneaking over while Rafe was at work so she could see her dog, but Gia informed her that her brother had elected to stay at home for the remainder of his vacation, and Larkin couldn't bring herself to confront him. At least, not yet. Not while recent events were still so raw.

Midway through the third week, word finally came that the repairs to her bracelet were completed. "Meet me downstairs in five and I'll drive you over," Gia called to say. "I think I'm almost as excited as you to see how it looks."

It wasn't until they made the turn onto Rafe's street that Larkin realized where they were going. "I thought the bracelet would be at Dantes," she said uneasily.

"Nope. Rafe has it." Gia spared her an impatient look. "You've done nothing but grouse about the fact that you haven't seen Kiko in weeks. Now you have the opportunity to see both her and the bracelet. You should be over the moon. Don't tell me you're going to let a little thing like my good-for-nothing brother spoil your big moment."

"No. No, of course I won't." Maybe not.

To her surprise, Gia pulled up in front. Instead of parking, she waved her hand toward the house. "On second thought, why don't you go ahead without me."

Larkin turned to glare. "You're setting me up, aren't you? You think if I go in there alone, maybe Rafe and I will resolve our differences."

Gia shrugged. "Worth a try."

"It's not going to work."

"Then it won't work. But at least I'll have given it a shot."

Realizing it was pointless to argue, Larkin exited the car. Snatching a deep breath, she forced herself to climb the steps of the front porch at a sedate pace and knock. A minute later the door swung open and Rafe stood there. They stared at each other for an endless moment before he stepped back to allow her past.

She didn't know what to say. Emotions flooded through her. Powerful emotions. Longing. Regret mixed with sorrow. Love and the sheer futility of that love. And overriding them all was pain. A bone-deep, all-invasive hurt.

"Where's Kiko?" she managed to ask.

"Out back." For some reason he couldn't seem to take his eyes off her, his gaze practically eating her alive. "The gentleman who brought the bracelet wanted you to inspect it before he left and I wasn't sure how well he'd take to having a wolf hovering over him."

She almost smiled, catching herself at the last instant. "But Kiko's okay?"

"She's fine. Misses you. But then, that seems to be going around."

She blinked up at him, not quite sure what to make of his comment. Not that his expression gave anything away. "I guess we shouldn't keep your associate waiting."

Rafe led the way to the den and shoved open the door. She could see her bracelet spread out across the empty glass-topped desk, captured within the beam of a bright spotlight. A man stood nearby, silent and attentive.

Larkin approached the table, her breath catching when she saw the bracelet. She swung around to glance at Rafe, tears gathering in her eyes. "It's beautiful. Please tell Francesca she did an amazing job restoring it."

The man beside the table cleared his throat. "She made a few minor changes. The fire diamonds, for instance. They're similar in size, but the quality can't be compared. And I understand she used Verdonia Royal amethysts. The color is stunning, don't you think?"

Larkin glanced at the man and smiled. "Don't tell Francesca, but I still prefer the original."

"Do you really?"

For some reason, he seemed ridiculously pleased by the comment. He looked directly at her then and she froze, riveted. He was far shorter than Rafe, maybe five foot six or seven and somewhere in his late forties. Eyes the color of aquamarines twinkled behind a pair of wire-rimmed glasses. And though his wheat-white hair was cut short, there was no disguising the wayward curls that were next to impossible to subdue. His nose was different from hers, stubbier, but they shared the same pointed chin and wide mouth. And she knew without even spending a minute of time with him that he used that mouth to laugh. A lot. Best of all, he made her think of leprechauns and rainbows and pots of gold. And he made her think of magic and the possibility of dreams coming true.

"I must confess," he said, "the old girl looks quite grand with all those fancy stones attached to her."

Larkin continued to stare at him, unable to look away. "Old girl?" she repeated faintly.

"The bracelet. She belonged to your great-great-great-grandmother."

"You're—"

"Rory Finnegan. I'm your father, Larkin."

She never remembered moving. One minute she was

standing next to the table and the next she was in his arms. "Dad?"

"You have no idea how long I've been looking for you." He whispered the words into her ear and they flowed straight to her heart.

The next few hours flashed by. At some point, Larkin realized that Rafe had slipped away, giving her and her father some much-needed privacy. Coffee would periodically appear at their elbow, along with sandwiches. But she never noticed who brought them, though it didn't take much guesswork to know that Rafe was behind that, too.

During the time she spent with her father, she discovered that her mother had called him shortly before her death. "She was horribly sick. Almost incoherent," he explained. "She just kept telling me I had a daughter but couldn't give me a name or location. By the time I tracked her down, she was gone and that bastard of a husband claimed he had no idea what I was talking about."

Larkin also learned that her name belonged to the same woman whose bracelet she'd been given. And she discovered that she had a family as extensive as the Dantes, and every bit as lovingly nosy. "You won't be able to get rid of us," Rory warned. "Not now that I've found you. I'd have brought a whole herd of the troublemakers with me, but I didn't want to overwhelm you."

When the time finally came for him to leave, they were both teary eyed. Standing by the front door, he snatched her close for a tight hug. "You'll come by this weekend. We'll throw a big welcome home party. And bring your man with you. Your grandmother Finnegan will want to look him over before okaying the wedding date."

"Oh, but—"

"We'll be there," Rafe informed him as he joined them.

The instant the door closed behind her father, Larkin turned to confront Rafe. "I don't know what to say," she confessed, fighting back tears. "Thank you seems so inadequate."

"You're welcome." He held out his hand. "I have something else I want to show you."

"Okay." She dared to slip her hand into his, closing her eyes when The Inferno throbbed in joyous welcome. "But then I'd really like to see Kiko."

"That's what I wanted to show you."

He pulled her toward the back of the house to the guest suite where she'd spent so many blissful days and nights. The door was shut and on the wooden surface someone had screwed a glistening gold placard. "Official Den of Tukiko and Youko" it read.

"You told me that was Kiko's full name. I looked up the meaning." He slanted her a flashing smile. "Moon child?"

Larkin shrugged. "It seemed fitting." She frowned at the sign. "But who is Youko?"

"Ah, you mean our sun child."

He shoved open the door. Where once had stood a regular bed, now there were two huge dog beds. The door to the backyard stood ajar and he ushered her in that direction. She gaped at the changes. In the time she'd been gone, someone had come through and transformed the yard into a giant doggy playpen. Rope pulls and exercise rings, doghouses and toys were scattered throughout the area. He'd even had a section of lawn dug up and a giant square of loosely packed dirt put in its place.

"For digging," he explained. "And burying bones. And for rolling around, if that's what they want."

Just then Kiko emerged from one of the doghouses and bounded across to her side, nearly bowling them both down in her enthusiasm. Larkin wrapped her arms around her dog and buried her face in the thick ruff.

"I've missed you so much." A small whine drew her attention back to the doghouse. Peeking out from the shadows was another animal. "And who is this?" Kiko darted back to stand protectively beside the newcomer, a dog who appeared to be part yellow Lab and part golden retriever. "Youko, I presume?"

"She's a rescue dog. Terrified of people, so I'm assuming she was abused. Kiko's helping me socialize her." He hesitated. "I'm hoping you'll help, too."

She stiffened. "A dog's a big responsibility. A long-term commitment."

"Fifteen. Twenty years, if we're lucky. Of course, Kiko's Pals will also be a long-term commitment."

Larkin stared blankly. "Kiko's Pals?"

"It's the rescue organization we're starting, if you're willing. A charitable organization to help dogs like Kiko. I'm hoping you'll run it."

"You've started—" She broke off, fighting for control. "You did that for her? For us?"

"I'd do anything for the two of you," he stated simply.

"I don't understand," she whispered. "I don't understand any of this."

"Then let me explain."

This time he took her upstairs, pausing outside his bedroom door. Another plaque had been attached. This one read, "Den of the Big Bad Wolf and his Once in a Lifetime Mate." He opened the door and stepped back, giving her the choice of entering or walking away.

She didn't hesitate. She stepped across the threshold and straight into hope. He closed the door and she turned. In two swift steps he reached her side and pulled her into his arms.

"I'm so sorry, Larkin. I was an idiot. You're nothing like Leigh and never could be. I've spent so many years protecting myself that I almost lost the only thing I've ever wanted. You." He cupped her face and kissed her, losing himself in the scent and taste and feel of her. "I love you. I think I loved you from the first minute we touched."

"Oh, Rafe." She was laughing and crying at the same time. "I love you, too."

He pulled back. "I still want you to be my temporary fiancée."

Her eyes narrowed. "You do, huh?"

"Definitely. A very temporary fiancée, followed by a very long-term wife." He swung her into his arms and carried her to the bed. "You'll have to remind me where we left off. It's been so long I can't quite remember."

She wrapped her arms around his neck and feathered a kiss across his mouth. "I'll see what I can do to refresh your memory."

"Nope. We can't do that. Not without breaking my promise to Primo."

He fumbled for something on the dressing table. Taking her hand in his, he slid her engagement ring on her finger, back where it belonged. The heat of The Inferno flared between them and even though he didn't acknowledge it aloud, she could see the acceptance in his eyes.

"It would seem this is the perfect ring after all," he told her.

"And why is that?" she asked, even though she already knew.

"Your ring is named Once in a Lifetime, which is fitting because if there's one thing you've taught me—" he kissed her long and hard "—it's that wolves mate for life."

* * * * *

&Desire™

2 in 1
GREAT VALUE

HONOUR-BOUND GROOM by Yvonne Lindsay

Alexander Del Castillo was betrothed from childhood. So the CEO doesn't expect his beautiful bride to get under his skin…

CINDERELLA & THE CEO by Maureen Child

Tanner found himself saddled with a gorgeous housekeeper he couldn't keep his mind—or hands—off, who also turned out to be his annoying neighbour!

BARGAINING FOR BABY by Robyn Grady

Queensland sheep-station owner Jack Prescott was all bad boy sex appeal, but he'd inherited his baby nephew and feisty Maddy!

THE BILLIONAIRE'S BABY ARRANGEMENT by Charlene Sands

Suddenly Nick Carlino was face-to-face with a woman from his past…and her five-month-old baby.

EXPECTANT PRINCESS, UNEXPECTED AFFAIR
by Michelle Celmer

Samuel Baldwin had seduced Princess Anne to quench his own desire. Chipping away at Anne's icy façade had been pure pleasure…

FROM BOARDROOM TO WEDDING BED? by Jules Bennett

He'd been faced with the toughest decision of his life—a future full of wealth and power, or the love of Tamera Stevens. What would it be, love or money?

On sale from 15th July 2011
Don't miss out!

Available at WHSmith, Tesco, ASDA, Eason
and all good bookshops

www.millsandboon.co.uk

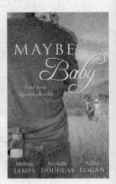

BAD BL**OO**D

A POWERFUL
DYNASTY,
WHERE SECRETS
AND SCANDAL
NEVER SLEEP!

VOLUME 5 – 17th June 2011
HEARTLESS REBEL
by Lynn Raye Harris

VOLUME 6 – 1st July 2011
ILLEGITIMATE TYCOON
by Janette Kenny

VOLUME 7 – 15th July 2011
FORGOTTEN DAUGHTER
by Jennie Lucas

VOLUME 8 – 5th August 2011
LONE WOLFE
by Kate Hewitt

8 VOLUMES IN ALL TO COLLECT!

www.millsandboon.co.uk

Royal Affairs – luxurious and bound by duty yet still captive to desire!

Royal Affairs: Desert Princes & Defiant Virgins

Available 3rd June 2011

Royal Affairs: Princesses & Protectors

Available 1st July 2011

Royal Affairs: Mistresses & Marriages

Available 5th August 2011

Royal Affairs: Revenge Secrets & Seduction

Available 2nd September 2011

LATIN LOVERS COLLECTION

Intense romances with gorgeous
Mediterranean heroes

Greek Tycoons
1st July 2011

**Hot-Blooded
Sicilians**
5th August 2011

Italian Playboys
2nd September
2011

**Passionate
Spaniards**
7th October
2011

**Seductive
Frenchmen**
4th November
2011

**Italian
Husbands**
2nd December
2011

FREE BOOK
AND A SURPRISE GIFT

We would like to take this opportunity to thank you for reading this Mills & Boon® book by offering you the chance to take a specially selected book from the Desire™ 2-in-1 series absolutely FREE! We're also making this offer to introduce you to the benefits of the Mills & Boon® Book Club™—

- **FREE home delivery**
- **FREE gifts and competitions**
- **FREE monthly Newsletter**
- **Exclusive Mills & Boon Book Club offers**
- **Books available before they're in the shops**

Accepting this FREE book and gift places you under no obligation to buy, you may cancel at any time, even after receiving your free book. Simply complete your details below and return the entire page to the address below. You don't even need a stamp!

YES Please send me a free Desire 2-in-1 book and a surprise gift. I understand that unless you hear from me, I will receive 2 superb new 2-in-1 books every month for just £5.30 each, postage and packing free. I am under no obligation to purchase any books and may cancel my subscription at any time. The free book and gift will be mine to keep in any case.

Ms/Mrs/Miss/Mr _____ Initials _____

_____

Surname _____

Address _____

_____

_____ Postcode _____

E-mail_____

Send this whole page to: Mills & Boon Book Club, Free Book Offer, FREEPOST NAT 10298, Richmond, TW9 1BR.

Offer valid in UK only and is not available to current Mills & Boon Book Club subscribers to this series. Overseas and Eire please write for details. We reserve the right to refuse an application and applicants must be aged 18 years or over. Only one application per household. Terms and prices subject to change without notice. Offer expires 30th September 2011. As a result of this application, you may receive offers from Harlequin (UK) and other carefully selected companies. If you would prefer not to share in this opportunity please write to The Data Manager, PO Box 676, Richmond, TW9 1WU.

Mills & Boon® is a registered trademark owned by Harlequin (UK) Limited.
Desire™ is being used as a trademark. The Mills & Boon® Book Club™ is being used as a trademark.